Dear K.

Thank you so much for your support.

Blissful Tragedy

A Novel

By
Amy L. Gale

There's more to love than Tragedy or Bliss.

♡ Amy L Gale

This is a fictional work. The names, characters, incidents, places, and locations are solely the concepts and products of the author's imagination or are used to create a fictitious story and should not be construed as real.

5 PRINCE PUBLISHING AND BOOKS, LLC
PO Box 16507
Denver, CO 80216
www.5PrinceBooks.com

ISBN 10: 1631120069 ISBN-13: 978-1-63112-006-0
Blissful Tragedy
Amy L Gale
Copyright Amy L Gale 2014
Published by 5 Prince Publishing

Cover Art by Viola Estrella
Author Photo by Guy Cali and Associates, Inc.

First Edition/First Printing February 2014 Printed U.S.A.

5 PRINCE PUBLISHING AND BOOKS, LLC.

Acknowledgements:

I am enormously indebted to many wonderful people who have believed in me and assisted in my journey to publication.

Carol Riccetti, my mother, who believes I can do anything. Chris Gale, my husband, who supported me through this journey and spent many nights watching television alone while I quietly wrote. Kelly Gazey, my friend for the last 25 years, who read and edited my book so many times she probably can recite it verbatim. Sharon Cometa and Rachel Capitano who formed our "Girls Bookclub", read and edited my manuscript, and encouraged me to follow this dream. My brother, John Paul Riccetti, who spent many hours creating a web presence for me. I'm lucky to have such wonderful people in my life and couldn't ask for better family and friends, I love you all.

My editor Sara Barnard, who polished my book until it shined and also served as my teacher, inspirational coach, and friend. My publicist, Sara Benedict from Gliterary Girls Media. My author friends from the Pocono Lehigh Romance Writers chapter of the RWA. Ellen Hartman, who encouraged me to join the RWA, and guided me on my road to publication. Doug Simpson, who recommended 5 Prince Publishing and suggested I join the team. And 5 Prince Publishing who made this dream a reality.

Dedications

To my husband, who rocks my world
To my mother, who believes I can do anything
To my "Girls Bookclub" Kelly, Rachel, and Sharon,
who taught me to follow my dreams

Blissful Tragedy

CHAPTER 1—THE CONCERT

An eerie silence takes over the dark night sky. I stare straight ahead and breathe slowly, trying to ignore the pounding of my heart. The crisp, cool, spring air caresses my body and heightens my senses. I shiver slightly. The bone-rattling drum beat pulsates through my chest. I jump up from my seat as the guitar screams its heavy ear-splitting shriek, like a choir of electric angels. A frenzy of loud cheers emerges, piercing through the calmness as hundreds of fans leap to their feet. The bright lights focus on center stage. I take a deep breath and stare at the silhouette slowly being illuminated.

Van Sinclair stands so close that if I lunged forward, I'd crash into six feet of pure muscle. My eyes fixate on his light-brown, shoulder length, perfectly messy hair that frames his chiseled face. Then, they travel down to the tight black T-shirt that clings to every sculpted muscle of his torso, flaunting them in just the right way. My lips part and chills flood my body causing the hair on the back of my neck to stand on end. I hold in a deep breath and slowly exhale as he grips the microphone stand, pulling it close to his body. He closes his eyes and begins to belt out the lyrics. His raw powerful tones, both decades old and brand new at the same time, resonate through the night sky. Hot lights shining down on the stage highlight a bead of sweat that runs down his arm, over the impeccably detailed dragon tattooed on his left bicep. He lifts his head and looks into the crowd. My heart races as I stare into his exquisite emerald green eyes, mesmerized.

"Oh my God, he's so hot!" Brooke yells into my ear, breaking my trance. "His picture doesn't do him justice."

"You can say that again," Sydney agrees.

Breathless, all I can do is nod.

Devil's Garden is promoting their best album yet. Even though the two-thousand-seat amphitheater is not the largest of venues, it's sold out tonight. A wall of bodies closes in, pushing us toward the stage. The hard wood against my palms keeps the crowd at bay. *Can it keep me from being crushed for the whole two hour set?* My skin glistens as the three of us sway, moving to the music. *Wait, is Van Sinclair watching me? Yeah right, like that would happen.*

∞

The band steps forward. "Thank you so much Lakeview University. You've been great. We'll be back next year, good night!" he yells to the crowd.

Sydney holds up her pass. "Hey girls, the concert may be over but our night is just beginning. Let's go backstage!"

I put my arm around Sydney, pulling her into a side hug. "You're the best sister in the world! Thank you so much for this awesome graduation present. Bryce must have called in one hell of a favor to score front row seats."

"You know Bryce doesn't settle for less than the best." Sydney says with a grin. "He picked me, didn't he?"

The three of us erupt into a mess of giggles. "I can't believe we're going to meet the band. When I met you freshman year, I never dreamed we'd be journeying backstage on graduation week," my best friend Brooke says.

"I would never leave you out. I couldn't have gotten through this week without you, or the last four years for that matter. You're the best friend and roommate a gal can have." I flutter my eyelashes.

She chuckles. "Aw, I think I might cry."

Sydney brushes her light brown hair over her shoulder. "Ok ladies, time to meet some hot rockers."

I tug at my new skirt, which hangs slightly past my underwear and hope they don't show. My silver tank top leaves nothing to the imagination and for once, my hair actually cooperates. I brush the brown curls that hang down my back over my shoulder and fiddle with my black headband. *Jesse would never let me leave the house dressed like this, but that's no longer his concern.* My stomach clenches and a sour taste develops in my mouth. I shake my head and banish the negative thoughts from my mind. *Tonight is all about fun. Plus, I won't be wearing this type of attire in the corporate world. Might as well live it up!*

I pat down the fabric as the crowd begins to dissipate. "If the wind catches the pleats in my skirt, I may be arrested for indecent exposure."

Sydney adjusts her body-hugging, hot pink T-shirt. "Think of going backstage as a woman's right of passage."

I haven't seen her wear those daisy dukes with the pockets that extend longer than the actual jean shorts since high school, and she's put on more make-up than I've ever known her to wear. Bryce would freak if he could see his soon-to-be bride now.

Brooke raises her eyebrows and pulls down her short black dress, which flaunts every curve of her perfect body, trying to make it reach her black thigh high boots. "I'm pretty sure Dean wouldn't approve of my look either, but what he doesn't know won't hurt him."

Dean would cringe if he knew his girlfriend left the house in that dress, especially to go backstage to meet a band.

Like three giddy schoolgirls, giggling and squealing, we make our way to the secret catacombs of the amphitheater's backstage area. We turn the corner and stop in front of a man of considerable size who looms before us, barring access to the stairwell. Sydney flashes him our passes and he moves aside, a knowing smirk on his face.

The stairs lead us to a long hallway. The aroma of damp musty air surrounds us as people carry equipment through the walkways, barely giving us a second glance. *This is not the glamorous fantasy I've always envisioned backstage to be! Oh well, who cares? We're still meeting the band. I can cross 'meeting someone famous' off my bucket list. Well, sort of famous anyway.* My face flushes as we continue through the hallway.

"You're the only one of us who's single. Sydney and I have to live out our rock star fantasies through you," Brooke says as she winks at me.

I press my lips into a hard line. "Oh please, I would never hook up with some rocker. They probably screw anything and everything walking." *Why would anyone want to be used? I hate to ruin it for everyone, but I'm not trying to score tonight.*

"That's why the Trojan company is so profitable," Sydney chimes in, snickering.

I scowl and grind my teeth. "I think I've been exploited enough for one lifetime, thank you!"

Why does it always have to be about sex? Devil's Garden creates amazing music and I can't wait to find out more about them; I bet they're interesting guys. Sure, they're all handsome, especially Van Sinclair. My heart beats faster. *Their talent is not merely skin deep.*

We stop at a room filled with people. Scantily clad women crowd the space while the smell of smoke and booze thickens the air. *We can't look as trashy as these girls!*

I step back and wipe my sweaty palms against my skirt. "Does everyone have a backstage pass? There's not even room to breathe in there."

Sydney turns and raises an eyebrow. "Come on ladies, it's now or never."

Fruity perfume from the groupies greets me as I turn sideways and graze a few of them. We push our way through the crowd, finally reaching the band members.

Van Sinclair is perched on a couch surrounded by an entourage of sleazy women. I glance around at the sea of miniskirts and tight T-shirts. My heart freezes and then begins to pound. His skin glistens under the glow of the fluorescent lights in the room. My hands tremble as he runs his hand through his hair. His bicep flexes as he moves. Steam should engulf the room from the energy radiating off his body.

I take a deep breath and slowly walk toward Brooke and Sydney, who have managed to join the entourage.

Van Sinclair looks up at me with those amazing emerald green eyes and my heart races. "Hey babe, want a drink?"

My muscles tense and my jaw clenches. *Sure, first they ask you if you'd like a drink and the next minute you're walking in on them screwing another girl. No thanks! There's no way I will be sweet talked into sex, no matter how enchanting this rock star is.*

"Listen, I'm not your *babe* and I'm definitely not sleeping with you!" I shout.

Oh my God, did I just say that out loud? My stomach knots as I replay the words in my mind. *I really need to establish some control over the filter between my brain and my mouth. I've just insulted the lead singer of one of my favorite bands while backstage at his show! Am I insane?* A pearl of sweat runs down my neck, trickling along my backbone. A red-head in stilettos and a thin piece of fabric she's trying to pass off as a dress snickers.

He raises his eyebrows, smiles, and chuckles. Without missing a beat, he resumes schmoozing with his fans. There's a harem of women holding shot glasses in their cleavage, begging him to drink. I can just imagine the other services they're willing to offer. Four shots later, he's back to signing an array of body parts and posing for pictures while women hang on his words, as well as his body.

Brooke and Sydney glare at me with the most sinister of looks. If they had the ability to shoot daggers from their eyes, I would be lifeless on the floor.

Why can't I stop my eyes from traveling toward Van Sinclair? I flinch when I catch him gazing back at me while socializing with the others. *Please let him forget my earlier outburst.* I play with my hair, twirling it around my fingers, as I stand like a wallflower away from the action.

Brooke runs her fingers along the bass players arm, catching her bottom lip with her teeth every time she smiles. *When did she turn into such a flirt? Jeeze, she's just about sitting on his lap.*

Sydney holds out her glass for a refill and downs another shot. *There's no way Bryce would've gotten us backstage passes if he knew she'd be drinking Jager bombs with the drummer. Thank God she's not our designated driver.*

Van Sinclair rises from the couch and walks toward an ice-filled tub. He grabs two beers, and continues in my direction, stopping in front of me.

"Hey *not-my-babe-and-definitely-not-sleeping-with-me*," he says with a smile, almost laughing. "How about that drink?" He hands me one of the bottles. "Come on, walk with me."

My heart is threatening to beat out of my chest. There are so many butterflies in my stomach that I think I might hurl. Instead, I take a deep breath, compose myself, and look into the flawless green eyes which are searching my face, waiting for my answer.

"Ok," I squeak.

We start to walk. I have no idea where we're going, but it's safe to say I would follow this man into the fires of hell if that's where he led me. *Dear God, don't let me say or do anything else to embarrass myself any further than I already have.* We walk through a hallway which leads us outside. I clutch my beer for dear life. *Please let me steady my hand enough to prevent me from spilling it.* We go up a few steps and I find myself on the backside of the stage, behind a curtain which separates us from the public's view. Van sits on the edge, letting his feet dangle. He gestures for me to sit down next to him. I lower myself beside him, discreetly trying to pull my skirt down to maintain my dignity.

"So, *not-my-babe-definitely-not-sleeping-with-me.* Do you have a name that's a little bit shorter?"

A heat wave flows from my neck to my cheeks. I lift my head and smile faintly. "Alexis Waters. Everyone calls me Lexie."

"Well Lexie, I'm Van Sinclair and I don't think we were properly introduced before." He turns toward me and holds out his hand.

Goosebumps erupt as our skin makes contact. My heart is drumming against the walls of my chest. A powerful surge flows from my head to my toes as if electricity surges through me. "I'm really sorry about before. I didn't mean to be rude. It's been a rough week and I think I may have temporarily lost my mind."

He raises his eyebrow. "First time backstage?"

"I'm sadly a backstage virgin." I breathe slowly, trying to steady my pulse.

"Not many of the other girls I met today can say that, judging by the things they were saying to me." He flashes a wry grin. "Nothing like what you said to me of course."

"I'm not a *use-me-and-lose-me* groupie." I press my lips into a hard line and cross my arms.

He smirks. "These girls come half-naked to our concerts with the hopes of banging a rocker for the sheer purpose of bragging rights. Now, who's using who?"

I look down at the skimpy outfit I'm wearing. *Wow, I never thought of it that way.*

"You look great," he says as if reading my mind. "Don't take this the wrong way, but do you honestly dress this sexy every day?"

I bite my lip and twirl my hair around my finger. "Halloween was the last time."

He cocks his head to the side and lowers his eyebrows. "You're not like my usual backstage guests. What's your story?"

Is that an insult or a compliment? Maybe it's just an observation. "I graduated from Lakeview University with my business degree a few days ago and I've accepted a position with an advertising company. Hopefully I can work my way up to an account manager. The next great slogan you hear may be from my mind." *Oh God, I'm babbling. If I could just control my nerves.* "I don't start until the week after Labor Day. So I'm basically just enjoying my summer off."

"I thought you said you were having a rough week."

My stomach hardens. "Does walking in on my boyfriend, make that *ex*-boyfriend, cheating on me count as rough?"

"Ouch." He grimaces and lifts his bottle. "To groupies and cheating boyfriends!"

My whole body ignites as his eyes burn through me. I lick my lips and raise my beer. We clink bottles and his fingers slightly brush mine. My skin tingles and my hand begins to tremble.

I steady it and take a sip. "So, how'd you come up with the name Devil's Garden? You don't seem satanic."

He rubs his hand along his jaw. "Seriously, you just want to talk?"

I nod. A flash of tingles spreads across my face like wildfire.

After a few blinks, he speaks. "The story's really not that interesting. The guys and I all went to Prairie View High in Silent Springs, Kansas; class of two-thousand-four. When we formed the band, our guitar player, Marcus, wanted to check out the music scene in Seattle. We jumped in his car for a road trip. Got lost in Lake County Oregon, and found this place called Devil's Garden. It's an awesome volcanic field that's hundreds of thousands of years old. It's really cool! We used the name for our band." He runs his hand through his hair. A few stray locks fall onto his perfectly chiseled cheek bone.

I breathe slowly and stare at his flawless face, barely able to comprehend what he just said as I lose myself in the emerald hue of his eyes. Shaking my head, I compose myself. "Wow, I like it even more, now that I know the story. Devil's Garden has a hint of a dangerous flare, like Black Sabbath meets Metallica. Nothing beats the classics!"

He jerks his head back and squints his eyes. "Huh, I always say that too."

"So, how's Seattle? It's on my list of places to visit."

Van pauses. "The music scene is amazing; so many clubs and festivals. You can hear anything from folk to grunge to indie. We spent a week just hitting the clubs, trying to hear as many different bands as we could. There's lots of talent out there. Our tour stops there the last week of August and I'm psyched to go back."

I exhale and continue to stare. "It must be awesome to travel the country doing what you love."

"Sometimes I think I'm going to wake from an awesome dream." He rocks his head backwards. "There are drawbacks too. Like the times when I just want to relax and hang out but have deadlines and time constraints. I never get to stay in one place for very long when we're on tour." He looks down at the ground and then back up at me.

My phone chimes. I let out a deep sigh. *Why couldn't I have left it on the coffee table tonight?* I check the message. It's Sydney.

Brooke and I will wait for you by the car.

I set the phone beside me.

Van snatches it up and starts pressing buttons. He presses his lips together, holding back a smile.

What reply could he be sending to Sydney? *Oh God, please don't let it be something I'll never live down.* I fidget with my fingers.

"My sister and roommate are waiting for me. I better go. Thanks for my backstage experience. I'm glad I can officially say I'm no longer a backstage virgin." I hop up from the stage.

A slow smile builds as the moonlight reflects off his chiseled jaw line. "The pleasure was all mine. This may have been the best time I've ever had backstage."

"I seriously doubt that," I smirk, rocking back on my heels.

"You'd be surprised. Walk with me," he says and holds his hand out to me.

My whole body tingles with pure adrenaline and my heart hammers as our skin makes contact. We start walking back, hand in hand, through the hallway. The butterflies return with a vengeance, fluttering in my stomach. It's unnerving how this man can affect me with just his touch.

"Hey Van, there you are," calls a voice in the hallway. It's the bass player.

"Hey Tyler, meet Lexie."

Tyler nods. "Hi."

Tyler has a true rocker look with long blond hair, soft blue eyes, and a few tattoos on his biceps and forearms.

"Hi," I answer, twirling my hair around my finger.

"See you on the bus buddy," Tyler pats Van on the shoulder and continues down the hallway. .

"Wow Van. Nice," another voice says.

"This is Chaz, our drummer."

"Hey, good for you buddy!" Chaz blatantly looks me up and down. *Wow, all those muscles really show off the tattoos covering his arms.* I glance up at his buzzed cut brown hair and brown eyes. Each of these guys is truly an individual. He strolls past us with a scantily clad blonde on his arm.

Van shakes his head. "Just ignore him, I do."

We walk back up the steps and out of the corridor to the parking lot. Van stops in front of a third guy. I recognize him from the show as the band's guitar player. If Van wasn't Devil's Garden's front man, Marcus would be the hot rocker of the band. My eyes ascend, focusing on his thick, light-brown, wavy hair that begs you to run your fingers through it. His clear blue eyes could pierce your soul.

"Did you enjoy the show?" Marcus asks.

"Definitely! You guys were great!"

An attractive woman, who could easily be Playmate of the Year, walks up to us and stands beside Marcus. She sweeps her long, wavy blond hair from her shoulder and lets it fall down her back as she turns toward us.

Van runs his hand through his hair. "Hey Jenna, meet Lexie."

Jenna looks at me with cold eyes. She lowers her eyebrows. "Please Van, I meet one of her every night." She rolls her eyes and walks away.

Van shrugs. "Sorry about that."

"No worries." *Jeeze, just because I'm with Van doesn't mean I'm his one-night stand.* I pull down my skirt as we make our way through the parking lot. *Maybe I misjudged the other girls backstage.*

We walk up to the only car left in the parking lot.

"Van Sinclair, this is my sister Sydney, and my roommate, Brooke."

Sydney jumps off the trunk of the car, a huge smile plastered across her face. "It's a pleasure."

"Pleasure's all mine," Van replies.

Brooke stares, her eyes traveling across our intertwined hands. "We loved the show."

Van slides his free hand into his pocket. "Thanks, I hope you girls can make it to another one."

Van lets go of my hand and turns toward me, his gaze meeting mine. My nerve endings stir and tingle. My body craves his touch. A little lightheaded, I look into those emerald eyes and lose myself for a moment.

He steps forward, slowly moving his face closer to mine. My heart hammers against the walls of my chest. Breathless, I close my eyes and clench my sweaty palms. His cheek brushes mine as he whispers in my ear. "I had a great time tonight. I hope to see you again sometime soon."

His soft lips graze my ear, sending a powerful surge to my core. Every cell in my body awakens. The hair on the back of my neck stands on end and the butterflies again take flight. I inhale quickly, catching my breath, before I melt into a puddle. "Thanks for a great night."

∞

I'm on the receiving end of a police interrogation during the car ride home. *Are Brooke and Sydney playing good-cop bad-cop?*

Sydney squints and stares right into my eyes. "Ok, spill it."

"Honestly, we just sat around and talked. I don't know why you two don't believe me," I maintain.

"Please, I saw the way he looked at you." Brooke raises her eyebrows. "Something *had* to have happened."

I pull into the driveway and make my way into the apartment. "I really wish my life is as exciting as you two think." I shake my head and disappear into my room. However, my huge smile refuses to extinguish as I change into my pajamas and get ready for bed. Lying down, I mentally relive the highlights of my amazing night. Just as I place my cell phone on the night stand, it chimes. *No doubt more ribbing from Sydney or Brooke.*

I grab my phone and look at the screen. *Am I dreaming?* I rub my eyes and look at the small bright letters. I turn on the lamp on my nightstand and focus my attention on the words I never imagined would grace my cell phone screen. Holy crap! I have a text, and it's from Van Sinclair.

CHAPTER 2—INVITATIONS

Hope you enjoyed your backstage adventure. I know I did.
P.S. Tell your cheating ex he's a moron.

Oh my God! My hands start shaking as I try to keep hold of my cell phone. *Van Sinclair is texting me?* I scroll through my contacts. I gasp and focus my eyes on the last entry. The words "Van Sinclair" glow like the light of a thousand candles. *Huh, when I thought he was replying to Sydney's message he must have actually been adding himself in as a contact and then discreetly calling his phone so he'd have my number.* Shivers surge through my body. *Van is planning to stay in contact.* The butterflies start their slow, steady flutter in my stomach and my heart threatens to beat out of my chest. *Now is the moment of truth. I have two options.*

Number one, I can ignore the text. Obviously, any type of relationship with Van will be doomed from the start. He's touring the country and never in one place for very long. To make matters worse, he's constantly sought after by sex-hungry women.

Number two, I can text back. I really have nothing to lose, unless you consider that I'll most definitely get hurt if this ends badly. *He's just so damn irresistible.* Every cell in my body awakens with his slightest touch. *Will it be fair to deprive myself the chance of ever having that feeling again?*

My window of opportunity is short. Sweat forms on the edge of my hairline. I hate making quick decisions! *What am I doing? It's not like he's proposing. No need to over-analyze the situation.* My face flushes and my body trembles as I press send. As usual, desire overrules rational thought.

I thoroughly enjoyed every part of my backstage deflowering ☺

My phone chimes again.

I'm proud to be the man to claim that honor ;)

Is it possible for him to be any more appealing? He just keeps getting better. My phone chimes again.

I hope you're not mad that I hacked your cell phone. I just don't want tonight to be the last time we talk.

My entire body trembles and my stomach twitches. As usual, my insecurities dominate my mind. *Why would someone like Van Sinclair want to get to know me better?*

There's really nothing special about me. I'm just a new college graduate with a BS in business who's starting my career in the fall. He's going to be utterly disappointed when he comes to that realization. I'm sure he can take his pick from all of his gorgeous fans. *Why me?* Regardless, I'm going to keep this conversation rolling. I wipe my palms along my soft cotton sheets and let my fingers dance against the buttons.

I'm not mad, I'm flattered…and technically its morning.

He's not nearly as intimidating when we're texting. Thank God for modern technology. My phone chimes again.

I guess it is morning. Well then, technically, we just spent the night together.

My face heats up as blood rushes through my veins. Spending the night with Van would be divine paradise. My tongue brushes over my lips. I pause and try to think of an equally clever comment. Then, my phone rings.

Van Sinclair appears in large letters on the screen. My heart palpitates and my stomach quivers. I twirl my hair around my fingers. My nerves are getting the best of me again. I'm not nearly as confident face to face or ear to ear. I take a deep breath, press answer, and hold the phone to my ear.

"Just so you know, I'd never spend the night with you and not call the next day. So, how's your morning so far?"

My heart flutters and my face is on fire. He's a romantic at heart! "It's off to an exceptionally good start. I hope it's an indication for the rest of my day. How about yours?"

"My morning's pretty awesome. I get to spend it talking to a beautiful and intriguing woman. On the down side, I'm looking at being stuck on the tour bus for the next few hours," he says.

Oh my God. Every word coming from his mouth makes my stomach flip flop. If my heart beats any faster I may have a heart attack. I can't contain the smile spreading over my face. *This handsome, talented, rock-god thinks I'm beautiful and intriguing? That clearly indicates he must be at least slightly psychotic, but hey, nobody's perfect.*

"Believe me, I'm far from beautiful or intriguing at this hour," I assure him.

"I should decide that for myself."

I lightly touch my throat as my body tingles again. "Where's your next stop on the tour?"

"We're headed to the Jersey Shore. Tyler's cousin is the entertainment manager at Bader Field in Atlantic City. He got us a gig. We probably won't fill the place but it looks really good that we got booked there. It's not prime shore weather yet, but its June next week and Atlantic City's always hopping."

"The beach is beautiful any time of the year. I think I owned an ocean house in a past life. I've always loved listening to the sound of the waves and digging my feet in the sand. It's very therapeutic. I hope you get some free time to enjoy it."

"We actually get to stay for two nights. I'll make sure to take some beach time for myself. When you live in Kansas you don't see much sand."

I chuckle. "You get to see everything on tour; from the mountains to the valleys to the oceans."

He laughs. "God Bless America! So what's on your agenda for today?"

"I'm my sister's wedding planning slave. I'm not exactly sure what she has planned, but I'm sure she'll insist that it's all part of my duty as maid of honor."

"Weddings rock. There's lots of food, booze, and cheesy music, and someone's usually drunk on the dance floor."

"I'm sure the trashed dancing machine will be from our side of the family. The wedding is at Sydney's fiancé's family plantation in Savannah, Georgia."

"Mint juleps can get you just as drunk as Jagerbombs."

"Well then, bring on the mint juleps! I'm actually pretty excited to see Savannah, even if it is to watch my sister become a Stepford wife."

"From the impression I got of your sister, she won't be turning into any Stepford wife but she might turn her fiancé into a Stepford husband."

I lay my head back against my pillow letting the tension in my muscles subside. "Her assertiveness is one of the things I love about her. Do you have any brothers or sisters?"

He sips a drink and clears his throat. "Nope, just me. I consider Marcus my brother and his parents my family."

"Marcus seems nice. However, that girl he was with may need anger management." *Crap. What's wrong with me? I've just insulted one of his entourage.*

He exhales and lowers his voice. "Jenna is Marcus's wife. They're high school sweethearts and got married right after we graduated. She really is a cool girl. She just hates groupies and assumed you were one of them."

A low growl forms in my throat. "That's understandable, although it's never smart to assume. I'm definitely not a groupie."

"You are most definitely not a groupie, Lexie."

I turn and look at the clock. 4:00 a.m. *I'm going to be like a zombie later but this is so worth it.* Loud voices invade our conversation.

He covers the mouthpiece, muffling the sounds. "How long will you be confined to wedding planning slavery?"

"Well, Sydney's picking me up at eight o'clock but didn't really let me know how long my sentence will be." I giggle. "I guess we're playing it by ear."

"Do you realize it's four o'clock and your sentence starts in four hours?"

"I'll be exhausted and useless to her, but it's worth it."

"Hopefully you still feel that way later," he says as he yawns. "I'm going to let you get some sleep and I'm going to grab some zzz's too."

"Ok. Goodnight, Van."

"Goodnight, Lexie."

I wait until the phone clicks indicating Van ended our call. There's no way I was going to be the one to hang up first. Even though I know I'm in store for a busy day, I can't sleep. The pounding of my heart and endorphins flowing through my blood are giving me a second wind. *Van Sinclair can do such amazing things to me with just the sound of his voice or the slightest soft touch.* He fills my thoughts as I finally drift off to sleep.

The alarm clock sounds like an executioner's bell. I frantically slam my hand around the night stand, desperately trying to hit the snooze button. After succeeding, I rub my eyes and stumble into the shower. I let the warm water hit me, hoping it will revive me enough to make it through the day. I finish getting ready and check myself out in the mirror. Amazing! I look pretty good. It must be from the adrenaline rush of my after-hours phone call. My face is glowing. Van Sinclair has turned me into a lustrous siren.

I walk into the kitchen to make myself coffee and find a note on the table.

Thanks for a great night! I had a blast at the concert with you and Sydney. Gone to Dean's. Catch ya later. Love, Brooke.

Brooke always leaves me notes knowing I usually forget my cell phone and will miss a text. Not anymore. My phone won't be leaving my side from now on.

The strong bold aroma of fresh ground beans heightens my senses as I sip my coffee in the quiet kitchen. I'm definitely not in the mood for more interrogation. I'm also not ready to tell Sydney or Brooke about the phone call. I want to keep it private for now. Today, however, is about Sydney. I'll put everything else aside and focus on her and her wedding. I'll be the maid of honor extraordinaire.

There's a knock at the door. I open it and find a man holding a bouquet of Gerber daisies.

"Alexis Waters?" the man asks.

"Yes," I reply and take the flowers into the house. My hands tremble as I set the flowers on the counter. *Wow, first a text, then a phone call, and now flowers.*

I tear open the envelope and remove the card. My jaw stiffens as my eyes flow over the blue handwritten letters.

Sorry for everything Lexie. Love, Jesse

Oh my God, does that creep really think he can win me back with flowers? Is there an appropriate gift to say, 'Sorry I fucked around on you, you should forgive me? Even Hallmark can't tackle that one. If he cared so much he wouldn't have cheated in the first place.

I throw the card in the garbage and move the flowers to the kitchen table. They're beautiful, regardless of their intent.

Just then, there's another knock at the door. I open it and flinch. Jesse stands in my entranceway, leaning against the frame while looking down at me. My heart hammers and my body freezes in the doorway. *Great! I was hoping I wouldn't have to face him again.* Alphabetical order already punished me at our graduation ceremony. Sitting two seats away was close enough.

"I understand that you're really pissed off. I want to tell you that I really am sorry and I promise I'll never let this happen again. Please, let's just get past this minor setback so we can move on with each other. It was a meaningless fling and it's over. Please forgive me."

My fists clench into balls and my body temperature rises. *How can he be so arrogant? He really thinks I'm going to excuse him for this 'meaningless fling'. Does he actually think he's entitled to my forgiveness? Well I've had enough.*

I shout through my clenched teeth. "You're a cheater and a manipulator. I don't know what I ever saw in you."

"Please, everyone knows what you see in me. Isn't it obvious?" Jesse says with a smirk.

"Go fuck yourself!" I shout and slam the door.

I press my back against the door, resting my weight against the strong hardwood, and momentarily stop breathing as the rate of my heart doubles and my chest begins to tighten. *Please don't let me pass out.* Why is there suddenly no air in the room? I breathe rapidly as tears form in my eyes. I cover my face with my hands, trying to stop them. A gut-wrenching sensation develops and a sour taste invades my mouth. I close my eyes and remember walking into Jesse's dorm room only to see him hovering over the blond. Why can't I stop replaying that night over and over again in my head? My pulse soars. I scroll through my phone and look through the texts Jesse sent to me right afterwards.

1. **I'm sorry. I screwed up.**
2. **I didn't mean it. It just happened.**
3. **Please talk to me, we can work this out.**
4. **It was a one-time mistake and meant nothing.**
5. **This was the first time it happened. I had a moment of weakness.**
6. **I drank way too much and didn't know what I was doing.**
7. **She followed me to my room and wouldn't leave.**
8. **I never slept with her.**
9. **I really screwed up and want to fix this.**
10. **I love you. Forgive me.**

I suck in a deep breath. Jesse's texts are basically a list of worthless excuses. Nothing he can say will erase the image I now have burned into my brain. There's no way I can ever forgive him. Our relationship is over. I exhale and clutch my stomach as my body begins to crumble on itself.

What am I thinking? Whatever this thing is with Van Sinclair is sure to be a disaster. Am I a glutton for punishment? I'm pretty sure walking in on a rocker doing God knows what with a groupie is a daily occurrence. Once is enough for me. I need to focus on my career anyway, and stay away from guys. Ugh, why can't I get Van off my mind?

Keys clink against my countertop and footsteps tap along the tiles of the floor.

Sydney takes a sip from her water bottle. "Good morning. Are you ready for the wedding planning extravaganza?"

I quickly wipe my eyes. "I'm so excited about it I couldn't sleep."

Sydney smirks. "Since you're so enthusiastic, we'll start with your maid of honor dress. We have an eight-thirty appointment at the Bridal Boutique." She raises her eyebrows. "Are you ok?"

I sigh. "Yeah, just some issues with Jesse."

She puts her purse on the counter and turns toward me. "I didn't want to bring it up at your graduation but I'm curious. Why did you guys break up? He didn't even come over to say hello to us."

"He cheated on me at the last Beta Omega party."

Sydney covers her mouth with her hand then lets it drop away. "Want me to kick his ass?"

Sydney is an amazing sister. She always has my back and there's no doubt she would tear Jesse a new one if I said the word. In sixth grade, when the 'cool girls' made fun of me for having braces, Sydney walked right up to Taylor Morgan and gave her a bloody nose.

I shake my head. "Screw him; he's not going to ruin our day. Let's start the festivities."

We drive into the city and pull over at an elegant Victorian building. There are ceiling to floor windows which showcase gorgeous bridal gowns. Sydney purchased her dress in a swanky Philadelphia boutique. When my time comes, I will prefer a shop like this one.

We walk inside and are greeted by a smiling woman, her face beaming brighter than her fiery red hair.

"Hello girls, welcome to Bridal Boutique. Please feel free to look around and let me know if you need anything."

"Thank you. We're looking for a maid of honor dress," Sydney replies.

"Right this way. My name is Anna. Holler if you need anything else."

We follow Anna to a wall of dresses, in an assortment of colors and styles.

I take a step back. "Sydney, you're the bride. I'm at your mercy."

"I'm thinking we should go with a light-weight material like chiffon since it's an outdoor ceremony. It can still be really warm on Labor Day weekend." Sydney explains as she looks through the racks of dresses. She stops. "This is perfect, go try it on!"

I take the dress and make my way into the fitting room. I'm a vision in peach chiffon! I run my hand along the cascading ruffle down the side. She's right. This dress is perfect. It fits like a glove and I look beautiful in it. I step out of the dressing room to get her opinion.

Sydney squeals. "You look fabulous! All we need are some silver strappy heels. Anna, we'll take it!"

Dress shopping was a breeze; hopefully the rest of the day flows just as smoothly.

Sydney is in a complete state of bridal bliss. Her sparkling hazel eyes gleam and she almost bounces when she walks. "I thought it would take hours to find the perfect dress. You must be my good luck charm."

"I think it's more like the other way around, Sis." I put my arm around her and give her a quick squeeze. If anyone deserves complete happiness, it's Sydney.

My pocket chimes. I pull out my cell phone and take a deep breath. My hand trembles as my eyes gaze over the bright letters on the screen. I try to relax my raising cheekbones as I read the text from Van Sinclair. It' a picture of the ocean.

My heart flutters as I text back.

Looks like you made some beach time.

My phone chimes.

I thought you'd like to see the ocean too. How's slavery?

I bite my cheeks. Sydney wouldn't be amused by my new title of wedding planning slave.

It's actually pretty fun. We got a lot done and are heading home after lunch. I type and press send.

I'm headed to the beach bar and grill. Our show's tomorrow night. Tonight's all about relaxing.

Is he deliberately trying to make me jealous? If he is, it's certainly working. I type quickly as Sydney walks toward me.

Wow, I'm jealous. Enjoy your free day. *TTYL*

"Who are you texting?" she asks, "You usually don't even remember to bring your phone."

I twirl my hair around my fingers and slide my phone back into my pocket. "Brooke. She's just letting me know I shouldn't wait up for her." I'm not ready to tell anyone about Van. I've only talked to him a few times and still don't know where any of this is going. *If it develops into something, I'll tell everyone. Until then, it's my secret.*

"She should've just left you a note. She's lucky you even got the text."

"I guess it was last minute," I lie again. "So, where we going for lunch?"

"How about Zena's Bistro? They have great Panini," she boasts.

We really worked up an appetite with all of our wedding planning. We inhale our grilled chicken sandwiches in minutes and head back to my apartment.

"Thanks for lunch, Sydney. I had a great time with you today."

Sydney leans her head against the headrest of the car. "We got so much done. I'm so relieved. I finally feel like I'm ready for this wedding. Well, I have to head back to Philadelphia after I drop you off. Next, Bryce and I have to agree on the cake."

"I'm sure he won't mind all the tasty sampling that goes into that decision. Just think, in a few more days we'll be back in Cherry Falls attending the shower of the year." I smile. "I can't wait to see all of Mom's planning come together."

"No doubt it will be over the top," Sydney says as she hugs me. "Thanks again for the help today. I'll see you next week."

I yawn and rub my eyes as I walk through the driveway. The lack of sleep is starting to catch up with me. On the way up the steps I notice a package on my porch. It's addressed to me but has no return address. *That's strange.* I place it on the kitchen table and search the junk drawer for scissors. *Please don't let it be another lame present from Jesse.*

My mouth falls open as I peel back the stiff cardboard. I blink repeatedly, trying to focus my tired eyes. Inside is a concert ticket to see Devil's Garden tomorrow night at Bader Field, a backstage pass with a note that reads, '*Your second backstage experience will destroy your first one*', and a postcard from the Sea Star Hotel in Atlantic City.

My heart starts racing again. I grab my phone and do something I never dreamed I'd do. I dial Van Sinclair's number.

"Hey," he answers.

I fidget with my fingers. "Hi. After serving my slavery sentence I found an interesting package at my door."

"Really? I can't imagine what it could be."

I bite my lip. "Well, it's kind of cryptic. Maybe it's from some psychotic serial killer."

"You need to watch out for those crazy bastards that go around killing cereal." He laughs. "You said you love the ocean. I'm hoping you'll want to come to the show and spend some beach time with me. I need someone to show me the ropes, or should I say the waves."

My heart literally skips a beat. Van wants me to stay with him, at the beach, in a hotel? The butterflies in my stomach flutter frantically. I know exactly what will be happening if Van and I share a hotel room. *What should I do?* I really want to see him again, but musicians aren't known to be the most faithful people. *Who am I kidding?* He may only want me for one night.

I pace around the room. Oh, but I meet with Owen Jenkins tomorrow morning. Well, there's really not much I can do to prepare for my new position yet. I certainly can use some fun, and I'm sure nothing will evolve from this anyway. I pull out a kitchen chair and sit. *Ah, a slumber party with Van Sinclair.* My whole body trembles and tingles. I'm breathless as heat radiates through my chest. I take a deep breath and swallow hard to relieve the dryness in my mouth; I try to act clever.

"Should I pack life jackets?"

He chuckles. "I think they provide that stuff here."

I twirl my hair around my fingers. "Ok, I have a meeting with my new boss tomorrow morning. I'll leave in the afternoon so I should be there around four o'clock."

"I booked a room at the Sea Star Hotel. It doesn't have a casino so we won't have to deal with any drunken gamblers," he says. "I have to go to meet everyone at Bader Field now but I'll see you tomorrow."

"See you tomorrow," I reply.

Did I forget to breathe again? I let my dizzy head fall back and slink into the chair. *Oh no, did I dream this up in a sleep-*

deprived daydream? I look over at the box on the table and pinch myself just to make sure. *Ouch, yep this is for real.*

CHAPTER 3—BEACH

Pure exhaustion finally allows me to shut my mind down and get some quality sleep. The alarm rings at 9:15 a.m. for my 10:30 meeting at Global Inc. I stretch and press the snooze button. *Why do they want to meet with me now? Eh, there's probably some agenda.* Besides, I'm lucky that I managed to obtain the assistant to the senior account manager position, a rarity for new graduates. Too bad it's not open until the end of the summer and I won't be starting until September.

I yawn and muster up enough energy to get myself out of bed and start my grooming ritual. *Now what's my most professional outfit?* I put on my gray business suit and pull my hair into a sophisticated ponytail. Truth be told, I'm more prepared for my meeting with my new boss this morning than I am for tonight.

∞

I pull into a huge parking garage and stare at the enormous building. I take a deep breath and look around at the endless sea of parking spaces. *I'll just be another number in this vast corporation.*

I sign in at the front desk and wait to be called. The reception area is large and filled with people hustling toward the elevators. The marble tile is exquisite and the wall to wall windows don't contain even one fingerprint. The soft music mimics that of a fancy hotel. *Hmm, what will I need to pack for my overnight excursion?*

My head jerks back slightly as I'm pulled out of my daydream and greeted by a handsome man in a dark gray suit.

"Hello Alexis, my name is Owen Jenkins and I will be supervising the advertising and marketing division for Global Inc."

I stare at him like a deer in headlights. "It's a pleasure to meet you, Mr. Jenkins." Our eyes break contact and I fidget with my fingers.

He holds out his hand. "Please, call me Owen."

I shake his hand, trying to keep a firm grip. *Can he be any more intimidating?* Owen Jenkins exudes the air of a man who's successful in all endeavors. Every strand of his thick brown hair is perfectly in place. In his late thirties, he's handsome and clearly rich. The subtle musk of expensive cologne trails him as he walks.

He adjusts the sleeve of his Versace business suit, showing off his silver Rolex watch. "Alexis, I called you in for a meeting to introduce myself, give you a tour of the facility, and let you know a little about our company. We will have one more meeting in August to finalize our goals and expectations."

"Thank you, I'm eager to learn the ins and outs of the advertising world."

Owen takes me on a tour of the mammoth building where I'll soon work. It's a safe bet that I won't remember half of what I'm being shown. He educates me about the various companies that Global Inc. represents and then outlines my job description. From what he explains, I'll be reading over business proposals and fetching coffee for department heads. Those tasks are fine with me. It's better than starting in the mailroom which is where most new graduates end up.

"I hope I've answered some of your questions, Alexis. I enjoyed meeting you. We will get together again in August, until then enjoy your summer."

"Thank you very much. I look forward to working with you."

The meeting takes longer than I expect. I rush home to start packing. Even though I'm only staying overnight, it's a crucial night that may decide what the future holds. Who knows?

Umm, should I even be thinking about a future with a rocker? He certainly doesn't have the most stable career. Sure, he's the essence of physical perfection but that only brings heartache. Especially with the droves of women that chase him after every show. I cover my face with my hands and shake my head. Here I go, overanalyzing everything again. I need to clear my mind and live it up! I pull a duffel bag out of the closet.

I check Brooke's room. She must still be with Dean. *Looks like I don't have anyone to help me decide what I should take.* I find a purple mini dress that'll be perfect for the concert. Ok, my black knee-high boots, and a long crystal beaded necklace knotted in the middle should finish the look. Now the all-important question of which underwear to choose. I find a sexy black lace bra and bikini panties that I bought from Victoria's Secret a few weeks ago but never got the chance to wear. *Perfect!*

I throw shorts and a tank top in my bag for the next day along with a brush, toothbrush, deodorant, and make-up. That should cover it. I jump in the shower, paying close attention to grooming all of the areas Van may glimpse over. I continue with my grooming routine, trying to look my best. My hair falls down, letting my curls hit my shoulders and back. I fasten the front with a crystal embellished headband and apply light make-up concentrating on a smoky purple eye and red lips. I'm all ready, except I'm not ready at all.

My heart races and I begin to hyperventilate. I haven't been with anyone other than Jesse for two years. That ended up a disaster; I hope my sexual skills are up to par. To make matters worse, Van Sinclair is gorgeous, confident, and no doubt very experienced. I don't even want to know how many women he has been with. There were at least fifty throwing themselves at him the night we met.

I go into Brooke's bedroom, open the nightstand drawer, and take out a sleeve of condoms. Even though I've been on the pill for years, I still want to protect myself. *I have to get rid of this nervous energy before I get to Atlantic City.* I must believe that Van has been texting and calling me because he wants to know *me*. He could easily have sex with much less effort if that was what he was after. I have to believe that he truly wants to be with *me* and there's no doubt I want to be with him, no matter what I try to tell myself. He awakens every hibernating cell in my body. I smile as I think through all of our conversations and texts. My little self-pep talk boosts my confidence. I grab my overnight bag and head for the car. I'm on my way to Van Sinclair.

It's a three-hour car ride from my apartment to Atlantic City. I really don't mind. The drive gives me some more time to think and convince myself that I'm the woman Van Sinclair wants. I begin to fidget and become more restless the closer I get to Atlantic City. My heart beats a little faster with every passing mile. I can't wait to see Van again. Plus, this time we'll be alone after the concert. I won't be in a room filled with other woman trying to compete for his attention. He'll be completely mine.

I twirl my hair around my fingers as I pull into the hotel's parking garage. Salty air and the cackle of seagulls greet me as I step outside. The hotel rests on the boardwalk and leads to a pristine white sandy beach. It's reminiscent of the long-lost glamour that Atlantic City possessed in eras past. I walk into the enormous lobby and admire the crystal chandeliers and marble tiles. I text Van, letting him know I'd arrived and set my bag onto the floor.

The elevator doors slowly open. My whole body erupts in goose bumps as the unique electricity flows through me. I glance down at the dark-blue ripped jeans that hang down on his hips just enough to flaunt his chiseled abs, and then focus my gaze to yet another tight black T-shirt that once again does not fail to show off just about every muscle in his perfect body. *Wow!* The fluttering in my stomach begins.

He walks up to me, rubbing the back of his neck. "You look great! Thanks for driving all this way. I'm sorry, I should've gotten a ride for you."

"I didn't mind the drive, it was relaxing," I say, fidgeting with my necklace.

He drops his arm. "So what do you think of the place?"

"It's absolutely beautiful." I take a step back and glance around once more.

Van lifts my bag with one hand and puts the other hand around my waist. Sparks flow through my body, drifting from my fingertips to my toes. I take a deep breath and try to steady my heartbeat.

"Come on, I want to show you our room." He guides me toward the elevator.

I follow him like a moth to a flame. Is there hidden meaning in his comment?

We're on the sixth floor. The elevator doors open and he leads me into the room. It's incredible, decorated in white and blue with a massive king-sized bed beside a huge window which offers a magnificent view of the Atlantic Ocean. There's also a sitting area with a table and chairs, and an enormous bathroom. I step over to the window, captured by the view of the sea.

"Van, it's breathtaking."

"Wow, I was shooting for nice," he says and flashes a smile. "We'll have to be at Bader Field around six so I thought we could order some room service and have dinner here. What do you like?"

I bite my lip. "Surprise me." I'm definitely not one of those girls who starve themselves. A man from Kansas can probably be trusted to order some savory cuisine, right?

He jerks his head back slightly and scrunches his eyebrows. "Huh, you want me to surprise you? Ok, get yourself settled and I'll order up some food."

He goes over to the phone and I unpack my things. Ten minutes later, there's a knock on the door. *Wow, I guess rockers get prime treatment here.* A man dressed in black pants, a white shirt, and a bow tie wheels in two trays covered with silver domes and a bottle of white wine. He lifts the domes to reveal two filet mignon dinners with baked potatoes, green beans, and chocolate cake. Van Sinclair is most definitely the perfect man.

"I hope you aren't a vegetarian."

"Yum!" It's hands down one of the best steak dinners I've ever had. The soft texture melts in my mouth and the flavor tantalizes my taste buds. *This is the best date I've ever been on. He really chooses hotels with all the bells and whistles.* I look out the window at the sun glistening off the ocean. It's an image you can print on a postcard.

Van glances at his watch. "We have about an hour before we have to head to the show. Do you want to walk with me on the beach?"

"Just give me a minute. These boots won't work so well in the sand."

Van's eyes burn through me as I disappear into the bathroom to quickly freshen up. My fruity perfume fills the air as I rub my wrists together. I slip into my flip flops and head out of the bathroom, ready for sun and sand. Van sits on the edge of the bed, waiting for me. His flawless skin glistens from the sunlight shining in through the window. My heart beats like a jackhammer. He's the epitome of perfection.

"Ready?" he asks as he runs his hand through his hair.

"Yes, definitely," I answer, hoping it will hold true for our entire evening.

It's an ideal spring day. The light breeze flows through our hair as Van holds my hand and we walk along the shoreline. My body tingles, sparked by the energy that's created when we touch. I inhale the fresh salty air as the cool water hits our feet, sinking me into the gritty sand.

"It's so beautiful here. Thank you for inviting me."

"I had to see you again. You said you love the ocean. It's the perfect bribe."

"You didn't have to bribe me, I would've come even if you'd invited me to a mud pit," I say with a grin.

"Well that could certainly be interesting," he says with a smirk. "I'll have to remember that for next time."

My pulse quickens at the thought of a next time. *He's planning on seeing me again?* I hope that holds true after tonight. I'm queasy just thinking about it.

As we pass an empty lifeguard chair, Van stops. "Come on, let's get a better look at the ocean."

We walk over to the chair and he boosts me up. My muscles tense as his hand touches my thigh. He puts his arm around me, running his finger along my arm as we sit, watching the sun glisten off the waves. Warmth floods my body and my breath quickens. A fluttering begins in my chest. I clench my hands briefly and release them, rubbing my palms against the bottom of my dress.

"I can see why you like the beach so much," he says.

"Especially on a perfect day like today."

We sit and watch the waves crash in perfectly choreographed rhythm. I take a deep breath and try to control the fluttering of my stomach.

"We better head back," he says reluctantly.

"Ok. Hey, in case I forget to tell you later, I had a great time tonight." I tilt my head and gaze into his eyes.

His lips slowly rise into a sexy smile. He climbs off the chair and glides his hands up my legs and onto my hips to help me down. I hold onto his shoulders and jump into the sand in front of him, slowly sliding my hands down his hard chest. My body trembles as my fingertips slip down the soft T-shirt. His hands, still on my hips, move up to my face. My heart races, faster and faster. His emerald eyes are locked on mine. He takes a step forward and brushes his lips over mine. My body is a blazing inferno, sending shockwaves from my head to my toes. I pull him closer, gripping his shirt as he massages his tongue against mine in a sweet, smooth motion. He gently sucks on my bottom lip and pulls away, keeping his eyes fastened on mine.

My lips part and I stare, hypnotized in a lust-filled trance. His look is extremely intense, like he wants to devour me at that very moment. My knees are weak. It's most definitely the very best kiss of my entire life. If this is any indication of what's to come, I'm way out of my league. I need to do something to prevent anything more from happening on the beach. Besides, I don't want him to be late for his show. No need to give the band members a reason not to like me. I reach my arms around and pull him into an embrace. He exhales deeply and puts his arms around me, slowly running his hands down my back. He slithers his fingers along mine, intertwining our hands and we start walking back to the hotel.

There are hundreds of people filing into Bader Field when we arrive. It's an impressive turn out for an up-and-coming band. Dozens of half-dressed women lurk near the entrances to the restricted areas. Van and I walk hand-in-hand to the meeting area in the back of the pavilion where Chaz, Tyler, Marcus, and Jenna are waiting.

"Nice of you to show up!" Chaz teases, waving his hand in the air.

"Yeah, I figured you wouldn't start without me," Van sneers.

Jenna's eyes travel from my boots to my face. "Umm, hi. I've never seen one of you twice. This is new. I guess I should introduce myself. I'm Jenna Crane."

"Hi Jenna. I'm Lexie Waters." I hold out my hand and we exchange a quick handshake. Even Jenna's smart ass comments can't ruin my pure euphoria.

Jenna and I stand at the side of the stage to watch the boys do their thing. My eyes fixate on the plethora of screaming fans waiting for the show to begin. Suddenly, it's show time. The lights shine down, illuminating the flawless face that leaves me mesmerized. I'm breathless! Van keeps looking over at me and smiling between songs.

I tilt my head and let out a soft sigh. *I'm the luckiest girl alive.* Not everyone gets to live out their rock star fantasy. Although I don't know how I'll feel tomorrow, tonight is shaping up to be one of the best of my life.

The band meets with a few fans and signs some autographs. I wait patiently for Van to finish.

"Hey guys, great show! We're heading back to the hotel. Catch you tomorrow at breakfast," Van says.

"More girls for me," Chaz replies.

As we step into the hotel room my breathing becomes rapid and my heart races. It's as if I've stepped into another dimension. I scurry into the bathroom to freshen up and give myself another pep talk. The moment that I yearn for, yet fear, has arrived. I unzip my boots and yank them off, letting the cool tile collide with my hot feet. Ah, the sensation invigorates my body. My palms rest against the granite countertop. I close my eyes and take a deep breath, slowly opening them and gazing at my reflection. *Come on Lexie, pull yourself together! He's just a guy.* Yeah right. I run my fingers through my hair, removing my headband and pull my necklace over my head, dropping it onto the counter. A quick spray of perfume on my belly and I'm as ready as I'll ever be.

I step into the bedroom, twirling my hair around my fingers. Van sits on the bed and lifts his eyes; they scorch through me, encircling my soul. He runs his fingers through his hair and stands. *God, he's so sexy. No matter what happens, I'll never forget this night.*

Keeping his eyes locked onto mine like a predator stalking his next meal, he slowly moves toward me. My heart is thrashing against my chest. He leans in, brushes a few strands of hair away from my face, and sweeps his lips over mine. A firestorm streams through my body. I reach around and slide my fingers over the solid muscles of his back and press myself against him. *Ah, he really wants me.* The deep passion intensifies as his tongue penetrates my mouth. I'm so out of my league. I start shaking.

He pulls away. "Are you cold?"

"Just need to warm up."

"I can help with that."

Holy crap, he can feel me shiver. I have to pull myself together. I'm my own worst enemy. I move my hands up his body and weave my fingers through his still-damp hair, re-igniting our make-out session. His soft lips glide across my jaw and down my neck, causing every hair on my body to rise. I run my hands down to the bottom of his soft T-shirt, slowly slithering my fingers over an array of peaks and valleys as I pull it up and over his head. My grip loosens and the shirt falls to the floor.

At last, a chance to admire his chiseled body. I rest my hands on his shoulders and lower my head. My eyes travel over the rugged terrain of his torso. *God, he's sexy.* My heart is pounding out of my chest. Can he hear it?

He reaches around and whisks my hair away from my back. His fingers softly caress my skin causing goose bumps to spread over my body as he unzips the back of my dress. I step out of it, revealing my black lace bra and panties.

He runs his hand along my face and down my side. "Wow, the view from this room just keeps getting better."

He scoops me up and places me on the bed. The silky blue sheets cool my blazing body. I'm breathing so fast I'm almost panting. All my negative thoughts are now replaced by an overwhelming need to touch and explore every inch of Van Sinclair.

He hooks his fingers under my bra straps, gradually slipping them down while placing soft kisses from my neck down to my breasts. Every hair on my body stands on end and I try to erase any physical distance between us. His flawless body stings my fingers, the unique electricity flowing through, as I move down to the waist of his jeans, pulling against the thick fabric. Finally the button gives, allowing me to release him from the denim stranglehold.

I reach down and slide my hand against the silky fabric of his boxers, exploring every inch of him. He groans.

He slips his index fingers on both sides of my panties and slides them down. My body quivers as I arch my back to help him complete the journey. He gently caresses my most sensitive areas while sliding his fingers inside of me. I'm in a state of complete bliss, desire building within. His hand pats the night stand as he searches the drawer and retrieves a condom. He kicks off his boxers, opens the packet, and slides it on. He crawls on top of me traveling soft kisses from my neck to my lips. He entwines his hands with mine as he pushes against me, slowly entering my body.

I gasp as he fills every inch of me. We start moving in a slow, steady motion. Every magical cell in my body awakens and my breathing increases once again. My body jolts into a frenzy of tremors and I moan as I find my release; the reaction from my intense pleasure results in him finding his shortly afterward. Our bodies lay entwined and our breathing slows.

He sits up on his elbow and turns toward me, his emerald eyes still locked with mine. "Lexie Waters, you have no idea what you do to me."

I mimic his movements. "Right back at ya." He ignites my body with the softest touch. It's truly amazing. He's my own personal catalyst of desire.

I excuse myself to freshen up. *Damn it! I forgot to pack something to sleep in.* I peek my head out of the bathroom door.

"Can I borrow one of your T-shirts?" I ask, meek as a mouse.

He roots through his duffel bag and pulls out a shirt. "You need one of these anyway," he says as he hands it to me.

Ooh, a Devil's Garden T-shirt. He's right, I do need one. As I pull the T-shirt over my head my body shivers. I breathe deep, taking in Van's scent which is trapped in every fiber. There's no way I'll ever wash it. I skip out of the bathroom and proceed toward the bed.

"It looks great on you," he says and pulls me under the covers. His strong arms surround me as we drift to sleep.

I wake to a dragon staring at me. I lift my head from Van's chest; the bright sunlight peeking through the window illuminates his body. With his arm wrapped around me, his tattoo is positioned directly in front of my eyes. He opens his eyes, squinting from the sunbeams.

He stretches. "Good morning."

"Good morning, it looks like another beautiful day."

He fastens his hypnotizing eyes on mine. "Definitely beautiful."

Chills run through my body and I smile at the compliment. He props himself on his elbow and turns toward me. I do the same, facing him and smiling. He reaches over and tucks a stray piece of hair behind my ear.

"Everyone's meeting at the diner around the corner for breakfast in about an hour. Then we have a radio interview before we hit the road."

"Ok, I think I'll take a quick shower first."

He tilts his head and raises his eyebrow. "You read my mind."

I'm suddenly being carried into the bathroom.

Van turns the water on and sets me on my feet. He places his forehead against mine and grabs the hem of my T-shirt, slowly pulling it up and over my head. My body tingles as he brushes his fingers along my skin. He grabs my hips and pulls me closer to his body, slamming every inch of his flesh against mine. I moan as he moves forward, backing me against the bathroom wall. The smooth tiles slide across my skin as he brushes his lips against me, placing kisses up my neck, against my jaw, ending at my lips.

My heart drums as the kisses become intense and passionate. I run my fingers through his silky hair, gripping at the strands.

He lifts me up and I wrap my legs around his waist, my body refusing to break my lips from his. He starts walking back to the bedroom and lowers me onto the soft sheets. I'm out of breath, panting like I've just run for miles. He slides his hands along my thighs and pulls off my panties in one smooth movement. Goose bumps erupt as he trails kisses down my chest and stomach and continues down to my nether regions. His tongue moves around my most sensitive areas.

I groan and my heart races as the desire inside me builds to an intense level quickly. I moan while releasing my pleasure. I crash my head down on the bed, trying to catch my breath and lower my pulse to an acceptable level. Now, soft kisses are moving up my body, over my belly and breasts, back up to my neck, over my jaw finally ending on my lips, much more intense than before. I reach down over the silky fabric and tug Van's boxers away to release him. Breathing quickly, he reaches into the nightstand, rips open the package, and thrusts himself inside me. I moan as his thrusts fuel my building desire. Our breathing becomes rapid and we both find our release together.

Finally, I catch my breath. Wow, that was the best sexual experience of my life. My whole body tingles as the intense pleasure continues to radiate through me.

Van holds himself up on his elbows and brushes a few strands of hair away from my face. "I lose all self-control when I'm with you."

I press my forehead against his and softly kiss his lips. "I think it may be time for that shower."

Van rolls over and holds out his hand to lead me to the shower. Steam from the running water fills the room and fogs the mirrors. Face to face, the warm water engulfs our bodies. We rub soapy bubbles over each other in between giggles and kisses. Ah, he has a fun, playful side as well as an intense, seductive side.

Why is time flying? Already, it's time to head to meet Jenna and the band. My new Devil's Garden T-shirt sends shock waves through me. The cells of my body are tricked by the faint smell of Van trapped in its fibers. *Looks like I have a new favorite T-shirt.* We walk down the sidewalk and arrive at the quaint diner. Van puts his arm around my waist and pushes open the door. I look over at the table full of his band mates, who are staring at me.

Marcus pulls out a chair. "Hey Lexie, nice to see you again."

I take a seat and twirl my hair around my fingers. "Hi everyone."

"Van, you really missed out this time. Atlantic City girls are hot and freaky," Chaz says.

Van looks over at me. "I didn't miss out on anything." My face heats as I think about our night together. I try to hold back a smile.

"Bader Field was awesome. The crowd loved us and we had a pretty good turn out." Tyler says, changing the subject.

"Yeah, it was awesome," Marcus agrees.

The waitress sets a smorgasbord on the table. My stomach growls as I inhale the aroma of blueberry pancakes, cinnamon French toast, bacon, and sausage. I guess I worked up an appetite. I fill a plate while the guys discuss which songs they'll promote at their radio interview.

"So Lexie, want to hit some stores while the guys do their thing?" Jenna asks. "The shopping here is great." She searches my face and sips her juice.

I raise my eyebrow and look at her. *Doesn't she hate me?*

Van glances over at me nibbling on a slice of bacon. "We'll catch up with you girls after the interview."

"Ok, sounds fun." This is strange, but also intriguing. *Why does Jenna want to be alone with me?* The boys walk across the street to the station and Jenna and I head toward the stores.

"Ready for some girl time?" she cocks her head to one side.

"As ready as I'll ever be."

CHAPTER 4—JENNA

The shopping district resembles a high-fashion avenue in the big city. All of the big name stores from Gucci to Burberry are at hand. Good thing I don't need to buy anything. Selling a kidney would be the only way I could afford to shop on this street.

The cool breeze blows my hair around my face, tickling my nose. I pat it down to the best of my ability and turn to Jenna. Her heels click on the sidewalk as she stands tall with her chin up to the sky, every strand of her hair perfectly flowing in the wind. *Why does she want to spend alone time with me? Everything she's said to me in the few times we've spoken has been pretty insulting.* I have to lay things on the table before we can have any real conversation.

"Look, I'm fully aware that I'm an outsider on your turf but I'm not a groupie or a punching bag."

Jenna stops, turns her chin toward me, and raises her eyebrows. "You're clueless. I want to spend some time with you to talk. I owe you an apology for acting like such a bitch. I just figured you were another one of Van's one night stands. Imagine my surprise when I saw you here with him. I'm honestly stunned."

Can she be any more insulting? "I'm sure it's shocking to you that Van would want to spend time with someone like me. I can imagine he meets women who look like they stepped off of a runway. Honestly, I'm still surprised by it myself." I scowl.

She pulls her shoulders back, returning her body to its natural perfect posture, and continues to walk. "That's not what I mean at all. When I said I've never met one of you twice, I meant I've never met a girl Van was with more than one time. I've known him since he was twelve years old. I don't mean anything about you personally."

What is she talking about? I'm sure Van dated during school. My head flinches back as I stroll. "He must've had girls chasing after him since high school. He's gorgeous. You can't tell me he's never dated."

She smirks. "Well, if you want to call his relations with the girls in school 'dating'. He was basically with them for a one night only show, if you know what I mean. I kind of thought he was an asshole for treating girls like that but they were much worse. They knew exactly what he was all about and did it anyway."

I'm not sure why Jenna is confiding in me. She's either trying to be my friend or trying to scare me away. Van has really never been in a relationship? That's a hard concept to grasp.

I narrow my eyes. "Why are you telling me this? Are you trying to let me know that I'm basically just being used and I shouldn't expect much?"

She shakes her head. "You're the first girl Van's taken to breakfast and that means something."

I smirk. "Well breakfast is the most important meal of the day. I can understand your excitement."

"You're a smart ass. I think we will get along just fine."

As we continue walking down the street the big shops are replaced with small boutiques. Large windows display distinctive merchandise, from handmade fudge to intricately designed Christmas ornaments. Everything's so unique. We pause at a vintage lingerie store called Betty's Boutique. Beautiful lace garments grace the glass store front, emanating old-school charm. The contents in this store can fill a pin-up girl's closet.

"Let's stop in here. We can get something for our men to enjoy," Jenna says with a wink.

I pull open the heavy wooden door. "I've only been on one date with Van. I don't have a *man*."

"You just don't realize it yet," she replies.

I smile at the thought of being Van's girl. Jenna obviously sees something that I don't. I can't imagine Van has been talking about me to Jenna; that's not his style.

The smooth sheer fabric caresses my hands as I rummage through the racks. I stop and examine an emerald green silk and lace nighty. Perfect. It's extremely sexy, yet tasteful. The beautiful deep green color mirrors Van's eyes.

"Looks like we both found something." Jenna comes up behind me holding a red camisole and panties.

"You guys are hitting the road in a few hours. I may never even get the chance to wear it for him." My eyes start to water. I quickly blink to suppress the danger of falling tears.

"Buy it, I promise you will get a chance to wear it. Besides, the color looks great on you."

I buy the vintage French lingerie, hoping I'll get a chance to model it soon. I'm not exactly sure what happens now. I'm going home and Van will be continuing on his tour. He'll be traveling from town to town, state to state, and meeting girls at every stop. He'll probably forget all about me. A wave of nausea flows through me as I think about never being with Van again. His voice, his soft touch, just the thought of him causes my skin to tingle. No one else will ever breathe such life into my body.

Jenna stares at me as if she knows exactly what I'm thinking. "There's a cute little café across the street. Let's get a drink and relax."

We sit down at a table overlooking the beach with our raspberry lemonades and cookies. It's a shame I can't admire the view from the café's prime seating. My mind is pure chaos. What will the future hold?

"Stop frowning," Jenna says. "He really cares about you; I've never seen him act this way. He's going to make sure he sees you however and whenever he can. You're basically his first date." She sips her lemonade.

I touch the back of my neck. "He didn't say any of this to me. I hope you're right."

"He's probably going to screw up and do idiotic things because he's clueless about women. Just be patient with him. It'll be worth it."

I hate to tell her but Van Sinclair is definitely not clueless about women. He knows exactly what to do and how to do it. She must be one of the few that doesn't know about his abilities. I blush at the thought.

I bite my cookie. "Thanks Jenna. I really am glad we had the chance to get to know each other better."

Jenna isn't the evil, ruthless creature I imagined her to be. She's a woman who loves her husband, in a world where he's sought after and tempted by other women all the time. Her tough exterior is a necessity. Underneath it all she's a sweet, caring person who can only let her vulnerable side be seen by those in her inner circle, which I'm gradually becoming a part of.

Marcus and Van are waiting for us outside the radio station. Van leans against the brick building and flashes a sexy grin as I walk around the corner toward him.

"So how was shopping?" Marcus asks as he kisses Jenna.

"I think you'll approve of my fashion choices," Jenna says with a seductive smile. "We had a really good time. It's nice to finally have a girlfriend. You guys are terrible fashionistas."

I turn toward Van. "So how did the interview go?"

"They let us take some calls and answer a few questions from the fans," Van replies.

"I told them everyone was married," Marcus says laughing uncontrollably, "Chaz almost had a stroke."

Van walks over to me and reaches for my hand. "I've got time for one more walk on the beach before we have to leave."

My body's in turmoil. My heart races as the electricity flows through me when our skin makes contact, but it's challenged by the hollowness in my chest. He'll be leaving shortly. I breathe deeply. Oh well, there's plenty of time to be depressed later. I'll enjoy the little time we have left together in Atlantic City.

"It's a date," I say. That phrase means so much more since my talk with Jenna.

Van and I walk down to the beach and along the water. The sun glistens off the waves, forming tiny sparkles throughout the vast sea. The light ocean breeze cools my skin. I take a deep breath, inhaling the scent of the salt water and Van Sinclair.

Van plays with my fingers as we walk down the beach. Jenna is right. He's different, a little nervous and unsure, not the same confident rock god I originally met backstage. Maybe he really is stepping into a realm where he's never been before. I want to snap him out of his trance, so I try small talk.

"Where to after New York?"

"A few more stops on the east coast. We have shows in Connecticut, Massachusetts, and Ohio. Then we make our way out west."

An ache forms in my chest. "Are you looking forward to having down time after your tour ends?" I ask, hoping to find out something about what the future will bring.

He grimaces. "Yes and no. I love to perform but it'll be great to be able to rest my head on my own pillow for more than a few nights. Are you excited to start work?"

I shrug. "I guess. It'll give me the experience and opportunity I need to eventually get to where I want to be."

"And where is it that you want to be?"

My heart races. Right now I want to be anywhere Van Sinclair is, but that's not an answer I'm ready to share. "I want to be happy with my career and my life. I'm not sure exactly where that'll be just yet."

"That's funny, I feel exactly the same way." He rubs the back of his neck, and then lets his hand fall down to his side.

As I turn toward him, his emerald eyes lock with mine. The intense need to hold onto him and never let go overcomes me. I take a deep breath and hold it in. Does willpower exist in the presence of Van?

He raises an eyebrow. "You know, there are beaches we can go for walks on in Connecticut and Massachusetts. Our tour takes us there the end of next week."

My heart skips a beat. I'm giddy, like a school girl being asked to the prom. I want so badly to be with him again. A huge smile erupts.

I bite softly on my bottom lip. "My sister's wedding shower is this coming weekend but after that my schedule is wide open."

Van pulls me close to him, wrapping his arms around my waist. He presses his forehead against mine. "Will you stay with me again? Since your schedule is wide open."

I creep my hands up to his shoulders and slightly moan. "I would love to."

He lifts my chin and places his lips against mine. My stomach flip-flops and my heart smacks the walls of my chest. The intense energy and passion in this deep sensual kiss is nuclear. I put my arms around his neck, entwining my hands in the soft strands of his hair. We kiss deeply and passionately for several minutes, neither of us wanting to pull back. He finally breaks away.

"Just so you know, I'm looking up all of the mud pits in the New England region. Don't think I forgot," he says as he tilts his head and winks.

"Are you trying to make me a dirty girl?" I ask, raising my eyebrows.

He rolls his eyes at me. "I want you exactly the way you are. This time you're not driving by yourself. I'll figure something else out."

"We'll figure it out," I say to him with a sweet smile, not just referring to next week.

He seems to understand what I mean. We walk back to my car at the hotel parking garage.

"Be careful driving, and let me know when you get home."

"I'll be fine."

He pulls me close, wedging me in between his perfect body and my car. I get chills as he brushes some loose strands of hair away from my face and speaks softly.

"I had an awesome time."

"Me too, the time of my life." I run my hands down his back and stop at the waist of his jeans. "See you soon."

He brushes his lips across mine and gives me a sweet kiss. Hesitantly, he steps away from my car and we wave to each other as I pull away.

As soon as I make it to the main highway, tears start to form in my eyes. *What's wrong with me?* I had a great trip, followed by a happy goodbye, and a plan to see each other again. Maybe I'm going crazy, or maybe my subconscious realizes something my rational mind does not want to comprehend.

How will a relationship with Van work? I guess I'll meet up with him at various hotels across the country until his tour is over. Then, I'll be back at my apartment and he'll be in Kansas. I sigh. Besides the long-distance issue, he'll be constantly enticed by half-naked woman, offering to please him in any way he can imagine. Plus, I'll be starting at Global Inc. before I know it. I'm certainly not going to jeopardize my career, I've worked hard for my degree.

I grip the wheel harder as more tears run down my cheeks. How did I end up in this position? What happened to my plan of steering clear of guys and focusing on my career? One concert and my whole life turns upside down.

It's almost as if we are doomed to fail, even before we start. On the positive side, he wants to try. He's never wanted to try with anyone else, but he wants to try with me. Warmth radiates through my body.

This drive is taking forever. The rational part of my brain is telling me this relationship will most definitely turn out to be a train wreck, but my heart doesn't care. From the day we met, a fire ignited inside of me. My body quivers and I become breathless every time he's near me. It's a unique experience, probably something I'll never encounter again. It's an undying passion flowing through every pore in my body.

Unfortunately, passion has the tendency to fade. *How can I be sure I won't be betrayed? Can I handle that again?* I just don't know if the pleasure will be worth the pain that may come. So here I am facing the extreme likelihood that I will once again be replaced by a blond fling. Is it possible to harden my heart and enjoy the ride?

CHAPTER 5—HOME

Finally! The infinite ride home is over. Thank God I didn't fall asleep driving. I plop my head against the headrest and shift the car into park. *Please let my mind prevail over the internal battle that's been waging these last few hours.* I need to clear my head and concentrate on Sydney's bridal shower. It's going to be great to see my sister again, especially in Cherry Falls. It feels like I haven't been home in years, even though I was just there a few months ago for spring break.

I turn off the engine and stretch my arms over my head and yawn. Uh, driving can be exhausting. I pull out my cell phone to text Van as promised.

Made it home in one piece. Have a great night.

He doesn't need to know how conflicted I am about our future, telling him will only complicate things. I'll have that discussion with him when I'm sure of what I want. My phone chimes.

Glad you're home safe but I can't have a great night unless you're with me.

Oh. If I could only just clear my head! *How am I supposed to get Van Sinclair off my mind, especially with him sending me such sweet messages?* He's so different than all of the other guys I've dated. There are no witty lines or cheesy gestures to impress me. He's a 'what you see is what you get' kind of guy. I exhale deeply as a smile creeps over my face. How refreshing! He really means everything he says, and he's saying he wishes I was with him. There's no way I can resist his charm.

Believe me, I wish I was there….except I'd probably fall asleep.

I yawn again and start gathering my belongings to take inside. My phone chimes again.

Get some sleep. Sweet dreams.

I walk into the apartment to find Brooke sitting at the table with her arms crossed, tapping her foot and glaring at me. *Oh no, I forgot about Brooke.* Well, it's not the first time I've stayed out all night; she's guilty of this as well.

"Hey, how was your slumber party with Dean?" I ask, raising my eyebrows.

"Are you serious? You, young lady, have a lot of explaining to do!" she scolds, waving her finger at me.

"Ok Mom," I joke. "Right now I'm exhausted. How about we talk while I'm trapped in a car with you for four hours on our way to Cherry Falls tomorrow?"

She unfolds her arms and walks over to me. "Are you ok? You don't look so good. Late night or something?"

"I promise I'll give you all the gory details in the morning. Please, just let me get some sleep."

Luckily, I packed everything for Sydney's shower last week. I'll just have to get up and go. I pull my new Devil's Garden T-shirt from my bag and close my eyes, holding it against my face. It still smells like Van. My body comes alive as I inhale its fibers and relive the highlights of our glorious night together in my mind. The tingling sensation continues to electrify my skin as I crawl into my bed and drift off to sleep.

I wake to the beautiful fragrance of Van Sinclair. Reality sets in. *Damn! It's just his T-shirt.* Despite my best efforts, I can't stop thinking about him, not even for a minute. He has managed to engrave his essence into my brain.

Time to start our journey to Cherry Falls. Brooke and I pack the car and get on the road.

I'm sure she can give me some advice. She's been in a relationship with Dean for the past three years and they're still going strong. If anyone knows how to make a relationship work, it's Brooke. I give her a run down on my beach retreat.

"You should follow your heart. No relationship is perfect and there's always some type of obstacle."

I tap my fingers on the steering wheel. "Believe me, I want to run to him and never look back, but life doesn't work like that. There's not always a happy ending and I can't take another tragic one."

"Stop over-thinking everything or you're going to miss out. There's more to it than tragedy or bliss. You're forgetting everything in between." She fidgets with the knob on the radio.

Brooke's right. I'm trying to make my decision based on two ends of the spectrum, ending up either overjoyed or devastated. There is a place somewhere in between where I can be content, the infamous happy medium.

She sits back in her seat. "Just go for it. Give it a shot. If it doesn't work out you'll be in the same place you are now."

Van is irreplaceable. Can pure passionate bliss even exist with someone else? "That's the thing. I won't be in the same place."

She places her hand on my shoulder. "You're just scared. Nothing great comes easy. Plus, I'll kick his ass if he even thinks about hurting you!"

I put my hand over my forehead and rub my eyes. She's right, especially about my fears. I just want to stop thinking about it.

Is it even remotely possible to stop thinking about me and Van? I sigh. "Let's focus on Sydney's bridal shower."

"I'm sure it's going to be way over the top."

Mom insists on hosting, planning, and executing Sydney's shower on her own. The only decision Sydney and

I are responsible for making is what dresses we will be wearing, and I am honestly surprised she didn't make that choice as well.

I shake my head. "Sitting by Cynthia Thomas for three hours may kill me. I hope they serve mint juleps. Maybe she'll loosen up."

We pull into Mom and Dad's driveway. I step out of the car and let the warm breeze engulf my body.

Sydney leaps up from the rocking chair on the porch. "Hi Brooke! Hi Sis! You're finally here! Mom planned a girl's night for us. We've got pizza, cookies, sangria and an array of chick flicks!"

I take a deep breath and stretch. "I could use a girl's night in."

Red and yellow tulips line the border of the sidewalk leading up to the white, cape-cod home. The aroma of fresh baked cookies pours from the open window. Yum, Mom's famous chocolate chip. My whole body relaxes as I close my eyes and tilt my head back. *Ah, there's no place like home.*

The strong aroma of nail polish fills the room. I slather on one last coat of Desert Rose Pink while glancing at *Steel Magnolias* on the TV. Slumber parties are great. Every woman needs some bonding time with the girls. Next on deck is *The Notebook*.

I walk into the kitchen to get more sangria only to discover my purse is ringing. I reach in and grab my cell phone. Van Sinclair appears in large letters on my screen. My face no doubt lights up the room.

"Hi." I twirl my hair with my fingers.

"How's Cherry Falls?"

"We're watching chick flicks and painting our nails."

"Damn! I'm missing out," he says as he chuckles. "We're on our way to Massachusetts. The show in New York rocked; the place was packed."

"No shocker there, you guys are great."

"Friday's show in Connecticut sold out. You up for more beach time?"

My heart races and my stomach flutters. *Another slumber party with Van!* "Can't wait for my feet to hit the sand."

"I got a driver to pick you up. Connecticut's too far to drive by yourself."

Thank God. Five hours alone in a car gives me way too much time to think. "I'll be ready."

"I gotta go. Still checking the New England area for mud pits. Have fun."

I shake my head. "Talk to you soon."

I hang up the phone and fill my glass with more of the sweet, fruity cocktail. There's no way to hide this smile plastered on my face. *Yay! I get to see Van on Wednesday.* No show until Friday means two whole days alone with him. Heat radiates from my head to my toes with the force of a super nova. My stomach twitches and my heart thrashes. Has world peace been declared? Even that couldn't measure up to another beach adventure with Van. My purse starts ringing again. I quickly pick up my phone and say, "Hey, did you forget something?"

"Uh yeah, I definitely did." My stomach clenches as I process the familiar tone.

"I guess I should screen my calls better," I say, as a grim frown slaughters my smile. "What could you possibly want, Jesse?"

"I want to talk. I miss you, it's time we work out our misunderstanding."

He seriously has the worst timing ever. My mind is in turmoil and he has the nerve to call me the night before my sister's shower expecting me to take him back? My fists clench and fire flushes my face. All the anguish built up inside bursts out.

"There is no misunderstanding you asshole! You cheated! We're over, I've moved on. That's it!"

"I'm sorry, I screwed up. I just want a chance to prove to you that I know I made a mistake. I don't want to lose you," he pleads.

"You've already lost me. I don't want to give you a chance. I don't want to talk to you. I don't want *you*!"

I hang up the phone and take a deep breath, trying to compose myself. *Would I have been strong enough to resist giving Jesse another chance if I hadn't met Van?* He doesn't deserve another chance anyway; once a cheater, always a cheater in my book. Besides, Van ignites every aspect of my being, sending my body and soul into a flurry of pure euphoria. I breathe in deeply, closing my eyes and let out a soft sigh.

I walk back into the TV room with my sangria and sit down next to Brooke.

"You should have yelled 'Fuck Off' into the phone before you hung up. That would have been the cherry on top." Brooke claps and then grips my hand, pulling me back onto the couch.

I grit my teeth, pressing my lips tight. "Sorry, I didn't realize I was so loud."

∞

Bright sunlight warms the air and birds chirp, creating a soft melody as we head to the Cherry Falls Country Club for Sydney's wedding shower. She could grace the cover of a bridal magazine with her hair pulled up and soft curls falling around her face. Pink is her color, and the silver flowers spread throughout the material on her dress sparkle next to those silver heels. I run my hands over my powder blue dress, trying to tame the static cling that tends to accompany chiffon. *Please don't let my slip show.*

As we enter the ballroom, the sweet scent of flowers fills the air. Mom has chosen a rose garden theme for the shower and the beautiful décor is overwhelming. The plethora of crystal vases hold dozens of multicolored roses and a four-tier cake, also engulfed in roses and complete with a lattice design wrapped around the side, sits in the center of the room. The chairs are draped in pink chiffon, and everyone receives a crystal rose broach as a favor.

Sydney begins to cry. "Oh Mom, thank you so much. It's beyond perfect." She hugs our mom.

"Nothing less than the best is good enough for my girls," Mom replies as she rubs Sydney's back.

∞

Sydney receives just about everything a soon-to-be bride could imagine, from bake ware to lingerie. She'll be starting her life with Bryce in style. As maid of honor, I get the task of packing up all her gifts and bringing them to the house. *Great!*

Brooke and Dean are leaving for their vacation in Mexico in the morning, so we have to watch the clock. I take the last box into the house and gather my few belongings. We still have a little time before we need to head out, so we sit on the porch with Sydney and sip sweet tea while I relay the tale of Van Sinclair.

∞

I turn up the radio and belt out the lyrics to one of my favorite songs. Is it legal to have this much fun while driving? I'm laughing so hard my cheeks are hurting. Brooke remembers way too much from our college partying days. We conjure up the memories of our glory days on the long ride home. Hmm, to be carefree and relaxed again. This is just what I need after the stress of the last few days.

I try to help Brooke pack for her trip before heading to my room. We need to be at the airport at 5 a.m., so turning in early is a must. Just as I'm getting ready for bed, my phone starts ringing. I frantically run to grab it while trying to suppress the butterflies in my stomach. My palms sweat as I propel myself across my bed and reach for my phone on the nightstand. I glance at the screen; Jesse Woods appears in large letters. The butterflies are gone.

CHAPTER 6—LONELY

Emptiness fills the pit of my stomach on the ride home from dropping Brooke and Dean off at the airport. I cringe and drop my keys on the table, glancing around at the barren rooms of the apartment. I'm all alone. Everyone's either graduated, left to start their new jobs, or has gone home for the summer. This thriving college town is now a ghost town.

I flip open my cell phone to check my call log. *Great! Four missed calls from Jesse since last night.* I huff and grind my teeth. *Does he honestly think I'm going to talk to him?* Not only did he betray me, but he ruined my plans for the future. Brooke and Dean were supposed to live next door. We were going to have Bar-B-Q's, vacation together, and basically share in all aspects of each other's lives. He single-handedly changed the whole way I envisioned my future.

I lie on the couch, staring at my phone on the coffee table. *Please ring!* I picture Van partying with the band, surrounded by girls who worship him like a God. We never talked about being exclusive, so he has no reason to turn down the advances of other women. My mouth becomes dry and a nauseous sensation develops. I can't imagine Van with someone else.

The intense attraction between the two of us is magical. It shouldn't be possible for that to exist for him with anyone else. He's a unique key that opens my lock to a dimension of pure pleasure and passionate bliss. A few tears start to fall down my cheeks as my phone starts ringing. I look at the screen; Van Sinclair appears in large letters. I wipe my eyes and clear my throat.

"Hello?"

"Hey. Hope you're getting ready for the beach!" he says cheerfully.

"Actually, I'm just lying on the couch." I hold onto my pillow, wishing it was Van.

"Are you sick?"

I sigh. "No. Brooke and Dean left for Mexico and no one else seems to be around."

"I honestly don't know what that's like anymore. I'm a little jealous."

I clear my throat again and try my best to hide my emotions. "Don't be jealous, it's no fun being lonely," I say, as a few tears escape my eyes.

"Are you ok? Something seems wrong."

I take a deep breath. How can I answer his question without revealing my insecurities?

I slowly exhale. "I'll be fine. I'm just going to order a pizza and watch a movie in my sweats." I sigh. "I'm sure you guys are hitting the town and partying. You don't have a show tonight, right?"

"Um right, we don't have a show tonight but I don't party as much as you think. Been there, done that. It's never worth the hangover." His tone deepens. "We're grabbing a bite to eat and hitting the road." He exhales loudly.

I sniffle as a few more tears escape. "I'm sure all of your fans are waiting for you," I say, as I think about the lucky girl that gets to be with him tonight.

"The only person waiting for me is Marcus. We're going over a new song before we go to eat."

My phone starts to click. I look at the screen and grimace. It's Jesse calling yet again. God, when will he get the fact that we're over through his thick skull? I take a deep breath and hold it in.

"Lexie, are you still there?"

"Sorry, I'm getting another call. My asshole ex has been pestering me all day."

"Oh, has he now?" Van asks sternly.

"I mistakenly answered my phone thinking it was you while I was at my Mom's house over the weekend. I thought all of the cursing I did would have given him the hint to leave me alone, but obviously it hasn't."

"Does he know you're alone in the apartment?"

"Well Dean is his best friend, so he knows they're gone away."

"You won't be home alone for long. Soon you'll be with me on another sandy beach," he says.

"Yep, I'll be your next sandy beach special," I say sarcastically.

Am I turning into a booty call, running around chasing a rocker, hooking up in hotel rooms? Not really what I envisioned myself doing at this point in my life.

"Did I do something?" he asks.

My chest gets tight and my stomach becomes upset. He really didn't do anything to deserve me acting like such a bitch. I certainly can't be mad at Van for things I concoct in my warped mind. At this rate, I'm quickly on my way to ruining a relationship that could potentially be great.

"No, you didn't do anything wrong. I'm sorry. I think I'm just stressed and irritated about these phone calls from Jesse. We're going to have lots of fun at the beach," I say, trying to sound more upbeat.

"Ok, well I'll keep my phone with me. I'm late to meet Marcus. Call me if you need anything. I'll talk to you later."

"Ok, talk to you later," I reply.

I really am an idiot and I seriously doubt Van will be eager to call me again after the way I've just acted. I'll have to call him later and apologize again. Why can't things be different? If he didn't have to travel so much we could spend more time together. I want someone who can be there for me when I need them, both physically and emotionally. Someone who can come over when I feel lonely, or could cuddle up and watch movies when I feel like vegging out. I guess this is just another one of those 'want what we can't have' moments in life.

On a brighter note, in a few days I'll be headed for another mind-blowing beach adventure with Van Sinclair. My heart races as I relive the memory of the passionate night we spent together. I can't wait to see him, feel him, and breathe him in. Everything about him is so appealing and inviting. *I'm in severe withdrawal.*

I stretch and wander to the kitchen. Ah, Brooke left two bottles of wine in the fridge. Some vapor escapes the bottle as I uncork the chilled white zinfandel and pour myself a glass. I take a deep breath and head to the bathroom. Mmm, a relaxing bubble bath will clear my head. I pour some vanilla scented body wash into a stream of hot water and sip my wine. No harm in trying to enjoy this quiet time alone. I close my eyes and breathe deeply as the warm water caresses my body, dissolving my negative thoughts.

I dry off and put on my Devil's Garden T-shirt. The scent the fibers hold ignites my body, causing my skin to tingle from the unique electricity flowing through me. I breathe deeply, inhaling the faint scent of Van. *God, I miss him.* Why can't time speed up? These few days seem like an eternity.

Oh well, since I'm alone I may as well be comfortable. My gray sweat pants are perfect lounging attire. I pull my hair in a sloppy ponytail, plop myself on the couch, and check the TV guide for a movie. *Yes! Sixteen Candles is playing!* I reach for my phone and order a pizza. Ah, now I'm completely relaxed. A bubble bath and some wine can do wonders for the soul.

Just as a commercial starts, my doorbell rings. Pizza Palace's delivery drivers have perfect timing. I open the door. My jaw drops and my eyes widen as I stare. Standing in front of me is Van Sinclair, holding a pizza.

"I ran into the pizza guy in your driveway. Nice shirt."

I start laughing and crying at the same time and run to Van, practically jumping into his arms. He puts the pizza on the table and holds me close, gently wiping the tears from my eyes.

"Hope they're happy tears," he says.

I nod.

"You seemed so upset on the phone. I hopped on a puddle jumper and got here in just a few hours."

I wrap my arms around his neck, pressing my forehead against his. Our lips meet softly and within seconds, our kisses turn into an intense frenzy of passion. My heart is racing. I jump up and wrap my legs around his waist. *Self-control is overrated!* My body aches for this man. I've never wanted anything more than I want Van Sinclair at this very moment.

He walks into the TV room and traps me against the wall. My breathing becomes rapid and my heart hammers as he slips his hands under my shirt and pulls it over my head. Electric shocks follow his fingers as they caress my breasts, sending the unique current through me. His soft lips place sexy kisses from my lips, to my neck, and finally to my breasts. My whole body is on fire! I'm breathing so heavy and loud. I can't take it anymore. This is torture. I need him, and I need him immediately.

"Van. Please. Couch. Now," I both demand and plead.

"Yes ma'am," he obliges and starts walking toward the couch.

He lowers me down and lies on top of me, smoothly moving his hand underneath my sweat pants and underwear, sliding his finger inside of me. I moan with pleasure and grip his back as ecstasy builds inside. I rip his shirt over his head and slowly run my fingers along the waves of his chiseled chest and abs, stopping at his jeans. The button pops open. I gently caress him while releasing the tight fabric.

He groans as he pulls off my sweats and underwear in one smooth motion, grabs a package from his jeans, and tears it open. Sliding his hands along my thighs, he grips my hips and jerks my body toward him. I gasp in delight as he slams himself inside me, filling me completely. My heart is about to beat out of my chest and my body is electrified. Warm kisses descend from my lips to my neck.

Van breathes heavy almost panting. "Oh babe, I missed you," he says in between breaths.

I'm in a trance, alternating in and out of reality. The perfect rhythm of his body's movements mimics a choreographed dance.

My whole body suddenly ignites with intense pleasure. I yell out and dig my fingers into his back as I find my release. Within minutes he finds his.

His eyes lock with mine as we lay silently, trying to catch our breath.

What a turn of events. "This is the most romantic surprise of my life."

He sighs and brushes a stray hair behind my ear. "I hate being so far away. Especially when your ex is bothering you and you're alone."

I purse my lips. "It sounds like you're a little jealous. Believe me, you don't need to be."

He runs his fingertips along my arm. "Yeah, I didn't see that coming."

Van doesn't want anyone to have me except for him! I glow brighter than the millions of stars in the sky.

We get dressed, heat up the pizza, and cuddle on the couch just in time to catch the end of *Sixteen Candles*. My phone chimes.

"Is that him again?" Van asks.

I pick up the phone and place it back on the table. "I can just shut it off. I only had it on in case you called."

Van snatches my phone and starts pressing buttons. His face grimaces as he presses send. *Hmm, how will this play out*? He sets my phone down and puts his arm around me again.

"What did you text him?"

"Oh, just a suggestion," he says. "I'll be right back, which way to the bathroom?"

"Down the hall to the left."

I pick up my phone and read the text Van sent to Jesse.

Stop texting me, my boyfriend is getting pissed.

Oh my God! Van Sinclair just called himself my boyfriend. A swarm of butterflies take flight in my stomach and my whole body erupts into a plethora of tingles. The grin on my face spreads so wide it actually makes my cheeks hurt. This day cannot get any better. Just as Van comes back, my phone starts ringing. It's Jesse.

"This guy is unbelievable," Van says as he takes my phone. "Hello? No, she's not talking to you. Dude, do yourself a favor and leave her alone." He puts the phone down. "He hung up on me." Van reclines on the couch. "He won't bother you any more tonight, now that he knows I'm here."

"Don't underestimate his stupidity."

Van shakes his head and looks over at me. "So, why were you so upset before, when we were on the phone?"

I take a deep breath and sink back into the couch. "I'm sorry. It was nothing, just forget it."

He raises his eyebrows. "From the second we met you've told me exactly what's on your mind. That's a rare find in a woman."

I sigh and twirl my hair around my fingers. "I was just thinking about the time we met backstage. I remember all of the women trying desperately to get your attention and it worries me."

He gently lowers my hand and tucks my hair behind my ear. "That shouldn't worry you. *You're* the woman who got my attention."

"Yeah, but I'm here and you're miles away. Someone else may catch your eye in my absence."

"So you think because we're not with each that I'll be with someone else after the show? Is that what you think of me?" His lips form a hard line and he stares intently into my eyes. This talk is not going according to plan. He's not getting it.

"It's not that."

"Then what?" he asks.

I take a deep breath and slowly exhale, wiping my palms against my sweatpants. *Well, I guess it's now or never.* "It's just that you're surrounded by women who want to be with you. They're gorgeous, half-naked, and persistent. There's no reason you shouldn't be with them since we never really talked about what's going on with us."

He jerks his head back slightly and lowers his eyebrows. "Since we never talked about what's going on with us, let's talk about it now."

Wow, this night is turning out to be nothing like I expected. My heart starts racing. Time's up! Stay or walk away? There's no way I can walk away from him, I've really known that from the beginning. No matter what the rational part of my mind tells me, I've been his from the first time those emerald eyes locked onto mine.

"I think I'm upset and jealous because I'm not sure how you feel about me or exactly what you want out of our situation," I say while fidgeting with my fingers.

"I want you and only you and I want you all to myself. That's how I feel and exactly what I want."

Wow! I have to give him credit. He really does tell it like it is.

I raise my eyebrows and tilt my head. "You do realize being apart makes this difficult, right? Especially when you have women throwing themselves at you every night."

He brushes my cheek and lifts my chin. "You do realize that you have an ex-boyfriend who's still in love with you, living a few streets away, right? That also makes things difficult, especially when you're lonely and I'm away."

I raise my eyes and stare into the emerald abyss. "You're right. Plus, we've really just met and trust takes a long time to build. The distance only makes it harder."

"Well, that's an easy fix," he says. "Come on tour with me."

CHAPTER 7—NERVOUS

My jaw drops and my eyes widen. All the air suddenly escapes from my lungs and I gasp. "Are you serious?"

"I've never been more serious about anything. It'll be great. You'll get the chance to travel the country, see the sights, and find a mud pit in every state."

I squint and pull my eyebrows together. "Have you really thought this through?"

He shrugs. "What's there to think about? We want to be with each other. I'm on the road and you have the next few months off. It's perfect."

The grin on his face and the gleam in those emerald eyes renders me helpless. *He's right and everything he's said sounds logical.* But reality doesn't always follow logic. *We've only been together three times so far which makes today our third date.*

"Um, do you realize that me going on tour with you means we'll be practically living together for the next few months? That's a pretty big step." I twirl my hair around my fingers.

His lips press together in a slight grimace. "As long as you don't turn into a werewolf when there's a full moon, we'll be fine."

I can't just make a decision on a whim; someone has to be the voice of reason. I need to weigh the pros and cons and have all the information before making a choice. *Yeah, that's easier said than done.* I can't think clearly when Van Sinclair is near me. Everything about him makes me come alive, as if there's an electric current flowing through my body breathing new life into it. How can I resist him? He's both my strength and my kryptonite.

Van falls silent, gazing at me as he interlocks his hands and stretches his fingers. He's obviously not thinking about the possibility of this turning into a disaster. He's following his heart, and frankly I'm jealous that I'm having trouble doing the same.

I think back to my conversation with Jenna at the beach. She basically told me that Van was never in a relationship with anyone, nor did he ever want to be in one, until he met me. *Ah, Van Sinclair wants me exclusively!* My heart flutters. Unfortunately, since he's never been in a relationship, he doesn't understand how one works, especially when you're together twenty four-seven. I guess ignorance is bliss and I've never seen him look more blissful than he does right now.

His eyes lock with mine. I'm a prisoner, restrained by burning passion. My body quickly ignites with the fire that only burns for this man. A unique energy charges through me, unmatched by anything else on earth. There's no way I can ever choose to let this feeling be lost. *No more thinking!* It's time to take a leap of faith.

"Ok. Let's tour the country together."

He exhales, grabs my cheeks, and plants a sweet kiss on my lips.

I pull away and slowly tap my lip. "No promises on the werewolf transformation, I haven't been in the midst of a full moon in a while."

He grips my hips and jerks me forward until our bodies meet. "It's gonna be so awesome!"

I lean in, placing my lips against his ear and softly whisper, "Well, we still have some alone time, which I imagine will be hard to come by when we're on tour."

"Excellent point!"

His fingers softly stroke my forearms on their travels to my cheek, causing an array of goose bumps to grace my skin. Leaning in slowly, he brushes his mouth against mine, gently sucking on my bottom lip. A burst of molten lava passes through my body as the passion in his kisses grows with each passing moment. Whoa, he scoops me up in his arms, his lips never leaving mine, and walks into my bedroom. Electricity surges through me, causing a plethora of tingles to encompass my body as he lowers me onto the smooth sheets, hovering over me.

His silky hair falls into my face and gently, but sensually tickles my skin. My breathing increases as his hand travels down my back, gently lifting the hem of my shirt and continuing underneath it. Every hair on my body stands on end when the soft fabric glides against my skin on its way over my head. An uncontrollable beat, races through my heart as passion floods my body.

I grasp the bottom of his T-shirt and yank it over his head, slightly touching the bumpy washboard of his sculpted body. The view is amazing. He slides his jeans down and rips off my sweats. We lay naked and vulnerable, side by side. My body boils into a frenzy as I press myself against his body, feeling every bit of him.

I open my legs slightly and wrap my arms around his waist, pulling him on top of me. Our breathing becomes rapid as his hands caress my breasts, fondling my nipples. I take a deep breath and slowly exhale as they move to my waist. My hands descend, gently rubbing and exploring his flesh. He moans and reaches down to his jeans, retrieves a condom packet, and rips it open. He hovers over me again, kissing my lips softly.

Our hands entwine as he slowly enters me. I gasp and let out a slight moan. We move in a slow and steady rhythm as he gently kisses my lips, his hands never losing their grip with mine. My heart is ready to beat out of my chest as every inch of his body gently meets with every inch of mine. I inhale and hold in a breath as he pushes himself inside of me. *God, he never fails to impress.* I exhale and groan in ecstasy. My thighs quiver and my heart drums as adrenaline surges through my body. Our bodies ignite with passion. I clutch his back, deeply pressing my fingers into his flesh as I find my release right in time with his.

There's no comparison between having sex and making love. I swear the earth just moved and I traveled into another realm. My entire body is awakened, not knowing what it was missing until this moment. My heart melts into a puddle. We lie in each other's arms and slowly drift off to sleep.

I wake, still in Van's embrace. *Ah, my favorite place to be.*

He opens his eyes and stretches. "Good morning."

I stifle a yawn. "Hope you're ready for a nice home cooked breakfast. One cannot live on diner food alone."

"I've been eating on the road for the past six months," he replies. "Home cooking sounds amazing."

Once in the kitchen, I start making coffee. *Huh, looks like I left the hall light on.* No shocker there. My mind's been a little preoccupied.

Van walks up behind me and puts his arms around my waist, reaching around to kiss my cheek. "Do you need any help?"

I lay my hand on his forearm. "No, I've got this. You relax."

The aroma of the fresh ground beans heightens my senses. My eyes travel over each peak and valley of Van's finely chiseled torso. *God he's so sexy, sitting at my kitchen table wearing jeans and no shirt.* I tremble as I bring him a cup of coffee, spilling a little on the table.

"I could get used to this," he says as he pulls me onto his lap.

I'm sporting my Devil's Garden T-shirt with panties. Apparently, my morning attire has the same effect on him as his does on me. I snicker and pull myself up to start cooking.

I'm barely able to steady my hands to crack the eggs. His eyes are burning through me as I whip up some scrambled eggs, pancakes, toast, and sausage. The aroma of the kitchen is mouthwatering.

"I had no idea you're such a great cook," he says in between mouthfuls of food.

I smile, catching my bottom lip in my teeth. "There's a lot you don't know about me, Van Sinclair."

"I can't wait to be enlightened." He raises his eyebrows.

"Oh, we'll have lots of time for enlightening," I say. "Since you don't have a show until Friday, are you opposed to staying here until then?"

"We can stay here. You can get your stuff ready and join the tour with me Friday," he says as he stabs a pancake with his fork.

Oh my God. I cover my mouth with my hand, and then quickly drop it to my side. *I only have a few days to pack for the next few months. Where do I begin?* "So, how does one pack for a cross country tour?"

"Just bring one or two of everything. We stop at Laundromats and we can buy anything you might forget." He sips his coffee.

This task sounds much easier for a man.

"Are two suitcases ok? I don't think I can get everything into one." I twirl my hair around my fingers.

"Sure, whatever you need."

I take a deep breath. "Did you discuss me joining you on tour with the rest of the band? I want to make sure everyone's ok with this, especially Jenna."

"I told everyone. They're fine with it. Jenna encouraged me to ask." He pats my thigh.

"Ok good. I certainly don't want to cause any animosity between you and your band mates." I let my head fall back. "I'll have to leave for a weekend in August for my sister's bachelorette party."

"We're always close to at least one airport," he says.

I tap my fingers on the table. "I wish I could reach Brooke in Mexico to let her know. I'll have to leave her a note. She can call me when she gets back."

Van winks. "Sounds like you have everything figured out. Now, you've got me here until Friday. What will you do with me?" He smirks. "Oh, I can think of a few things."

My insides vibrate and quiver as I clean up. *Who would've thought I'd be dating the lead singer of a rock band and going on a cross country tour?* Never in my wildest dreams did I imagine this. It's almost surreal.

Van is mine for the next few days. No star struck fans, no crowds, no time constraints and no agendas. Every second counts! It won't be long before the chaos of touring resumes.

Van retreats to the couch. "We're all set. We fly to Connecticut Friday morning, and then we're off," he says, barely able to contain his smile.

I grin from ear to ear. "What would you like to do while you're here? Are there any local places you want to see before we take off?"

He scrunches his eyebrows. "Are you kidding me? I don't want to see anything but the walls of this apartment."

I plop next to him on the couch and lean back, sinking into it. "Well then, it looks like we're having a date night right here."

We talk about music and movies, our favorite sights to see, and foods to eat; just like a real date. I'm sure he'll eventually get bored hearing about Sydney and her upcoming wedding, college life at Lakeview University, and my roommate Brooke. I'm confident I'll discuss those topics to death while on tour. He listens intently to the saga of me and Jesse, right down to the tragic end.

"I think you've got more excitement in your life than I do," Van says. "You make me sound boring."

I bite my lip. "There's not a boring bone in your body."

He raises his eyebrows. "Miss Waters, are you flirting with me?"

"I wouldn't dream of such a thing, Mr. Sinclair."

My fingers ache, desperately wanting to touch him. He's so irresistible sitting shirtless on my couch in his perfect fitting jeans, just like a model in the middle of a photo shoot. Can he be any more enticing? I may not get many opportunities like this on the road so I need to strike while the iron is hot, and it doesn't get any hotter than this.

I stand up and stretch my arms over my head. "Well, I think I need a shower," I say as I pull my shirt over my head, dropping it on the living room floor. I slide down my panties, shifting my weight from side to side and creating a small pile.

His mouth falls open and his eyes widen.

"Are you coming?"

He leaps off the couch and quickly slides out of his jeans, leaving them on top of my clothes. "Let's go!"

I turn on the water and move closer to Van, rubbing myself against him. He lets out a deep sigh and holds me close, pressing his impressive body against mine. I wrap my arms around his neck, raking my fingers through his hair. His eyes lock onto me, burning through my soul. I'm rendered breathless, captivated by this enchanting man. My skin prickles and each of my nerve endings stir. He presses his lips against mine, gently running his tongue along them. My heart beat races, strong and steady like a raging river. We step into the shower and let the warm water engulf our bodies. The heat and steam heightens my senses, adding to the passion.

He wedges me against the wall of the shower, kissing me and caressing every inch of my body. We're so close, not even air can get between us. I'm breathing so hard I'm about to explode. I need him and I need him now. I raise my knee, positioning it against his waist and lift my hips to push myself against his erection. He backs away from me.

I exhale deeply and narrow my eyes. "What's wrong?"

"My jeans are in the other room," he says, touching the back of his neck.

Why is he so concerned about his jeans? Brooke is in Mexico so there's no chance of anyone walking in on us. I inhale deeply and pull him close. Ah, I finally understand. I start kissing his neck and softly whisper in his ear, "I've been on the pill for years. It's fine."

"Are you sure? I've never been with anyone without using one."

I'm breathless. A radiant smile forms. Of all the women in his past I'll be the first to experience Van Sinclair flesh to flesh.

"Yes, I'm one hundred percent sure."

I push him against the wall of the shower and explore his body with my hands. My fingers slide down his chest, gradually working their way down. The soapy water accentuates every chiseled muscle of his body. Running my tongue down his sculpted abs, I continue my seduction. He groans and lets out a sigh as I consume him with my mouth.

I bring kisses back up his chest and neck to his lips as my hands continue to caress his manhood. He grabs my hips and pulls me toward him. Slowly and sensually, I graze my fingertips against his torso and move them up to his neck. My heart hammers against the walls of my chest. I jump up, wrapping my legs around his waist. He holds me against the wall and enters my body. We both moan with pleasure as he thrusts himself inside of me over and over again. Pleasure fills my core and I find my release. He yells out as he comes inside of me.

We face each other, letting the water hit our bodies. I'm breathless, panting for air. He places his forehead against mine and brushes my hair away from my face. His emerald eyes stare deeply into mine. My heart is still beating out of my chest.

"That was intense," he says. "It's a first for me."

I just had Van Sinclair in a way no one else ever did.

"I'm glad I was your first," I say as I chuckle. "We're like teenagers, I'm yours and you're mine."

"I'm definitely yours and I hope you're mine," he says, nuzzling his lips against my neck.

"I'm completely yours, Van Sinclair."

∞

I thaw some frozen pasta sauce, boil some spaghetti, and continue to revel in the afterglow of our sensual shower. The classic *Halloween* is playing on the horror channel at eight o'clock. Spaghetti always pairs well with a slasher film and after finding out both of us love horror movies, it's the perfect activity for tonight.

I take a deep breath. Is my mouth watering from the sweet smell of the tomatoes and garlic or from the perfectly chiseled rock god sitting beside me? I scoot closer and rest my head on his shoulder. *Ah, I'm in paradise.*

∞

Looks like it's time to start getting myself ready for the tour. I carefully select my outfits and accessories. As usual, I over pack, trying to think of everything I may possibly need. The first thing that goes in the suitcase is four months worth of birth control pills; more than I need, but also something I don't want to run out of. *How did I end up with a whole suitcase filled with shoes, make-up, and hair products?*

Van peeks his head in the doorway. He laughs as he peruses the amount of items that I'm packing.

How the hell can guys live out of a duffel bag?

I did it! I managed to cram my life for the next few months into two suitcases. I'm ready, and this time I'm truly and completely ready.

CHAPTER 8—THE TOUR

Connecticut welcomes you, boasts a sign along the road. My palms start to sweat. It's tough to be the outsider among friends who have known each other for years. Hopefully, I'll make a good impression so they'll welcome me into their circle. I take a deep breath as the taxi pulls up to the front of the amphitheater. Jenna is standing outside.

Van tips his chin. "Hey Jenna."

She waves. "Hey. The guys are inside setting up for the sound check." She nods toward the backstage entrance.

"I've got to get ready for our show. You should check out the tour bus. We've got a hotel room for tonight and we hit the road tomorrow morning." Van gives me a soft kiss on the lips and flashes a sexy smile.

Jenna holds her hands to her mouth, forming a homemade megaphone and yells after him. "Don't worry Van, I'll show her the ropes!"

Van turns to us, pointing at Jenna. "Don't scare her away Jenna, I'll know who to blame if she's not here when I get back."

"I don't scare very easily. You should know that after watching *Halloween* with me last night." I shout, giggling. Judging from the death grip I had on his arm for first hour of the film, it's safe to say I both love and fear scary movies.

He rubs his arm. "Yeah, I think your finger prints are still embedded in my bicep." He yells and shakes his head as he walks toward the amphitheater.

Jenna smirks. "Welcome to the highway of hell."

I roll my eyes. "Don't downplay all the luxury that awaits."

Around the corner of the parking lot in the back of the amphitheater is the silver and black tour bus. It's really nice from the outside, much larger than a passenger bus. I pull my bags toward this iron horse that I'll call home for the next few months.

"I'm not gonna lie to you, life on the road sucks. It's cramped inside and we're all basically on top of one another. We have to put up with each other's annoying habits and there's really nowhere to run."

I shake my head. "You make it sound so glamorous."

"Don't freak out. I'm really glad you're coming with us. It's hard being the only girl with four guys. Now I can finally talk about things other than which actress has the best ass."

"I can't wait for such intellectual conversation." I laugh.

She snickers as she raises her eyebrows at me. "Honestly, Van is the happiest I've ever seen him. I don't know what you did to tame the wild beast."

"I don't know either, but I hope I keep doing it."

My suitcases barely clear the hallway as I walk onto the bus. *She's right, it is cramped.* On the left is a small kitchen with a stainless steel sink and black granite countertop equipped with a hot plate that's ideal for cooking nothing more than grilled cheese. A few wooden cabinets hang above and below the sink. My eyes travel across the kitchen to the two tables and benches that resemble restaurant booths. *I'll scratch cooking breakfast off my list, so much for trying to impress everyone with my culinary skills.*

Down the hallway are two massive black couches facing a huge big-screen TV mounted on the wall. There's a table in the middle of the floor, along with a stocked bar against the far wall. *We can all relax in style, assuming we can all agree on a movie.*

Past the TV area is a small sitting space with a large bathroom to its left. *Cool, there's a shower.* Beyond the sitting area are some drawers, cabinets, and closets. Last but not least is the sleeping area. More like glorified bunk beds, two on the top and two on the bottom, on each side of the bus. I sigh and exhale deeply. *How am I supposed to sleep like this?* Thank God I'm not claustrophobic! These are clearly the worst sleeping arrangements. Sardines in a can have more space.

Jenna glances at me, noticing my look of disgust. "Welcome to motel hell," she says as she waves her arms. "Don't worry, we usually get hotel rooms. We only sleep on the bus if we have a long way to travel without time to stop. I already cleared out two drawers for you and you can share Van's closet."

∞

Yay! Everything surprisingly fits into the spaces I'm provided. *Things are looking up.* I gaze around and examine the area. What have I gotten myself into? Jenna flips through the channels on the TV and we sit on the couch. She's being extremely nice to me and going out of her way to make things comfortable. I guess she's been lonely too. If I wasn't here she'd be alone, waiting for the guys. *A Walk to Remember* is on the movie channel.

My mind wanders to thoughts of Brooke. *How am I going to survive without her?* We haven't been apart for more than two weeks in the last four years. Thank God for cell phones and modern technology.

Footsteps smack against the floors of the bus. *Jeeze, it's like a herd of horses are stampeding.* The guys plop on the couch next to us.

"Oh God, now we have two chicks to fight over the TV with. I can't watch this shit! It might make me sterile!" Chaz puts his hands on his head and sinks into the couch.

"Well that would be a plus for humanity," Tyler replies.

Jenna slaps Chaz's arm. "Way to make her feel welcome, asshole."

"I'm only kidding. Lexie, welcome aboard. It's gonna be a fun, wild ride. Plus, with you here I'll get double the girls, mine plus Van's." Chaz is actually serious.

"Glad I could help," I say with an eye roll.

"You'll just have to ignore Chaz, the rest of us do." Van shakes his head. "What do you think of the bus?" He places his hand on my thigh.

I grimace before I can stop it. "It's nice although I'm not really keen on the sleeping arrangements."

"It won't be that bad, I promise." Van puts his arm around me, holding me close.

"I'm excited you're here Lexie, now Jenna has a shopping buddy. Apparently, I don't have the best fashion sense," Marcus says.

What a nice guy. He's truly happy that Jenna will have a girlfriend on the road. How can she survive without female companionship? Every woman needs her girlfriends.

"Thank you."

"Guess what Lexie, I've planned a late dinner for the four of us after the show tonight. We're going on a double date to Villa Italia!" Jenna exclaims.

Thank God Jenna is so excited to have another couple in her midst. It's nice to know someone other than Van wants me on tour.

"Awesome, then Chaz and I have the bus to ourselves tonight," Tyler says.

"Well, to ourselves and some fine ladies," Chaz interjects, slapping Tyler a high five.

Wow, I hope I don't kill the two of them in the next few months. Jenna must have the patience of a saint.

"We go on stage in an hour. Who wants a drink?" Tyler asks.

"Definitely me," I reply.

Van looks at me, wrinkling his brow. "I know it's a lot to take in at once. When you get past the initial shock, it's actually kind of fun."

Tyler grabs us each a bottle of beer. We relax on the couch and watch TV, waiting for the show to begin. It's like we're all hanging out at a friend's house.

"It's just about show time," Marcus announces as he stands up, grabbing Jenna's hand.

"Ok, move 'em out!" Chaz exclaims.

We all exit the bus, and head toward the amphitheater. I walk slowly, twirling my hair around my fingers as the chatter of hundreds of people fill the air. My heart beats faster. *Is it possible to get stage fright when you're not even in the band?* I lift my eyes and scan the crowd. Scantily clad female fans stare at us and cheer for the guys as they make their way toward the stage. Chaz blows kisses at some of the more attractive ones. I guess half-naked groupies are now part of my everyday life.

Jenna and I stand on the side of the stage while the guys gather their equipment for the show. Chaz walks out onto the stage first, taking a seat behind his drums. The fans start to hoot and holler. The euphoria from thousands of people cheering for you has to be magical. Next, Tyler and Marcus walk out and start playing their intro music. Van lifts my chin, plants a kiss on my lips, and then runs onto the stage to start the show. My heart goes wild, skipping beats and racing. *Please don't let me pass out.* The enormous smile stretching along my face lights up the amphitheater.

Van's so sexy onstage. Every inch of him is always incredibly appealing, but onstage everything is amplified. The bright lights illuminate his perfect body, accentuating every peak of hard muscle underneath that T-shirt clinging to him, and the energy he conveys through his music is unmatched by anything else. Everything about him radiates.

I'm weak in the knees! Is it possible to resist the urge to tackle him and ravish his body? My sexual side is awakened.

Jenna turns toward me and winks and then focuses her attention back to her guitar hero.

My hair tickles my back as we sway to the music and dance at the side of the stage. Our boys look over at us every so often, flashing a sexy smile. Jenna and I have an odd connection as very few people would know exactly how it feels to be in this situation.

The guys gradually make their way to us. My self-control is at an all-time low. I'm breathless and every hair on my body is standing on end from the unique electricity flowing within me. My sexy rock god is walking toward me, smiling. I wrap my arms around his neck and kiss him hard on the lips. He pulls me into a tight hug.

"I'm pretty sweaty; I can't believe you want to be near me right now." Van flinches back, brushing his wet hair back with his hand.

I lean in closer, trying to erase any distance between us. After watching him have complete control over the crowd, I yearn for his body to overpower mine. "You've never looked sexier!"

Van presses his forehead against mine. "I'm sorry, but we have to hang around for a little while, sign autographs, and meet the fans; the whole nine yards. Jenna will kick everyone out when it's time for dinner. We've got a hotel room for tonight so you can explain to me again exactly how sexy I look." Van raises his eyebrows, seducing me with his smile. He wipes himself off with a towel, grabs two beers from the ice bucket, and takes my hand.

Déjà vu floods through me as I remember meeting the band after their show a few weeks ago.

"You were backstage before so you know what it's all about. These people are our fans who support our music. It's only right to give them some of our time so they know we appreciate them."

"I understand, and I think it's great."

"Just remember I'm only interested in anyone I talk to as a fan. It drives Jenna crazy to see Marcus talking to girls. Remember the first time you met her backstage? Don't get mad or upset. This is just P.R. You're the only one I want, ok?" He fixes his emerald eyes onto mine as he waits for my response.

"I know what you're saying. I'm a pretty jealous person by nature but I promise I won't take it out on you. I know you're just doing what you need to do." I softly kiss his lips.

The room looks similar to the one at the Lakeview amphitheater where I met Van. There are droves of half-naked women running up to the guys, asking for their autographs, and professing their love. My muscles tighten and I grind my teeth. I already can't stand watching these women flirt with my man.

Ugh! Really? There are actually girls asking Van to sign their chests. A lump forms in my throat as I watch them pose for pictures with him. I close my eyes tight and take a deep breath. *What's wrong with me?* He just told me this is all P.R.

Jenna walks over to me, her arms crossed over her chest. "This is definitely my seventh level of hell." She glares at the women talking to Marcus.

"Wow, now I can understand why you were such a bitch to me the first time we met. I want to kick everyone's ass in this room." I fold my arms and sneer at the scantily clad women in my field of vision.

"I know. It comes with the territory, but it definitely sucks. I guess misery loves company because I'm happy you're just as annoyed as me. Luckily, it only lasts about an hour." She glances at her watch and sighs.

"I'm starting to think that this experience is going to make me a bitter person."

"I'm living proof of that," Jenna says, "I used to be a cheerleader."

We both start laughing.

Finally, schmoozing time is over. The four of us take a cab to the Villa Italia while Tyler and Chaz continue to entertain some chosen females back on the bus.

Jenna's smile is radiant. She bounces in her chair. "This is so exciting! We're actually going on a double date."

I chuckle. "I think I just caught a glimpse of that cheerleader poking out."

Marcus laughs. "Captain of the squad."

"Yeah, and Marcus was the quarterback and captain of the football team," Jenna replies while rubbing his back.

I look over at Van and bite my bottom lip. "And what did you do in high school?"

Marcus interjects. "Well, if there was a golden gloves team he would have been their captain. He was a brawler in high school."

Jenna slaps Marcus's arm.

I look at Van, raising my eyebrows.

"I had a lot of anger issues back then," he says, slightly wincing.

He's definitely holding something back, but I won't press the issue.

We have the place all to ourselves, one of the perks of being the last patrons of the night. I brush my hand over the white linen tablecloths and snatch the fancy linen napkin peeking out from under the plate. A rainbow of sparkling light illuminates the table from the candle reflecting off the exquisite crystal water goblets.

The waiter gawks at Van and Marcus. "Uh, do you guys want to hear our specials?" He repeatedly clicks his pen.

Jenna smiles and flutters her eyelashes. "Yes, and we'd like a bottle of champagne."

He blushes. "We have a chicken marsala special served family style with pasta with vodka sauce, meatballs, and salad."

Marcus cracks his knuckles. "We'll have that."

The waiter takes a step back and looks Van and Marcus up and down. "Coming right up." He jots down the order and leaves.

I take a sip of my water. "I guess he's not used to tattooed rockers."

Van shakes his head. "He better not spit in our food."

Jenna grimaces. "Ugh, gross. We're in a fine dining restaurant. Plus, it's family style and he wouldn't do that to Lexie and me."

We both burst into an array of giggles.

The waiter returns with our champagne. He tries to hold in a smile as he pops the cork and fills Jenna's glass.

Marcus grabs the bottle from him. "Ok dude, we'll take it from here." He grits his teeth.

The waiter holds up his hands and walks away.

Jenna puts her head on Marcus's shoulder. "Jealous are we?"

Marcus exhales and pours us each a glass of champagne. "Yeah, I know. You have to put up with the groupies, I have to put up with the waiter."

Van rolls his eyes.

We each raise our glass while Jenna makes the toast: "To a great night, with great friends, new beginnings, and an awesome tour!"

We all clink our glasses and drink.

My breathing slows as my eyes prickle with tears. I'm already missing Brooke. Toasting had become our tradition during college. Tomorrow, she'll find my note. My stomach rolls. I'm sure she'll have a lot to say about this rash decision. Regardless, I still can't wait to hear her voice.

The conversation, company, and food are superb. Jenna's full of surprises. Who would've thought she'd go out of her way to welcome me? It's the perfect end to my first night on tour.

I yawn as I enter the taxi cab. Van and Marcus booked rooms at the Marriot a few miles away, although, in reality Jenna most likely took care of the details. The long day is catching up with me but I'm definitely not too tired to stay awake with Van. I guess I have to adjust to a rocker's schedule, up late into the night and asleep most of the day.

Van pushes open the door to our hotel suite and gently pulls me inside. He quickly closes the door and traps me in between his perfect body and the cold, wooden door. "Now, you mentioned something about me never looking so sexy."

His soft breath caresses my face. Goosebumps erupt and my stomach quivers as the unique electricity flows through me. "I don't know if that was true. You're looking pretty sexy right now," I whisper and nibble the lobe of his ear.

He lets out a deep sigh and places his hands on my hips. His body presses against mine; *Hmm, even the thick denim of those jeans can't hide how sexy he is*. He slams his lips against mine with animal-like passion. Our hands are all over each other as articles of clothing are quickly being removed and scattered all over the hotel room. My heart hammers and my body trembles. I'm just about panting as I push him onto the bed and jump on top of him. Feverishly kissing his neck, I run my hands all over his body. He breathes heavily and rolls on top of me, kissing my lips, neck, and breasts, while caressing me from head to toe. I want him so badly, I can't take it anymore.

"Van, please, I want you now."

He drives himself into me and groans. Electricity sparks through my body spreading a current through each and every cell. I moan as he thrusts repeatedly in a strong, steady motion, filling me completely. My heart pounds and my whole body scorches with pleasure. Passion builds quickly. I find my release twice, before he finds his and collapses on top of me. We lay there, satisfied and sweaty.

Finally, I'm able to catch my breath. *Ugh, I'm a hot mess!* I roll myself out from under Van.

He pulls me close to him again.

"I think I worked up more sweat than you did on stage. I saw the bathroom on the tour bus and I think I'd prefer to shower here."

"Sounds like a plan, but I can't promise you won't work up a sweat again tonight."

"You're certainly making me a very dirty girl, Mr. Sinclair." I catch my lip between my teeth and raise my eyebrows.

He gently runs his fingers up my body and sweeps my hair away from my neck. "Maybe I need to clean you up. Let's start here." He softly kisses my neck, running his tongue along my moist skin.

Goosebumps erupt all over my body and chills run along my skin. My heart palpates and my breathing increases. My muscles tighten and desire aches throughout

my core. *Self-Control, where are you?* I need him again. Time
for round two!

∞

    Completely disheveled, a shower is now a necessity. I
walk into the bathroom and start the water. *Oh no, all of my
toiletries are on the bus.* Good thing the hotel provides some.
Strong arms wrap around me as the warm water washes the
day away. We playfully kiss and tease one another while
cleaning our steamy, sweaty bodies.

    Just about every muscle in my body is completely
relaxed. I crawl onto the bed and cuddle with Van while he
flips through the channels on the TV. My cell phone rings.
I glance at the screen and begin to fidget with my fingers.
It's Brooke. I don't want to have this discussion in front of
Van, but I have to talk to her. I grab the phone and answer.

    I twirl my hair around my fingers. "Hi Brooke! How
was your trip?"

    "My trip was great but how about we discuss this note
you left me?"

    I look at Van and cover the mouthpiece. "Hey Van. It's
Brooke, I just need a minute."

    "Take your time."

    I walk into the bathroom and close the door. Sweat
beads form on my forehead. "I didn't want to call you in
Mexico and I basically made a spur of the moment
decision. I'm sorry you had to find out through a note."

    "I can't believe you dropped everything to go on tour
with Devil's Garden. That's the craziest thing you've ever
done."

    "I know. Since I have the next few months off anyway,
I figured I'd give it a shot. I just want to try to make it work
with him. You know, follow my heart for once. I couldn't

just let him go. I know it's really fast and sounds crazy but he means a lot to me."

"Thank God! I've been trying to tell you to go for it for the last week and you're finally doing it. I'm going to miss you this summer. Make sure you call me and text all the time. I guess I won't see you until Sydney's bachelorette party."

I let out a deep breath and a smile spreads across my lips. "I promise to drive you crazy with my calls and texts. Thanks for understanding. The next show is in Ohio, so that's where I'm headed."

"Be careful. Have fun and call me."

"I will. Bye."

A weight lifts from my shoulders. I breathe easier knowing my best friend is behind my decision. I'm sure Van heard my whole conversation. I fidget as I walk back into the room and put my phone on the nightstand. I crawl into bed and cuddle up next to him.

"Everything ok at your apartment?"

"Yeah, everything's great." I pull Van closer; the heat of his body warms my skin.

We're just about to drift off to sleep when my cell phone chimes.

Van picks it up and looks at the screen. "You've got to be fucking kidding me."

I rub my eyes and look up at him.

He hands me the phone with a sinister look.

There's a text from Jesse.

I can't believe you ran off to be some rocker's groupie. You really will let anyone get in your pants.

CHAPTER 9—OHIO

"God help that asshole if I ever see him. I swear to God I'll put my fist right through his face." Van grinds his teeth and clenches his fists, his knuckles turning white.

"He's just jealous that you have me and he doesn't. Please don't let him ruin our night. He's not worth it." I put my arms around Van and lay my head on his chest.

He takes a deep breath and pulls me close, turning my chin toward him. "No one talks to you like that and gets away with it."

"Van, he wants a fight. Why else would he send me that text? He wants to get a rise out of us. I'm just ignoring him. That'll piss him off more than anything." I run my fingers along his chest in soft circles. Tiny electric impulses surge against my fingertips. "Thanks for defending me, it's really sweet." I lift my head and kiss his cheek.

He sighs, softly caressing my arm. "I'll always defend you."

Goosebumps spread across my body like poison ivy. My whole body begs for his touch. I take a deep breath and cuddle up next to him, letting the warmth of our bodies merge. The soft tones of Van's heartbeat relax my tense muscles. Exhaustion finally takes over and we drift off to sleep.

The sun blares in my eyes, blinding me as I try to open them. I squint for a few seconds until my body adjusts to the beaming rays. *I've got to remember to close the curtains next time.* Morning is here way too fast and it's already time to check out of our hotel room and head for the bus.

"Marcus and Jenna want to share a cab." Van pulls a T-shirt over his head. The muscles in his back flex, creating exquisite peaks and valleys as he pulls the fabric down.

My eyes follow the thin material until it reaches the waistline of his jeans, blanketing his skin. They travel down, over the thick black belt and perfectly tailored denim. I blink slowly, immersed by the alluring vision.

"Earth to Lexie."

I jerk my head back and rub my eyes. "Ok." My face heats up like a blazing inferno. "Is caffeine in my future?"

He picks up our bags with one hand and grips my hand with the other. "Let's check the lobby."

My eyes widen as they travel over the buffet table. Yum, complimentary continental breakfast! My stomach growls. I pour a cup of coffee and take a few blueberry bagels on our way out. No time to stop for a meal. We have a ten hour bus ride ahead of us. *Ugh, looks like showering and getting ready on the bus is unavoidable.* I wish there was some sort of schedule to follow, but it sounds like it is every man for himself.

Before we hit the road, Van introduces me to Bob, our bus driver. What does Bob think of me, a girl, joining the tour halfway through? I'm sure he's seen and heard some unbelievable things while driving for Devil's Garden.

I stare at my bagel. What happened to my healthy appetite? It's probably absent because I have to deal with Jesse while trying to adjust to a whole new lifestyle. He's never going to stop hassling me. Tormenting people until he gets what he wants is his best skill. *What made me think of him as admirable and ambitious? He's just abusive and annoying.* I sigh and rub my brow. Maybe I should change my number or block his calls. If he keeps this up there's a good chance Van will make the trip back to Lakeview U just to kick his ass. *Hmm, what's the best way to handle this situation?*

A slow throbbing begins in my temple. *Trying to come up with a resolution will make this long ride pure torture. A little relaxation can only help.* I close my eyes and sit back, letting my head sink into the soft leather. Finally, we all agree on the programming. *The Lord of the Rings* trilogy is playing on the movie channel, so that takes care of the entertainment for most of our ride. Van lays his head on my shoulder and dozes off half way through *The Two Towers.*

I stretch my legs and gaze around as the bus slows to a stop in front of the amphitheater. Everyone is napping, the rhythm of the road having soothed us all to sleep.

Van rubs his eyes and glances at his watch. It's five o'clock, just two hours before show time. He winks at me. "Hey guys, let's let the girls get ready in peace while we do our sound checks."

Jenna jerks her head up and rubs her eyes. "Was I dreaming or are you guys finally acting semi-human and letting the ladies go first?"

"We just don't want Van to beat our asses," Chaz replies.

"You have quite the reputation, I'm glad I get to reap the benefits." I kiss Van softly on the lips, running my hand along his cheek. *He's really trying to make it as easy as possible for me to adjust.* I guess he wants this to work as much as I do. Jenna is also reaping the benefits, which makes things even better. Our friendship is essential to both of us since we're in the same position. We need to stick together.

For once I don't have to rush. We take our time getting ready without any interruptions from the guys. Luckily, Jenna and I are the same size. I check myself out in the mirror. Wow, the backless, black dress and studded belt I borrowed from her fits me like a glove. She always looks great, but purple is her color. *Why can't I have her fashion sense?* The zebra scarf she tied around her waist makes the dress runway worthy. I brush my soft curls over my shoulders, letting them fall down my back. The hot rocker chicks are ready.

The door slams shut and the guys trudge their way back on the bus. Five minutes later, they're showered, dressed, and ready. It must be nice to be able to look so great with no effort. I stare at Van and shake my head as he finishes his quick grooming routine.

I step out of the bus and take a deep breath, inhaling the sweet scent of the summer air. It's a clear night in the middle of the state of Ohio. The stars gleam and twinkle like thousands of fireflies lighting up the sky. I want to take in every part of this experience, not allowing myself to overlook a thing.

So much for the serenity of the moment. The same familiar scene. Half-naked women line the entrances while drunken fans make their way to their seats. My eyes gravitate toward Van and the whole world fades away. A few locks of his damp hair fall against his cheek as we make our way to the stage. His bicep dances as he runs his hand through the light brown strands. My face flushes and my heart pounds, drumming against my chest. *When will I be able to compose myself?* I'm mesmerized by everything about him.

The crowd roars as the guys take their places and begin to play. The acoustics of the amphitheater, along with the perfect rhythm of the band, creates an awe-inspiring performance. The fans plead for an encore, echoing cheers through the air. A chill runs through my body causing my nerve endings to tingle as Van belts out the lyrics and works the crowd. I can't take my eyes off of him! His muscles tense and pulsate as the energy and passion flows through him into his music. Ah, my sexy rock god! I'm weak in the knees.

He glances over at me, flashing a quick smile. I exhale deeply and fear I may faint from pure bliss. The power this man has over my body is exhilarating.

Thousands of eyes follow Van as he walks off the stage. I wipe my palms against the thin fabric of my dress. No drug in the world can produce this euphoria. My heart is hammering. I yearn for the moment when this delightfully sweaty man embraces me. He's showing the world that I'm his, and there's nowhere I'd rather be than in his arms.

I'm falling for him, deeper with each passing moment. I'm out of my realm and in a place I've never been before. Oh, how I ache for his touch, to hear his voice, to feel his body. Everything about him appeals to me. He mesmerizes my soul, putting me in a hypnotic trance.

Van places his hands on my hips and pulls me toward him. I inhale and try catching my breath as he holds me close, claiming me as his. The sweet, sweaty embrace sends shivers through my body as he places a soft kiss on my temple.

I weave my fingers through his damp hair and press my body against his as we wait for Jenna and Marcus at the bottom of the stage steps.

"Awesome show guys, the crowd was amazing! We definitely have to come back here." Marcus's face lights up as he professes his love for the concert-going residents of Ohio.

"Come on Tyler. Let's find us some hot Ohio chicks. I saw a few fine looking specimens who can't wait to get their hands on us." Chaz bobs his head, flashing a half smug grin.

"I hear you brother," Tyler echoes as he follows Chaz.

Van and Marcus walk slowly behind them. It's obviously no secret that Jenna and I hate this part of the tour.

Jenna crosses her arms. "Huh, I bet walking to the electric chair is less annoying then meeting groupies."

I huff. "Yeah, or being mauled to death by grizzly bears."

Marcus sighs. "The fans come out to see our shows. We're nothing without them."

I nod. Well, if this is the worst I'll have to put up with I should run off to Vegas and marry him right now. Unfortunately, as much as I want to pretend Van is perfect, I'm sure he has his faults just like anyone else, and I'll be destined to see them at some point.

It's 'meet and greet' time. Great! We make our way to the meeting room underneath the amphitheater. Luckily, there are bottles of beer in an ice bucket right near the door. We're certainly going to need a drink tonight. I grab two and hand one to Jenna. It's amazing how our animosity for other women has brought us closer.

Jenna rolls her eyes and shakes her head. "Welcome to the bitching hour."

We had coined the term at our last venue.

"They can look all they want, but the guys come home to us." I twirl my hair around my fingers and sigh. "Does this part ever get easier?"

"I wish it did, but no. There's always some skank that tries to take it too far. I never thought I'd be forced to look at so many tits." Jenna slugs her beer, almost finishing the bottle in one gulp.

"Well, I'll try to make sure you don't have to see mine."

Seeing each other half naked on the cramped tour bus is a definite probability. *I'll have to be more careful when changing.* I really don't need any of the guys seeing me indecent.

The parade of trashy girls is much longer in Ohio than usual. In fact, there appears to be more Devil's Garden fans here in general. Maybe their music is just hitting the east coast which means that we should be seeing bigger crowds as we make our way west. Bigger crowds are a double edged sword. Sure, it's more success and exposure for the band, but it also means more irritation for me and Jenna.

The amount of women vying for our men's attention increases with their growing success. I need to find a healthy way of dealing with my aggression toward female fans.

"The bitching hour is taking longer than usual. Want to take a slow walk to the bus?" Jenna asks.

"Definitely, but I don't want Van to think I bailed on him. Let me tell him quick." I grimace as I trudge through the mass of half-naked women, getting pushed and elbowed on my way. *Finally! I've almost made it to Van.* I cross my arms and narrow my eyes. *What's this woman doing?* She's determined to keep me from getting through the crowd.

He spots me trying to reach him and shouts, "Hey, let her through, she's my girlfriend!"

Ah! They're the sweetest words in the English language. Van Sinclair just announced to the groupies of Ohio that I'm his girlfriend. Chills run down my spine and my whole body tingles. I love the way those words sound, rolling off his tongue. My smile can light up the amphitheater, no doubt. Oh no, I almost forgot what I came to tell him in the first place.

"Jenna and I are walking back to the bus. I just wanted to let you know where I'd be."

My smile must be infectious. A huge grin appears on Van's face too.

"Ok, I'll see you in a few." He gives me a quick kiss on the lips.

I wave and catch up with Jenna.

"Wow Lexie, I didn't know that rubbing elbows with a bunch of slutty women makes you so happy." Jenna smirks. She locks eyes with Marcus, raises her chin, and points toward the door.

He nods, seeming to know exactly what she's trying to say.

My cheeks hurt from the huge smile that refuses to extinguish from my face as I walk. The sound of crickets chirping in the fields breaks through the calmness of the night.

Jenna stops and puts her hand on my shoulder, turning me toward her. "Ok, spill it. What did he say?"

"When one of the girls wouldn't let me by, he yelled *Let her through, she's my girlfriend!* And that's the first time he's ever said it out loud." My cheeks are starting to hurt.

She raises her eyebrows and tilts her head. "You couldn't figure that out on your own? He invited you to go on tour with him. That should tell you something."

"I know, but it's different when you actually hear it said, especially from someone who's been pretty anti-relationship from what you told me."

"Yeah, you're right. It's a big deal for Van to announce that he has a girlfriend." Jenna smiles, validating my excitement. "Come on, let's get these heels off and relax. I hate to be the bearer of bad news, but guess where we're sleeping tonight?"

"Ugh, I figured. At least we'll get to stay at a hotel during our next stop, right?" *Please let her follow up this bad news with some good news.*

"Yep, thank God."

We stroll through the huge parking lot. The tour bus is parked in the back, away from the crowds, in a designated area. I run my fingers along the chain link fence that lines the perimeter of the lot. Its purpose is to separate the band from the public, but it's low enough to jump over so it's probably not that effective. Some fans are still on the other side of the fence, but most are walking to their cars while others continue to tailgate after the show. *Is it still considered tailgating at this hour?*

A few guys hoot and holler at me and Jenna as we make our way through the lot. She gives them the finger but a small smile comes across her face. There's always a small part of a woman that feels good knowing guys find her attractive, like we've still got it. At age 22, I really hope I still got it, especially since I'm trying to keep a man like Van Sinclair.

As I reach the far end of the parking lot someone yells my name. I quicken my pace, but the sound becomes louder. *You've got to be kidding me! Please let me be hearing things.* The blood drains from my face and my body tenses.

"Why does that guy know your name?"

"That would be my scumbag, cheating ex." *What the hell is he doing here?* I try to lose him and dash back to the bus, but he easily catches up with me, yelling my name over and over again. *Thank God he's on the other side of the fence.*

"What!" I turn and yell, placing my hands on my hips.

Jesse glares at me through the chain links, gripping the fence. "Wow, I had to come and see it to believe it. You really did run off with some rocker. Are you insane?"

"The only insane thing I've done in my life was date you. Why the hell are you in Ohio? It's a five hour drive from Lakeview U," I scream, throwing my hands up in the air.

"I came here to see you and talk some sense into you. I had no idea you turned into some groupie whore."

"Watch your mouth asshole, we're not groupies!" Jenna yells through gritted teeth. The fire in her eyes is unmistakable.

"Yeah ok, whatever you want to be called honey."

Jesse's arrogance won't fly with Jenna.

"Um, first of all, I'm not your honey, and from the looks of you neither is anyone else. And you can call me Mrs. Crane. My husband is in the band you asshole!" Jenna storms off leaving me there to handle Jesse on my own. I guess I can't blame her, why should she have to deal with my leftover baggage?

"I have no idea what you came here to see, but I hope your curiosity is satisfied. Now you can go home and leave me alone." I glare at him, willing him to turn around and leave.

"Jesus, Lexie, look at you. If you had been half as much of a whore as you are now maybe I *wouldn't* have cheated."

Footsteps stomp up behind me. I turn around. Jenna, Marcus, and Van are walking quickly toward me. Jenna didn't leave me to fend for myself, she went to get reinforcements.

Jesse's mouth falls open and his head jerks back when Van puts his arm around my waist. *Is he in disbelief that such an attractive man would be interested in me?*

Van looks at me, lowering his brow. "Lexie, are you ok?"

"I could care less what this asshole thinks of me," I say, pointing at Jesse.

Jesse smirks. "Oh please, I don't need shit from you and your band friends."

"Dude, you're the one who drove out here and paid to see our show," Marcus shouts.

"I just came to see what a slut Lexie's made of herself. It certainly looks like you've excelled with that." Jesse sneers and begins to back away.

Van walks toward the fence. "What did you just fucking say? No one talks to her like that."

Rage is smoldering in his eyes as his nostrils flare. His hands are balled into fists and shaking like a volcano about to erupt. He locks onto Jesse like a lion about to take down its prey. I have to stop Van before this gets out of hand. I step in front of him, and put my hand on his chest. He looks down at me.

"He's not worth it. Let's just go. He can go home alone like the worthless piece of trash that he is." I throw my arms around Van, praying I can get him to come back to the bus with me.

He lets out a deep sigh, puts his arm around me, and turns around. We start walking away from Jesse.

"That's alright, you can have her. I was just about done with the tramp anyway!" Jesse yells.

A low groan sounds from Van's throat. He drops his arm from my shoulder and darts back toward Jesse, jumping the fence and charging at him. Jesse's eyes widen as six feet of pure muscle collides with his body. Van is like a rabid animal. He punches Jesse in the face, his eye swelling immediately to the size of a golf ball. Blood splatters onto Jesse's shirt as Van pummels him, busting his lip and nose. Even though Jesse falls to the ground, Van continues his assault, kicking him in the ribs then hovering over him, punching him in the mouth.

These few minutes last an eternity. Marcus jumps the fence and pulls Van off of Jesse, while Jesse curls up into a ball and lays helpless on a small patch of grass. Van and Marcus jump back over the fence and stand next to us.

"Maybe his mouth will swell enough to teach him when to shut it," Van turns toward me and lifts my chin. "I'm sorry. I know you wanted me to walk away, but I couldn't. I don't care what anyone says about me, but no one insults you and gets away with it." Van presses his forehead against mine.

I grip his biceps and slam my lips into his. "Thank you for defending my honor."

"I'm pretty sure he won't bother you again." Marcus is bent over catching his breath; his hands on his knees.

I guess I have to relive the story one more time for Tyler and Chaz. Van's knuckles are swollen and bloody. My stomach turns and tears fill my eyes as I gently clean the fresh wounds. *Why did Jesse have to show up and run his mouth?* If he didn't learn his lesson tonight he never will.

Good thing we still have ice. I take some from the bucket, wrap it in a paper towel and hold it onto Van's knuckles. We cuddle up on one of the bottom bunk beds. *Hmm, I may have misjudged these sleeping arrangements.* I wrap my body around Van's and rest my head on his chest. The strong, steady beat of my white knight's heart lulls me to sleep.

CHAPTER 10—FOURTH OF JULY

The next several days bring more driving than anything as we continue moving westward. Devil's Garden plays a few small arenas; all sold out shows. Time is flying. The Fourth of July is just about upon us.

I close my eyes and sink my head into the soft cushion. Back home the Water's Barbeque should be televised nationally. Bursts of red, gold, and green fireworks light up the night sky, and the mouth-watering aroma of the fifteen-foot buffet fills the air throughout the whole town of Cherry Falls. Mom may be wearing a black veil over her face this year. The family name is tarnished. Not only am I touring with a rock band over the summer, but I'm also missing the Fourth of July festivities. In my parents' eyes, musicians are the stereotypical unfaithful, tattooed, drug addicts with no respect for women. They clearly know nothing about Van Sinclair.

I look down at Van, who's resting his head in my lap as he lies on the couch. The soft, silky strands of his hair tickle my fingers as I brush a few locks away from his eyes, exposing the green abyss. I'm hypnotized. Blinking slowly, I reach for his hand and entwine our fingers. The skin on his knuckles is almost healed and back to its smooth flawlessness.

Fortunately, Jesse hasn't bothered me since the fight. All it took was six stitches in his lip and a black eye. *Oh well. He got exactly what he deserved.* Luckily, Brooke and I chat almost every time Van is working out at the hotel's gym. She keeps me in the loop about everything going on back home. Her high-pitched tones flow through the phone lines like a cheerleader whose team just won the big game. A good friend understands your heartache; a great friend makes your enemies hers. Jesse is at the top of our evil nemesis list.

I glance out the window as the tires screech and the bus comes to a stop. Large buildings scrape the clear blue sky and bumper to bumper traffic surrounds us in the Windy City. The steps leading to the hotel shine like the stairway into heaven.

Riding non-stop for days wears on your patience. Chaz will be missing a few fingers if he doesn't stop biting his nails and spitting out the pieces. Yuck! *Am I more excited to get off the bus or to get into the hotel room with Van?* Alone time is hard to come by and I'm going into withdrawal. I clutch my overnight bag and dart for the door, almost knocking Van over.

He raises his eyebrows. "I'll take that as a compliment."

I pull my bag through the aisle and step off the bus. "I'm shocked you're taking so long. You better not be getting sick of me."

Van gives me a seductive grin. "If I live to be 1000 years old, I won't get enough of you." He takes off, racing me to the door.

Giggling like children we dash, our feet barely hitting the pavement, until we reach the front desk. Jenna scowls at us, her hand on her hip. *When did she become so mature?* Van grabs my face with both his hands and kisses me hard on the lips. My knees get weak and my head is spinning. I drop my bag and press my whole body against his, running my hands down his muscular back.

Jenna places her hands on both of our shoulders and pulls us apart. "I made a dinner reservation for us at seven o'clock. We'll meet in the lobby at six forty-five." She passes out our room keys, shaking her head.

We rush off, everybody going their separate ways. After spending every second of the last week together, a break from each other is as necessary as oxygen is in the air.

Another spectacular hotel room! We're right on Lake Michigan with a full lake front view. The enormous king size bed, and marble fireplace scream romance and the chilled bottle of champagne and chocolates on our pillows are perfect for those of us in need of some passion.

Every spark of energy I lost from traveling quickly reignites. I walk into the bathroom and turn on the water in the oversized Jacuzzi tub, adding body wash to produce some bubbles. The musky aroma heightens my senses, awakening the seductress inside. I pull my hair into a loose bun, snatch the two glass flutes along with the bottle of champagne, and set them on the tile surrounding the tub. I peek out. Van is lying on the bed, stretching out over the crimson comforter.

"This room has quite the view." I wet my lips and crawl onto the bed, pulling him up into a sitting position as I straddle his body.

He puts his arms around me, sliding his hands underneath the hem of my shirt while kissing my neck. Goose bumps erupt as he moves his fingers along my spine, slowly removing the slinky fabric. My breathing is rapid. I hold Van's hands tight and pull him off the bed.

"Guess it's bath time." He steps forward, kissing my lips. His hands move from my hips to my back and continue up my spine, unhooking my bra and dropping it on the floor.

My heart quickens. I grip the hem of his soft T-shirt and slide it up his body. My eyes follow the fabric over each and every sculpted piece of flesh, before tossing the shirt to the side. I move my hands to the waist of his jeans and frantically pull at the button. Finally, it gives. I unzip them and pull down his boxers, allowing him to step out of his clothes.

He slithers his hands inside my shorts and places his fingers on each side of my bikini underwear, slowly easing them down while his lips descend along my neck. A trail of fire follows his fingertips, right down to my ankles. I step backward until the cool porcelain hits my legs and pull Van toward me. We both get into the water and lay side by side in the warmth, covered with bubbles.

He wraps his arms around me, holding me against him. Every hair on my body stands on end as a frenzy of tingles flow through me. I turn, meeting his lips with mine. He sucks my bottom lip, running his tongue along the inside rim. My breathing becomes rapid. I part my lips allowing his tongue to enter my mouth and slowly massage mine. My heart pounds as I run my hands down his chest and abs, continuing down to massage every inch of him. He groans and deeply inhales, pulling me on top of him. I straddle his body, one hand on each side of the tub, and bend over to kiss his neck. He holds onto my hips, slowly easing himself inside of me.

I moan as he fills my body with his manhood. I rock back and forth as he guides my hips with his hands. We move faster and faster, the pleasure building within, sending water and bubbles splashing over the side of the tub. My heart is hammering and my breathing's brisk. I let out a loud moan, digging my fingers into his shoulders and clenching my muscles as I find my release. Holding me close, he lets out a loud groan as he finds his within seconds. I let my body collapse onto Van's, my muscles completely weak.

Wow, that was intense.

I roll to the side, still panting and rest my head against the tub, reveling in the afterglow. My breathing evens out and the jets massage my muscles. *Is it possible to be any more relaxed?* I pour two glasses of champagne, handing one to Van. The bubbles tickle my nose as I take a sip.

"Pure perfection," I say as I close my eyes, breathing in the sweet scent.

He winks at me. "Best bath of my life."

Soaking in the water erases the negativity from our long ride. I look up at the clock. How can it be time to get ready for dinner already? Since our meals over the last week or so consisted strictly of fast food, a real dinner is an exceptional treat. *Yay! I get to eat something not covered in grease or cooked in a microwave.*

I slip on a slinky red dress over my black lace bra and panties. The cool silky fabric slides down my skin, causing the hairs to rise. My crystal embossed head band holds my brown curls in place. I gaze into the mirror one final time. Just the look I'm going for, sexy but not provocative.

"We may not make it to dinner." Van looks me up and down, rubbing his tongue slowly along his lips.

I smile seductively, bending over and pushing my breasts together to tease him with my cleavage. He reaches for me and I pat his hand away. "Dinner before dessert."

He presses his lips together and tilts his chin. "I enjoyed the appetizer."

I shake my head and roll my eyes.

Van is a vision of pure perfection, dressed in black jeans and a green button down shirt, which flaunts the hue of his emerald eyes. My heart flutters as I stare at the glorious sight. He's right; if we don't leave soon we won't make it to dinner.

My stiletto heels click on the marble floor. Van takes my hand as we exit the room, making our way to the elevator. As we start going down, he wedges me against the wall. I press my body against him and glide my hands up to his neck, weaving them in his damp hair. We passionately kiss until the bell rings and the door opens.

"Really guys, can't you control yourselves for five minutes?" Jenna raises her eyebrows and crosses her arms as she and Marcus enter the elevator.

"I have no self-control when she's near me," Van says as he pulls me close.

I blush and pull away, running my fingers down his arm until our hands twine together.

Jenna's strapless black dress is breathtaking. The sheer waistline shows just enough skin and the backless design is racy yet classic.

"Wow, that's some dress," I say, glancing up and down at the dark fabric.

Jenna twirls around, showing off her whole ensemble.

"Yeah, I hope I can make it through dinner." Marcus pulls Jenna close, slamming his lips into hers.

"I never noticed your ink before. That's a beautiful tattoo." I stare at the intricate, colorful bird that graces the skin of Jenna's upper back.

"It's a phoenix, and Marcus has a Chinese dragon. They represent the yin and yang; two parts of a whole, a give and take."

Marcus rolls up his sleeve to show me his tattoo. The colors of his dragon compliment Jenna's phoenix.

"I love the symbolism," I say as I examine the exquisite artwork. "Van, your dragon is different. Any reason behind your piece?" I touch his bicep, slowly running my fingers over his impressive tattoo.

"I have a medieval dragon. I always liked them when I was a kid, so I got the tattoo the day I turned eighteen."

Jenna looks over my body. "Do you have any tattoos?"

"Nope, I'm a blank canvas. I've always wanted one though," I answer as we step into the lobby, just about to enter the restaurant.

"There are some great artists in Chicago. Are you up for some ink after dinner?" Van rubs his thumb across my fingers as we walk to our table. "Since you like symbolism so much, I'll get something to match yours."

Oh my God, Van wants to get matching tattoos. My heart flutters. I've always wanted one, and I'm not opposed to having something to forever commemorate this time in my life, but it just seems so permanent. It's sort of romantic, Van and I branding our bodies forever with the same image.

"Ok, I'm up for it." I sit down at the dinner table, sipping my wine and trying to choose something to order that won't clash with my nervous stomach. I twirl my hair around my fingers. I'm not a big fan of pain or blood.

"So Lexie, what are you guys going to get?" Marcus asks as he sips his beer.

After looking at Van's medieval dragon and thinking about the tour, I have the perfect idea. "I was thinking it would be cool to get an asphodel flower. In Greek mythology, it was believed to dominate the fields of the dead in the underworld. It seems appropriate while on a Devil's Garden tour, since it's the flower that would actually be in the devil's garden." *Ha! My mythology elective did come in handy.*

"Very cool! I'll get some put in my dragon's claws, like he's carrying them from the land of the dead."

The gleam and sparkle in Van's eyes is hypnotic. I stare into them, helplessly captured by the warm, green tone. My hands start to fidget and tremble. I take a deep breath and grip the napkin on my lap.

We all order steaks for dinner, clearly not the most easily digestible food. The soft texture of the divinely flavorful beef melts in my mouth. Wow, it's one of the best things I've ever tasted. I should probably eat light, but can't help myself.

According to the concierge, there's a reputable tattoo parlor across town. We all jump into a cab and make our way through the city. A sour taste engulfs my mouth and my stomach grows queasier with every passing minute. *Please don't let me pass out and make a fool of myself.*

The tattoo studio is housed in a big building painted in bold primary colors with a neon sign reading 'Best Ink'. The burgundy walls hold images of hundreds of different designs. Everything looks hospital-grade clean. *Whew! That's a pleasant surprise.*

A tall, lanky man walks up to us, both his arms covered in a variety of intricate tattoos. My eyes focus on the large holes in his earlobes, filled with neon green spacers. *How can he wear that stocking cap in this weather? It is July.*

The man nods his head, holding on to his sketch book. "Hey, you guys want some ink?"

Van takes my hand and walks forward, almost pulling me. "Yeah, my girl and I both want one."

"Let's get started, I'm Jared."

I explain to Jared what I have in mind. He makes the perfect sketch. It's time to start.

"Who's first?" Jared wipes his chair down and spreads out some white paper.

Sweat builds up on my hairline around my forehead as he prepares his color palate. I'm up first, no going back now. I straddle the chair and lean forward to brace myself against it. I'm greeted by the aroma of fresh leather and rubbing alcohol. Van is sitting in a chair facing me, holding on to both my hands.

"You ready babe?" Jared asks.

Van grips my hands tightly, clenching his jaw. "Her name is Lexie." His tone is deep.

Great! Nothing like pissing off the guy who's about to pierce my skin repeatedly with a moving needle.

"Here we go, Lexie." Jared pulls on rubber gloves and wipes my skin down.

The buzzing of the gun roars through the shop. I begin to breathe heavily and my hands tremble. Van squeezes them, placing a soft kiss on each of my knuckles. My heart races as the artist begins. Van holds me tighter as the tattoo gun makes contact with my skin. I close my eyes and cringe, then slowly relax. It's not nearly as painful as I anticipated. Forty-five minutes later, I have a perfect image of a pink and grey asphodel flower on my left shoulder blade. Sexy and tough, just like the woman of a rocker. Van is up next. He sits like a rock while the flowers are added to his piece. We're now branded with the same image forever on our bodies. Our connection is eternal.

We take another cab back to the hotel room and crash into our massive bed. I lay on my stomach, my head resting against Van's chest. The slow, steady beat of his heart relaxes every cell in my body. *Dear God, don't let me roll over onto my fresh tattoo.* I don't want to ruin the perfect image.

A dull ache pulls me out of my slumber. Cool air caresses my body, which is now erupting into shivers. *Jeeze, the air conditioning must be set at fifty degrees.* I slowly slide off the bed, trying not to wake Van. Tall shadows cover the walls, growing larger every time I move. I tip toe over to the thermostat. No wonder I'm freezing, it's set to sixty degrees. I turn the dial to seventy degrees and calmly walk toward the bed.

Bright moonlight shines through the sliding glass doors, reflecting off the tranquil water. The blaring sun has woken

me for the last time. No reason to get up early tomorrow.
The floor creaks as I gradually make my way over to the
balcony. *Tonight I'm closing the curtains and sleeping until noon.* I
gently crawl back onto the bed and cover myself with the
silk sheets, drifting off to sleep.

Piercing whimpers ring through the dark room. I jerk
my head back and open my eyes. The bed is shaking,
bouncing my body all around. I sit up, gripping the sheets.
Suddenly, Van's body collides with mine and I'm pushed
through the air. *Smack.* I hit the hard hotel floor. Rubbing
my eyes, I take a deep breath and grab for the light switch.
Finally, I reach it and turn it on.

Van is trembling, his body flailing back and forth across
the crimson sheets. I jump on top of him and place my
hands on his arms. Sweat is pouring off his body, covering
him from head to toe. His breathing is heavy and intense.

"Van, wake up!" I shake him as hard as I can. "Van,
please. Wake up!" I move my hands up to his face, yelling
into his ear.

He gasps and leaps up into a sitting position, catching
his breath. I straddle his lap and sweep his hair out away
from his face.

I give him a quick hug and pull away to give him some
air. "Are you ok?"

"Bad dream." He covers his face with his hands, wiping
the sweat off and slicks his hair back. "Sorry I woke you."

I brush my hand across his cheek. "Want to talk about
it?"

He takes my hand and kisses my fingers. Placing my
hand on his chest, he pulls me on top of his body and holds
me close. "I just want to get some sleep."

I'm just about to fall asleep when I remember I left the
night stand light on. No harm done, Van's already fallen
back to sleep and I don't want to risk waking him.

∞

I awaken, lifting my head to admire the gorgeous view. Ah, pure perfection sleeping right next to me. I stretch. *Ouch!* A sharp pain radiates along my left shoulder blade quickly reminding me of my new artwork. Van wakes up when I flinch.

"You'll probably be a little sore for a day or two. We'll have to think of something to keep your mind occupied." He winks as he tucks a stray hair behind my ear.

"I'm more than confident you can achieve that goal." I nuzzle my nose against his cheek. "Last night was pretty intense."

He props himself up on his elbow and tilts his head. "Intense is my specialty."

I blush and my face heats up. He certainly is a talented man with many gifts. "I meant your nightmare."

"I can't even remember it." He exhales deeply. "Let's check out our ink."

We remove the gauze and examine our artwork, revealing it to the world. My heart races and adrenaline rushes through my body as I gaze upon the smooth, intricate lines that are now part of my body permanently. Van and I have a forever connection.

I'm not taking any chance of pulling off the colorful scabs. *Ugh! I won't be able to wear anything but halter tops and strapless bras for the next week until it heals.*

We order room service for breakfast and sit poolside in the afternoon. It's like we're alone on a vacation. I close my eyes and let the sun shine down upon my face. There's no way it could glow brighter than my smile. I'm in a state of pure bliss for a split second before reality sets in.

Chairs scrape the concrete as the guys and Jenna join us at the pool. I slide my sunglasses up to the top of my head and squint.

Jenna hands me a frozen concoction, with a pink umbrella hanging over the side of the glass. "You've got to try this, better than sex."

I catch my bottom lip in my teeth, slowly releasing the flesh. "Not possible." I turn toward Van and take a sip.

He leans over and sips the melting cocktail. "Not even close." He lifts my chin and places a soft kiss on my lips. "Be right back, cold beer is more my style."

The guys head over to the patio bar and grill while Jenna and I snatch a table. The bamboo roof, along with the tiki torches surrounding the perimeter of the property, turn the resort into an island paradise. We drink our cool beverages and relive our adventure at the tattoo shop. Tyler and Chaz quickly find some ladies to focus on, so the rest of us order some poolside snacks.

"I can't believe tomorrow's the Fourth of July. I'll be sleeping in my own bed before I know it." Jenna's sips her drink, and tosses a nacho in her mouth.

"I've never been to the mid-west before." I'm picturing flat meadows and windmills, like a scene from *The Wizard of Oz.*

"You probably won't be that impressed, but home is home," Marcus says as he takes a gulp.

Van slugs his beer. "No place like it."

We head back to the room to get ready for the night's show. The temperatures soar to 90 degrees and the hot breeze mimics a convection oven, blowing my flowing, blue, halter dress all around. I pat it down, praying I didn't flash the mob of fans. A few loose hairs escape from my bun, sensually caressing my face. My new ink gleams in the sunlight, showing itself off to the world.

The spectacular show quickly turns the people of Chicago into hard core Devil's Garden fans. The energetic crowd roars, echoing cheers throughout the small arena. While the band greets their fans, Jenna and I save ourselves some anguish and wait for the guys on the bus.

"You guys are getting better; that was pretty quick." Jenna wraps her arms around Marcus, kissing him softly on the cheek.

Chaz grabs a beer and winks at Jenna. "Tyler and I have some hot chicks waiting for us at the hotel so we're pretty psyched to get back there."

She folds her arms and shakes her head.

The bus takes off and we're back at the hotel in record time.

Van places his hand on the small of my back and leads me into our room. I reach around and take it, pulling him toward the bed. He holds onto my hips and pulls me close against his body. I run my hands underneath the bottom of his shirt and slide my fingers across the various peaks and valleys of his abdominal muscles. Oh, he's sculpted like an impressive piece of art. I pull his shirt over his head, tracing my fingers along the mounds of pure muscle slightly tinged with sweat. He places his arms around my back gently squeezing me and then quickly flinches away.

"It doesn't even hurt anymore; you don't have to treat me like I'm going to break." I press my lips into a hard line.

"What, I'm not rough enough for you?" he says with a wry grin.

I purse my lips as I stare into his eyes. "Yes damn it. Now come over here and ravish me."

He's holding back a smile. "Be careful what you wish for." He walks over and pulls me hard by my hips, slamming my body into his as his lips collide with mine. I moan.

Almost immediately, our clothes are in a pile on the floor. He backs me up to the wall, placing one hand on my waist and the other against the wall, to prevent my back from contact. My breathing increases and my heart hammers. I bend my leg, resting my knee on his waist. He quickly and forcefully thrusts himself inside of me. My nerve endings stir and tingle, shocking my body into hypersensitive mode. Every inch of me explodes with passion. I find my release within minutes, and he continues his sensually forceful assail on my body until he finds his.

I look into his eyes as I try to catch my breath. "That's exactly what I needed."

He kisses my lips softly as we make our way to the bed, allowing sleep to overtake us. "I can never deny a damsel in distress."

∞

It's the Fourth of July, and we're spending it at the Navy Pier festival. Restaurants and quaint shops line the walkway while entertaining acts such as jugglers and magicians wow the crowds. The view from the giant Ferris wheel is almost as spectacular as the taste of my first Chicago hot dog. Van and I soar above the skyline, looking down on the massive structures throughout the city. Bursts of colorful fireworks light up the night sky, reflecting the shimmering sparks off the dark lake. Van and I sit on the edge of the pier, dangling our feet as we watch the impressive display. I cuddle with him and lick the sweet, sticky cotton candy from my fingers. *Can it get any better than this, or do all good things have to come to an end?*

CHAPTER 11—SEX, DRUGS, AND ROCK AND ROLL

The bus slows to a stop, gently rocking backward as the engine silences. The bright sunlight and warm summer air greet me through the screen of the window as I gaze out into the infinite sea of black pavement. This monstrous parking lot is endless and will be jam-packed by early evening. Devil's Garden is about to play their biggest show yet. Opening for a prominent, mainstream, metal band may propel their career forward leaps and bounds. Vengeful Wrath always sells out, and there's not even one seat left in the huge Des Moines arena for tonight's show.

Jenna walks over to me and interlaces our arms together. "Now Lexie, we'll partner up and use the buddy system so we don't get separated. Make sure you call 9-1-1 if you can't find me." She rolls her eyes.

Marcus presses his lips into a hard line. "Excuse me for trying to prevent my wife from being trampled to death in a mosh pit." His face reddens and his tone deepens. "You don't realize how rough these kinds of concerts get, and your smart mouth won't save you. Plus, if we all get separated and you don't have your pass, the bouncers are sure as hell not going to let you back in."

Jenna walks over and puts her arms around Marcus, giving him a kiss on the lips. "I love that you're so worried about me," she pauses, "oh, by the way, I'm confident I can get backstage without a pass if I needed to." She winks at Marcus, flashing a sexy smile.

Marcus sighs, throwing his hands in the air.

"Why are you busting his balls? You should be happy he cares." Van narrows his eyes, gawking at Jenna with a pinched expression.

"Jeeze, don't get your panties in a bunch, I'm only kidding. I appreciate everything Marcus does for me and I'm lucky to have such a great guy." Jenna pulls Marcus close.

Within minutes, they disappear to the back of the bus.

"Please, be careful tonight. Vengeful Wrath concerts get crazy. They'll probably rush us through the hallways to the stage, so stay close to me."

"I promise I'll be on you like white on rice."

"Hmm, not sure what that means, maybe you should show me now." Van walks toward me and sets his hands on my hips, weaving his fingers into the belt loops of my jean shorts. He pulls me close, slamming me against his body.

My hands travel up his hard biceps, and over the colorful serpent that graces his skin. I wrap my fingers around the back of his neck and press my forehead against his.

"Alright, enough of the lovey, dovey shit. I'm gonna throw up all over the bus from the four of you constantly doing that. Let's take it down a notch," Chaz yells, his arms crossed.

"Sorry buddy. I'll save it for the hotel." Van gives me a quick peck on the lips and steps away. "Let's grab some grub before we head inside."

Chaz nods and knocks on the door to the sleeping area. "Move 'em on out," he shouts with a smug grin.

Jenna and Marcus emerge, slightly disheveled.

My eyes settle on the blond strands, tangled and sticking up in a variety of directions. "Are you going for the grunge look?" I press my lips together, holding back my laughter.

"Bumpy bus ride." She blushes and runs her hands through her hair, securing it in a loose ponytail.

"Time to fuel up before the show". Tyler shuffles through the aisle and hops off the bus.

The rest of us follow suit and dash across the unending lot onto the sidewalk. Luckily, there's a pizzeria a few blocks away. I close my eyes and inhale, taking in the aroma of fresh bread and garlic that fills the quaint eatery, adding to its old world charm. The hand-stretched dough flies through the air before it's placed on a tray and baked in a wood fired oven, just like in Italy. My stomach growls and my mouth waters; I'm suddenly starving. I easily inhale four pieces.

"Jesus Christ, Lexie. How the hell can you eat like a trucker and stay so thin?" Tyler asks, staring at me in awe.

"I'm on the Van Sinclair workout plan," I reply, raising my eyebrows and sporting a devious smile.

Van licks his lips and grins. "You may need an extra session."

Chaz exhales loudly and shakes his head.

Jenna drops a piece of pizza crust on her plate. "I think we ate enough to feed a third world country."

I slouch in my seat. "Yeah, maybe we'll burn some calories on the hike back to the bus."

∞

Ah, time to relax and digest. There's nothing on the TV, so we turn on the classic rock station. I sway to the familiar chords.

"You guys are playing for about 10,000 people tonight. Are you nervous?" I tilt my head and look into Van's eyes.

Does he ever get stage fright? I'd be in a state of sheer panic. It's got to be stressful and scary to lead a band, especially in front of a huge crowd like this one.

"No, not really. I do my thing and hope the crowd likes it."

"If I had your talent I wouldn't be nervous either." I trace my fingers along his arm, stopping at his cheek and guiding his chin toward me.

He nibbles my lip and pulls me onto his lap. I wrap my arms around him and nuzzle my head on his shoulder. *Chaz can look elsewhere if he's offended.* Every ounce of my being gravitates toward Van, like a magnetic force. It's impossible to stop the attraction.

With twenty minutes left until show time, Jenna and I bolt for the bathroom. Getting ready together saves time and stress. I gently tug my silky, black nylons, stretching them up the length of my leg. *Hmm, this outfit may become part of my bedroom attire.* Jenna and I emerge, our hair hanging down over the stiff fabric of our tight, black mini dresses.

Van's eyes widen and his head jerks back. I smack my red lips together and blow him a kiss. He walks toward me and leans forward, slowly running his hands up my dress. He stops at my waist, turns my backstage pass so it's clearly visible, and steps back.

I let out a deep breath. *Such a tease!*

"Alright everyone, time to go," Marcus says as we start filing out of the bus.

I link my arm with Van's and hold his hand tightly as we walk into the arena.

Van looks at my face, wrinkling his forehead.

"You're holding on to me for dear life."

"I can't imagine why, you were only lecturing me all day about getting lost or abducted." I stare at him. How can men be so oblivious?

"That would never happen. I just need you to stay with me the whole night." Van squeezes my hand and kisses my cheek.

I gently nibble his neck, returning his squeeze. "I'm not leaving you for a second."

We're pushed through the musty, dim-lit halls of the arena by an entourage of large men in yellow *EVENT* shirts. *These heels wouldn't do well in a marathon.* I click along the concrete floor, barely keeping up with the group.

"Stop," Van yells.

Everyone halts and turns toward him.

The large man wrinkles his forehead and tilts his head. "Is there a problem?"

Van lifts me into his arms and continues forward. "No, we're good now."

My heart is racing faster than the quickest thoroughbred racehorse and my body is a raging inferno. Van is my gallant rock god! A smile sprawls across my face reaching the heavens and beyond. I wrap my arms around his neck and press my cheek against his. "Thanks for the lift, I'll return the favor later," I whisper in his ear.

His face flushes and he runs his tongue along his lips. "No harm in being a few minutes late."

"Good things come to those who wait." I kiss him softly on the cheek.

He exhales deeply.

We head through the corridor to an office-like area. The light grey walls boast posters of the headliners who've performed throughout the year. Van sets me down on one of the three black leather couches. *Wow, this room is massive.* We venture toward the full bar in the back of the room, stocked with drinks, pretzels and nuts.

Might as well have a few beverages while waiting for instructions. We fill our glasses and plop onto the cool leather. The guys are extremely quiet. Van is rubbing the back of his neck and Marcus is scraping his hand through his hair. Tyler bites his lip as he stretches. Even Chaz is silent, which is really scary. Before long, Vengeful Wrath joins us in the room.

The foursome sport leather pants, black T-shirts, and motorcycle boots. I raise my eyes, quickly perusing the multitude of tattoos and array of scantily clad women. The singer, James, approaches us.

"Hey guys, good to meet you. Feel free to party with us before you go on and afterwards if you're game."

"Thanks man," Marcus replies.

The group takes over two tables and lets their entourage use their laps as chairs. James unzips a duffel bag, placing all sorts of objects on the table. My eyes widen and my heart starts to race as I gaze at the vials of white powder, baggies of yellowish powder, needles, and joints. I've never been around drugs other than pot. These guys aren't screwing around. Their stash covers just about everything imaginable. I swallow hard and lean back. No way in hell will I be partying with them.

Van looks over at the table and grimaces. "No one moves from this couch. Junkies are unpredictable." He puts his arm around me, shielding me from any threat of imminent danger.

Jenna slides over to us. "Guys, I feel like I'm in the middle of a really bad after school special."

"We're here to open for their band, not become friends. We'll cut out after our set," Marcus replies, rubbing his hands on his jeans.

A putrid odor flows through the air as the guitar player heats up some powder in a spoon, draws it up into a syringe, and injects it into his arm.

Why can't I look away?

He lets his head fall backwards, closes his eyes, and inhales deeply. My stomach churns. *How can someone who's living the dream just throw their life away?*

A skinny blond leans over the table, holds back her hair and snorts lines of the white powder with a rolled up dollar bill. More of them follow suit. Laughing and giggling like drunken sorority girls, they continue to take turns until the powder is gone. *How can they be oblivious to the realization that they're practically killing themselves?* My chest tightens and my posture becomes stiff. *Someone needs to slap some sense into them.*

Marcus grabs us a few more beers. No way am I moving from our area. I want to be far away from all the action. I take a deep breath, inhaling the familiar scent I grew accustomed to throughout college. I glance around the room and spot Chaz smoking weed with his new drumming friend. They both air drum with their sticks.

"If he attempts to try anything more than pot, I'm definitely stopping him." I turn to Van, clenching my jaw.

"He won't. None of us are into the drug scene. It's the downfall of most bands. We're all about the music, not that bullshit."

Thank God Van feels as strongly as I do about steering clear of drugs. Musicians tend to get stereotyped into that kind of behavior and I won't be with a junkie. What a complete waste of talent. There's so much excitement traveling on a tour bus with a band. What about the natural high from performing? Why would drugs need to be added to the mix?

Is time moving backward? An eternity can't take this long. I glance up at the clock on the wall. Finally, it's 7 o'clock and time for the guys to hit the stage. My insides start to quiver. I jump off the couch and grip Van's hand, holding him close and ensuring my pass is easily visible. Now is *not* the time to get lost.

I walk up to the stage and gaze out at the vast sea of people. There are so many faces that I'm starting to get stage fright. Loud cheers emerge as the guys take their places on stage and began to play. It's instantly clear that the size of the crowd has no effect on their ability to perform. A perfect set! The crowd goes wild, quickly becoming fans. Van resembles a golden god as the bright lights illuminate his body. I guess I'll always be a star struck fan, no matter how many times I watch him sing. How did I manage to make this gorgeous, talented rock god mine?

Chaos reigns as the unruly crowd waits for Vengeful Wrath to grace the stage. I twirl my fingers around my hair and focus on their ornery fans. Loud screams echo through the packed area and the mass of people in the first few rows step aside, parting the angry mob like the red sea. An uncontrollable mosh pit forms in front of the stage. *Violently slamming into another person is a form of dancing?* It's very barbaric. Ah, that's why Van and Marcus are so worried about us.

Van clutches my hand tightly as we watch Vengeful Wrath from the side of the stage. I rest my head on his shoulder, trying to get as close to him as possible. His damp hair tickles my face as I press myself against his hot, sweaty body. Bitching hour better be quick.

Despite the many substances in their bodies, Vengeful Wrath plays an astonishing set. *How impressive would they be if they were clean?*

It's that special time, when Devil's Garden meets the fans with backstage passes. The drunken, drug fest doesn't start for a few more hours, after Vengeful Wrath returns from the stage. Elbows smack into my sides, and hair flies in my face as Jenna and I trudge through the women-filled hallways, getting pushed the entire way to the meeting room. Only those with backstage passes make it through security. We sit at the bar, munching on pretzels and nuts while our guys greet the fans. *Wow, so many more people than usual.* We kick off our shoes, settle in, and grab a few beers.

"What the hell, we may as well make ourselves comfortable. These women seem worse than usual. I can't stand them hanging all over Marcus. If I don't turn my chair away I'm going to punch one of them."

"I'm with you. I think Van may have to shower before he touches me. I don't want some slutty groupie disease."

Jenna and I laugh. Aren't smiles known to hide frustration? Since the guys don't want us to go anywhere without them we have to make the best of the situation.

"That's fucking gross!" Chaz screams.

A drugged-out girl stumbles, wiping her face. She heaves her whole body in a spasm as she spews out the putrid contents of her stomach all over Chaz's shirt and Van's jeans. Chaz immediately takes off his shirt and throws it in a trash can. He lifts his chin and stands with his shoulders back. Removing his shirt attracts double the women. Van better not plan on throwing his jeans in the trash or he'll be facing a fate worse than death, a pissed off girlfriend.

He walks toward us, grimacing and slightly gagging. "I've got to go back to the bus and change. I can't sit here with puke on my jeans, plus I reek." He swallows and jerks his head back, his face distorts. "Hope I don't hurl on the way. I'll be back."

About ten minutes pass, Marcus comes over. "Hey girls, we're just about done here. Tyler and Chaz already left with two chicks so let's meet up with Van on the bus and go to our hotel."

"That's the best thing I've heard all night. This place is like a skank-a-palooza." Jenna looks around the room once more and shakes her head.

I carry my heels and march across the mammoth parking lot. God knows what I'm stepping on, but my feet had enough of these shoes. The air is stagnant, not even the hint of a breeze. I take a deep breath and carry on. *Hey, looks like the party never stops.* Droves of fans sit on their cars, drinking and smoking, swaying to the music from the radio. Reaching the bus is like walking to Mars. *Why does it have to be so far away? Strange, we didn't pass Van on the way to the bus.* He should've changed and been on his way back by now, especially after his lectures to stay close all night. He was pretty grossed out, maybe he needed a shower.

We're back at the bus and there's still no sign of Van. Emptiness fills the pit of my stomach. *Where is he?*

"Lexie, I think you should go first. I don't want to walk in on him if he's not decent," Jenna suggests. "He's not going to be expecting us."

Yeah, she's probably right. I open the bus doors and head up the steps.

"Hey Van, we're back! Where are you?" I yell through the bus.

I stop dead in my tracks as all the blood in my body rushes to my face. I gasp, releasing the grip on my shoes and cover my mouth. They bang against the steel floor as I take a step back. My trembling hands drop and ball into tight fists. My heart bangs against my chest, pounding in my ears. *Unbelievable!* Van is on the couch of the bus with a blond girl straddling him.

I'm in the middle of a nightmare. Déjà vu overcomes me. *Why am I in the same position I was in a few months ago?*

Van quickly throws the girl off of him and walks toward me, his face white and pallid.

Tears fill my eyes and stream down my face. My heart is racing. A sour tang consumes my mouth as my stomach heaves. Spots are flashing in front of my eyes and my lungs constrict. My teeth clench as I quickly and forcefully inhale.

The blond girl, acting as if I'm invisible, grabs for Van. He pushes her away and stares at my face, frozen. He lifts his hands in the air and shakes his head, squeezing his eyes shut. Clawing at his cheeks, he drags his fingers down his face.

Adrenaline surges through my body. I lunge at the blond, tackling her through the aisle. She screams, begging me stop as she frantically grabs at my hair. My body is numb. I push her on the couch and hover over her body, punching her in the eye, then the mouth. With my grip firmly on her straggly hair, I drag her through the hallway of the bus. When I reach the door I kick her, sending her flying down the steps. I shake uncontrollably as an adrenaline rush fills my veins.

Jenna and Marcus stare at me with open mouths as I follow the girl through the bus doors and straddle her, punching her face. Marcus pulls me off of her while I'm frantically swinging my fists in the air. When the blonde is finally able to focus, she runs toward the arena, away from me.

"What happened?" Marcus asks as he holds my arms, restraining me.

I pull myself away from him as Van appears in front of me.

"It wasn't what it looked like." Van takes a deep breath and gazes at me with a pained stare.

"Are you fucking kidding me? I just walked in on you with some whore on top of you. The picture was clear. No need to spell it out for me."

Jenna gasps, holding her hands to her face.

"It's not what you think." Van sighs and exhales loudly. "This is just a misunderstanding." He lowers his head toward the ground and rubs the back of his neck, slowly shaking his head.

"Are you serious? Did you just call this a misunderstanding?" I grind my teeth and clench my jaw.

"I'm sorry; I shouldn't have used those words. Can--"

Smack! I cut him off mid-sentence with a slap across the face. I jerk my head back. *Oh my God, did I just hit him?* I rub my hand over my forehead and let out a deep sigh as the tears continue to fall.

He stands still, his hands at his side. "Can I please tell you what happened? I know what it looked like but I can explain."

"A picture says a thousand words, Van. I just can't do this right now. I have to get away. I should have known this relationship would be over before it began. I just want to go home. I can't handle any more devastation."

"No!" His lips tremble as beads of sweat begin to form. "Please don't leave."

"I'm sure you won't be lonely for long. There are a million women who'll be lined up to be with you."

"There's only one you and I don't want anyone else." He takes a step forward and reaches for me, but I turn away. "Please, just listen to me. I didn't do anything, I swear. I started washing my jeans off in the sink, and then got changed. This girl must have snuck onto the bus earlier and hid in the closet. She jumped out and knocked me on the couch. That's when you walked in. I swear, that's the truth." Van paces frantically, running his hands through his hair.

I start walking away; I need some time to process. My face is on fire, like molten lava is flowing through my veins. My heartbeat slows, but there's a painful tightness that remains in my throat. I'm not even twenty feet away and Van is standing in front of me. I stop and glare at his face. Tears stream uncontrollably over my cheeks as my eyes lock with his. Even if he is telling the truth, things like this are bound to happen again, in another town, with another girl. *How can I handle the constant worrying about other women?* The tears continue to fall.

Van sighs, walks toward me, and puts his arms around me. I push him away, banging my hands against his chest. He picks me up over his shoulder and walks back onto the bus.

"Put me down!" I'm slamming my fists into his back.

He gently lowers me to the couch and kneels in front of me, placing his hands on my legs. He rests his head against my stomach and moves his hands to my waist, pulling me close. I sit straight and rigid, trying to suppress my need to hold him tight.

"I always tell you guys to lock the fucking door of the bus! See what happens?" Jenna yells at Marcus loud enough for us to hear her through the window.

Van sighs and looks up at me. He swallows hard. "Please, talk to me. The only thing I did wrong was forget to lock the door. Believe me I'll never do that again." He lays his head in my lap and grabs my waist, pulling me close.

This is really happening? More tears fall as I pull Van's chin up to look at me. "Van, I need some time. I'm going for a walk."

"No! Please, don't leave. I'll go, you can stay here. I'll wait for you outside." He wipes away my tears, kisses my cheek, and leaves the bus.

I am in love with him. That's why this is so hard. I grab my cell phone and start texting.

CHAPTER 12—CONFESSIONS

I pull the thin curtain aside and gaze out the window at Van. He lowers his head and wraps his arms around his knees as he sits on the hard blacktop. His hair falls forward, covering my view of his face. How am I going to muster up enough energy to talk to him? I'm out of breath, drained from the night's events.

Ouch. A sharp pain radiates through my hand, it's throbbing and twice its normal size. I actually got into a fist fight! Never thought I had it in me. Then again, my feelings for Van are strong, so strong they make me act crazy.

His story is most likely the truth. Why would you betray someone you care enough about to invite on tour with you? How do I handle this situation? I guess I have to weigh my options. *Should I move on to protect myself from getting hurt again?* Maybe I should be alone for a while; after all, I did start dating Van right after Jesse and I broke up. *Should I give Van another chance since he most likely wasn't doing anything wrong?* I take a deep breath, close my eyes and rub my temples. I need to talk to a girlfriend, someone who'll understand. My phone chimes.

Ok, I'm on my way

Jenna approaches Van on her way to the bus. He raises his head to look up at her.

"The princess is summoning me. Should I just walk onto the bus, or do you want her to hang her hair out the window so I can climb up it?" Jenna's voice drips with sarcasm.

Van looks back at the ground.

"Seriously Van, possessive much?" Jenna walks onto the bus and sits beside me on the couch. She puts her arm around my shoulder.

Tears run down my cheeks as quickly as I can wipe them away.

"Don't cry. I really don't think he did anything with that girl." She gently rubs my back.

I wipe my eyes and lower my head, slowly shaking it. "I'm not sure what to do. How can you handle this lifestyle? I don't think I can do it."

"You've been doing it. You're a strong, independent woman. Stronger than I thought after seeing that tramp's face." She smirks and raises an eyebrow. "I'm impressed."

Jenna examines my hand, which is really swollen now. I can barely move my fingers. She bags some ice and holds it to my knuckles. Ah, the pain turns to beautiful numbness, like the rest of my body.

"Only you can decide what's right for you. I would walk through hell to be with Marcus, and sometimes I feel like that's exactly what I'm doing, but I can't imagine my life without him. He's my soul mate."

I turn toward her and lift my puffy eyes. "It's different for you and Marcus. You two dated all through high school and are committed to each other."

Jenna tilts her chin and raises her brow. "Look around. Someone can be yours without being married to you and being married to someone doesn't necessarily guarantee that they're yours. Whether you want to admit it or not that man sitting outside is yours."

My heart beat quickens. She's right, Van Sinclair is mine. He isn't perfect and he makes mistakes, but I'm in love with him. I take a deep breath, absorbing my newfound comprehension of our relationship. Now the ball is in my court. *Do I trust in Van or walk away?*

My heart can't take the pain of living without Van Sinclair. He's as important as oxygen is to my lungs, a necessary part of my existence. My life is complete when I'm with him. Every part of my body comes alive whenever he's near me. I can't lose him, and I'm not going to let some trashy blonde hiding in a bus ruin this.

"You're right, I overreacted. I just lost it and took it out on that girl."

"Oh, she deserved everything she got. You may have even taught the guys to lock the door." Jenna pulls the curtain open and gazes out the window. "I'm glad you're giving him a chance. He is so pathetic moping around out there."

Van sits with his head hung low, pinching the skin between his eyebrows while he waits for me to decide his fate.

"Don't get me wrong, if he ever cheats, I'm gone." I sweep my arm through the air pointing at the door.

She hits her fist against her palm. "You won't have to leave; I'll kill him for you."

"Deal. Will you please ask him to come in so we can talk?" I take a deep breath and slide back, pressing my body into the couch.

"Sure, no problem." She gives me a quick hug. "If you need me, just call."

"Thank you Jenna, for everything."

I watch out the window as she walks over to Van, she puts her hand on his shoulder. Apparently the bus is not sound proof since I hear everything she says.

"Hey Prince Charming, Cinderella's ready to talk to you now."

Van stands up, and exhales while he raises his eyes.

"Just take your time and talk everything out with her. Marcus and I are heading to the hotel. See you guys there, ok?"

"Ok. Thanks, Jenna." He wipes his hands on his jeans and turns toward the bus.

Jenna pats Van on the arm and walks away with Marcus.

He slowly shuffles through the aisle, his shoulders curling over his chest and his chin slightly quivering.

I look down and stare at the floor until black boots enter my field of vision. My eyes quickly travel up the perfectly fitted dark denim and continue over the black fabric clinging to his sculpted body. Finally, they stop at the slack expression on a flawlessly chiseled face. The strands of his perfectly messy hair fall down over his cheeks as he raises his head. My body starts to tingle. *Not fair*!

He places his hand on my thigh and turns toward me. "I'm so sorry. I promise. I won't screw up again."

My heart beat slows as an aching comes over my throat. I just want to grab him and hold him tight, but he needs to know this is a serious situation. "I'm sure we're both going to screw up every once in a while. That's not the issue. I believe nothing happened between you and that girl, but you need to understand that I won't tolerate cheating, ever, so please don't let yourself be in a position like that again. I can't handle it."

Van takes a deep breath and slowly exhales. He stares straight into my eyes. "Don't you understand? I'll never cheat on you. I don't want anyone else. I've been all over the country and I've met thousands of women. There's only one you, and by some miracle you're mine. I can't lose you. I'll do anything. Please, don't leave me." He brushes the hair away from my face and softly kisses my lips.

My skin tingles as every hair on my body stands on end. "Let's just take a breather until we get to the room, then we can talk for the rest of the night. I need to clear my head. Come on, let's get a cab and go to the hotel."

Van holds out his hand to take mine. He stands in front of me and presses his forehead to mine. "Are we ok?"

I sigh. "Yeah, we're ok."

The silence is deafening during the cab ride to the hotel. Van rests his hand on my thigh, gently stroking his thumb across my skin. His slight touch sends sparks through me. My mind in is pure turmoil. *Why is my body ignoring it?* At least one good thing has come from all this, I know exactly where I stand and what I mean to him. All of the doubts disappear when you hear the words out loud. Technically, he didn't say those three magic words but I heard them anyway. We still have a lot to talk about. Trying to define a relationship in a heated moment is not for the best, although sometimes it takes pure passion to realize what's important. Our love is priceless and essential to both of us.

We walk into our hotel room and find a chilled bottle of champagne with a card attached:

♥ Jenna

That's so sweet. She's really turning out to be a great friend.

I drop my overnight bag, let out a deep sigh, and rest my head against the door. My muscles quiver and my heart rate starts to rise. I'm dizzy and my lungs are constricted, there's no air in the room.

Van turns toward me, his eyes locking with mine.

Without warning, I burst into tears as everything inside me spills out. I cover my face with my hands, trying to hold them back.

He walks over to me and holds me tight in his arms as I let out a few last sobs. "Please don't cry." Van sighs as he pulls me closer. His eyes start to water and his shoulders droop.

I have no energy left so I rest all of my body weight against him. He picks me up and walks over to the bed, gently placing me down. He wipes the tears from my eyes and lies down beside me, propping himself up with his elbow he turns to face me.

"I know you said we're ok, but we're not. How do I fix this?" Van brushes the hair away from my eyes.

"I'm ok. I just have to work out some things in my head." Not an easy task to define a relationship while beating up on some girl and screaming at your boyfriend. Jenna and Marcus are probably ready to have us committed.

"I've never done this before, but I need to be honest with you." He lifts my chin. "Trust is everything right?"

What else does he want to tell me? I wrinkle my brows and stare into his eyes.

He takes a deep breath. "I've never wanted to be with anyone until I met you. Everything in my life is actually kind of perfect right now, and I won't let anything ruin it." He brushes his fingers across my face, softly touching my lips.

I prop myself up on my elbow and turn toward him, focusing all my attention.

He clears his throat and sighs. "I was pretty much alone my whole life. My mother was a teenager when she got pregnant. Raising a kid was no fun so she ran off with her boyfriend, my father, and left me with my grandma. When I was two, grandma got the call she was dreading. Both of them were found dead in a car. Drug overdose."

My heart sinks as I gaze into those beautiful emerald eyes, tinged with pain. *Abandoned by the two people who are supposed to love you more than anything; how can you recover from that*? Tears well up in my eyes and my chest begins to ache. I reach out and place my good hand over Van's.

He stares down at our hands and swallows hard. "My grandma raised me until I was seven. One day, when we were grocery shopping, she collapsed on the floor of the market. By the time the ambulance got there she'd already passed away."

My body becomes cold and my chin trembles.

His mouth twists grimly. "I have no other family, so the state got custody of me. From the time I was seven until the time I was twelve, I lived in nine different homes. All white trash families, who took in foster kids for the check attached to them." He winces as his voice cracks.

Tears stream down my cheeks; I picture the man in front of me as a child, scared and alone, with no one to love him. My chest becomes tight and my heart aches.

"Don't cry. There's a happy ending, look where I am right now." He kisses my cheek and I pull him into a hug. He moves back, and takes a deep breath, desperate to finish his sad story.

"Anyway, when I was twelve, I was placed in a home in Silent Springs. My foster father, if that's what you want to call him, was a drunk and liked to slap me around a lot. When I started school at Prairie View, it was in the middle of the semester. Marcus was my lab partner in Science class. He was scrawny back then. This big guy, Randy Jones, used to bully Marcus all the time. One day, after class, Randy had Marcus up against the lockers, threatening him for his money. I gave Randy the beating of his life. He never bothered Marcus again."

"I guess that's how you got your bad boy reputation." I smile, trying to make light of this horror story.

He shrugs. "Yeah, some of it I guess. Marcus and I got close. He was friends with Chaz and Tyler, so we all became close. One day after my foster father came home plastered, he drug me out of bed to teach me what happens when we leave the kitchen light on. The prick used to lock me in the closet in complete darkness when he didn't want to deal with a kid. I hated it so I always tried to leave a light on. A little light always managed to find its way under the door. Better than nothing."

Oh no! Did he have that terrible nightmare because of me? I'll keep my hands off all curtains and light switches from now on. My chin drops as a few more tears start to fall.

He brushes his hand along my cheek, wiping away the stray tears. "Anyway, I went to school the next day with a black eye. My teacher reported him to child services and I was on my way to another foster home. Marcus's parents heard what happened and wanted to help me. They took me in and I stayed with his family until the band got our break and I was able to afford my own house. I don't know where I'd be if it wasn't for them." He tears up.

He's a survivor who was dealt a lousy hand in life but still managed to prosper and better himself. Thank God he found music to pour his heart and soul into. I throw my arms around him, and hold him close to me. His heart pounds, pulsating throughout his body. I squeeze him tighter.

I hold his face in my hands and gaze into the emerald hue. "I'm sorry. No one deserves to go through that."

He places his forehead against mine. "According to the shrink I was forced to see once a week until I was eighteen, I have *a desire to be wanted and a need to make others feel unwanted.* I don't buy that."

Wow, that shrink is half right. If I didn't blurt out *I'm not sleeping with you* when we met backstage, would I be here right now? But he's never made me feel unwanted, anything but.

"From the second we met, I couldn't get you off my mind. I needed to see you again. Everything's better when you're with me. How can I prove it to you?"

Chills run through my entire body. No one has ever said anything so beautiful to me. How did I win the heart of this amazing man?

"Telling me is proof enough and I feel the same way."

He smiles, locks his eyes on mine, and touches my cheek with his hand. My heart is beating like a drum. Van brushes his lips across mine, softly but passionately kissing me. He pulls me closer. I return his embrace, resting my head near his heart.

As we lay in each other's arms, I replay Van's story in my mind. His life was heavily impacted by unprotected sex and drugs. That explains his aversion to drugs; however, he has been far from abstinent.

"Jenna informed me that you were quite the ladies' man in high school."

He squints and lowers his brow. "Did she now? She better watch out, because I know a hell of a lot about her skeletons too."

I hope I'm not overstepping my boundaries. "I'm just curious. Since your mother was a teen mom, weren't you worried the same thing may happen to you?"

He inhales deeply, slowly rubbing his chin.

It's clear he wants to avoid this subject like the plague.

His posture becomes rigid. "The girls in high school didn't deserve more than one night of my time. I was worthless to those bitches when I was twelve, they only acknowledged my existence to bust my balls, but once we hit high school they couldn't keep their hands off me? And groupies are the same deal." His lips press together in a small grimace. He pulls in and slowly releases a deep breath. "I told you I was careful about protecting myself. You're the only person I've been with without using anything. I told all of them I'm not a relationship kind of guy; sex is sex, not love. I wanted to be sure they didn't confuse the two."

Van is quiet for a while; he rubs the back of his neck and fidgets with his fingers.

Does he think I'm going to bail on him? His troubled history makes me love him more. I want to show him that true love can erase the pain from his past, and promise him an amazing future.

"Just for the record, I don't recall you ever telling me not to confuse the two," I say as I twirl my hair around my fingers.

A sexy half smile forms on his face. "You're different. Everything with you is different. If anything ever happened, I wouldn't be devastated. I'd be ecstatic to spend forever with you."

My heart is in danger of beating out of my chest. My skin tingles as the heat of a thousand suns radiates throughout my body. The smile on my face is barely containable. I run my fingers slowly along Van's arms, desperately trying to resist the urge to jump on top of him and erase any distance between us, but instead I preserve the sweet moment.

"Forever isn't long enough to spend with you." I kiss his lips.

We both lay silent, looking into each other's eyes, nothing but love flowing between us. *Will anything be the same after tonight?*

CHAPTER 13—KANSAS

Ouch! The throbbing pain in my hand pulls me out of my deep slumber. Van's still asleep. I tip toe to the bathroom to grab ibuprofen from my overnight bag. Shadows dance across the room as I slowly make my journey. I glance out the enormous picture window at the sun which is just beginning to rise, signaling the start to a new day with wonderful possibilities. Orange rays shine onto the tan walls as the night sky turns to gold.

Crack! I trip over the champagne chiller, propelling myself onto the bed. Van jumps up, startled. "Rise and shine." I giggle. "Sorry, I'm not very coordinated in the dark."

Van yawns and stretches. "Now, we both know that's not true." He licks his lips and raises his eyebrows.

Warmth spreads across my face like wildfire. "Looks like we still have some ice left." I stick my hand in the bucket. Ah, immediate relief!

Van turns on the light and examines my hand. "Should we go to the hospital to make sure it's not broken?"

"No, it's fine, I can still move it. Plus, I don't want to explain what happened." *No need to relive that portion of last night.*

He flinches, and then holds my hand up to the light, tilting it back and forth while gently caressing my knuckles. "Keep the ice on it. It always works for me. Come on, let's sit on the balcony and watch the sun come up."

He takes the soft fluffy comforter from our bed and wraps it around the two of us as we watch the sun rise over Des Moines. The heat rising from his body turns our balcony into a sweltering inferno. I lean back and nestle my head into his chest. The rhythm of his heart steadily speeds.

Feather light fingers graze my shoulder, moving up and down the length of my arm. I tense; his soft touch ignites the wild animal-like craving inside. All the pain in my hand is erased.

I lift my chin, catching his lips with mine. The intensity and passion deepens, growing with every passing second. He slides one arm under my knee and the other along my back. Swish, I'm suspended in the air. My hands automatically wrap around his neck, clutching his warm skin while his hair tickles my knuckles.

He walks slowly, his lips never leaving mine and carries me back to the bed, gently placing me on the cool satin sheets. Every nerve in my body tingles as he reaches his fingers under my shirt, lightly touching my skin while pulling the thin fabric over my head. A slow deep inhalation fills my lungs. His magic fingers travel over my breasts, stomach, and nether regions in a slow, teasing manner.

I hold my breath and slightly arch my back, allowing him to slide his fingers along my hip bone and underneath the sides of my panties, slowly removing them. I grip him tight, bringing his body closer to mine and run my tongue along his neck. My fingers wander down his body and venture under his sleek silky boxers. A low moan bursts from his throat. I manipulate my hips until he is pressing against me and slowly pull him close allowing him to enter me. Our rhythm increases causing my heart to explode in an overabundance of reckless beats.

The electricity that only Van Sinclair can provide flows through me at lightning speed. Everything's different this morning, more comfortable, more intense, better. Passion builds up inside of me. I grip the bunched up covers with my good hand as I find my release, yelling out in pleasure. Loud moans emit from both of us, cutting through the silent dawn. He continues to thrust himself into me at a slow, steady pace until I find my release again, just in time with his.

I lie in the safe strong sanctuary of Van's arms and sigh with content as my muscles relax. I'm the luckiest girl alive. I've got it all, an amazing boyfriend, who's also a red-hot lover, a great friend, and a talented rocker who's taken me with him to travel the country. What else could I possibly want?

"We head to Kansas today. I'm pretty psyched to sleep in my own bed. Want to meet up with Jenna and Marcus or do you want to catch a flight?" He kisses my forehead.

I jerk my head back as I'm yanked out of my daydream. "Let's catch a flight; I want to be alone." I hold Van close and squeeze him tight. I'm greedy to keep him to myself for just a little while longer.

"You got it." He kisses my cheek and gets out of bed to snatch his cell phone.

I fling a few toiletries and garments of clothing into a duffle bag, pressing it together with my thighs while I struggle to zip it up. *Voila! I'm packed. Silent Springs, Kansas; here I come.*

I better give Brooke and Sydney a quick call to finalize our plans for the bachelorette party. Talking to my friends and family every chance I can is a must. It's easy to lose touch with reality when you're on the road so much and I don't want to lose myself in this process.

"We're all set. We leave as soon as you're ready." Van's eyes are wide and glowing. Whether he wants to admit it or not, I think he gets homesick.

Hoards of Devil's Garden fans pack the space of gate two, filling the small airport almost to its capacity. Hundreds of arms brush against me on my journey through the crowd. Why am I shocked, shouldn't I be used to this by now? The fans pat Van's back, congratulating him on the new album and expressing their love for the various tracks. He makes small talk and signs autographs until the mass of people disperses. *Am I with a movie star?* Kansas certainly shows a warm welcome to their hometown heroes.

We hail a cab and cuddle in the back seat on our drive to Van's house. *Ah, a boyfriend who owns his own home.* I stare out the window at the specks of light illuminating the sky. Fire flies dance through the air, swirling to and fro. The driver veers off the highway and onto a long stretch of dirt road.

"Wow, you live in the Kansas wilderness." I rub my hand against his and grip it tight.

"Yep, in the middle of fifty acres of land. I see enough people on the road." He brings my hand to his lips, delicately kissing my knuckles.

That makes sense. He's constantly entertaining people, and then meeting with them after the shows; I can't blame him for wanting privacy.

We pull up to a large yellow house with a beautiful stone chimney. It's breathtaking, classic and modern all at once. The cab driver drops us off at the door, wishing Van luck, and refusing to take the fare. We step onto his huge wraparound porch, decorated with hanging baskets and a big wooden swing. This is definitely the type of home I would choose for myself.

"Your house is amazing." I place my hands on the wooden railings and lean back, looking up at the two-story splendor.

"Glad you like it. I had my cleaning service take care of everything so we can just relax and hang out." He takes my hands from the railings and guides me toward the door.

We walk into a large open foyer with ceilings at least twenty feet high. I take off my shoes and let my stockings slide along the hard wood, leading me into a giant room with a big screen TV and enormous green leather sectional. The motif is neutral, with a few paintings gracing the walls. I run my hand along the hard leather and continue toward the kitchen and eating area.

Granite countertops, stainless steel appliances, all the bells and whistles! The small dining room is perfect for intimate dinners and a music room is more or less required when you're a touring musician. Does he really need four bedrooms and two bathrooms upstairs?

"Wow Van, this is a really big house for one person. You must get lost in here." I swivel my head, examining the spacious rooms.

"The guys like to hang out here and play since it's in the middle of nowhere. No neighbors to complain about the noise." He holds up his finger. "Ah, I haven't shown you the best part yet."

Ooh, his bedroom? We follow a trail of lush tan carpet downstairs to a finished basement, separated into three rooms. The only normal room is the bathroom. My eyes widen, finally focusing on a huge theater room complete with a popcorn machine. Add polite to the list of Van's appealing qualities. It must have been pure torture for him to stay in my tiny apartment. I turn my head and feast my eyes on the third room containing drums, a microphone, two guitars, a large wet bar, three televisions, and a gaming system. Wow, an extreme man cave.

"Very cool! I bet you guys have lots of fun down here."

"Yeah, but you and I have the place to ourselves. I'm not taking any company." Van slithers his arms around my waist, pulling me close. "I want you all to myself."

The doorbell rings.

I jump, slightly startled. "Umm, so much for being alone."

"No one even knows I'm home yet." He scratches his temple.

I follow Van back upstairs. He peeks through the blinds before opening the door. A woman with blond hair and a brown bag full of groceries walks inside.

"Hi Sweetheart. Marcus told me you were coming home today, so I thought I would bring over some dinner." She sets the groceries on the table.

"Thanks, I missed your cooking." Van hugs her and walks over to me. "This is my girlfriend, Lexie Waters." He puts his arm around me as he introduces us. "Lexie, this is Leslie Crane, Marcus's mother."

"Hello, it's wonderful to meet you." I hold out my hand to shake hers, but she smiles and hugs me instead. I finally get to meet the wonderful woman who gave Van love and compassion when he needed it most. She's an incredible human being.

She pulls a large container out of the bag. "It's great to meet you too. I hope you like pasta."

"Mmm, I love pasta." I could sense the two of them want a minute alone. "I'm going to get settled, if you'll excuse me, I'll be back in a few minutes." I walk upstairs and into the bathroom. I can still hear them talking.

"She seems like a very nice girl. I think it's wonderful that you finally found someone. I can't believe you have a girlfriend. I had to see it for myself after Marcus told me."

"Yeah, she took me by complete surprise."

"Well, that's usually the way it happens. I'm having a barbecue tomorrow, I hope you'll both come."

"Wouldn't miss it! Thanks again for the food."

The front door closes. I head out of the bathroom as footsteps get closer.

"Hey, looks like we're going to a barbecue tomorrow at Marcus's parents' house."

"Can't wait, I've heard great things about Kansas cooking." I kiss Van softly on the lips and slowly bring my hands over his forearms and up to his shoulders. "Leslie seems really nice. It's sweet of her to bring you dinner."

"She just wanted to see if the legendary Lexie Waters really exists." He moves his hands to my waist and takes a step toward me.

"Wow, I didn't know my legend precedes me." I guess with Van's loner reputation, a girlfriend is big news.

"This house has an interesting history." He raises his eyebrows and presses his forehead to mine.

Wait, this is new construction. Barely two years old. "What? Ghosts?" I tilt my head.

"None that I know of." He chuckles and moves his hands up and down my arms. "There's never been a girl in my bedroom." He smirks at me.

It's time to break that trend. "I'm dying to go where no woman's ever been before."

"It wouldn't be the first time you've done that." He lifts my chin and sucks on my bottom lip, taking my hand and leading me forward.

I follow Van through a set of French double doors into a large room. The moonlight blares through the ceiling to floor windows, casting intricate shadows on the king size bed covered in purple satin sheets that fills the middle of the room. A stereo system rests on top of the triple dresser and connects to a large TV nestled inside the armoire. More light shines through a doorway on the far end of the room. I peek around the corner and feast my eyes on the marble and granite bathroom containing the largest whirlpool tub I've ever seen indoors. Memories of our sensual baths consume my mind.

"Since I'm the only girl to grace this room, it's only right to christen it." My tongue slowly darts out of my mouth and moves along my top lip. I walk toward Van, removing an article of clothing with each step.

Van's eyes enlarge, focused intently on my body as I continue my escapade. I finally reach him and hook my fingers into the belt loops of his jeans. I yank hard, forcing his body against mine. A low groan stems from his throat, his lips pressed together in a line, slightly upturned. The hidden seductress inside comes out full force. I grasp the hem of his shirt and tear it over his head, exposing the perfectly carved flesh that makes every pore in my body sweat. Our hearts beat fast and furious as I lightly graze my fingernails over each and every curve of his muscular torso, stopping just below his belly button.

I glide my tongue down his chest, continuing over his abs and stopping just where my fingers rest. His smooth salty skin drives my body wild. Every inch of my flesh bursts into an array of electric impulses. The loud groan coming from his throat proves it has the same effect on him. I drop to my knees and fiddle with the button of his jeans. It finally gives. I jerk down the thick denim, tangling his boxers in the fabric and taking them down as well.

My eyes ascend onto the glorious sight in front of me. His head tilted back, eyes closed and hands balled into loose fists. He wants me bad, just as much as I want him. I touch the tip of my nose to his thigh, gently teasing him as my head makes its way up, traced by the slight touch of my fingers. He sighs, wetting his lips. My tongue swirls and spins in an assortment of twists and turns along every inch of him. His body shudders and trembles as I engulf him, sucking slowly and intensely. He grips my shoulders and steps back, releasing my hold.

"If you keep that up we won't get to christen the bed." He bends down and kneels in front of me, softly brushing my cheek and moving his hand around to the back of my neck.

God, I want him so bad. What was I thinking? Willpower is required to seduce the irresistible.

He tugs my neck toward him, our lips slamming together. A familiar trail of tingles follow the path of his descending fingers from my neck, down my chest, and finally to my waist. He wraps his arms around the tops of my thighs and grips them tightly.

I'm airborne, my hair whisks around, sticking to the glistening skin of my back. I hold onto his neck, trying to balance my weight.

Van lays me on the bed and crawls on top of me, his heart pounding through his chest, sending shockwaves through my core. His hot sweaty forehead presses against mine. "You're now literally where no woman has ever been before," he mutters.

Is there a double meaning to that sentence? The cool satin sheets caress my body while the electric sparks flow through me. Drenched strands of hair tickle my neck and shoulders. I run my fingers through the sleek locks, as Van hovers above me. Our eyes lock and a frenzy of passion erupts. Any minuscule speck of willpower that may have existed is nowhere to be found. I heave my body toward him and crash my lips against the soft pink flesh of his. My hands frantically explore every smooth surface of his hard body from head to toe. In a wild craze, my entire state of being flustered, like a shark sensing the slightest drop of blood.

Van holds my hips, steadying me as I sink into the covers. I gasp, desperately trying to catch my breath. He thrusts himself inside me hard, quickly gaining a strong rhythm. I moan and dig my fingers into the hard flesh of his back.

We roll around the purple satin sheets, loving each other in just about every way imaginable. My nerve endings burst out into a rage of euphoria. I yell out and weave my fingers in his light brown strands as my body convulses. He grips the sheets and moans into the calm Kansas night as he explodes inside me. My breath stalls and I try to reorient myself to my surroundings, just an after effect of toe-curling, passion-filled love. *Why can't I stop time and stay in this moment forever?*

Complete devastation yesterday and utter euphoria today? Life with Van Sinclair is certainly a roller coaster ride. We lay in the sea of purple for a few minutes, catching our breath.

I prop myself on my elbow and turn, letting my fingertips slightly graze Van's chest. "It would be a shame to let that pasta go to waste." I'm sure he worked up an appetite as well.

"You read my mind, let's go."

Van microwaves our pasta and sets the table while I slice the Italian bread. Just like a normal, everyday couple. The aroma of fresh garlic and tomatoes flows through the air, turning Van's house into a summer garden.

I shovel a forkful into my mouth. "I'm in for a treat if the barbecue is half as good as this pasta."

Van slurps up his spaghetti. "I know. I can't believe Marcus isn't fat."

I pour us each a glass of wine and head outside. That porch swing has been calling me. I sprawl out, lifting my feet onto the swing and nuzzling next to Van. Crickets chirp, singing their unique melody to the creatures of the night. The warm breeze flows through my still damp hair as we slowly rock. I stare out onto the landscape of grassy knolls as far as the eye can see. Ah, it's as if we're cut off from the rest of the world, on our own private island.

I breathe in the scent of the summer air. "Van, this is incredible and very peaceful."

"I actually write a lot of new music out here."

"I'd love to be the first to hear your new stuff, but I know you're constantly playing for people so it's ok if you don't want to."

He turns to me and raises his eyebrows. "You're not people, and I'll serenade you any time you ask." He walks into the house and returns with an acoustic guitar.

My own private concert! We sit outside as Van plays to his audience of one. These new songs are destined to become hits. I sway to the melodic tones of his voice. What a range. He can sing anything from hardcore rock to the sweetest lullaby. He's truly a talented man, in every sense of the word.

∞

The sun blares into the wall of glass, burning through my lids. Morning arrives quicker than usual. I open my eyes and slowly focus on Van sleeping in a sea of purple satin. *Best view in the world.* He must sense my stare. He slowly blinks and smiles.

"Good morning. How'd you sleep?"

I stretch my arms over my head. "Like a log. This is the most comfortable bed I've ever been in. I don't want to get out of it."

"That can be arranged." Van raises his eyebrows and smirks, as he pulls my body close to his, kissing my cheek. "Want breakfast in bed?"

"I would actually love some coffee out on the swing."

"Your wish is my command." Van waves his arm as we get out of bed and head downstairs.

Golden beams light up the meadows and trees. My eyes travel across the endless lush greenery as I sip my coffee and glide my feet against the wooden porch, slowly propelling the swing. I love it here, definitely a place I can see myself settling down.

Does time move faster here in Kansas? It's already time to get ready for the Crane's barbecue. My brown curls hang down over my shoulders in a half ponytail. *Jeeze, I hope this isn't a formal event.* I gaze in the mirror at my purple sundress. Since Van looks perfect as usual in his blue T-shirt and jeans, I better step it up a bit. Some fancy jewelry and beaded flip flops should do the trick.

Much better! I fidget and twirl my fingers around my hair. I'm meeting Van's only "family". God bless him when it's time to meet my parents.

I lower myself into the sleek leather of Van's black Dodge Charger and run my fingers over all the lights and buttons. *Is this the Bat Mobile?* It is a muscle car to the extreme.

A short dirt road leads us to a gorgeous brick ranch home. The large tent in the backyard covering several tables, chairs, and two large grills indicates a decent size crowd is expected. My stomach clenches and flip-flops. *Please let me be able to eat!* I take a few deep breaths and calm my nerves.

My eyes travel over the vast amount of unfamiliar faces. "Van, I thought you said this was a small barbecue. I think Leslie invited half the town."

"Yeah, I should've warned you. The Cranes tend to overdo things." Van parks the car and opens my door for me like a true gentleman. I flash a goofy grin.

Dinner music echoes throughout the yard. My mouth waters as the aroma of smoked hickory engulfs me. *Mmm. If the food tastes half as good as it smells, I'll be in heaven.*

We walk into the party, holding hands and giggling, totally engrossed in each other. A dark haired man with glasses comes up to us and gives Van a big hug.

"It's great to see you back! We missed you." He pats Van on the back.

"I missed you guys too. Mitch Crane, meet my girlfriend, Lexie Waters."

He holds out his hand. "It's nice to finally meet you. I've heard wonderful things from Marcus and Jenna. Welcome to our home."

I smile and shake it. "Thanks for having me. Everything smells delicious."

"Enjoy yourselves. I've got to help the missus get everything ready."

I spot two empty seats at Jenna and Marcus's table. *Thank God.* I really didn't want to force small talk with total strangers.

Marcus stands up and pulls out a chair. "Hey Lexie, ready for some Kansas cuisine?"

I lick my lips. "Oh yeah, it smells heavenly."

Van leans in and whispers into my ear. "If you keep doing that I'll have to show you the backseat of the Charger."

I roll my eyes and shake my head.

"I guess the lovebirds are back in paradise." Jenna gives a quick thumbs up.

"Thanks in part to you, everything's perfect." I give her a quick hug.

Is there special livestock in Kansas? These steaks are the best I've ever tasted, perfectly cooked and seasoned, so tender they melt in your mouth. Everything's top notch. Leslie Crane is truly a culinary genius. *Thank God I left room for dessert!* My eyes practically bulge out of my head, never leaving the buffet as they focus on a tray of decadent brownies and beautifully decorated cupcakes. I lick the fudge icing off first, and then finish the spongy cake. Yum.

Van stares directly at my face, his mouth opened and his eyes locked onto me like a lion stalking his prey. I lick the rest of the icing off my fingers, wrapping my lips around each one and sucking hard.

He exhales deeply. "We'll have to put those skills to good use when we get home."

I lick the remaining icing from my bottom lip and slowly catch it in my mouth. "That can be arranged."

A bead of sweat forms on his forehead. "Let's get a drink before I give you a tour of my old bedroom. It's far from soundproof."

Wine is being served near a small area opened up for dancing. I take two glasses and hand one to Van. I sway to the slow ballads as guests take to the dance floor.

"Wanna dance?" Van holds out his hand.

I set my glass down and, take it. "More than anything."

He leads me to the dance floor, twining his fingers with mine. We sway back and forth to the slow rhythm. Nothing in the world compares to Van's strong arms around me. Our lips meet as we dance, showing the world around us that we belong to each other.

As we exit the dance floor I glance around at the other guests. *Why are those girls staring at us, smirking and laughing, as they whisper to each other?* They watch me as I walk around the party.

I nod my head toward them. "Who are those girls?"

Van spots the brood of cackling women. "Just some girls we went to high school with, I think Jenna's still friends with them. They aren't worth your time."

"You do see them laughing at us, right?" I place my hands on my hips and glare at the table, inadvertently tapping my foot.

"Ignore them; they're probably still pissed I wouldn't take any of them to prom." Van pulls me close, kissing my lips and giving the girls something to stare at.

"I guess Jenna turns into one of them when they're together. Huh, I thought we were friends." I'm not able to peel my eyes away. *Is she looking over and laughing as well?*

Van notices, puts his arm around me, and leads me away. I frown and my posture becomes rigid. For the first time since taking up with Van, I'm a complete outsider.

"Screw them. It's me and you against the world." He kisses my forehead and squeezes me tight.

"I wouldn't want to fight the world with anyone else." I kiss him deeply, creating more of a show. There's more snickering as I pull away.

"Come on. I'm going over to introduce myself. If they want to stare at me, they can see me up close."

CHAPTER 14—FRIENDS?

Hand in hand, Van and I walk to the table where Jenna and her girlfriends are sitting. The heat from the setting sun blaring on my back adds fuel to my internal fire.

My lips curl, showing a glimpse of my teeth. "Hi Jenna, I thought I should introduce myself to your friends."

She narrows her eyes. "Umm, ok. Guys, you all know Van, and this is his girlfriend, Lexie. Lexie, these are my friends from high school, Taylor, Claire, Ashley, Hailey, and Kara."

The girls gaze at me with blank faces. I hold out my hand to shake theirs as Jenna introduces us.

"Why is your hand purple?" Taylor flinches as she wrinkles her nose.

I glare. "Oh, that's just a war wound from the last bitch that offended me."

Taylor's eyes widen. She sinks back in her chair and turns her head away from me.

Van lets out a faint chuckle. He wraps his arm around my waist, obviously trying to deter me from starting a brawl. I have no intention of fighting with anyone, but I want to make it clear to these girls that I won't put up with their bullshit.

Claire looks me up and down and lowers her eyebrows. "So, I hear you're a groupie that Van met on the road."

Thank God Brooke and I always avoided girls that act like they're better than everyone else. It looks like I'll have to stoop to their level to prove a point. "I hear you're some chick that Van wouldn't take to the prom."

Claire sighs, rolling her eyes. "God, Van, what do you see in her?"

Van glowers and flattens his lips. "Everything." He kisses my temple.

"Alright, that's enough," Jenna interrupts. "Lexie's not a groupie. She's really great and I'm sure you guys would all love her if you got to know her. Let's get past the fact that she got the guy no one else could. No need to be jealous." Jenna smiles at me. "Plus, she and I are very close, so enough with the nonsense."

Van rolls his eyes. "Whatever. We'll catch you later, Jenna." He slides his hand across my back and down my arm to my hand, interlocking his fingers with mine as we walk away.

"Wow. She actually stood up for me." I tilt my head up and lift my eyes.

"Too bad she turns into that I'm-better-than-you cheerleader when she's around them. Forget about it, you proved your point." He squeezes my hand.

We walk away from the party guests and onto a grassy path.

Emerald fire stares down at my face. "Walk with me."

Volcanic lava flows through my veins. I sigh. He's utterly irresistible when he says those words to me.

"This was my home away from home when I lived here with the Cranes."

I clutch Van's hand and follow him through the field, up into a clearing on the top of a small hill. Countless twinkling stars illuminate the clear night sky. We sit down on the ground, admiring the beauty of the night. Van puts his arm around me, pulling me closer to him.

"Can I ask you a question?" I twirl my hair around my fingers.

He tips his chin toward me, searching my face. "Ask me anything."

I bite my lip and look toward the ground. "What is it that you see in me?"

Van lifts my chin, turning it toward him. "You let those girls get to you. Don't give them the satisfaction."

I fidget with my fingers. "Maybe, but I honestly want to know. I'm just an average girl, nothing special."

He lowers his eyebrows. "Is that how you think of yourself? An average girl? You're so wrong." Van kisses my lips and locks eyes with mine. "The first night when we met backstage, I couldn't take my eyes off you. And when you blew me off, I wanted you more. I had to have you. No girl's ever put me in my place like that."

I smirk. "So you were attracted to the fact I was a bitch to you? I haven't heard that one before." I wink and press my lips together, trying to hold back a smile.

He tilts his head and cracks a slight smile. "You're real. You don't give a shit about my looks, rocker status, or money. None of that impresses you. You aren't the kind of girl who can be bought."

I lick my lips and narrow my eyes. "You figured I wasn't a gold digger so you were intrigued?"

"No, that's not it."

I bat my eyelashes. "Then why?"

He brushes a stray piece of hair away from my face. "You're beautiful, funny, caring, and smart. You always tell me exactly how it is. There are no games with you. You care about me, not some front man of a band, but the real me." His eyes remain locked with mine. "The short answer is I'm happiest when I'm with you and I can't stand it when we're apart. No one else in the world makes me feel like you do."

My heart melts as I stare into those emerald eyes. My knees are weak, the heat of a raging inferno floods through me as I bask in the glow.

He parts his lips slightly. "A better question is why are *you* with me? An orphaned, foster child with anger management issues."

"That's not who you are. You're talented, smart, exciting, absolutely gorgeous and easy to love." I take his hand and play with his fingers, softly kissing each one. "You make every part of me come alive. I never knew these feelings existed. Life is so much better with you by my side. It's a high I can't achieve from anything or anyone else."

"I don't know what I did to deserve you, but I swear I won't screw this up." He brushes his hand across my cheek, sending chills through my body. Moving in closer, he kisses my lips and eases me down onto the cool grass, while cradling the back of my head.

"Umm, sorry to interrupt, but Regina's here and she wants to talk to us." Marcus stands a few feet away, looking down at the ground.

"On my way," Van says as he pulls me up onto my feet.

"Who's Regina?" I ask as we start walking back to the party, pursing my lips.

"Our manager." He nods in her direction. "She probably wants to meet while we're in town."

Why's everyone staring at us? *Jeeze, these people are starting to give me a complex.*

Jenna walks over to me and brushes the grass out of my hair. "Were you guys having a good time?" She asks, barely able to keep a straight face.

My face flushes and fire spreads across my cheeks. How did we manage to become so disheveled in such a short amount of time? There's grass all over me and my hair is a hot mess. Great! Now I look like some tramp that Van brought as his play toy.

Van brushes the rest of the grass off me and places his hand in the small of my back. "Regina this is my girlfriend, Lexie Waters."

Regina raises her eyebrows. "Pleased to meet you."

I smile meekly. "Nice to meet you, too."

"Ok guys, I want to meet tomorrow for lunch to discuss plans to record your new album. The record company wants to plan a tour to promote it as well. No offense ladies, just the band."

Jenna's face explodes into bright crimson as she shoots Regina a sinister look. "Lexie and I will have our own lunch date. Don't worry, we'll be consulted before any decisions are made anyway."

Marcus pulls Jenna away. "We'll be there tomorrow."

The party slowly dies down and everyone goes their separate ways. Tomorrow's a busy day. Besides Van's business lunch, a big show at the arena is scheduled for later in the evening.

Why does time move so quickly when I'm alone with Van? Good thing we actually got a good night sleep. Van pulls me into the TV room right before we need to leave for his meeting.

"Sit down with me for a minute." He sits on the couch and pats the cushion, gesturing for me to join him.

I take a seat beside him and twirl my hair around my fingers. My muscles begin to quiver. What could this be about? "What's on your mind?"

"I'm guessing our meeting with Regina is to explain the details for recording our new album. We'll record in LA, probably right after the tour ends." He runs his fingers through his hair. "How do you feel about all this? I need you and me to work out."

"The new stuff is great. I think it'll boost you guys into mainstream music." I look over at Van. This is not the answer he's hoping for. I take a deep breath and slowly exhale. I place my hand on his thigh and look up at his face. "I start my new job after Labor Day weekend. I'll see how my schedule is set up then. We'll do whatever we have to do to make it work. Make your plans for the new album and we'll work around them."

What does he expect me to say? I certainly can't drop everything I've worked for to follow his band. We'll have to see how things go and make adjustments as necessary. We're deeply in love and our bond won't be broken by time, space, or distance.

"Ok, that's what I'll do." He breathes deeply and sighs, wrinkling his brow.

∞

We drive into town for our separate lunch meetings. Van and the guys meet Regina at a steakhouse, while Jenna and I choose a small delicatessen.

"This place is great! I wish there was a deli like this at Lakeview U."

"We've been eating here for years. I used to come after cheerleading practice to fuel up." She bites her pickle. "I'm sure the guys will be a while. You're going to love LA! Lots of sun, shopping, and great entertainment. I can't wait to show you all the amazing stores." Her eyes sparkle and gleam as she sips her diet soda.

I exhale deeply and drop my turkey sandwich back on the plate. "I don't know how everything's going to play out. I do start my new job after Labor Day."

Her eyes widen and her head flinches back. "Are you thinking of bailing on Van? Please don't, it'll kill him."

I sigh. Van is probably thinking the same thing. "No! I just have to do the long distance thing until we figure everything out. My career's important to me and I don't want to end up resenting him."

She sits back in her chair. "There's nothing in the world like true love, don't forsake it. That's all I'm going to say to you." She bites her sandwich. "Make your decision, but remember whichever bed you make is the one you have to lie in."

A wave of nausea flows through me. There goes my appetite. I have to stay positive to keep my sanity. "Like I said, we'll see what happens."

Jenna is as quiet as a church mouse, a stony expression on her face. We finish our lunch in silence.

The steak house is a street over from the deli. The warm breeze flowing through my hair and across my skin comforts me. Our heels click against the concrete sidewalks as we approach the restaurant. The boys emerge, holding a stack of papers and schedules.

"So what's the verdict?" Jenna rests her head on Marcus's shoulder.

"We record in the beginning of November and start another nationwide tour to promote the new album in March." Marcus picks Jenna up and swings her around.

The guys are smiling ear to ear and talking about their future plans to further their careers. Well, all the guys except one. Van walks over to me, with his head down. He flashes a meek smile. My stomach hardens. *Great, more silence.* When we reach the car I slide into the seat and turn down the radio.

"Congratulations! I'm so proud of you. Three albums is quite an accomplishment."

Van lips are in a hard line. "Thanks."

"Wow, try to control your enthusiasm."

The tires screech against the black top like a war cry, leaving a trail of skid marks and burning rubber. Van slams the car in park. "Don't you realize my happiness is directly related to you?"

I take a deep breath and close my eyes, trying to hold back my tears. "I told you we'll work it out. As long as we love each other, everything will be fine."

He lets out a heavy sigh and rests his head against the steering wheel. "I wish that were true. I can see from Jenna and Marcus that relationships take time and work. If we're apart we have a lot working against us." Van looks down, taking a few minutes to himself before locking his eyes on mine. "You can always stay here with me. I'll do whatever it takes to make that happen."

My hands start to shake and twitch. I let my head fall back and squeeze my eyelids shut, trying to keep my tears at bay. I fail miserably. "We have time to figure things out. At least a hundred new graduates applied for the position I've managed to get. I worked hard for my degree and I plan on using it." A river of salty tears falls down my face.

He looks into my eyes and brushes his hand against my cheek, wiping them away. "Ok, but please think about it." Van kisses my lips and pulls back onto the road. We continue home.

I glance at my watch. Not much time before we're due at the arena for the show. Van's so quiet. *Is he trying to avoid me?* I want to assure him that we can be physically together, but I'm not sure if that'll be the case.

Now, what outfit will make me look extra special for his hometown show? I root through my clothes. Perfect! My red tank dress fits me like a glove and looks extra sexy when paired with black high heeled boots. Van needs some kind of distraction. Ah ha, my emerald green French lingerie from Betty's Boutique. Maybe this is the special occasion I've been saving it for, plus it'll keep up the sexy look after hours.

"It's time to go." Van calls upstairs, his voice stern with the hint of a quiver.

"Here I come." I walk down the steps as Van comes around the corner.

He stops in his tracks and his eyes widen. "Wow! You think anyone will care if I'm a little late?" Van comes up to the steps and puts his arms around me, pulling me close to his body. I run my fingertips over his shirt, tracing his sculpted muscles through the thin fabric. "We better go now or I won't leave the house."

"Hmm, sounds like a plan to me." I pull Van closer, rubbing myself against his body, softly kissing his neck.

"I hate myself for saying this but we better go." He takes my hand to lead me out the door.

I stop and touch his chin, turning it toward me. My heart races as his eyes burn through my soul. "Van Sinclair, I love you more than anything. I want to make sure you understand that. You're extremely important to me and we'll be spending forever together, don't look so sad."

Van steps forward and presses his forehead against mine. "I love you too babe, and I hope forever happens for us." He exhales deeply, his eyes closed.

"It will." I grab his cheeks with both my hands and smack my lips against his. *How can I reassure him that I'm not going to bail on him?*

He pulls away, still quieter than usual and leads me out the door.

The parking lot is packed with cars parked bumper to bumper. It looks like the entire town of Silent Springs has come out to see Devil's Garden tonight. We make our way backstage and meet up with the rest of the band. Jenna's hanging out with her cheerleader friends while Chaz and Tyler entertain a group of ladies. Van and I walk up to Marcus, who's talking with his parents.

"Have a great show kids," Mitch says to the guys. He and Leslie wave as they make their way to their seats.

Van and the sound technician are finalizing the playlist. Guess that leaves Marcus and me alone.

"Hey, I never seem to get to talk to you." He nudges my arm.

I smile and narrow my eyes. "Yeah, we're not alone much."

"You know he'd do anything for you, right?" Marcus gestures toward Van.

I raise my eyebrows. "What's on your mind?"

He stares at me, letting out a deep sigh. "Look, he's my best friend, my brother. I just don't want you to crush him. Jenna told me you're probably not coming to LA."

Seriously? Everyone's acting like a nuclear disaster is eminent. I don't think starting my new job and using the degree I've worked so hard to obtain is such a tragedy. I want Van more than anything and I'll do whatever it takes to make our relationship work. "God, why is this so hard for everyone to understand? Van and I will figure things out once I know where I stand with my new job." I throw my hands in the air.

He looks down. "It's really none of my business."

I sigh and rub my hand across my forehead. "No, I'm sorry, you're just looking out for your friend. It's ok."

"Time to hit the stage." Tyler yells.

Ah, the cherry on top. I get to I watch the show beside Jenna and her friends. I stand on the side of the stage a few feet away from them, my arms folded.

The bright spot lights shine down on our boys, signaling the start of the show. They sound better than ever. I guess they naturally put out extra effort for their hometown fans. I sway to the music as I watch Van take control of the crowd. His hair glistens under the gold lights.

All the energy radiating from his body increases with each song. His shirt begins to cling to him, the hot lights moistening his skin. My heart skips a beat as the beads of sweat roll down his perfect body. My mouth is a sweltering rain forest. I lick my lips as the boys play their last song of the night.

Strong arms wrap around me and pull me down to the ground. I gasp, struggling to breathe and desperately trying to pry loose the hands holding me down. Van turns, his eyes following mine as I hit the floor. Of course, the bouncer is preoccupied with a female fan.

The overpowering stench of alcohol emits from the large man who's trying to touch just about every inch of my body. I kick and squirm. *Please, let me get away from this guy.* Van's nostrils flare and his lips pull back, baring his teeth. He drops the mic and rushes over, violently ripping the man away from me. Van swings wildly, his fists making contact with every blow. Blood spatters over my face and chest as Van continues his assault. Finally, the bouncer steps in and pulls Van away from the man. I crawl across the rough wooden floor, away from the brawl.

"I hope you know you're fucking fired! How can you let some drunken asshole attack my girl?" Van slams his hands against the bouncer's chest, shoving him into the wall. He kneels next to me, looking me over head to toe.

"I'm fine, just a little shaken up. Sorry, I didn't even notice that scumbag near me." I look up at Van, my eyes begin to water.

His bloody fingers match the hue of his face. "Not your fault. Come on, I've had enough for tonight."

I'm almost jogging through the parking lot to keep up with Van. The wind wildly blows my hair around my face. A tornado would be a perfect end to this horrid night.

I grab his arm and jerk him back toward me. "Should you leave? What about the band?"

He stops and pulls his arm away. "Yeah, what about the band? Everything I do is for the band. Maybe it's time I do something for me." His tone is deep as he paces and holds his hands onto his head.

I wrinkle my eyebrows. "What are you talking about?"

He glares at me and flattens his lips. "You know what I'm talking about. You don't want to come with me to LA and I don't want to be without you. Maybe I should just take off and stay with you while you start your life. At least we'll be together." He kicks a few stray pebbles and gets into his car.

My chest tightens. "You don't mean that. These are your friends; you can't let them down and ruin their lives." I open the door and slide into the cold leather.

His lips press in a slight grimace. "I certainly don't want mine to be ruined. I think I've put up with enough bullshit for one lifetime." He grips the steering wheel. "You're starting a job that's two-thousand miles away. How am I going to protect you when we're so far apart?"

My eyes begin to water. "We'll work it out. I want to be with you, but I can't have it both ways."

"Can't or won't?" Van leans in and presses his forehead against mine. He lets out a heavy sigh. "I can't do this, it just won't work.

CHAPTER 15—HOMEWARD BOUND

I'm suffocating. All the air in my lungs is suddenly gone. My heartbeat thrashes in my ears and a sharp pain radiates in my chest. Everything's closing in on me. Streams of tears roll down my cheeks. Oh my God, did he say what I think he said? I start to hyperventilate, becoming dizzy. I close my eyes. *Please let this be a terrible nightmare.* I slowly open them and clear my throat, trying to gather enough energy to speak.

A few more sobs escape as I struggle to hold myself together. "Are you breaking up with me?" My body trembles and begins to collapse, crushed by emotion. I muster enough energy to turn and look at Van.

Van looks over at me. His wide eyes search my face. "What? No!"

He swerves over to the far end of the parking lot where it's desolate and slams on the brakes. He grabs my face, wiping the tears away. "No baby. I never want to break up with you. I said I can't do this as in I can't let us be apart. I'll do whatever it takes to keep us together. If you can't be with me, then I'll be with you."

I take a deep breath, leveling my heart rate. The tension releases from my body. "I'd be devastated if I lost you. I need you." I try to stop the tears from flowing down my cheeks, but I just can't shut them off.

Van holds me as close as he can in the cramped sports car. He eases the driver's seat backward and crawls into the back seat, pulling me with him. "Please stop crying." He wipes away more tears with his thumbs as he holds my cheeks. He softly kisses my lips, staring into my eyes, he slowly pulls away.

Finally, I catch my breath and press my forehead against his. "We have to stop trying to plan out our lives. It's tearing us apart. Your tour ends in October and I start work in September. By that time we'll know what we need to do to be together, but we will be together, no matter what."

Van slowly brushes my hair behind my ear. "I'll do whatever it takes for us to be together in the end." He holds my hands, bringing them up to his face and kissing my fingers without breaking eye contact.

What's that black residue on his fingers? I look into the rearview mirror. Ugh! I am a complete mess. There's mascara running down my face, my hair looks like a rat's nest, and my dress is ripped.

I try to wipe the black make-up off my face with a piece of my torn dress. "Oh my God! I look like a raccoon that just crawled out of a dumpster."

"We make quite the couple tonight." Van holds out his hands, black with mascara and covered in blood from his busted knuckles.

I lunge toward him, sealing our lips together and desperately pulling at the button of his jeans, unable to unfasten it fast enough to satisfy my desire. My heart hammers in my chest. I need to feel him, to be close to him right now. I push the seat as far as it will go to give us more space and I free him from the dense fabric of his jeans. I breathe heavily, my whole body electrified in an array of tingles. I hike up what's left of my dress, exposing some of the silk lingerie and slip out a leg out of my panties. I want to feel him inside of me. I slam myself onto him as quickly as I can. I gasp as he fills me.

He lets out a loud groan as he guides my hips, meeting my thrust with his. Our bodies move in a perfect choreographed rhythm. I need to please him after this trying night. Pure adrenaline surges through my body as we both find our release in unison.

I collapse onto Van, panting heavily, and wrap my arms around his neck. I lay my head on his shoulder, still keeping him inside of me. My pounding heart begins to slow as we catch our breaths. We have such a unique physical connection. *What was I thinking? We can't have a long distance relationship for a lengthy period of time. Six weeks is going to be pure torture.*

Van kisses me softly as he eases himself out of me. He tucks my hair behind my ears. "We better get home before security shows up."

Dark shadows bounce off the fogged up windows. "I feel like we're sixteen years-old in my parents' car." I wipe the window with my hand. "Please take me home. I've had enough of the real world for tonight."

Van helps me back up to the front seat of the car and we drive back to his house.

I'm afraid to walk past a mirror. I follow Van like a duckling. He heads to the kitchen, pours two glasses of wine, and then continues up to the bedroom. At least the whole night isn't ruined. Romance is still in the air.

He leads me into the bathroom and starts the water, adding some musky body wash to make bubbles. "I think we need to relax." He sets the wine on the tiles and takes off his clothes.

I remove what's left of my dress and drop it to the floor.

His eyes travel along the silk green lingerie. He runs his tongue along his lips. "Damn, you're beautiful. Make sure you save that."

I look down at my tattered nighty, and then back up at Van. He holds out his hand, taking me into the sea of bubbles. We let the warm water wash away all the negativity of the day.

∞

No rest for the weary. We wake up and start packing our things. *Time to get back on the road. Van still has another two months on tour.* I head downstairs and pour a glass of orange juice while he makes a quick phone call to check in with Marcus and the guys.

I can't believe it's already the middle of August. Sydney's bachelorette party is next week. *I better give Brooke a quick call to finalize our plans.*

"Hey Brooke, is everything ready for the party?"

"I double checked and we're all set with the hall, the limo, and most importantly the stripper." She meows into the phone. "It's going to be a blast. How are you and the rock god?"

"We're awesome," I pause, "Better than awesome actually. I'm really excited to see you. Life isn't the same when you are minus your best friend."

"Aw, I miss you too. I've got to get back to work. See you Saturday."

I hang up the phone and sink into the couch. *Finally, some time with my favorite girls.* I'm sure there'll be an extensive inquisition from both my family and Brooke. Ugh, Van's going to have to meet my family soon. How long can I procrastinate? It's going to go as smoothly as a train wreck, but if we plan to be together in the long term, they need to at least talk to him. Soft lips brush against the back of my neck.

"All set for the big bachelorette party?" Van raises his eyebrows.

I raise my eyes and lift my chin. I managed to plan the whole party while on the road. "All we have to do is show up."

Van plays with my fingers. "I'm not thrilled about some greased up stripper having his hands all over you. In case you didn't notice, I get jealous."

"Well I'm not thrilled about skanky groupies hanging all over you, but you do what you got to do, right?" I smirk and fold my arms. There's no way he can ever win this argument. "In case you haven't noticed, I'm insanely jealous all the time."

"Oh, I've noticed." Van pulls me close, kissing my lips. "Too bad you're wasting your time. I only want you and no one else even remotely compares."

My heart is about to beat out of my chest. An overabundance of electrical impulses drifts from my head to my toes. I jump up and tackle him onto the couch. Alone time is hard to come by on the road so these last few minutes need to be used wisely.

∞

We're on the road again. Devil's Garden is pulling in larger crowds with each passing show. The concert in Oklahoma saw the largest crowd that the band brought in on their own to date. Our next stop is Texas, where two shows are scheduled. After the second one, I fly back to Cherry Falls for the party.

Van holds on to me every free moment we have. I love the extra attention, but we're both being overly dramatic. *I'll only be gone for a few days.*

∞

Time passes quickly once again. It's early Saturday morning and we're on our way to the airport. My maid of honor duties are calling. *Jeeze, am I in a romance movie?* I stand with Van until the last possible minute, holding him close and hugging him tightly. I weave my fingers through his hair and plant a long passionate kiss on his perfect soft lips.

∞

I trudge through the aisle of the plane, launch my carry on into the overhead compartment, and plop into my seat. I close my eyes and take a deep breath, trying to hold back my tears. *What's wrong with me? We'll only be away from each other for a few days.* I rub my face with my hands and let my head fall back against the headrest. At least the other passengers at the gate got a show. We must have looked like star crossed lovers to the rest of the crowd.

∞

I land in Cherry Falls and shoot Van a quick text, telling him I've arrived. I glance around the crowded airport. *Where are Sydney and Brooke?* They spot me and run toward the gate, frantically waving their hands in the air. I'm crushed into a three way hug. Maybe I have an affinity for cheesy airport scenes.

∞

Sharing a bathroom with four women is quite a challenge. Time is of the essence. I fling my bag onto my old bed and start getting myself ready. Brooke and I ordered black tank tops customized with neon pink martini glasses on the front and the phrase *Sydney's bachelorette party* underneath. On the back of Sydney's shirt we added the word *BRIDE*. The required uniform for the evening is the tank top paired with jean shorts. Sydney sports a silly veil and a sash which reads *bachelorette*. Even my mom is ready for a wild night.

∞

The Cherry Falls Community Hall looks like a flashback to the 70's. A huge silver disco ball hangs from the ceiling, casting various hues and patterns as it spins. The floor blocks are each a different color. Sydney does the hustle over to me and pulls me into a hug. "Oh my God, you did an awesome job! I love it."

I hope she doesn't cry. "You deserve it! It's your last time to party as a single woman." I hug her back tightly.

"Let's have a shot to celebrate Sydney tying the knot!" Brooke exclaims, holding a tray of shot glasses she took from the bar.

I smile as we all raise our glasses and down our shots. "To a lifetime of love and happiness and a night to remember!"

We continue to drink and dance as a small buffet of pizza, hoagies, chips, and crackers are brought out by the wait staff. I'm starving. It's been a long day. Of course, I overindulge and stuff myself.

Screaming sirens echo through the room. I cover my ears with my hands and raise my shoulders. The head waiter comes over, talking loud enough to drown out the noise but trying not to yell. "Sorry for the inconvenience folks. There's a small grease fire in the kitchen which triggered the fire alarm. We need to wait for the fire company to come and shut it off. They should be here shortly."

Wow, that was quick. The alarm is silenced by two firemen who walk into the hall. They stop in front of Sydney. She's trying to hide her frown.

"Are you girls alright? There's a fire burning pretty hot."

"Yes, we're fine. Thank you for checking on us," Sydney says.

"I'm afraid it's going to get even hotter in here ma'am," the fireman says as they both tug on their outfits, ripping them off at the same instant the D.J. hits the music.

We all hoot and holler at the sexy men grinding against Sydney. Her cheeks flush and she covers her face with her hands. *Oh boy, she's going to kill me.* The two hot guys are wearing nothing but G-strings with flames on the front. They sandwich Sydney. A bead of sweat forms at the base of my neck. I look down at the floor. *Please don't let her kill me.* I raise my eyes, at about the pace of a snail, and look up at her face. Her huge smile lights up the make-shift disco hall. *Thank God she's a great sport.* She downs another shot and starts dancing and laughing along with the rest of us. *These guys don't have half the sex appeal of Van. He, however, is only allowed to strip for me.* I guess I am pretty jealous and possessive.

Enough embarrassment for Sydney tonight! We jump into the limo to start our night of bar hopping. Ugh! My mother enjoyed the strippers more than Sydney; did she have to let them lick whipped cream off her neck? I really need to drink that image out of my mind.

The first stop is called Cherry Hollow. Tonight they are featuring a local band playing classic rock. Emptiness forms in my chest, forming an empty pit. I miss Van. The band is good, but they don't compare to Devil's Garden. Of course, they notice our bachelorette party. Time for round two. Sydney is called onto the stage to dance while the band plays Foxy Lady. Thank God I remembered to bring my camera. Sydney may only remember bits and pieces of the night.

The next few bars don't offer any entertainment, so we make our own. Dancing like drunken sorority girls, we commandeer the jukeboxes while Sydney tries to accomplish a list of quests we gave her earlier. She has to get two guys' phone numbers, get someone to buy her a shot, get three kisses on the cheek, and lastly dance with five random guys. *Wow, she really can't ignore a challenge.* The guys she's flirting with have to be at least sixty. Brooke and I are so hysterical, we can barely breathe.

The limo takes us all to my mom's house after a full night of bar hopping. Sydney passes out in the back seat. Great! I had my fill of cardio from all the dancing. Brooke takes her legs and I take her head. We lug her out of the limo and into her bedroom. I leave two Advil and a glass of water on her nightstand. *She'll thank me in the morning.*

Brooke camps out in my room. Thankfully, she falls asleep as soon as her head hits the pillow. I'm way too drunk and exhausted to talk anyway, plus I could use a good night's sleep. I cringe and curl up in my bed. *How long will the inquisition last tomorrow morning?* I stretch, relax my muscles, and burrow my head into the pillow. Van's right. Even though I haven't lived here in years, there's nothing better than sleeping in your own bed.

∞

The sun peeks through the window, blaring through my eyelids. I squint and glance at the clock. No way, it's noon? A slight throbbing pulsates in my temple. I sit up and grimace. *Brooke must be downstairs already.* I snatch my cell phone from the nightstand. *Ooh, a new text from Van.*

**Hope you're feeling alright this morning. The
strippers better not have been too frisky.**

I chuckle. Is he really jealous of a stripper?

I think they were just frisky enough.

My phone chimes.

Yeah, not funny. I miss you!

Flames shoot through my body.

I miss you too. I wish you were here with me.

I press send and pull on shorts and a T-shirt. My phone
chimes again.

Me too. We'll be together soon.

I can't wait to see Van again. The very second he's in
my field of vision I'm launching myself into his arms. Long
live the cheesy airport scenes! I put my cell phone in my
pocket and make my way downstairs. Mom, Sydney, and
Brooke are having coffee at the kitchen table.

"You're the last one up. I guess you're used to rocker's
hours." Brooke smirks at me.

"Van texted me, so he was technically up first." I rub
my temple. "I haven't been bar hopping in a while. I must
be out of practice." I go over to the coffee pot and pour
myself a cup. The aroma of the fresh grind alone helps perk
me up.

Sydney looks up at me. "Thanks for the Advil sis. It
was a God-send. Was that a trick you learned on the road?"

I lower my eyebrows. "No, that's a trick I learned from
rooming with Brooke for the last four years." I add some
sugar and stir.

Brooke and I look at each other and start laughing. I
take a seat next to her.

My mom asks, staring at me. "Since we're on the
subject Lexie, what exactly is it like to be on the road with a
band?"

Ah! The inquisition begins. "It's actually pretty great. The bus is equipped with everything, even a kitchen and shower." I sip my coffee. "We very seldom sleep on the bus; we usually stay in really great hotels. Whenever we stop we try to see some attractions, plus there's great music all the time."

She raises her eyes and taps her cup. "What's your relationship with this guy in the band?" Her tone is deep, almost scolding.

She clearly has no idea that I am in love with Van and whatever she says isn't going to change that. "He's my boyfriend." I set my cup down. "We're great together and once you get to know him I'm sure you'll love him just as much as I do." Sweat forms on my forehead. I prepare for battle.

Mom sighs. "Really Lexie? You fell in love with some musician? They party all the time, they cheat, and if anything goes wrong with their music career they have nothing to fall back on. Look at how he's corrupted you already. Don't think I didn't notice that tattoo on your shoulder." Her lips are in a hard line.

Uh oh, I forgot that my family didn't know about my tattoo. "Mom, I'm not going to argue. I'm an adult and I'll make my own decisions. I'm sorry if you don't approve, but nothing you say will change how I feel about him." I push my chair back and stand up.

She folds her arms and glares at me. "Your father and I are not happy about your choice. If he's a gentleman he should have at least met with us before shacking up with our daughter and dragging her all across the country."

My heart speeds as I grind my teeth. My lips flatten. "Mom please, you'll meet him soon. Unfortunately, all of his shows are scheduled so we'll have to find time in between to get together."

"I'll believe that when I see it." She jumps up from her chair and stomps out of the room.

Sydney turns to look at me. "Don't worry about Mom. She's just insanely overprotective. She'll get over it." She smiles and sips her coffee.

"I think she's jealous," Brooke adds.

We all burst out laughing.

"I can use a hot lunch. Let's head out to Burger Palace." Sydney pulls out her chair and heads upstairs. "Meet you guys down here in 15 minutes."

Today is definitely a ponytail day. I quickly apply make-up and pull on a pair of jean shorts. I miss Van, especially after explaining our relationship to my mother. I hold my Devil's Garden T-shirt up to my face and inhale deeply, hoping the fibers still contain Van's scent. They don't disappoint. I breathe in his essence and yank it over my head. *Why is Mom on the steps waiting for me? Aren't we finished with the inquisitions?*

She rubs my arm. "I'm sorry about before. You're right, you're an adult and I need to respect your decisions. I'm sure Van is a nice man but I still want to meet him face to face."

I hug her. "Thanks Mom. I promise you'll meet him soon." I wave goodbye to her and head out with Sydney and Brooke.

Burger Palace is right around the corner. I follow the scent of fresh buns and French fries. Even though I've traveled half way across the country, nothing tastes as good as the food you grow up with. I inhale my double cheese burger, fries, and vanilla milkshake while the three of us recount our night of strippers and bar hopping.

My purse rings, pulling me back into reality. I reach for my cell and look at the screen. My eyes widen. Seeing those letters is like waking up on Christmas morning. I can't contain my smile no matter how hard I try. Van Sinclair flashes across my screen. *Ah, the most beautiful words in the English language.* I quickly answer.

"Hello?"

"Are you enjoying your trip?"

I twirl my hair around my fingers. "Yeah, last night was a blast. I miss you."

"Glad you had fun. Nice shirt by the way."

I look down and narrow my eyes. *How does he know what I'm wearing?* My heart hammers. I stand up and glance around the crowded restaurant. Suddenly I freeze.

Van rises from the counter holding his cell phone, a sexy half smile gracing his perfectly chiseled face.

CHAPTER 16—PROMISES

My mouth falls open, gradually turning up at each end. I spring up from my chair and throw my phone on the table. *Is that really him?* I rub my eyes and focus. Dark jeans hanging right below perfectly chiseled abs, a tight black T-shirt clinging to a plethora of sculpted muscles, and the familiar glow of the most unique emerald eyes. I charge at him like a freight train. He slides his phone in his pocket and slams his lips against mine, right in the middle of the diner. All eyes are upon us as I pull away. My cheeks rise to the heavens. *Will this smile plastered on my face ever fade?*

I bounce on my tip toes and pull him into another embrace. "What are you doing here?"

Van licks his lips and stares into my eyes. "You said you wished I was with you, so here I am."

I'm breathless. Every time I'm lonely, Van shows up. Maybe he misses me just as much as I do him, or maybe he can't stand the intense ache that occurs from being isolated and cut off from love. A thickness forms in my throat. *He would know what that's like more than anyone.*

Everyone in the crowded diner is still staring at us. I grasp Van's hand with both of mine and walk backwards toward the table. My eyes travel from his black boots to his perfectly messy hair. I'm hypnotized. Ah, my enticing rock god! Goose bumps cover every inch of my body.

My legs back up into the cool metal strip along the table. "You remember Sydney and Brooke?"

He quickly waves his free hand. "Yeah, great to see you girls again."

We park ourselves in the vintage red chairs. Van runs his fingers through his hair and turns toward me. *Wow, can he be any sexier?* My heart hammers and my body is on fire. I lift my trembling hand and pick at the few fries that are left on my plate.

"When did you get into town?" Sydney asks.

Really? She can't take her eyes off of him. *She has a handsome fiancé; would it kill her to be a little more subtle?*

"About an hour ago. Perfect timing!" Van holds me close, nibbling at my neck.

Brooke exhales, resting her head on her hand.

"That's the most romantic thing I've seen in a while." Sydney sips her milkshake. "Where are you staying?"

Umm, not at Mom and Dad's! No way is that happening.

He guzzles my milkshake. "The hotel on the next block over. It's really nice."

Sydney's face lights up. "It is amazing! I was contemplating having my wedding there if we didn't decide on Savannah."

Oh no! Am I the most absent minded person in the world? I still haven't invited Van to Sydney's wedding. *I'll save that talk for later.* A wave of nausea flows through my body along with emptiness in the pit of my stomach. Van's going to have to meet my parents since he's in town. They already have a preconceived notion that he's a no good, cheating, drug-addict. This has disaster written all over it.

"Our parents are dying to meet you," Sydney says, avoiding eye contact with me.

I kick her chair hard underneath the table, just missing her shin.

Van rubs the back of his neck. "Maybe we can meet while I'm in town. Any chance they're music fans?"

Sydney almost chokes on her shake. "They're not really into music."

I scowl at Sydney, the fire of a thousand hells burning in my eyes. "If you don't want to, that's ok. You can meet them another time. You came here to see me, not to be harassed by my family."

Van turns to me and smiles, stealing a fry. "No, she's right. We should get together while we're all in the same town."

Brooke raises her eyebrows and shrugs.

Has she ever been this quiet? She's louder in the library. I guess she knows how this will go down. Luckily, she's on my side no matter what, which is good in case I need back-up.

I twirl my hair around my fingers. "I'll talk to Mom and make plans. Brooke, you should join us too."

"Sure, I'm definitely in." She tries to cover up her grimace with a smile. "So, where are you guys off to next?"

Who's she kidding? She wants to know when I'll be back at our apartment. I'm a horrible roommate. I just took off and left her with all the upkeep. I've got to make it up to her when I get back. I sigh. Reality hits soon.

He finishes the last of my fries. "Next stop is Tucson in two days. The rest of our shows are on the west coast before we end the tour in a few months."

"I hear Arizona's beautiful," Brooke says.

"If you guys ever want to meet up with us on tour let me know. I'll hook you up with tickets and a hotel." He wipes his hands on his jeans.

"Dean and I may take you up on that offer someday." Brooke flashes a quick smile.

"I'm going to the hotel with Van. Can you tell Mom I'll be calling her soon?" *It's the least you can do after embarrassing me.*

Sydney waves. "Sure thing. Catch you guys later."

Sydney and Brooke leave the diner, giggling to each other as they walk out the door.

I turn to Van and place my hand on his. "This is the best surprise ever."

"Maybe there'll be more where that came from." He kisses my lips softly. "Come on, walk with me."

We stroll through the quiet streets of Cherry Falls. The warm summer air caresses my body as we walk hand in hand. Birds chirp, spreading their melodic song throughout town. The hot sun shines, lighting up the clear blue sky. Has it always been this breathtaking or does Van make everything better?

The Empress Inn, a beautiful Victorian style hotel, stands in the center of town. The round turrets and large wrap-around porch emanate old world charm. Green and gold silk curtains adorn beautiful windows that are large enough to walk through and intricate woodwork graces the lobby. The paintings are so spectacular they should be hanging in an art gallery. We head to Van's room on the fourth floor, allowing for a splendid view of my small hometown.

I glance out the window onto the familiar streets. "I've never seen Cherry Falls quite like this in all the years I've lived here." I turn toward him.

"The view is impressive." He stares directly at me, emerald flames burning through my soul.

Heat radiates through my face, creeping across my cheeks. I run my tongue along my bottom lip. *Did it just get ten degrees hotter in here?* Every cell in my body aches for his touch. He walks toward me; his eyes locked directly on my face as he grabs my cheeks with both hands. Butterflies flutter in my stomach and my heart slams against the walls of my chest. Van brushes his lips against mine, softly at first, slowly increasing his intensity with each kiss. My God, I want him!

I wrap my arms around his waist and pull him close, pressing him against me. A low moan emits from his throat. He slides his hands under my Devil's Garden T-shirt, lightly brushing my skin while slowly lifting it up and over my head. Hmm, that T-shirt sure has seen its share of hotel room floors. He slithers his hands down my stomach, then unbuckles my jean shorts, sliding them down until I stand before him in my blue bra and panties. He takes a step back.

"Not a more beautiful sight in the whole country." He moves closer, softly kissing my neck.

My mouth becomes moist. I clutch the hem of his shirt and rip it over his head, flinging it onto the floor. He's certainly right about the view. I run my hands over his flawless body. His skin shimmers from the heat radiating from his pores. I trace my fingers down, ending at the waistband of his jeans. *Why is this button my nemesis?* Finally, I unlatch it.

My heart is about to explode. No shirt and unbuttoned jeans; the ultimate eye candy. The steamy seductress inside me surfaces. I tackle him onto the bed, entwining my hands with his and pressing them against the cool sheets above his head.

He rolls over on top of me and grinds himself against my body, taking complete control. Ah, he wants me bad. I arch my back and thrust my pelvis toward him. He groans and exhales deeply, almost panting. His strong fingers slide between my skin and silk panties, slipping them off. An extraordinary rush of passion engulfs my body as he places them inside me, gently moving them in and out. A shiver that brings complete pleasure comes over me. I moan as his thumb brushes my most sensitive area. My body reacts immediately. I call out his name as my body quivers in pure delight.

I'm breathless, barely able to focus. Van pulls down his jeans and slams into me, hard. I dig my fingers into his back and yell out as he thrusts himself inside me again. My heart is pounding; I pull him as close as I can, making him fill my body as deeply as possible. Passion floods my core. I scream his name again. He groans as he finds his release in time with mine.

Van rolls over and I nuzzle against his chest, trying to hold tight to the amazing feeling. He wraps his arms around me as we lay there, catching our breath.

I trace my fingers up and down his chest. "That hotel tour gets a five star rating."

"Tour guide was a close second, right behind musician." Van kisses the top of my head as I lay in his arms.

"There are still a few things we need to talk about." I sit up resting on my elbow.

"What's on your mind?"

"Well, the first thing is my sister's wedding Labor Day weekend. Will you be able to go with me?"

He smirks. "I don't know. I haven't been asked to be anyone's date yet."

I roll my eyes. "Van Sinclair, will you do me the honor of being my date at Sydney's wedding?"

He chuckles. "I've already checked and we don't have a show that weekend. What's next on the agenda?"

I sigh. "I guess next would be meeting my parents. I'm not really optimistic on this one." I twirl my fingers around my hair.

Van narrows his eyes. "Why? Do your parents have some kind of issue with us being together?" He tucks my hair behind my ear.

An ache forms in the back of my throat. Why are my parents so difficult? I'm a grown woman, not a child. I don't want to scare Van off but I have to make sure he's prepared for whatever inquisition they have planned. "They don't like the fact that I've run off to tour the country with you." I pick at my fingernails. "They also apply the musician stereotype to our relationship, but once they meet you they'll know they couldn't be more wrong."

Van bites his lip. "So basically, it's going to be like walking into a war zone. I'll be bombarded with questions and assumptions, and it's my job to prove to them that I love and respect you and that we have something special." He leans back and exhales.

He hit the nail on the head. "Yeah, that's probably how it'll go." I shrug and bite my nails. *I can't believe he has to go through this.*

He puts his hand on my chin and lifts my head. "You're worth it." He kisses my lips as we collapse back on the bed for round two.

∞

I dial Mom's number. My stomach flip flops and the nausea increases with each ring. She finally answers.

"Hi Mom. I'm sure Sydney told that you that Van came to surprise me. It looks like you guys will get to meet him sooner rather than later."

Why is my heart beating a mile a minute? Jeeze, it's not like it's the first time I brought a guy home. I'm a grown woman. *Ugh, will I ever stop vying for my mother's approval?*

She clears her throat. "Yes I heard. That was sweet of him to surprise you. Do you guys want to go out to dinner or would you rather eat in?"

I nibble at my fingernails. "I don't want Dad and Van having a pissing contest about who'll pay the bill so let's have dinner at home. I know its last minute, so don't fuss.

Pizza's fine." The more casual the better. I don't need Mom's stuck up friends eyeing Van all through dinner. I'm sure it'll be uncomfortable enough.

She huffs. "I am certainly not ordering a pizza for a dinner we're hosting to meet the man you love. Would you rather lasagna or steaks on the grill?"

I roll my eyes. Of course she's being overdramatic. "Go with lasagna. You can't expect a man from Kansas to be happy with one of our steaks." I twirl my hair around my fingers. "What should we bring?"

"Just bring yourselves dear." Yeah right. All Van has to do is show up empty-handed and he'll be labeled *Lexie's inconsiderate boyfriend.*

I sigh. "Mom, can you please talk to Dad. Van's coming over to meet you guys, not to be insulted, ok?"

"Yes, I understand. We'll be on our best behavior."

"Please, he's important to me." I bite at my fingernails.

"Stop worrying. It'll be fine. See you at seven."

I hang up the phone and walk over to Van. "We're having dinner at my parents' house at seven. Mom's making lasagna."

"What do you want me to wear?" Van asks, cracking his knuckles.

I slightly jerk my head back and lower my eyebrows. "Wear your jeans and a T-shirt." Does he think I want him to be someone he's not to impress my parents? No way, I love him just the way he is and wouldn't change a thing.

I fiddle with my hair, trying to fix the disheveled locks. Oh no, what am I going to wear? "All of my clothes are at my mom's house and since we're not going there until later, it looks like we may have to go shopping."

We walk down the cobblestone sidewalk and stop at a small boutique. Vibrant colors light up the wall of glass across the storefront. A red strapless dress catches my eye.

Ooh, I have to try it on, especially since my last red dress was torn to pieces.

Van's eyes widen as I step out of the dressing room. "That was made for you." His lips part and his eyes travel from my flip flops up to my face.

Sold! That's more than enough to prompt me to buy it. *Let's hope it has the same effect every time I put it on.*

We continue to slowly walk around town, looking in all of the store fronts. The aroma of cinnamon and fresh baked bread fills the air as we walk past the Cherry Falls Bakery.

"Should we get something to bring to your parents for dessert? I would buy wine, but I don't want them thinking I'm an alcoholic."

"Great idea." *Too bad they already assume he's addicted to drugs and alcohol.*

My eyes are just about to bulge out of my head and my mouth waters as I look into the case of confections. Everyone has their weaknesses and mine are Van Sinclair and desserts. Cannoli makes a great accompaniment to lasagna and a dozen should be more than enough. By the time we get back to the hotel room though, there are ten left. Oh well, willpower is nonexistent when we're together.

We're short on time, so it only makes sense to shower together. Steam fogs up the mirror. Warm water mixed with Van Sinclair's scent always drives my body wild. My heart is pounding in my ears. I run my hands over his hot, wet body. *My God, he's enticing. Will I ever get enough?* I take a deep breath, desperately trying to find any shred of self-control. I've got to behave myself. Walking into my parent's house late and disheveled will certainly not help the situation.

∞

Forty-five minutes later, we're just about ready to go. How can he always look so perfect? That green T-shirt brings out the beauty in his emerald eyes and those jeans. They cling to him just right.

Van stops, takes my hands, and presses his forehead against mine. "No matter how this goes, promise me it won't change anything between us."

I lift his chin and gaze into his eyes. "Of course not, I promise."

We make it to my parents' house five minutes early. The aroma of pasta sauce and garlic bread fills the air. Maybe I can relax once the introductions are out of the way. I find my parents in the living room watching the end of the news cast.

I twirl my fingers around my hair. "Hi Mom and Dad, we're here." They get up from the couch and walk over to us.

I smirk when I notice my mother staring at Van as if she's never seen a handsome man before. I take a deep breath. "Van Sinclair, meet Erin and Richard Waters."

Van wipes his hands on his jeans and shakes hands with my mom and dad. "Nice to meet you, Mr. and Mrs. Waters." My mother continues to stare, slightly blushing.

"It's great to meet you too. Lexie's told us a lot about you."

We make our way to the kitchen where Sydney and Brooke are setting the table. Van places the box from the bakery down. "Hope you guys like cannoli. We couldn't walk by the bakery without going inside."

Sydney opens the box to look at the Italian pastries. "Mmm, I'll make sure I save some room for these."

We all take our seats at the table. Van runs his hands down his jeans and bites at his lip. He starts to bounce his knee.

I place my hand over his and squeeze, interlocking our fingers.

"Ok everyone, what are we drinking tonight?" Dad asks, scanning the room waiting for an answer.

"I'll have a diet coke," I reply.

"Me too," Van says.

He passed test number one.

"Diet cokes all around!" Brooke exclaims.

Mom's secret lasagna recipe never fails. I miss her cooking, especially Sunday dinners. Now we only have these kinds of feasts for holidays and special occasions.

Sydney pours coffee to accompany our dessert. The cannoli is to die for. Everything's going *too* well. My muscles begin to twitch. When's the other shoe going to drop?

My dad clears his throat. "So Van, why don't you tell us a little about yourself?"

Van puts his hand on my thigh. "Ok. I'm from Kansas, I'm 26, and I'm the singer of a band called Devil's Garden."

Dad sips his coffee. "Yes, we knew all of that already. How do you like being on tour and traveling the country?"

"Being on the road has some perks. I get to see the sights doing what I love." He bites a cannoli.

Dad places his cup on the table and folds his arms. "Will you be attending Sydney's wedding? I can imagine it's hard to keep your commitments while traveling."

Ah, and it begins. The insulting assumptions.

"We schedule our shows so we all get the personal time we need. I'm lucky Lexie has the summer off and is able to tour with me." He bites at his nails.

"Do your parents still live in Kansas?" Mom asks.

Van lets out a sigh. "No ma'am, my parents passed away when I was two."

I give my mother a dirty look, even though I know her question was completely innocent.

Mom squints and frowns. "Oh, I'm sorry to hear that Van, I didn't know."

"It's ok, my grandmother took care of me until she passed away, and then my guitar player and best friend Marcus's parents raised me throughout high school."

I rub my temple. *For the love of God, please change the subject!*

Mom sips her coffee. "Losing any family member is very traumatic, especially at a young age. It's nice to see that it didn't hinder you, and you made a nice life for yourself with your music career."

Van flashes a meek smile. "Thank you."

"Lexie starts her new job soon. Will you still be touring?" Dad taps his fingers on his coffee cup.

A low growl forms in my throat. "Dad, we're figuring all that out after I see my work schedule. I know what you're getting at, and yes, Van will be touring until October." My tone hasn't been that snotty since high school.

"Sorry honey, we're just looking out for you and want to know what intentions the two of you have for the future. I don't want to see you get hurt sweetheart." Dad places his hand on mine, but I pull away.

Van takes a deep breath. "Listen, Mr. and Mrs. Waters. I would never hurt Lexie. I'll do anything I can to keep her happy." Van looks over at me, with a gleam in his eyes.

"I'm sure the two of you are very smitten with each other, but it must be hard to nurture a relationship in an environment where lust and partying can get in the way.

Especially when you'll be away from each other," Mom says, folding her arms.

I slam my coffee cup down on the table. "Ok Mom, enough!" I push back from the table.

Van places his arm over mine. "It's ok." He turns to my mom. "I can promise you that partying's not a problem. I loathe the drug scene since my parents died from an overdose."

My mother puts her hand to her mouth and flinches as she continues to listen to what Van has to say.

"I don't want anyone else, so lust isn't an issue either. We're working on the distance thing." Van exhales.

Did Sydney and Brooke turn into mutes? They both sip their coffee and stand against the counter on the far end of the kitchen. *Hope they're enjoying the show.*

Mom drops her hand and drums her fingers against the table. "You're making quite a long list of promises and I sincerely hope you're able to keep them all."

I clench my jaw, and then slowly release my tense muscles. *Really? He's not a child. No need to scold him.*

Dad smiles and extends his hand to Van. "Lexie seems very happy so I hope she stays that way. We appreciate you coming over to talk with us. It was nice to meet you."

Van stands up and shakes Dad's hand.

Van handled himself so much better than I would have. *It's like I'm back in high school.* Thank God that's over; it could've most definitely gone awry. I gather my belongings and say my goodbyes to my family and Brooke. We leave for Arizona in the morning, but in a week we'll be celebrating Sydney's wedding together, so it is really more of a *see you soon.*

Back at the hotel, we quickly get ready for bed and jump under the covers. Just as I'm drifting off to sleep, my phone rings. I pick it up and look at the screen. Here's my reality check.

CHAPTER 17—OBLIGATIONS

Global Inc. flashes across the screen of my cell phone. My body lacks all energy and my breathing slows. I let it go straight to voicemail with a sigh. There's no way I'll be able to sleep without checking the message. I dial my pass code and hold the phone to my ear.

Owen Jenkins wants to meet with me one more time before I start working, but I'm not ready to start my life in the real world just yet. How am I going to survive without Van? It's pure torture when we're apart. My chest becomes tight. I'll be far away while half naked women hang all over him.

Damn my parents! Was their whole plan to put doubt in my mind? I place my phone on the nightstand and hold Van tightly. I need to soak up every second I have left with him before we spend our six weeks apart.

Beams of sunlight shine through the windows of the Empress Inn, gently warming my skin and waking me before the alarm sounds. I stretch, inadvertently awakening the extremely handsome man by my side. *How he can look so great all the time?* I look like I've just emerged from a tornado, but he always looks perfect.

"Hi. How'd you sleep?" I roll over, kissing him on the cheek.

"Surprisingly well. The Empress Inn is second best to my own bed." He stretches his arms over his head and glances at the clock.

I slightly frown. "I was so exhausted last night that I didn't get a chance to apologize for all of the obnoxious questions my parents were asking you."

He brushes his hand over my cheek, tucking my hair behind my ear. "I thought it'd be worse. It went ok."

Every cell in my body radiates. "I promise that when you meet the rest of my family at Sydney's wedding it won't be nearly as intense. When they hear that you're a musician they'll probably ask you the same questions your fans ask. It's a very intriguing profession."

"That I can handle. You worry too much about what other people think. In the end you and I are the only ones who matter." He runs his fingers lightly down my arm.

"You're completely right," I say as I kiss his lips, steadily increasing my passion.

Van pulls away and sighs. "As much as I hate to say this, we have to be at the airport in a half hour." He grimaces and gets out of bed.

Time seems to be my enemy lately. It appears to move so quickly, pulling me out of the moments I want to cherish. I'm sure it'll feel like it just about stops while I'm waiting for the weeks to pass when Van and I are apart.

∞

We land in Tucson, Arizona five hours later. As we step outside, a warm blanket of heat envelops my body. It's extremely hot, but not uncomfortable. The humidity I'm accustomed to is absent, which makes the air light and dry. I put on my sunglasses and walk with Van to the cab. Huge red mountains meet with the blue skies and create a postcard-worthy image. It's my first time to the southwest. The desert terrain is awe-inspiring. *Finally, I get to see a real live cactus!*

Jenna and the guys are waiting for us in the hotel lobby as we walk inside. The coolness from the air conditioning jolts my senses.

"I missed you. You have to fill me in on all the details of the bachelorette party, and make *sure* you don't leave anything out!" Jenna pulls me into a big bear hug.

I wink. "Don't worry, I'll give you all the gory details."

Van raises his eyebrows. "I think I want to hear the gory details too."

I roll my eyes at both of them. "When we get to our room I have to call Owen Jenkins back to schedule a meeting."

Van looks toward the floor. Reality is slowly creeping in. "Here's the key. I'll head to the restaurant with Jenna and the guys. Come down when you're done."

"Ok, sounds good." I kiss Van and make my way to the hotel room.

I pass a mirror and glance at my reflection. My head hangs low and a frown forms. Where's the girl who's taking the advertising world by storm? Working for Global Inc. is an unbelievable opportunity. I try to get myself back to that place in my mind before dialing. Just then my phone chimes.

Do you want me to order for you? They specialize in fajitas.

My frown turns into a full blown, ear-to-ear smile. At least there's no show tonight. He's all mine.

Get me chicken fajitas. I'll be down soon.

He certainly has a gift for distracting me from the task at hand and making me focus my thoughts on him. I take a deep breath and dial Global Inc., hoping I correctly calculated the time zone change.

I twirl my hair around my fingers. "Hello. This is Alexis Waters, returning a call from Owen Jenkins."

"I'll put you right through Miss Waters."

"Hello Alexis. Nice to talk to you again. I want to schedule our last meeting before you join the Global Inc. team. Are you free tomorrow?"

Wow, talk about last minute. A little advanced notice would be nice. "Unfortunately, I am currently in Arizona and I'll be in Savannah next week for my sister's wedding. I return home the day after Labor Day."

"You seem to enjoy traveling, Alexis. That's quite a cross-country trip. Does the Wednesday after Labor Day at ten a.m. work for you?"

"Yes Owen, that's perfect. Thank you."

"Looking forward to seeing you again."

"Yes, me too."

I let my head fall back and take a deep breath. Thank God, quick and painless. I grab my purse and belt out the door. Every second away from Van is like an eternity.

∞

The restaurant is elegant with a southwestern tone. The orange and turquoise theme mimics the hues of the desert.

Our food is just being served as I arrive at the table. "Hey guys, sorry I'm late. Business matters to tend to," I hang my purse on my chair.

Chaz grimaces. "Just don't tell us about the bachelorette party over dinner. I can't think about naked men while I'm trying to eat."

"I'll try to control myself." I sit down at the table and join the group. I'm now part of another family. One that travels together, eats together, fights with each other, but also sticks by one another. Not only will it be complete devastation to be apart from Van, but I'll also miss Jenna and the guys. *Who would've thought it would be so difficult to leave?*

I quickly shake my head, hoping to banish the negative thoughts. I need to make the best out of my last few stops of the tour.

I slather some sour cream on my fajita. "I would love to come back to Arizona. It's so beautiful." Doesn't anyone else feel the same way?

"We have some extra time before our show tomorrow. Wanna sign up for a desert tour? Anyone else in?" Van dips a tortilla chip in salsa and takes a bite.

Everyone nods in agreement.

Van and I visit the concierge desk and book a tour of the Northern Sonora desert region. We'll be riding in a jeep so we can get the full effect of the area. Our tour leaves at eight a.m. and returns to the hotel at two. Great! We still have time to nap before getting ready for the show.

I run my fingers along Van's arm. "Thanks. I'm stoked to see a real-life desert! No one else seems too interested. I know they're doing this for me."

"I'm sure you do lots of things for us that you're not really interested in. I'm pretty psyched to see the desert too. It's my third time here and I've never seen any of the sights." Van pulls me close, kissing my lips softly.

I wrap my arms around his neck, weaving them in the silky strands of his hair. "I know what you're doing and I love you for it." I hold my breath, trying to control the tears which are starting to form. *Why can't I forget about the future and enjoy the present?*

He pulls me closer. "I know how upset you are about missing out on Seattle."

The tour stops in Seattle the same time I have to be in Savannah for Sydney's wedding. Isn't that something right out of Murphy's Law? The one place I really want to see throughout the entire tour and I can't go. Time's certainly flying. Sydney's wedding is Saturday.

Jenna and Marcus are in the hallway looking into the hotel bar. There's a sign at the entrance of the large room: KARAOKE NIGHT.

"How fun would it be to join Karaoke night?" Jenna tugs on my arm, easing me toward the bar's entrance.

I take a step back. "I'm a terrible singer. I may clear the place out."

Jenna grabs my hand and pulls me into the bar.

"Most people are terrible singers, including me. That's what makes it so fun."

There's a decent size stage in the back for local entertainment, a large bar in the middle, and plenty of tables leading to a small dance floor. On the plus side, it's really dark. It must be the place to party on the weekends because it's packed. Apparently, I'll be embarrassing myself in front of a huge crowd. *At least none of these people will ever see me again.*

Our heels click on the gray concrete floor as we snatch an open table. Van and Marcus get us a round of beers.

"If I'm going to get up there and sing, I need something stronger than beer. Preferably something that won't make me cringe." I sigh, looking up at the stage. The bright spotlight shining down is sure to illuminate anyone who gets up there.

Van and Marcus come back with a tray of shots and the songbook for karaoke.

"I signed us up. Our table is fifth in line. Drink up girls, you'll be lighting up the stage soon!" Marcus lifts his shot glass and downs the clear liquid.

I shake my head and turn toward Van. "I hope you still love me after this."

He tips his shot glass and swallows hard. "I signed up too."

I shake my head and slam the shot, grimacing from the burning sensation in my throat.

"That doesn't count, you're a singer!"

"Let's do something together. Something sexy, then we can have fun with it and no one will care how we sound." Jenna flips through the pages of the songbook. "I found it, we're doing this one!"

I look at Jenna's choice and tip my head toward her. "Seriously? I'll need another round of shots. Van, you have to go after us, we can't follow you."

He puts his arm around me. "I usually don't get to watch the show from this side of the stage. I'm excited."

I turn toward Marcus and lift my eyebrows. "And what song will you be doing?"

"Oh no, I'm buying the drinks. I vow to stay away from all stages when I'm not playing. It's like going to work on your day off." Marcus takes off toward the bar for some much needed refills.

Jenna and Van go up to the karaoke coordinator to give him our song choices. *Hmm. Will Van do a Devil's Garden song?* Probably not, he likes to keep himself incognito when he's offstage.

"Get ready. You're up next." Van gestures toward the karaoke coordinator, letting him know he'll sing after we finish.

Thank God for small favors. The guy ahead of us did a horrific version of *Hungry like the Wolf,* which is proof that some songs should not be available in the karaoke songbook. I down one more shot. My face is hot and my heart begins to palpitate.

Marcus and Van cheer loudly. I have the intense urge to throw something at them. No need for any more attention than I'm already getting.

Jenna pulls me up on the stage. "We're gonna dance really sexy, ok?"

"Yep, I'll follow your lead." I sigh as the music to *Like a Virgin* starts.

The crowd cheers. Well, mostly the male members of the crowd cheer as Jenna and I shake our hips and sing. Huh, we're better than I expected, but I'm fairly sure that our male audience enjoys our dancing much more than our singing.

Jenna starts grinding back-to-back with me; the crowd goes wild. She runs her hands over her body and pulls her fingers up through her hair. *Was she a stripper in a former life?* The drunken men yell for us as if we're the rock stars. Alcohol and testosterone sure make an interesting combination. The whistling continues as we walk off the stage and back to our table.

Jenna winks at me, nudging my arm. "That was awesome! The crowd loved us."

"I'm sure it was our heavenly voices that won them over," I shake my head and sip my drink. "Van, you're up next."

He approaches the stage with confidence, and puts the microphone in its stand as if he is headlining an arena. "Hi everyone. I'd like to sing this song for my girl, the lovely Lexie, who just finished entertaining you." Van chuckles as a few men clap.

I expect to hear something like *Cherry Pie*, but instead the beautiful chords of a ballad begin. *Faithfully*. My heart races and my eyes water as he looks directly at my face. Everyone else is invisible. My mouth falls open as the clear beautiful tone of his voice sings only to me. The words tell a tale of a romance between a musician and his girl while he's on tour, apart from the one he loves. A tear rolls down my cheek as he professes his love the best way he knows how, through his music. The crowd cheers, giving Van a standing ovation. His eyes are focused on me, nothing else. He walks toward me and grabs my face with both his hands, placing an extremely passionate kiss on my lips.

My whole body tingles, the unique electricity flows through my core. *Can it get more romantic than this?* My stomach flutters as I pull him closer and slide my hands up his soft T-shirt to his neck. Talk about being swept off your feet. Van scoops me up and walks out of the bar, our eyes locked. He nudges the elevator button. The bell chimes and he steps into the elevator, pulling me into a lip-lock.

He carefully slides the key into the hotel room door and opens it, with me still in his arms. He kicks the door, slamming it shut behind us and lays me on the bed. I grip the bottom of his shirt and pull it over his head, exposing his rock hard body. *Please let this image burn itself into my brain.*

Keeping with the romantic theme, he nudges his nose along my neck, slowly placing sweet kisses along my jaw. An intense fire burns within me. I run my fingers over his chest tracing the lines of his muscles while barely touching his skin. His entire body quivers. His warm, soft lips travel over just about every inch of my body, pausing on the more erogenous zones. *Are his talents limitless?* A soft moan escapes as he slowly enters me, while interlocking his fingers with mine. I'm breathing heavy, almost panting. I gasp as he fills and empowers my body. We slowly and steadily continue our beautiful love-making. My toes curl as I find my release twice, before Van finds his. We lay entangled in one another's arms, gazing into each other's eyes not saying a word.

I wake to soft lips brushing against my cheek, causing the hairs on my neck to rise. When did I drift off to sleep? I rub my eyes and focus on the flawless face hovering above me.

"Rise and shine sleepy head. The Arizona desert awaits."

I yawn and stretch. "I want to make sure I bring my camera. I think it's still in my purse from Sydney's bachelorette party."

Van holds up his hands. "Whoa. I don't want to see those pictures."

I roll my eyes. "Don't worry, I'm only planning on showing them to Jenna."

∞

Like everything else, the morning flies by. I grab my camera and sunglasses and we're off. Jenna and Marcus are waiting in the lobby for us.

"Tyler and Chaz won't be joining us. They hit the town last night and still have some company." Marcus winks.

"No problem. The fabulous four will ride out to the desert." Jenna slides her sunglasses from her head to her eyes.

The tour is amazing. The guide explains the history and culture of the desert and educates us about the wildlife. Sky Island and the Desert Seas are the big attractions. Thank God I remembered my camera. I scroll through my photos. *Did I really take twenty five pictures of cactus?* Oh well, I've always wanted to see one in real life and now at least I've captured the moment.

Rockers' hours are not for early birds, especially when you factor in the desert heat. We all look like we just downed a bottle of whisky each. Sunglasses are a godsend. At least we have time to crash before the show. I crawl onto the cool sheets and cuddle up with Van.

∞

Warm sunlight blares through the window. I squint and turn toward the clock. We've got two hours left. It's only fair to let Van sleep until the last possible minute, he's technically working tonight. I head to the bathroom and start my grooming routine. Will my red strapless dress have the same effect as it did the last time Van saw me in it? Only one way to find out.

I finish up by pulling my hair up in a loose bun, exposing my neck, and throwing on black high heeled sandals. I dial room service and order a pizza and bread sticks. Last thing on the agenda, wake up Van. I graze my lips in between his belly button and the sheet draped over him, softly kissing his skin. He moans and rolls toward me.

I lightly run my fingers across his stomach. "Time to get up sleepy head."

"I'm way ahead of you, especially after those kisses."

Warmth creeps across my cheeks. "Very funny. I ordered some room service so you can eat and shower before the show. It doesn't look like there's time for much more."

Van pulls me on top of him and kisses my lips. "I'll always make time for you babe."

Knock, knock.

"Pizza's here!" I leap toward the door.

Van sits up in bed, covering his lap with a sheet as I pay the waiter.

My body tingles as his eyes burn through me. I guess the red dress is a keeper. I bring the pizza over to the bed. We turn toward each other and eat picnic style.

How can he get ready in two minutes flat? My lips part as I watch him step out of the bathroom wearing only jeans. Ah, my rock god has emerged. He runs his hand through his damp hair and throws on a faded-blue fitted T-shirt.

Damn. He looks perfect. I take a deep breath and fight the urge to tackle him on the bed. We head to the lobby, where Jenna and the guys are waiting.

The arena is bigger than I expected and fully air conditioned, thank goodness. Even though the humidity is absent, it's still extremely hot. They play a perfect set. Are they're getting better from performing so much, or do they want to step it up for the last leg of their tour? My adrenaline spikes and blood rushes through my veins as my sexy front man works the crowd, giving every ounce of energy he has. He comes alive on the stage, as if the music is literally flowing through his veins. I need to memorize this image of him and etch it onto my brain. Only one more show before I leave the tour. Why must my life be so bittersweet?

It's time for Devil's Garden to meet their fans backstage for a few hours. Hours seem like seconds. Next stop is Salt Lake City, Utah, and a twelve and a half hour bus ride before the concert at the Red Butte Amphitheater.

∞

These half-day bus rides are a killer. I stare out the window holding my head up on my hand. Ooh, I spot a sign that reads *Salt Lake City*. Finally! Van puts his arms around me as we step off of the bus and into the warm summer air. I close my eyes and breathe deeply, desperately trying to memorize every second left. Bleakness is closing in on me.

I tug at my short, tight, purple, halter dress and brush my curls over my shoulder, letting them fall across my back. If Van and I have to be apart, I want him to remember what's waiting for him.

Devil's Garden is really starting to pack the venues. This show has to be sold out. I breathe in deeply, trying to inhale the beauty of the evening. The sun is just starting to set across the endless Utah sky casting an orange and pink glow along the horizon.

"I've seen some beautiful places these last few months." I wrap my arms around Van's neck and gaze into those emerald eyes that bring me to my knees.

"This is the best view I've seen anywhere." He brushes a few stray strands of hair away from my face.

Intense flames of passion rush through my body and my heart slams against my chest. His hands slide around my waist and pull me forward. I press myself against him, trying to feel every inch of his body through the dense denim.

He presses his forehead against mine. "I feel sorry for the rest of the fans 'cause I'm never as good as I am when you're here. Every song I sing tonight is for you."

Goose bumps form, causing all the hair on my body to rise. I hold in a deep breath, trying to suppress the tears threatening to release. I bring out the best in him? I exhale slowly. "Your biggest fan can't wait."

"Come on guys, we have to go in if we want to start on time!" Marcus yells.

Van and I walk, hand in hand, to the backstage of the amphitheater. His eyes never leave mine for more than a few minutes as he checks his equipment. With everything ready to go, we enter the large room backstage and wait until show time. I sit on his lap and play with his hair as he holds me in his arms, resting his head on my shoulder. We couldn't get any closer to each other if we tried.

"You two are your own worst enemy." Jenna rolls her eyes and walks past us. "It's going to go by quicker than you think. It's not even a goodbye, it's a see you soon."

Van looks up at me. "Yeah, and I'll be with you in Savannah on Saturday."

"I'll be counting the minutes until I get you all to myself in that hotel room." I attempt a sexy look. I'm pretty sure I fail.

Van's eyes widen as he holds in a smile. "And what are you planning on doing to me when you get me all to yourself?" He raises his eyebrows.

"Anything and everything I please," I whisper.

"Let's go. It's show time!" Chaz yells, pulling me away from my blissful thoughts.

Jenna and I take our usual places at the side of the stage. Van holds my cheeks, planting a heartfelt, passionate kiss on my lips. I weave my fingers through his hair and press myself against him. The lights on the stage are no match for the heat radiating from our bodies. My heart hammers against my chest, drowning out the sound of the drums. The bass and guitar break my trance. Van pulls away at the last possible second and runs onto the stage, leaving me breathless.

Star-struck is an understatement. My sexy, rock god looks over at me as he belts out his lyrics to a packed amphitheater. My knees are weak and my body trembles. *Will I always be in awe?*

Van walks toward me as Marcus's guitar solo starts. I run my fingers through his damp hair and pull him close. He wraps his arms around me, and slams his lips into mine. My heart melts. I'm dizzy and my body is tingling. Does he think he has to impress me tonight? I'll have to tell him later that everything he does impresses me, but tonight he's bringing his A-game. He pulls away and runs back to center stage to start his next set.

One thing's for sure, this is the best I've seen him perform. Every note is spot on. The last song is a ballad, telling the story of a couple whose love can endure anything. I know it's a song that Marcus wrote for Jenna, but tonight Van's singing it directly to me. My heart skips a beat when he comes over and takes my hand as he sings. He pulls me out onto the very edge of the stage where a good number of people can see me. As soon as the song ends, he walks forward and pulls me into another passionate kiss. My heart is about to explode. He scoops me up and carries me offstage. Marcus thanks the crowd, his voice echoing in the distance.

Van finally sets me down at the edge of the parking lot. I giggle, still giddy from the romantic gesture. A limo pulls up to us and a chauffeur quickly jumps out, opening the back door to let us in.

"I want your last night of the tour to be special." Van tilts my chin up to kiss my lips. "Your chariot awaits."

I slightly gasp, momentarily forgetting to breathe. "Every second I spend with you is special."

Van takes my hand and leads me into the limo, cuddling as close to each other as we can once inside. We might as well make the most out of the short ride to the hotel. I lower myself onto the cool leather seat, pulling Van down on top of me, our lips meet, erupting into a frenzy of passion. He slowly slides his hand up my thigh and under my dress. I let out a moan and lay my head back. The chauffeur opens the door, clearing his throat.

My face flushes, the sensation creeping across my cheeks. Oh well, I'm sure this guy has seen worse. I sit up and adjust my dress before exiting the limo.

I jiggle the key to the hotel room and open the door. The glow of candlelight fills my vision. There are at least thirty candles lit around the room and a bottle of champagne lies in a chiller near the bed. I'm breathless. I place my hands over my mouth, smiling from ear to ear underneath. I drop my hand and turn toward him. "This is absolutely spectacular!"

"I love the way your face glows in candlelight." He brushes his lips across mine, slowly invading my mouth with his tongue.

My entire body trembles and nuclear energy flows through each and every pore. My heart hammers as blood rushes through my veins. An uncontrollable yearning fills my soul. I pull Van closer, pressing every part of my body against his.

He gently slides the straps of my dress down my shoulders, placing soft kisses along my neck. Shockwaves emit throughout my entire body. His fingers lightly brush my skin creating an array of goose bumps as he continues to ease my dress down in a slow sensual motion. I step out of it and stand before him in a black bra, panties, and black high heels. He takes a step back.

"You are the sexiest, most beautiful woman I've ever seen." He licks his lips and then slams them into mine.

My entire body shivers in pure delight. I slither my hands under the soft fabric of his T-shirt and slowly pull it over his head, revealing his hard, chiseled body. I softly run my fingers over every intricate muscle of his chest, trying to memorize every part. I trace down to his abs and stop at the waist of his jeans. I tug at the button, desperately trying to release him from the thick fabric. It finally gives. I reach my hand in between his jeans and his boxers. Ah, he wants me badly. He gasps and lets out a soft moan as I ease them down. He steps out of them and gently eases me onto the bed, his lips never leaving mine.

My body immediately energizes as the weight of Van presses against me. My heart rate rises steadily as we remove the last few pieces of clothing, allowing our bodies to meet. I graze my fingers against his back and sway my hips back and forth while pressing against him. He slowly slides inside me, filling me completely. I wrap my legs around his waist, pushing him deep inside me.

The inferno of passion builds as we move in time with each other. The beautiful rhythm we create drives my body wild. Desire fills my core. I'm gasping for breath and panting as I find my release three times to the slow, steady motion. The intensity is building again as Van takes his time, catering to my body's every need. I moan in pleasure as adrenaline rushes through me and I find my release once again, this time with his.

We lay on the bed panting, trying to catch our breath. I close my eyes and wipe the sweat from my forehead. *Wow, that was by far the best sex I've ever had; he knows just what to do and when to do it.* It's more than just physical pleasure. It's truly an intimate experience. Nothing else even comes close. The connection between us produces an amazing experience. There's no way either of us could achieve this with anyone else.

I quickly freshen up, snatch the champagne bottle from the chiller, and crawl onto the bed with Van. The cool sheet drapes just below his waist. My heart skips a beat. *Can he be any sexier?* He pops the cork and pours two glasses, handing one to me.

He raises his glass. "To enjoying every second we have together, and hoping time passes quickly when we're apart."

I raise my glass and sip my champagne. "Van Sinclair, I have no idea how to spend a second without you. I want you to know that these last few months have been the best of my life and I can't wait until this tour ends and we can be together again."

Van flashes a sexy half-smile and takes a deep breath. "Chaz and I used to bust Marcus's balls about Jenna. I couldn't understand why he was so into her. I felt sorry for guys like him. I never thought I'd become one of them yet here I am, under the spell of Lexie Waters."

I raise my eyebrows and tilt my head. "Are you insinuating I'm some kind of witch?"

He chuckles. "I just never understood it until I met you. It's like my whole life before doesn't even matter."

It only takes a few words to make everything complete. *Can our love really erase the pain of his past?* I set my glass down and throw myself on top of him, ripping the sheet away from his body. A few drops of champagne from his glass spill onto my back. He tosses the glass and rolls on top of me. Time for round two.

∞

Sweat pours from my body and my heart is pounding like a jack hammer. I hop up to a sitting position and gasp for air. Great, a nightmare! Thank God I didn't wake Van. The clock reads three a.m. I quietly creep out of bed and splash some water on my face, making sure I don't turn off the light on my way back.

I crawl back into bed and gaze upon the flawless face sleeping next to me. *Will he sleep just as peacefully when I'm away?* I sink my head back into the pillow. I haven't had a nightmare since I was a kid. Maybe all this stress is getting to me, or maybe my heart won't listen to my brain. Am I destined for a tragic ending?

CHAPTER 18—WHITE WEDDING

The blaring tone of the hotel wake-up call pulls me from my peaceful sleep. *Ugh, is it really morning already?* I glide my fingers over Van's rock hard chest and hold him close to me one last time before forcing myself to leave the bed. Time, now my mortal enemy, has passed quickly and I only have an hour left before I need to check in at the airport for my flight to Savannah.

Van pulls me on top of him and grazes his fingers up and down my back. "I'm not so sure I can let you go yet. I may need one more memorable activity." He raises his eyebrows as he gently caresses my skin.

"The next memorable activity is going to be you, getting me a cab. I miscalculated the wake-up call and I'm super late." I hop out of bed and head to the bathroom.

I pick at my fingernails. This is the first time Van and I will be attending a family gathering together, and it just so happens to be the most important day of my sister's life. *Please let this weekend go well!* Since I'm going to be his only sister-in-law, Bryce will have many fun filled years of me embarrassing him. No need to start today. His parents are very prim and proper, so we have to be on our best behavior. I certainly don't want to offend them in their own home. A few beads of sweat form on my neck. Van will be meeting my entire family. Is it possible for them to refrain from doing or saying something insanely embarrassing? Yeah, I'm pretty sure my parents already covered that.

Good thing I'm taking Van's clothes with me so he can travel light. He's basically jumping on a plane right after his show in Seattle in order to make it to Savannah on time. I sit on my suitcase and pull the zipper closed. We're all packed. Yay! I still have a few extra minutes to spend with Van. I crawl onto the bed toward him and wet my lips.

Knock Knock.

I sigh. Who could that be? I pull the door open. Jenna and the guys are standing outside the room with a service cart.

"Hope you don't mind. We're all having breakfast together before you leave us!" Jenna exclaims as Tyler and Marcus push the cart into our room.

Marcus fills the coffee cups. "Airport food sucks and this hotel has a four star restaurant."

Chaz lifts the silver domes covering each plate to reveal eggs benedict with fresh fruit. "I left some chick in my bed just to have breakfast with you. I hope I'm not turning into Van." He laughs and Van throws a pillow at him.

Jenna pours orange juice into beautiful crystal goblets and hands everyone a glass. She holds hers up. "Here's hoping that the six of us are all together again for Devil's Garden's next tour."

We all raise our glasses and sip our juice. My eyes began to water as I pull in a deep breath. *Everyone wants me to join the next tour?* Jenna and I have become very close, but I've also gotten attached to the rest of the band over the last few months. I'm sure going to miss these guys.

My extra few minutes seem like seconds. Everyone hugs me as we exchange our goodbyes. I swear to call Jenna at *least* twice a week. Chaz pesters me to send him pictures of hot girls from the wedding even though there's no way he could put up with the uptight women who are friends with Sydney and Bryce. Everyone clears out of our room. It's just about time to leave.

Van sits down on the bed, pulling me next to him. "I know we have all of about five minutes, but I want to give you something."

I wrinkle my eyebrows and twirl my hair around my fingers as my heart rate quickens. "You already give me everything. Plus, I'll see you Saturday."

"Yeah, I know, but I saw these on my way to dinner in Arizona. They're perfect for you." He opens the nightstand drawer and clutches a red velvet box.

My heart flutters like the wings of a hummingbird. I tremble as I brush my fingers over the soft red fabric. Slowly and gently, I open it. A beautiful pair of flower shaped diamond earrings. I gasp! *They must have cost a fortune.* An army of a thousand men couldn't contain my smile. I place them in my ears and turn toward the emerald eyes searching my face. "I love them! Thank you."

He tucks a few stray strands of hair behind my ears, showing off the precious gems. "They remind me of the flowers in our tattoos. I've never seen anything like them. They're made for you."

I jump into his lap and tackle him on the bed, brushing his hair away from his face. My lips crash into his and my hands travel over the mountainous terrain of his chiseled body. A few tears escape my eyes as I look over to the clock. My time has run out. "They're perfect for me, just like you."

∞

The airport is extremely crowded today. I run to my gate just minutes before the plane starts loading passengers. Van hooks his fingers around the belt loops of my jeans and pulls me toward him. Our bodies smash together, meeting at the lips. Ah, the intense energy radiating from this passionate kiss could fuel the plane. My knees are weak and my entire body is tingling. I'm going to miss him so much; especially when I have to see everyone else with their significant other. *Saturday, please get here fast!* We both keep looking back at each other, waving while he walks away. He finally fades into the crowd and I continue through the gate.

Security is a nightmare. My name's being called? Why do they want me at the front desk? Did I pack something I shouldn't have? I bite at my lip as I approach the flight attendant.

"Alexis Waters, this is your new boarding pass. You've been upgraded to first class."

I let out a deep breath and all the tension in my body releases. Wait, what did she just say? My cell phone chimes.

Just thought you should travel in style. The food in first class is great.

My mouth falls open. I blink a few times and take my new boarding passes; first the earrings, now this? I start typing into my phone.

You are definitely my Prince Charming. I'll have to thank you Saturday ;)

I shut off my cell phone and step onto the plane. Wow! These seats are enormous! Finally, time to relax. Van will be heavily rewarded for all this pampering. Two glasses of champagne later, I recline my seat while enjoying the in-flight movie before dinner. The menu is shrimp cocktail, salad, ravioli, and cake. This is definitely the way to travel; I'm getting spoiled. My heavy eyes close. I jolt up as the flight attendant announces that we're beginning our descent to the Atlanta airport. Just one more flight to go; I hop on a puddle jumper to the Savannah airport.

Even with the first class flight, it's still a long day of traveling. I yawn, grab my carry on, and step out of the gate. Sydney, Brooke, and Dean wave frantically when they spot me. Sydney and Brooke run toward me, the three of us colliding in one big group hug. Dean stands shaking his head.

"I missed you so much! It's great to have you back. I even cleaned your room so you can actually relax when we get back home to our apartment." Brooke bounces on her toes and squeals.

Finally, I get to see my best friend again. "I had the time of my life, but nothing's better than sleeping in your own bed." I wince slightly. If I could only be as excited as Brooke, but being without Van for six weeks will be pure torture.

"Wait until you see the Thomas's plantation. It's so big we each have our own rooms. Isn't it great? We can all stay together." Sydney nudges my arm. "Don't worry; you and your rocker boyfriend will still have your privacy."

I roll my eyes. "Good, I have to find some way to thank him for upgrading me to first class." I flash a devious grin.

Brooke winks at me. "Nice! Are we still allowed to go for pizza or are you too high class for us now?"

"I could go for a pizza and beer," Dean adds.

I slap Brooke on the arm jokingly. "Let's find a pizzeria, smart ass."

"Sorry guys, Bryce's parents have dinner set up for us tonight and for the rehearsal party tomorrow. Pizza and beer will have to wait until after the wedding. Lexie, when's your boy toy getting here?" Sydney asks.

"I've really missed all the ball busting." I shake my head. "Van won't get here until Saturday morning. He has a show in Seattle on Friday night."

Brooke gently pushes me and laughs. "Didn't you always want to go to Seattle? Maybe he'll bring you a T-shirt."

I sigh. "Come on guys, it's been a long trip. Now show me this impressive plantation."

We pull into a huge driveway, closed off by a wrought iron gate embellished with the letter T.

My eyes travel up the black metal structure as the gates slowly open. "Wow, this is worse than the security at the airport." We continue up to an enormous white house with a ton of windows and several large white pillars. White wooden rocking chairs sway on the huge wrap-around porch. *Jeeze, am I at the white house?* I gather my belongings and walk up to a sizable wooden door adorned with a heavy knocker. Sydney presses the doorbell and within seconds Cynthia Thomas greets us.

"Alexis, it's a pleasure to see you again. Welcome to our home. I'm sure you'll want to freshen up after your trip. Your room is the first door on the right, second floor. We'll all meet for dinner in the dining room at five o' clock." Cynthia smiles and walks away.

Brooke and I just look at each other, raising our eyebrows, as we make our way upstairs.

"Charming isn't she?" Brooke rolls her eyes.

"Sydney's going to have a great time with her as a mother-in-law." I shake my head.

When was the last time I've had dinner so early in the evening? The time change is taking its toll. Please don't let the Thomas's have anything else planned. I yawn and lug my bag into the room. A king-size four post bed with at least fifteen red and gold pillows covering a matching paisley comforter sits in the middle of the room. All of the wood, including the hardwood floors, is cherry. A white and gold fan hangs from the middle of the ceiling creating a soft breeze. Southern hospitality is sure living up to the hype.

My bridesmaid dress already hangs in the closet, along with my shoes. I quickly unpack and slide into gray sweatpants and my Devil's Garden T-shirt. I step into the hallway in search of the bathroom. Sydney is standing outside the door to her room.

"Very nice, is that what you're wearing for dinner?" Sydney looks me up and down.

"Well it will be if I don't get a shower. Where the hell's the bathroom?"

"Last door on the left." She places her hand on my shoulder. "Thank you for putting up with all this crap to be my maid of honor. I know Cynthia can be a pain in the ass."

I place my hand over hers and tilt my head. "You know I'll do anything for you. You do realize she'll be your mother-in-law after Saturday, right?"

"It's a shame we'll be living so far away." Sydney presses her lips together, holding back a smile.

We both laugh.

Hot water trickles down my skin reviving my body. I'm always grimy after traveling. A thickness forms in my throat and my eyes start to water. *What's wrong with me*? I guess my body isn't used to this. I haven't showered by myself in quite a while. I wrap my hair in a towel and head back to my room to get ready for dinner. Now, how can I look like a southern belle? I root through my clothes and choose a sundress with a light sweater. Perfect! It's just about time to make my way to the dining room.

"I hope everyone's all settled in. Mr. Thomas and I want you all to be comfortable and enjoy your stay in our home. Tonight we'll be having buttermilk fried chicken tenders, sweet potato casserole, corn, biscuits with honey, and peach cobbler for dessert. Please bow your heads as Mr. Thomas offers a blessing and Mabel fills our glasses with sweet tea."

Brooke lets out a slight chuckle. I squint at her and kick her under the table. She raises her eyebrow at me and bites her lip, holding back her smile. It's going to be tough to live up to the standards of Cynthia Thomas for the next few days.

Dinner conversation is light. I'm quiet; God only knows what may be construed as offensive. Sydney and Bryce are smiling from ear to ear throughout the meal, in a complete state of bliss. *They deserve every minute of it. I imagine I look the same way when I'm with Van.*

"Alexis, your earrings are beautiful. Where ever did you find such exquisite jewelry?" Cynthia's mouth opens as she touches my earrings.

"Thank you, my boyfriend bought them for me when we were in Arizona." I tuck my hair behind my ear, exposing a perfect view of my large diamond earrings.

"Whoa, those are some rocks!" Dean says, staring at them. "What'd you have to do to get those?" He raises his eyebrows.

"Wouldn't you like to know?" I whisper, and then roll my eyes. Guys really do have a one track mind.

First the earrings and then the first class plane ticket, Van is becoming a romantic right before my eyes. *How did I get lucky enough to win his heart?*

Eight o'clock and we're still at the dinner table. Mr. Thomas tells us the history of the plantation and all about the Thomas family. *Dear God, don't let me fall asleep!* This jet lag is killing me; time is again my enemy.

"We're going out to the porch to have a few drinks, you coming?" Brooke asks, pulling my arm.

I yawn stretching my arms over my head. "Sorry, I'm beat. Pencil me in for tomorrow night."

"It's a date." She hugs me and skips off to the porch.

I make my way up to my room and get ready for bed. I inhale deeply while pulling my Devil's Garden T-shirt over my head. Adrenaline rushes through my blood. Amazing!

Van's scent is still captured in its fibers. I don't want to call him; they're definitely hitting a club in Seattle tonight, so I send a quick text message and shut off my phone, allowing myself to catch up on some much needed sleep.

Counting the minutes, until Saturday. Miss you.

The bright rays of sunlight warm my face, gently waking me. I open my eyes, stretch, and look at the clock. Holy crap, its noon! Wow, I really slept in today. I must've needed the extra rest. Luckily it did the trick. The jet lag is gone and I am back to my old self. My parents should be arriving shortly. *Hmm, what am I in for?* I twist my hair into a loose ponytail and quickly dress in a skirt and tank top. I head downstairs to find everyone having lunch.

"Hello Alexis. I'm sorry you missed breakfast, but please join us for lunch," Cynthia says as she pulls out a chair for me.

My stomach hardens and tingles sweep across my face to my ears. "Thank you. It seems like the time zone change caught up with me last night." I pat down my skirt and sit.

"Maybe it's the party all night, sleep all day lifestyle you lead with the rock stars," Brooke sarcastically mutters under her breath, flashing me a quick smile.

I glare at her and take a bite of a turkey sandwich.

The Thomas's give us a tour of the plantation grounds after lunch, showing us where the wedding will take place. The aroma of thousands of flowers fills the air as a beautiful menagerie of brightly colored petals peek out through the lush green landscape. There are already several companies setting up tables and tents.

We return to the house just as my parents are stepping out of the cab.

Sydney runs up to our parents, pulling them into a bear hug. "Hey Mom and Dad! How was your flight?"

"Everything was fine sweetheart." Mom kisses her on the cheek. "You're absolutely glowing. Are you nervous?" Mom locks her arm with Sydney's and Dad and Dean grab their suitcases.

"Just excited," Sydney replies.

"Hi Mom and Dad." I give them each a quick hug. *Am I an outcast?* I know its Sydney's big day, but my parents are acting as if I'm invisible.

"Where's Van? Isn't he coming?" Mom asks with a hint of anger in her voice.

I guess she's still secretly hoping that he'll screw up. *Great! Let the fun begin.*

"He has a show tonight in Seattle. He'll be here in the morning," I say, twirling my hair around my fingers.

"Good, I was hoping he isn't letting you down already. You know how musicians can be; self-absorbed." Her lips press into a hard line.

I let out a heavy sigh and cross my arms. *Really?* They haven't even been here for fifteen minutes. I roll my eyes and walk away before the conversation escalates into an all-out battle.

"The rehearsal will start in two hours. We'll all meet outside near the gazebo," Mrs. Thomas shouts to everyone.

"I call dibs on the first shower." I gather my toiletries and head to the bathroom, away from the conversation.

∞

I have some time before the rehearsal starts. There's no way I'm heading out any earlier than necessary. I quickly dress and sit on the bed. Damn, I forgot to turn my phone back on after I woke up this morning. I power it up; it chimes.

Going crazy without you. Call me after your rehearsal tonight.

At last, something to brighten up my night! I get to talk to Van later. My body erupts into an array of tingles. *Please let time fly tonight.*

I glance down at my watch and mosey downstairs. It's rehearsal time. We're quickly instructed on the details of the ceremony. The grand ballroom of the plantation is being set up for tomorrow's big event, so we retire to the formal dining room for tonight's elegant five course meal.

Sydney and Bryce tell cute and funny stories about their relationship as we enjoy an exquisite meal of glazed ham with all the fixings and berry pie for dessert. I slump my shoulders and look down. *Am I the only person at the table without their significant other?* These sweet stories are making me miss Van. I'm quiet throughout the night and specifically avoid my parents. I'm sure they're dying to say something about me being alone.

It's just about eleven o'clock and time to retire to our rooms. Everyone needs a good night sleep before the big day tomorrow. I can't wait to hear Van's voice again. It's like we've been apart for an eternity. My fingers dance across the buttons as I dial his cell phone.

"Hi there," he says in his sexiest voice.

My heart races and my body tingles, aching for his touch. "Hi. How'd the show go?"

"Great. Seattle fans rock, I promise to take you here sometime soon."

"I'm definitely holding you to that, Mr. Sinclair."

"Hey, we got some exciting news, but I don't want you to get upset." He exhales loudly.

My head flinches back slightly. "Well, I usually don't get upset from excitement. So what is it?"

"We're offered a show at the Key Arena, opening a two hour set for Cryptic Mayhem." His voice trembles.

"Wow, they're the biggest metal band around! I can't believe you're not more excited. Why would you think I'd be upset?"

Van sighs and clears his throat. "The concert is tomorrow. There's a last minute cancellation which is why we're offered the gig. A show like this can push us mainstream," he pauses, "It looks like I won't be able to make it to Savannah."

I gasp, a river of tears stream down my cheeks. My night has gone from bad to worse. Nausea flows through me and my breathing becomes fast and irregular. My hands shake, barely able to keep the phone to my ear. I sob so hard I can barely get air into my lungs. A tightness forms in my chest along with an ache in the back of my throat. I'm dizzy; my lungs constrict making it difficult to breathe. Spots flash through my vision. *Is it possible to physically feel your heart break?*

"Lexie, are you there? Please say something."

How can he do this to me? He promised he'd be here. No, this can't be happening. I grind my teeth and my body tenses. "I'm here."

"I promise I'll make it up to you. If it was only me I would blow off the show, but I can't let the guys down. They depend on me." His voice is shaky, full of desperation.

My hands ball into fists and my nostrils flare. My pulse speeds as my muscles quiver. *Is this what my future holds, empty promises?* There's no way I'm going to be anyone's silver medal. "Well guess what? You let me down instead. I left my family, my friends, my life to travel with you for months. I would drop anything for you, I'd do anything, and you can't even keep your word to be here for me the one time I ask? If I can't count on you, what do we have?"

He exhales loudly. "Please, can I talk?"

"I think you've said it all." My voice cracks as I break into sobs. "There's nothing you can say or do or buy to change the fact that you're breaking your promise and bailing on me." I take a deep breath and clear my throat. "I just can't do this. We're over."

I slam my phone shut and throw it at the wall. Tears flow down my cheeks like an endless ocean. I bring my knees to my chest and cover my face with my hands. A painful tightness forms in my throat. My perfect life has taken a tragic turn. *I get it, his career is important and so is mine, but trust is essential. If he can't keep his commitments, what does that say?* My mind wanders back to the groupie on the bus. *Oh God, if he breaks one commitment, will he break others?*

Brooke can't even give me a pep talk. What would she tell me? Things like, 'You'll find someone better'. Clearly that isn't true, no one can compare to Van Sinclair. I'd rather spend my life alone than be with someone else. Isn't he my soul mate, the one person who's perfect for me?

I've been sucker punched. My body curls in a lump as if all the wind has been knocked out of my lungs. I wrap my arms around my body, trying to hold myself together and take a deep breath. I need a half decent excuse so I'm not totally embarrassed tomorrow. Maybe I can say his flight is delayed.

My mother will be gloating, since she and my father are just waiting for Van to screw up. I'll wait to tell them that we broke up when I'm safely back at my apartment. I'm in no mood for the *I told you so* speech all weekend.

I open my eyes and look at the clock. Six a.m. Wow, I literally cried myself to sleep. I'm such a cliché. I turn on the TV to occupy my mind with something other than Van.

Of course I fail. Within seconds, tears stream down my face. *How can I live without him?* I'm fated to know I can be electrified by a touch, to be breathless from looking into the most beautiful emerald eyes, to have my body come alive, and to be damned to never feel that way again. It's like living in hell on earth. There are no more tears left to shed. *Why am I still sobbing?*

I stare at the clock until seven. I better turn my cell phone back on in case Brooke or Sydney is trying to get in touch with me. I flip it open and examine the screen. Thank God, it didn't break. It chimes continuously. I have forty-two missed calls from Van, but no voice mail messages.

Knock, Knock.

It must be time to get my hair done. I wipe my face for the millionth time and pull open the door.

Brooke jerks her head back and wrinkles her brow. "Are you ok? You look like you have pink eye."

I rush to the mirror. My eyes are swollen, red and puffy. If I were stung by a hundred bees I wouldn't look this bad. "I must be allergic to something." I can't come up with a better answer at the moment.

Brooke tips my chin toward her and examines my face. "Come on, let's hope our make-up artist can work wonders," she says as she leads me downstairs.

Sydney wants my hair in an up-do of formed curls with soft tendrils hanging down. I wear a tube top so I can slip it off without messing my hair when it is time to get dressed.

Cynthia gasps as she walks behind me. "Oh my, Alexis! What is that desecration on your back?"

What's she talking about? Oh, she's referring to the tattoo on my shoulder blade, clearly visible with my hair up. Great, another thing to remind me of Van, and this one is permanent. My stomach clenches. "Don't worry; we can airbrush it out of the pictures."

Cynthia walks away with a look of disgust on her face. I can already foresee some fierce battles between Sydney and Cynthia in the future.

Our make-up artist *can* work magic. She does a fabulous job of hiding the huge bags under my eyes. I grab a few crackers and go back upstairs. Soon it will be time to get dressed. I clutch my arms to my chest and take a deep breath. When should I tell everyone that Van won't be coming?

Knock, Knock.

Sydney bursts into my room with tears in her eyes. "Look, the whole bottom hem has come out of my dress. I can't walk down the aisle like this. What am I going to do?"

At least there's one thing I can repair. "Calm down. We can fix this. I promise you will not walk down that aisle any less than perfect. Ok?" I find a bunch of safety pins in the drawer and start fixing her dress, hiding the pins in the lush satin. When I finish, the hem looks perfect.

"You're my savior!" Sydney hugs me tightly.

I squeeze her back. "You make a beautiful bride. I'm so happy for you."

Sydney smiles at me. "Don't worry sis, I'll return the favor on your wedding day."

My smile slowly turns into a frown. *That day may never come.* It's just about time to head downstairs. I pull on my peach chiffon dress and touch up my make-up. My heart hammers. *Ugh, I have to tell everyone about Van when I get downstairs.* I wait as long as I can.

Knock, Knock.

"Oh no, did the hem fall out?" I pull the door open and my jaw drops.

"Wow, you look absolutely beautiful," Van says as he stands in front of me in the doorway.

My heart pounds and tears well up behind my eyelids; my muscles weak. I throw my arms around him and start to cry. He steps into the room, closes the door behind us, and wraps his arms around me, holding me tight like he'll never let me go.

"I'm sorry. I'm an idiot. I promised you I'd be here and I'm here now. I hope it's not too late."

"It's not too late. It's never too late."

"Please don't cry. I want to make you happy, not sad. I love you, Lexie."

"I'm happy. I'm so happy you came here for me." The warmth of his embrace erases the pain. The familiar sparks that I feared I'd never feel again encompass my body as Van runs his fingers along the top of my back. He presses his forehead against mine, and slowly kisses my lips.

"Lexie, we're meeting downstairs in five," Brooke calls, pulling me out of my moment of bliss.

Van holds me tight in his arms. "I hope there's time for me to change. I'm pretty sure Bryce's mom would have a heart attack if I showed up to the ceremony in jeans."

I chuckle and wipe my eyes. "I have to get some pictures taken. The shower's the last door on the left and your clothes are in the closet," I say, still clinging to Van like he's my lifeline.

He pulls away, lifts my chin and places a long, sweet kiss on my lips.

How could I have doubted him? He does keep his commitments. *He is my soul mate*!

I grasp his arm as he starts walking toward the door. "I love you."

He steps forward and grabs both my cheeks, planting a knock-your-socks-off kiss on my lips. I'm breathless, my knees shaking. He flashes a quick smile and leaves the room to shower.

I glance in the large hallway mirror on my way downstairs. Do I need any make-up touch ups after our emotional reunion? I actually look pretty good. It's amazing what love can do for one's complexion.

I pose for more pictures than a Hollywood starlet. Finally, I escape the wedding paparazzi to meet Van as he makes his way down the stairs. My heart races as I stare in awe. *Wow, he does wonders for that suit.* I've never seen him in clothes other than T-shirts and jeans. Boy was I missing out. He looks like he just walked off the pages of a magazine. My eyes travel across the charcoal grey suit up to a white shirt and silver and black tie. His hair is combed back, bringing more attention to his sparkling emerald eyes. My eyes widen and my heart pounds against the walls of my chest. *Please don't let me faint.* Van Sinclair is mine and I am the luckiest girl in the world!

I shoot a death glare at two girls who are expressing the things they want to do to him in a not-so-lady-like way. *Where's Cynthia Thomas when you need her?* My mouth falls open, rendering me speechless as Van walks up to me and places a sweet kiss on my lips, putting his arm around me. I fight the sudden urge to throw the finger to these girls. Today is a day to act like a lady.

My mother does a double take as Van and I walk out to the garden where the ceremony will take place, hand in hand. She turns to me and smiles approvingly. I introduce Van to my extended family. Amazingly, not one of them did or said anything to embarrass me.

Everything's absolutely perfect. Bryce even sheds a few tears when he sees his beautiful bride. Dad grips Sydney's arm and holds her close as he walks her down the rose-petal filled aisle. He'd never admit it, but he doesn't want to give away his little girl. Would he feel the same way if it was me up there, walking toward Van? My heart flutters. *Ah, to*

be Van's forever. My eyes flock to him like a moth to a flame.
They travel over his still damp hair, each strand perfectly
placed, and his gleaming emerald eyes staring right back at
me. Our eyes lock, trapping each other in our perfect
world. *How can I spend a second away from him?* Spending
eternity with Van isn't even close to long enough.

Cheers and claps fill the air, slamming me back into
reality. I jerk my head back and get my bearings straight.
Sydney and Bryce skip down the aisle, stopping to smooch
every few minutes for the photographer.

Cocktail hour starts immediately after the ceremony.
Perfect timing, I can use a drink tonight. A few more
pictures and I'm a free woman. Now I can focus my time
on Van. *Do I have enough self-control to keep my hands off of him
until later?*

I notice several women staring at Van. Oh, hell no. Not
tonight. I sneer and press my lips tight. I walk up to him,
kiss his lips, and pull him into an embrace, claiming him as
mine. I put up with enough of the groupies on the road.
Dean, Brooke, Van, and I find a table in the back and have
a few drinks while we're being served hors d'oeuvres.

"Lexie, it looks like you better eat up. You'll need your
strength to take out all the women staring at your man,"
Brooke says as she sips her appletini.

"These girls are nothing compared to the groupies on
the road, and I have better things to save my energy for
than that." I pop a grape in my mouth.

Dean furrows his eyebrows and flashes a grin.

Does he think Van's going to entertain him with tales
of groupies past? *Yeah, not going to happen.* I shake my head
and banish the negative thoughts from my mind.

By the time my maid of honor duties are fulfilled,
cocktail hour lasts about thirty minutes. The night is flying
by and it's already time to proceed into the grand ballroom

for the reception. The band announces the wedding party and introduces Sydney and Bryce as a married couple. They emerge into the ballroom to the theme from Star Wars. Who knew Bryce was a closet sci-fi nerd?

I get chills as everyone stands and claps for the newly married couple. I turn my gaze toward Van and freeze. He's staring at my face. Heat spreads across my cheeks as a smile forms. I pull him close and rest my head against his arm.

We dine on surf-n-turf as sweet melodies from the string quartet set the mood. After dinner, another band plays party music and we all hit the dance floor. Van's an exceptional dancer. Mom stares at him as his feet glide across the wooden floor. I cross my arms and squint.

She looks at me, jerks her head, and turns away. I chuckle. Caught red-handed. *I should've known his body can move on the dance floor based on the way it moves in other places.* We sway to the slow songs, sweetly kissing as we stare into each other's eyes. *And I thought my high school prom was special.* Van makes everything astonishing.

This night exceeds all my expectations. Van's proven to me and my entire family that he keeps his promises. My face is sore from smiling so much, but I just can't hold back my blissful joy.

Van takes off his jacket and tosses it on the back of his chair. "Want another drink? I'm thirsty from all this dancing."

"I'll have a Cosmo," I say, swigging down the last few drops from my glass.

As soon as he walks away his jacket chimes. *Should I check it for him?* Maybe it's something important. I pull out the phone from his pocket and glance at the screen. It's a text from Chaz.

I cover my mouth with my hand.

If you don't answer your fucking phone I'm going to smash you with it when I find you.

CHAPTER 19—CHOICES

I quickly slide Van's phone back into his jacket pocket. His decision to keep his promise to me has clearly caused some friction with the band. I pin my arms against my stomach, trying to suppress the nausea. Am I the most selfish person alive? I forced him to choose.

My eyes lock with his as he approaches me carrying two drinks. How can he keep this from me? It must be eating him alive inside. I twirl my hair around my fingers, hoping the dance music drowns out the pounding of my heart.

"Miss me?" His fingers brush mine as he hands me my Cosmo.

"Every second you're away from me." I sip my drink, trying to work up the nerve to broach the subject.

Alcohol has been known to give me liquid confidence. No need to let Van know I looked at his text. I don't want him to think I have trust issues. I'll go with another approach.

"I haven't talked to Jenna since I left Utah. I better call her soon or she'll kick my ass the next time I see her." I take another slug of my Cosmo and set the glass on the table.

Van rubs the back of his neck. "Maybe you should wait a few more days. Regina just gave us a list of deadlines for the new album. Everyone's on edge. Jenna's super bitchy." He sips his drink.

I laugh, playfully smacking his arm. "I didn't know she could get any bitchier."

He's not laughing. Instead he looks at me with an empty smile. *Ok, time for the truth.*

I put my hand on his and wrinkle my brow. "Is something wrong?"

He looks down at the table and takes a sip of his drink, tapping his fingers on the glass. "Everyone's pissed at me because I left them high and dry when I backed out of the Cryptic Mayhem show. As far as I know we're not speaking and I think that includes you and Jenna."

I take a deep pained breath and close my eyes. *Why am I so selfish?* Not only did I drive a wedge between Van and his band, but I also caused a group of best friends to fight. My stomach knots. Yeah, I can see why he doesn't want me to call Jenna; I'm the villain in this scenario.

I place my hand on top of Van's, gently brushing his fingers. "I'm sorry. Everyone should be pissed at me, not you. I need to realize that you can't always be here with me, and that's just the way it is."

He looks up at me and places his hand on my cheek. "You didn't do anything wrong. If I make you a promise I should keep it. You should be able to count on me. If I have to make a choice, it'll always be you."

Tears well up in my eyes. *How did I get lucky enough to find a man like Van Sinclair?* My insides flutter. *And I may have just ruined his career and cost him his friends.* What the hell is wrong with me? I have to fix this before it gets out of hand. I never want him to resent me and causing his band to break up is definitely grounds for resentment.

"Come on, the wedding's just about over. We're going upstairs and I'm calling Jenna. We're resolving this before it goes any further and then I'm going to show you just how much I appreciate you and everything you do for me." I take Van's hand and lead him upstairs to our room, closing the door behind us.

He takes off his jacket and loosens his tie as I grab my cell phone and dial Jenna's number. She picks up on the second ring.

"Hello?" She already has attitude in her voice.

My heart races. "Can we please talk?"

"I guess someone should, now that Van has abandoned everyone."

I sigh. "Please don't be so theatrical. I really want to fix this before it gets out of hand."

"It's already out of hand. I'm surprised there isn't a bounty on Van's head, or yours for that matter," she shouts.

I twirl my hair around my trembling fingers. "Blame me; let everyone blame me. I pushed him to it. I made him choose."

"Yeah you did. Before you came into his life he'd never abandon the band. Out of all the shows on the tour, this one was most important to Devil's Garden's future and you wouldn't let him stay. It was Lexie's way or the highway, and now we all have to suffer. But hey, you got to have your boyfriend at your sister's wedding so everything worked out." Her voice drips with sarcasm.

A low growl erupts in my throat. "That's not fair. I'm sure you've faced some situations like this with Marcus. I don't mind taking a back seat to the band for many things, but this was really important to me and my family, and I needed him. I'm sorry it turned into a shit storm." Tears well up in my eyes.

"You're right; I've faced situations like this. We shouldn't always come second to the band, but sometimes we have to and this was one of those times."

My face is hot and my jaw clenches. I take a few deep breaths to calm myself down. Jenna is my only hope of correcting things, so fighting with her isn't going to help my cause. "I understand that now, but what's done is done. What can we do to fix things and get back on track?"

"I'll let the guys know that you called and see what they want to do. Please promise me that you won't let him pass up any more huge opportunities from now on unless it's *your* wedding day. Maybe not even then."

Wow, she is something. I exhale loudly. "I promise. Call me back and let me know what needs to be done."

I close my cell phone and turn to Van, who's sitting on the bed taking off his shoes. "She's going to call back after she talks to the guys. I'll make sure we fix this. Too many women are blamed for bands fighting and I'm not going to be one of them."

I reach around and unzip the back of my dress, letting it fall to the floor. My heels click on the hardwood floors as I step out of it and walk over to the bed. Slowly, I crawl onto the smooth sheets and straddle Van. "You do wonders for this suit, but I prefer what's underneath." I softly kiss his neck and gently tug at the buttons of his shirt, exposing his perfectly chiseled chest.

"I would miss anything in the world for this." Van pulls my hips toward him, grinding my body against his.

My heart rate accelerates and my skin flushes. I slide off his shirt, toss it to the floor, and push him backwards, lowering him onto the bed. I lay on top of him, pressing my body against his.

He rolls to his side so we're facing each other and lightly brushes his fingers over my breasts, down my abdomen, and under my panties.

My muscles twitch as adrenaline rushes through my veins. My body aches for him. "Oh Van, I need you."

"No reason to rush tonight. For once, we have time." He continues his sexy assault, gently rubbing my most sensitive areas and slides his fingers inside of me.

My heart pounds and my breathing is quick and heavy. A loud groan escapes from my throat. He moves his talented fingers in a perfect rhythm, causing my body to erupt with pure pleasure. Once I regain focus, I roll Van over and straddle him, pressing his wrists against the bed.

He wets his lips. "Now that you've got me, what will you do with me?"

I brush my lips across his and send soft kisses down his body, bit by bit. I run my tongue over his salty skin, tracing every peak and valley. He moans and his muscles tighten when I glide my tongue across his stomach, ending just underneath his belly button. I take my time, sweeping my lips along the rim of his boxers, slowly pulling them down. I slide my tongue over the tip of him and his breathing becomes erratic.

"My God, you're killing me. Don't stop."

My mouth engulfs him, gently sucking, aiming to alleviate his frustration. I stop after a few minutes, leaving him wanting more. He looks up at me with those emerald eyes, feverish and over-bright. I creep up and ease myself on top of him, slowly rocking my body back and forth. I'm breathless. We both groan as I run my hands behind me, over his body. Our breathing accelerates. He grips my hips tight and rolls me over. I gasp and dig my fingers into his back as he thrusts inside of me, starting off slow and easy, and increasing his intensity with each thrust. My nerve endings prickle and I wrap my legs around him, squeezing tight and pulling him as deep inside of me as I possibly can. I groan as he fills me. We meet each other thrust for thrust, our bodies giving in to the passion and exploding with desire at nearly the same time.

Van buries his head in my shoulder, catching his breath. He looks up at me and tucks my hair behind my ear, brushing his hand against my face. "You're so beautiful." He gazes into my eyes, gently placing a kiss on my lips. "Other than Marcus's, this is the only wedding I've been to. Do they all end like this?"

"They will now." I push Van's hair out of his face, stealing another kiss. My eyes travel down to his impeccably sculpted torso as I pull away. That thin sheet lying over his waist is the only thing separating me from intense pleasure. My heart races again. *God, he's sexy.* Time for round two.

My phone rings, interrupting my seductive thoughts. I inhale deeply and check the screen. It's Jenna.

"Hello?"

"I talked to the guys and they finally decided to end their pissing contest. Everyone wants to straighten this out."

Thank God. I let out a deep breath. "I hope it's more talking than fighting and that they can all come to an agreement."

"Umm, it's not going to be that easy. Since you and Van are together now, we all need to talk this out, including you and me. When do you start work?"

Why am I part of this? It should be between Van and the band, but if the guys consider Jenna and me part of the package, then I better be there. "I have a mandatory meeting on Wednesday, and I start the next Monday. What did you have in mind?"

"Our next show's in Idaho on Tuesday. Can you guys come to Kansas on Monday? Then you can head back home and we can get back on the tour."

I turn to Van and fill him in on the plan. "Ok, we'll meet you at Van's house on Monday."

I close my phone and take a deep breath. Emptiness fills the pit of my stomach. I run my hands over my face and turn to Van, who's drifting off to sleep. *Please let my mind turn off so I can do the same.* How will this meeting go? Everyone's pissed at us, especially at me, and from what I've heard about Van's temper, things can quickly go awry. I just want to get this over with as quickly as possible.

The morning sun floods the room with a vengeance, blinding me. I stretch, rub my eyes, and greet the new day. Van's still sleeping peacefully. His hair scatters around his face in a sexy mess while his body slowly moves with each breath, allowing the sun to accentuate his muscles. My heart rate quickens. Even in his altered state of consciousness, Van Sinclair is perfect.

He wakes and catches me staring at him.

My face flushes.

He smiles his sexy half smile. "Like what you see?"

"Best view in the world." I lean over to kiss his cheek. "Not that being rushed is anything new to us, but Bryce's parents are having a brunch downstairs in forty-five minutes."

"I was hoping we could stay in bed all day." Van sighs. "Ok, let's hit the showers." He playfully smacks my behind.

I hop out of bed. "I'm showering first. I'm sure my Dad doesn't want to meet us coming out together."

He scrunches his eyebrows. "They know we were on tour together for months. Do they think we were sleeping alone in all of those hotel rooms?"

"It doesn't seem right to throw it in their face." I snatch my toothbrush and head to the bathroom.

The invigorating shower relaxes my tense muscles as well as my mind. I return to our room to find Van on the phone making airline arrangements.

"Guess it's my turn." He grabs his jeans and a gray T-shirt and makes his way to the shower.

Who would have thought we needed a full wardrobe for this weekend? The only clean outfit I have left is my red, strapless dress, while Van only has his suit, jeans, and T-shirts. Cynthia may have a nervous breakdown when she sees us. I'm sure my mother will have some comments, too. I finish up my make-up as Van enters the room.

"Wow, you look hot." Van stands behind me, wrapping his arms around my waist and kissing the back of my neck.

"Right back at ya." *How can he look so great without even trying?*

He runs his fingers through his damp hair, causing it to become the perfect balance of sleek and sexy.

Knock Knock. "Wakey, wakey, eggs and bakey," Brooke calls.

Van opens the door, letting Brooke and Dean into our room.

"Are we going to a stuffy brunch or a concert?" Brooke chuckles and looks me up and down. "Cynthia's going to freak out."

"Great! I'll be known as the slut of the brunch." I roll my eyes and grab my small purse.

"You may have earned that reputation already. These walls are either really thin or you were having the time of your life last night." Brooke raises her eyebrows and smirks at me.

Dean looks down at the floor, holding his lips together, trying not to smile.

I cover my mouth with my hand. Ugh! My parents' room is not very far from ours. I can't even blame Sydney since she spent her wedding night in a lavish hotel. I drop my hand. "You know what? I may as well play the part. Anyone who sees Van will understand why I can't keep my hands off of him."

"You go girl!" Brooke nudges my arm and we make our way downstairs.

I hold on to Van's hand for dear life as we enter the ballroom. My mother's eyes widen. She crosses her arms and shakes her head. Everyone in the room is staring at us. Why doesn't this bother Van? He stands with his shoulders back and his head held high. I guess he's accustomed to judging eyes staring at him.

My mother walks toward us. "Really Lexie? We're at an elegant southern plantation and you chose to wear that?" She waves her hand in front of me.

"I didn't know I needed a million outfits mom, so this is what I have left. Sorry to disappoint." I grip Van's hand tighter and clench my jaw.

"You're the most beautiful woman in the room no matter what you wear." Van kisses my cheek. Our eyes meet as we stand facing each other, blocking out the rest of the world.

My mother sighs. "Come on you two. Let's sit down before you bring any more attention to yourselves."

We follow my mother and join everyone at the table.

My dad speaks first. "So kids, did everyone have a good time at the wedding?"

"Oh yes, Mr. Waters. Lexie was just telling us about what a great time she had last night." Brooke flashes a devious grin at me.

I kick her under the table and give her a death stare. "We had lots of fun Dad."

"Do you need me to take anything back to our apartment for you?" Brooke asks.

"Nope, I have most of my stuff and I'll get the rest soon. We're making a quick pit stop at Van's house but I'll be back at the apartment on Tuesday." I shove a forkful of eggs benedict into my mouth.

She wrinkles her eyebrows and sets down her crystal goblet full of orange juice. "I thought you were coming home later tonight. Tomorrow's Labor Day." Brooke's face reddens.

"It's Labor Day, not Christmas. No biggie. I'll be home Tuesday. I have a meeting with my boss on Wednesday, and then I'm free until Monday. Don't worry; we'll have lots of time to spend together." I blow her a kiss and sip my coffee.

Brooke sighs. "I was going to throw a surprise welcome home cookout for you tomorrow, but I guess that plan is shot to hell." She drops her fork onto the table.

I certainly have a gift for pissing people off lately. "That's really sweet of you to do, but my life is on a constant schedule now. Surprises aren't included." I grip my napkin.

She shakes her head. "What was I thinking trying to surprise my best friend with a party?" She looks away. "If that's what you still are."

I let out a deep sigh and drop my napkin. "Please just cut me a break. I'll be home Tuesday."

Brooke flashes a meek smile and nods her head slowly. "Tuesday it is."

The whole table is absolutely quiet. *Jeeze, am I at the library?* It's not like we had a battle royal at the brunch. Everything's fine. Thank God the guys finally make small talk about sports and music to break the tension. I pick at my fingernails and patiently wait for brunch to be over; it seems like it is taking days. Finally, Van and I head back to our room.

"Well, that went well. I guess we'll have to clone ourselves to make everyone happy." I violently shove my clothes into my suitcase.

"It doesn't really matter, as long as we're happy." He grasps my arm and pulls me into an embrace.

I wrap my arms around his neck and hold him close to me. "I'm glad we're going to your house tonight. I need a night to be with you and only you and forget about the rest of the world."

"I got us on a three p.m. flight, so we'll be at my house by the evening." Van tilts my chin up and softly kisses my lips. "You should probably leave some of your stuff at my place so you'll have it when you need it. I'll clear out a few drawers for you."

My heart rate spikes and my stomach flip-flops. It isn't like we're moving in with each other, but it's a step in that direction. "You should probably leave some of your stuff at my apartment too."

"Sounds like a plan."

I change into jeans and a T-shirt and quickly say my goodbyes. Brooke's gotten over our fight. Thank God, I don't need any drama when I see her on Tuesday. We thank Mr. and Mrs. Thomas for having us at their home and quickly hug and kiss my parents.

I sigh as I step inside the plane. Tomorrow will consist of a horrible battle before any resolution is made. Fortunately, tonight is the calm before the storm. My heart flutters; a night completely alone with Van. No distractions. No time constraints. Just two people in love, enjoying some much needed quality time with each other. I turn to the stunning man sitting next to me as he holds my hand in his lap.

My mind wanders during the flight. Why are all our friends turning against us because we choose each other over anything or anyone else? Jenna and Brooke are hypocrites; they would certainly choose their men too. Everything in life comes with a choice, and I choose Van Sinclair.

CHAPTER 20—KANSAS, REVISITED

The plane follows the setting sun, reflecting golden rays through the window as we land in Kansas. Luck is on our side, we're able to stroll right out and catch a cab. All the fanfare is absent. No screaming fans, no autographs to sign. Ah, a nice surprise. It's probably because this is an unplanned and unannounced trip. The short cab ride leads us to a dark, isolated house. I rest my head back and gaze out the window. It's the most welcoming sight I've seen in the last few months.

Van clutches our bags with one hand and puts his arm around me with the other as we walk up to the huge wrap-around porch. I sit on the swing and take a deep breath, inhaling the fresh summer air while he fumbles with his keys. Finally, the porch light turns on, illuminating our path. I follow Van into the house. Everything's exactly as we left it.

"We only have soda and water. I guess we should've stopped for some food." Van holds the refrigerator door open and searches its contents.

I glide my hands up his back and kiss his neck. "I think there's still some pasta sauce left." I open the freezer and remove a frozen pint. "I can boil some noodles and put a bottle of wine in the fridge."

"You can make the best out of anything. One of the many things I love about you." He spins me around and pins me against the refrigerator, smashing his lips into mine. The door slams shut. "Let's get our stuff upstairs."

Van carries our bags up to the bedroom. He drops them and collapses onto his bed. "I've missed you." He hugs a pillow and professes his love to the bed.

I giggle while he rolls around on his purple sheets. He's more content than I've seen him in a while.

He suddenly sits up and lunges for me, grabbing me by the hips. I squeal as he pulls me backwards onto the bed with him. The smooth satin sheets cool my skin. How refreshing. It's great to be carefree and playful. He rolls on top of me with his face hovering above mine. "I consider this *our* bed since you're the only woman who's ever been in it." He kisses my lips softly, staring into my eyes.

"I'm proud to earn that honor." I raise my eyebrows placing a quick, sweet kiss on his lips as his hair tickles my face. "Well, since it's *ours*, which side is *mine?*"

Van gently rubs his nose against mine. "Lady's choice."

"We'll have to see what side I end up on later."

Van pushes himself up. "I'm losing track of why I came up here." He stands up and walks toward a tall chest of drawers. "Are three drawers enough?"

I nod.

"Bouncing between here and your apartment's gonna be tough. Then I guess we'll see what happens." He sighs, his lips forming a hard line.

Ugh. Please don't let him bring this up again. We're not making a decision until I get settled with my new job and he finds out the details of his new album and tour. No need to re-visit the fight we had the last time we were in Kansas. How can I change the subject quickly?

"I'm all out of clean clothes." I twirl my hair around my fingers.

"There's a washer and dryer off the bathroom in the hallway." He opens a drawer full of T-shirts. "I'll share."

I take a gray one and throw it on the bed. He licks his lips and stares as I slip out of my clothes and into his shirt, leaving only my panties underneath.

I lick my lips, catching the bottom one in my teeth. *Will we ever stop wanting to ravish each other?* If I don't leave this bedroom now I may never have clean clothes. I carry my bag to the hallway and start sorting my laundry. I return to the bedroom. Van has the drawers cleared out for me and also gives me some space in the closet.

I tilt my head and lower my eyebrows. "How do you feel about me leaving my toothbrush here?"

"My toothbrush is dying for company." He leads me to the bathroom and places my toothbrush next to his in a ceramic cup. He backs me against the sink and presses every inch of his impressive body against the thin fabric of my T-shirt, gently kissing my neck.

The cool porcelain sends goose bumps throughout my body. I slide my hands down Van's chest and push him away. "Tonight's a date night. I want dinner first."

He sighs and places his head on my shoulder.

I giggle and step away. Grabbing his hand, I lead him downstairs to the kitchen. I rummage through the cupboards, find two pots, and start boiling the water for the pasta and defrosting the sauce over low heat. Van sits on a kitchen chair watching me. *How can he always look so sexy?* I walk over to him and sit on his lap, softly kissing his neck and nibbling his ear.

"You're quite the tease tonight." He nudges me away from his neck.

"I'm just trying to keep you wanting more." I straddle him and run my finger over his lips.

"I never get my fill." He grabs my face, slamming his lips against mine.

I quietly moan as he presses against the thin fabric of my panties. My breathing increases as he grows. I squeeze his biceps tight and press my body harder against his until

I'm grinding myself against him. My heart is racing, adrenaline pumping through my blood.

He pulls my T-shirt over my head, dropping it onto the kitchen floor and lifts me up onto the table. The cool tabletop is no match for the heat radiating from my body. He leans over me, kissing my neck, then breasts, and slides my panties down. Goosebumps erupt on my skin following the path of his hands. He caresses my inner thighs, gently spreading them apart as he continues to move his lips down my body.

My heart is hammering. I moan as his tongue travels over my most sensitive areas, twisting and turning. I gasp and my breathing becomes erratic. Suddenly, my body explodes like an atomic bomb into a frenzy of passion. I groan, loudly calling Van's name. He stands up, grips my hips, and thrusts himself into me. We both moan as his body rhythmically moves in time with mine. I dig my fingers into his back and wrap my legs around his waist, urging him deeper inside of me as my climax starts to build. I yell out as I find my release. Van yanks my hips against him, roaring in ecstasy as he finds his.

We take a minute to catch our breath.

"I wonder if the water's boiling yet." I slide off the table and gather my two articles of clothing.

"So much for dinner first." Van flashes a sexy smile.

I can never resist him. Hey, everyone wants to enjoy dessert before dinner anyway. "Why don't you see if you can find us a movie to watch while I finish cooking? We'll just do everything backwards tonight." I snicker and push Van into the living room.

The water is already boiling and the sauce is heated. No surprise there. I grab two wine glasses and uncork the bottle, pouring us each a glass. I take a sip, letting the sweet flavor invade my mouth, and head into the living room while waiting for the pasta to finish boiling. I hand a glass to Van and sit down on the couch beside him. "Find anything interesting?"

He runs his hand along my thigh. "Nothing more interesting than what's right next to me." He raises his eyebrows and sips his wine.

What a perfect night; just the two of us. Alone time is hard to come by. Maybe that's why I cherish every second I have with Van. I sigh, I guess everyone wants the things they don't have. Dean and Brooke don't realize how lucky they are. I frown, tonight is flying by. I head back to the kitchen, finish preparing the pasta, and fill our plates. Van joins me at the kitchen table.

I lightly brush my fingertips along Van's forearm. "This is one of the best nights ever. I'm looking forward to next time. Any idea when that will be?"

Van narrows his eyes and turns toward me. "I thought you wanted to get settled with your job before we make any more plans."

Are guys really this clueless? "Yeah, before we decide what we're doing after your tour ends. We still need to plan to see each other until then."

He twines our fingers together. "We have a show in Wyoming on Friday. I'll come to your apartment Saturday and we can do something special to celebrate the start of your job."

My face erupts into a huge smile. "I would love that! I'll bring some of your stuff to my apartment so you can travel light. Since I've developed a habit of keeping your T-shirts, this one's coming with me." I stand up and spin myself around, modeling my newly acquired tee.

"I've never loved that T-shirt more than I do right now," he grins, "except maybe when it's lying on my kitchen floor." He raises his eyebrows.

I suck on my pointer finger. "Maybe we can see how it looks on the floor in my apartment soon."

Van lets out a quiet sigh and stares at my mouth. "Ready for dessert?" He walks toward me, pulling me into an embrace. His soft lips brush against mine, softly at first, and then increasing in intensity with each passing moment. He traces his hands down to my hips and lifts me up, holding me against his waist as we continue to kiss.

My body trembles. I wrap my legs around him tightly and we began to move. He carries me up the stairs and into his room. The soft satin sheets caress my body as he gently places me on the bed, running his tongue over every inch of my skin. I need to feel him inside me; time for round two. My body erupts with pleasure as I collapse into a sea of purple satin.

I eventually muster up enough energy to make my way to the bathroom and freshen up. My toothbrush is leaning against Van's in the cup on his sink. What a glorious sight! It's never been at a home other than my own, and represents a milestone in our relationship. I stare at it for a few minutes, and then quickly brush my teeth, returning my toothbrush to its cup.

"We better get some sleep. Tomorrow may be exhausting." Van pulls me close to him.

I'm sure it will be a drama fest, plus I'm flying out on a red eye back to my apartment so I had better catch some Z's. "Good night, I love you." I rest my head on Van's chest and listen to the strong rhythm of his heart as it slowly lulls me to sleep.

∞

A familiar sea of purple greets me as I wake and roll over to face Van. The soft rays of sunlight peeking through the window glisten over the peaks and valleys of his chiseled abs, accentuating them. He's propped up on his elbow, bare-chested, with the sheet covering his waist. My heart pounds out of my chest. *Wow, he could grace the cover of a romance novel.*

"Good morning." He tucks a few loose strands of hair behind my ear. "Looks like the left side is yours."

"Left side it is." I sink into my pillow and yawn. "Are you sure we can't stay here all day?"

"Maybe someday," Van runs his hand along my cheek, "but not today. Everyone will be here in about an hour so we should get dressed."

I take a deep breath and stretch. Van's bed really is comfortable. My body moves in slow motion. "Any chance there's coffee in my future?"

"I'll make a quick stop at the donut shop while you're getting ready." He slides out of the satin sheets and slips into his jeans and T-shirt.

Oh well, time to haul myself out of bed. I finally sit up and get myself moving. My clothes are still in the dryer. Guess I lost track of time, no surprise there. *This meeting with the band is going to be intense.* Even though I have no issues with confrontation, I need to keep myself in line. I certainly don't want to ruin any of Van's friendships, so I better watch what I say.

The front door closes and the sound of jingling keys fill the house. I'm just about ready, so I head downstairs.

"I wasn't sure what kind of donuts you like so I got us a variety." He places a box on the countertop.

"Great, I'm starving." I take my cup of coffee and snatch a donut from the box.

Boston Cream, my favorite! The swing is calling me. We both make our way to the porch to enjoy our breakfast along with the beautiful scenery. I could certainly get used to this life.

My muscles tense as a car pulls up the dirt road and into the driveway. Van lets out a deep breath and stands up, cracking his knuckles.

"Hey Van. Should we head downstairs?" Marcus tips his chin.

"Yeah, you guys want anything?"

"Nope, we're good."

Chaz walks past us with his head down not even saying hello. Tyler follows suit. *Well, this is starting out just great.*

"I've missed you." Jenna smiles and gives me a hug.

I squeeze her back. "I've really missed you too. It's nice to know at least one person doesn't hate me." I look down at the ground.

"No one hates you. It always ends up a heated discussion when there's too much testosterone in the room." She rolls her eyes.

Jenna and I follow the guys downstairs into the finished basement. They're all sitting on the couch as we walk in, completely silent. *God, I hope this doesn't turn ugly.*

"We're all here so let's get this shit settled." Van rises from the couch and begins pacing around the room. "I know you're all pissed at me for blowing off the show but I had no other option. Sometimes we have other obligations."

"Are you fucking serious man?" Chaz leaps up, his hands clenched and his knuckles white. "Your obligation should be to us, your friends and your band. You fucked us all over for your chick." He grinds his teeth. "Marcus is married and he doesn't even pull that shit."

Here we go. I'm the evil one who's sabotaging the band.

"Chaz, don't be an asshole. I have obligations to the band and to Lexie. She doesn't ask me for much, so when she needs me to do something for her, I'm doing it." Vans face flushes and his hands ball into fists.

"I think all of our lives were better before you met her. Women are everyone's downfall." Chaz points his finger right at me as he mutters the words. The vein above his temple throbs.

"Watch your fucking mouth!" Van charges Chaz, shoving him hard. Rushing forward, he grips Chaz's T-shirt and pushes him once more, holding him against the wall. Crimson fire spreads across Van's face and his lips pull back, baring his teeth. His arms tremble, right down to his pure white knuckles. He pulls one arm back, keeping Chaz pinned against the wall with the other.

I cover my face with my hands, tears stream down my cheeks. They're going to kill each other and it's all my fault.

Marcus steps firmly in between them. "Stop! You two are acting like idiots." He holds his arms out, separating them the best he can. "You can be committed to the band and to your girl. I do it every day so I get it."

"Yeah man, you chose the chick over us." Chaz jerks his arms and breaks free from Van's death grip.

Van pushes Chaz's shoulder and points his finger in Chaz's face. "Don't make me choose. It will always be her." He steps back.

"You're such a pussy. You would never say something like that a year ago." Chaz throws his hands in the air.

"Fuck you! You don't even know what you're talking about." Van storms toward Chaz again, his lips flatten into a hard line.

This is going nowhere. I jump in front of Van right before he reaches Chaz and throw my arms around his neck. He exhales deeply, a low growl in his throat, and wraps his arms around my back. The ferocious beating of his heart pounds through his chest as he holds me tight. I loosen my hold and take a step back.

"Listen everyone. I know this is my fault and I'm sorry. I asked Van to be my date for my sister's wedding last month. Before he committed, he checked the schedule to make sure you guys weren't playing. If he cancelled he would have looked undependable and irresponsible to my whole family. Since the show was last minute he decided to keep his commitment to me. I only have one sister and this was her wedding. It's over and done with. Nothing like this should come up again but if it does, I promise to talk to all of you about it and we'll make a decision that's best." My hands are shaking as ten eyes stare at me.

"Please, the decision that's best will always be what you want. You women are all the same. You have us by the balls and if we don't do what you want, you threaten us." Chaz rubs his hand over his head and pinches his lips together.

"That's the stupidest thing I've ever heard. You're such an ass. If you've ever even *had* a girlfriend you'd know that isn't true." Jenna glares at Chaz, shaking her head. "Lexie is trying to make things right so we can prevent this from happening again. Give her a break, asshole." She folds her arms across her chest.

Ah, there's the Jenna that I know and love.

"Don't you morons realize that this show would've been huge for us? Opening for Cryptic Mayhem is like playing at the White House for bands like us. We passed it up because Van had a wedding? That's so fucked up I can barely believe it myself." Chaz pinches the bridge of his nose.

Tyler stands up and grabs a beer from the fridge. "Everyone realizes what happened. Lexie's trying to make things right. Van's back on board. What more do you want?"

Chaz rolls his eyes "I want to know that this won't happen again. I don't even have a chick and I'm suffering. All the aggravation and none of the pleasure."

"It won't happen again. I promise." I walk over to him with tears in my eyes. "I'm sorry."

He has a much easier time fighting with Van. Maybe he does have a soft spot for women.

Chaz shakes his head, finding himself unable to yell at me. "It's a shame I like you so much." He exhales loudly. "I'm holding you to that promise. Don't fuck me over."

I place my hand on Chaz's shoulder. "I won't."

"Alright, are we done fighting? I'm ready for some pizza and beer." Marcus grabs the phone.

Chaz and Van shake hands and everyone sits down on the couch. *Wow, girl fights are so much more destructive.* It's as if nothing ever happened. The guys play video games, eat pizza, and drink beer. Hmm, this is kind of like hanging out at the frat house in college.

Unfortunately, the real world awaits me. I excuse myself and go upstairs to pack my things, and a few of Van's to take to my apartment. Jenna comes up to help me.

"I'm going to miss you. I have to put up with all these guys by myself. It's like having four husbands." Jenna laughs and folds a few T-shirts. "I may have to keep a journal to hold as evidence in case I kill them." She lowers her eyebrows. "So, what happens after our tour ends? Are you staying here while the guys work on the record, or are you going to keep doing the long distance thing?"

That's the million dollar question. If I only had the answer to it. "I'm going to see how it goes when I start work and decide then." I toss my toiletries in my bag.

"You better feel sorry for me. I have to put up with a lovesick Van who has no idea what's going to happen after the tour. Ugh, I'm doomed." She rubs her hand along her temple.

Is she trying to win an Oscar? I zip my bag shut. "I don't think it'll be that bad."

"You don't have a clue how into you he is. He'd do anything for you. Are you planning on coming with us on the next tour?"

I sigh. "You're asking a lot of questions that I don't have the answers to yet. My heart tells me to run away with Van, to go on the tour, and to live happily ever after. I would love it to work out that way, but what if it doesn't?"

She grabs my arms and faces me. "I really think it will, but you need to take risks to achieve anything great in life. I took a risk and ran off with Marcus, and I love my life."

I drop my bag onto the floor and sit on the bed. "I know, but you and Marcus have a strong commitment, you were married first. I've been dating Van for about four months. I'm scared that my fairytale could be over someday and I want to make the right decision."

Jenna sits beside me and puts her hand over mine. "I can understand that. I also know that Van is head over heels in love with you and if you need some type of commitment, you can get it from him."

Is she saying what I think she's saying? "If all of that's true then we'll make it work, no matter what."

She raises her head and stares into my eyes. "I just know that I'll be at your wedding someday."

I jerk my head back and gasp, my mouth falls open. If she's waiting for me to say something she better get comfortable. It's not like I haven't thought about it, but that's a conversation I should have with Van, not Jenna.

I finish up and we head back downstairs. Van's still playing a video game when I walk into the room.

"All packed?" He rests his head against the back of the couch and turns toward me.

I glance at my watch. "Yeah. We'll need to leave in a half-hour."

He puts the game controller down and stands up. "Wow that went by fast." He grabs my hips and pulls me into a tight hug, softly kissing my lips.

"We're heading out. Meet us at Marcus's after you get back from the airport." Tyler cleans up the last few beer cans and the gang makes their way out.

My stomach rolls and a sour taste invades my mouth. No matter how many times I do it, saying goodbye never seems to get any easier.

Van sits back on the couch and pulls me backward until I plop down next to him. He eases me across the cool leather until I'm sitting on his lap.

"Here we are again. Another 'see you soon' moment." I wrap my arms around his neck and try to suppress the tears forming in my eyes.

He presses his forehead against mine. "It won't always be like this. Who knows, maybe you'll eventually stay with me. I know you said that after the tour ends we'll be together one way or another. You know you can stay here, right?" Van nibbles on his bottom lip.

"That's why I left some clothes and my toothbrush." My heart beats faster, pounding against my chest.

"You can bring all your clothes and toothbrushes here permanently." He bites at his lip, slowly lifting his eyes.

Oh God, is he suggesting we live together? I do love it here, but am I ready for that yet?

"We'll talk about everything after you finish your tour. One thing at a time." I press my lips against his, weaving my hands in his hair.

I'll have lots of time to think about our future while he's away. No need to make any rash decisions now.

He pulls away and exhales forcefully, blowing his hair around his face. "I can't wait until this tour's over." He wraps his arms around me and presses his forehead against my shoulder.

We stay in each other's arms until it's time to leave for the airport.

Time for another cheesy airport scene! We arrive at the terminal and Van walks me to my gate. We hug and kiss each other until the last possible second, then Van disappears into the crowd and I make my way to my seat.

The plane is only half full so I have a row of seats all to myself. Ah, the silence of the red eye! I stretch my legs, place my head onto a pillow, and begin to drift off to sleep. The exhaustion of the day has caught up with me and I just want to shut my mind off so I can relax. I reach into my purse for a mint. What's this? I wrinkle my brow as I pull out a box. Huh, my name's written on it, in Van's handwriting.

CHAPTER 21—REALITY

The pounding of my heart blares in my ears, cutting through the silence. My fingers shake as I glide them over the soft blue velvet. What could this be? My mouth is as dry as the desert sand. I swallow hard and stare at the small silver strip of ribbon wrapped around the box. Does this have anything to do with Jenna's comment about commitment? My stomach flutters. Since I don't have x-ray vision, it's now or never. I take a deep breath, quickly tear off the paper, and open it up. It's a key, hooked on a heart-shaped silver key chain, along with a note:

You already have the key to my heart, so I want to give you the key to my home.

Hopefully our home someday.

Nuclear energy flows throughout my body. I hold the key to my chest and close my eyes. My cheeks erupt into a smile so wide they're on fire. No chance of sleeping now. What would life be like if I live in Kansas with Van? I'd wake up every morning in a sea of purple satin, next to the most magnificent and enticing man alive; enjoy coffee on the porch swing and stare out into the endless green meadows, secluded from the rest of the world. I sink into the leather seat.

Why can't I stop time and stay with Van, in a true utopia? Reality is getting in the way of my happiness. I let out a deep sigh and press my head into the headrest. These next few weeks are going to be torture. The worst part is that I need to come to a decision soon. My stomach clenches. I want to stay with Van, but I don't want to give up this dream job. How can I have it all?

∞

"We will begin our descent, fasten all seatbelts and shut off electronic devices," the flight attendant announces, pulling me out of my deep thoughts.

I gather my belongings and head to the baggage claim. I yank my suitcase off the belt and roll it onto the concrete floor.

"Welcome home! Our apartment wasn't the same without you." Brooke lunges at me, almost knocking me over, and squeezes me tight.

I hug her back with my free arm. "Aw, I missed you too. I can't wait to get back and relax in my own bed."

Luckily, the airport is only fifteen minutes from our apartment. The short ride will come in handy when I'm dying to see Van. I let out a deep sigh, I already miss him. We pull into the driveway and make our way inside.

I roll my suitcase to my room and collapse onto my bed, letting the sheets and mattress envelop my body. Ah, I get to sleep in my own bed. I stretch out as if I'm trying to make a snow angel in the sheets.

"Jeeze, that's starting to look erotic. Should I give you and your bed a minute alone?"

I roll my eyes and sit up. "I think we're just about done."

She walks over to the bed and sits down next to me. "Now that you're back home, I want to talk to you about something."

I lower my eyebrows and turn toward her. "What's up?"

"Well, it was pretty tough staying here all alone while you were gone with Van, so Dean's been staying here with me." She bites at her lip.

My chest tightens slightly. "That's good, at least you weren't lonely."

She fidgets with her fingers and looks at the floor. "I'm hoping it'll be ok with you if he stays here permanently with us. We could split the rent three ways and I'll make sure he helps with the chores." She stares at me and waits, rubbing her fingers as she watches me.

I place my hand on her shoulder. "That's a great idea. Van will either be here or I'll be visiting him so we'll be in and out anyway."

Brooke squeals and pulls me close, hugging me tightly. "Thank you so much!" She jumps up off the bed, bouncing on her toes.

I lug my suitcase onto the bed and open it. "Don't feel obligated to watch me unpack, I'm beat anyway."

She skips off into the hallway. "We'll start fresh in the morning."

Hmm, I missed comfy sweats. I twist my hair in a ponytail and prepare for a relaxing night. Finally, I finish unpacking. My heart flutters and my face flushes as I pull the box out of my purse and attach my new key chain to my everyday key ring. Why can't I stop smiling every time I look at it? I reach for my cell phone and quickly text Van.

I'm home and exhausted. I love my key more than you know.

I pull the covers over my chest and rest my head on the pillow. My phone chimes. I dart up and check the screen.

Hope you use it soon. Miss you already.

How am I going to get through the next six weeks? It hasn't even been twenty-four hours. This bed seems so empty, like my heart. I let out a heavy sigh and sink into the mattress, trying to alleviate the dull ache in my chest. My head falls back on the pillow; I'm physically and emotionally drained. My heavy eyelids descend, covering my field of vision and allowing me to drift off to sleep.

∞

Is Brooke banging around every pot and pan we own? I rub my eyes, stretch and roll out of bed. My mouth waters as I enter the kitchen. The aroma of fresh coffee, eggs and bacon fill the air. I inhale deeply, letting the delectable scent overcome my senses.

"I figured it's been a long time since you've had a home cooked meal." Brooke whisks a bowl of scrambled eggs.

"I can't remember the last time I've eaten something homemade." I pour myself a cup of coffee, pull out one of the kitchen chairs, and take a seat.

"We should have a girls' day today. A little shopping, a mani/pedi, and some chick flicks later while you tell me your stories from the tour." She fills our plates and brings them to the table.

"Sounds great. Will Dean be included since he's our new roommate?" I bite my toast.

"He would love girls' night," she laughs, "but he's staying at his own place for now. His lease isn't up until October." She nibbles on a piece of bacon. "I'll stay at his place when Van comes to visit. My virgin ears don't want to hear the things that may go on."

"Your ears may be your only body part that's still virgin." I wink.

Brooke rolls her eyes and throws a potholder at me.

∞

The steam from the shower perks me up, invigorating my senses. I dry off and slip my Devil's Garden T-shirt over my head, deeply inhaling as I pull it down over my body. Goosebumps form from Van's scent, still locked in its fibers.

Brooke should advise celebrities on their fashion choices! I plop a pile of clothes on the checkout counter. Wow, five new outfits that I can mix and match to make ten different looks, plus a gray business dress that'll be perfect for my meeting with Owen Jenkins tomorrow. Do I need anything else?

We continue down the sidewalk, glancing in the enormous storefront windows. How convenient, a high end lingerie store. My eyes travel across the room as we walk inside. Dozens of racks grace the walls of the quaint space and feature every style imaginable. What should I choose to make a lasting impression?

We root through the racks, trying to find the perfect item. I stop and pick up a velvet hanger holding a red and black lace bra with rhinestones and matching panties, a black garter belt, and red thigh high stockings with black musical notes on them.

"Perfect!"

Brooke's eyes widen. "Rocker chic and sexy. You need to buy it."

Amazing, I manage to acquire a new wardrobe for work and some sexy extras for my unforgettable nights with Van. *What's he doing right about now?* I glance at my watch. It's three o'clock. *What time zone is he in today?* Thank God Jenna is so good at managing the groupies. I shake my head, trying to block those particular thoughts from my mind as we enter the spa.

It's great to be pampered. I haven't had the luxury of a mani/pedi in quite a while. "This is just what I needed." I lean back in the massage chair and close my eyes.

"The day is still young."

We walk down the strip, showing off our crimson nails, and browse through a few more stores. Evening is approaching. I twirl my fingers around my hair. *It is almost time for Van to hit the stage.* A thickness forms in my throat and I lower my gaze. Brooke is trying so hard to make the day special for us and my mind is somewhere else entirely. What kind of friend am I?

"Let's head home for phase two of our fun day." Brooke opens the car door and slides into the driver's seat.

"I'm ready for more. What chick flick do you have in mind?" I pull my door shut.

She taps her fingertips on the steering wheel. "Hmm, how about *Pretty Woman* followed by *Thelma and Louise?*"

I chuckle. "Hookers and outlaws. Perfect."

Time to change into our sweats and make popcorn. We lay a blanket on the floor and lounge in front of the TV, picnic style. Emptiness fills the pit of my stomach. *Does everything have to remind me of Van?*

"I got some cheap champagne for us to commemorate the occasion." Brooke pours some bubbly into two plastic cups and hands one to me. "To a new chapter of our lives filled with more wonderful and crazy adventures!"

We clink our plastic cups and sip the champagne. The bubbles tickle my nose. I guess I'm a cheap date. I've always preferred sweet wines and champagnes to the dry ones that cost a fortune.

"Speaking of new chapters in our lives, are you excited about starting your new job?" She shoves some popcorn into her mouth.

I sigh and my stomach rolls. "Excited but nervous. I hate not knowing what to expect. Plus, my boss is so confident, it's intimidating." I twirl my hair around my fingers.

"Seriously? Your boyfriend is a rock star. If he doesn't intimidate you, no one should." She sips more champagne. "What's going to happen with you guys now?"

How am I going to find the answer to that question? I take a deep breath. "I have to make a decision when his tour ends. He wants me to move in with him in Kansas while he works on his new record, and then join him on another tour."

"Wow, that's big." Brooke pulls me into a side hug. "I don't want to lose you, but I want to see you happy."

Tears well up in my eyes. I close them and rest my head on her shoulder. "I don't want to lose me either. I did go to college and earn a degree that I'd like to use."

"You'll know what's right when the time comes. Don't over-think everything and you'll find your answer." She rubs my shoulder.

"You're right." I wipe a stray tear from my eye and sit back up. "Enough of this serious talk; let's get back to girls' night."

The champagne is going down way too smooth. I rub my eyes, trying to clear my fuzzy vision. Of course I drank more than I should have; time to call it a night and get some rest before my meeting tomorrow. I glance at the clock. Almost midnight. I dial Van's number, he should be finished entertaining his fans by now. My heart skips a beat when he answers on the first ring.

"Hey."

"How was the show tonight?"

"Not even close to as good as when you're here."

I blush and my cheeks lift into an ear to ear smile. "Can't wait till Saturday."

"My ticket's booked. I'll be there at noon. I miss seeing those four walls of your apartment."

My body tingles as his sexy voice electrifies me. "You may only see the four walls of my bedroom."

"Even better."

Goosebumps spread across my skin. "My meeting's early tomorrow morning but I had to hear your voice before I go to bed."

"Good luck. I love you."

"I love you too. Goodnight."

∞

I open my eyes and glance at the clock, two minutes left before my alarm sounds. I quickly shut it off, stretch, and gaze out the window. Ah, a clear, sunny, beautiful day; not a cloud in the sky, just an endless view of blue. *Maybe this picture-perfect scene is an indication of the rest of my day.* Let the beauty routine begin. My new gray business dress looks great with my simple jewelry and black pumps.

I pull into the Global Inc. parkade and step into the reception area. A blond sits behind the desk, her eyes following my every movement. My heart races as I walk up to her. *Why am I so jumpy?*

I clear my throat. "Hello, I'm Alexis Waters. I have a ten a.m. meeting with Owen Jenkins."

"Hello Alexis, Mr. Jenkins is expecting you. Please go right in." She points toward a dark wooden door.

I walk into the large office as my boss begins to walk toward me.

"Alexis, hello again. Please, have a seat." He gestures toward a large office chair and sits behind his desk.

I pat down my skirt and lower myself onto the cool leather chair.

"Well Alexis, I hope you've enjoyed your summer. I'm looking forward to working with you. Do you have any questions about the position you will be starting on Monday?" He swivels his chair toward me and taps his pen on his desk.

I twirl my fingers around my hair. "No, Owen. I think you explained everything to me the last time we met. I hope it's ok to ask questions after I start. I may have some then." In reality I only need the answer to one burning question.

"Of course, please ask me anything," he says as he grabs a folder from his desk and starts rummaging through the pages. "I'm sure you know Global Inc. represents a variety of products, from soft drinks to cars. I'm working on a project now which involves marketing and advertising for a jewelry line. I'm hoping to work on this project with you. You can show me what you've learned in college and I will teach you Global Inc.'s way of marketing a product for the masses."

Wait, am I hearing him right? This is a *huge* opportunity. New graduates seldom get to work on a project like this one. Maybe I really do have a prosperous future at Global Inc.

My eyes widen. "That sounds wonderful, Owen! Thank you for this opportunity. I won't let you down."

"Alexis, I'm a good judge of character. I can tell you won't disappoint. Your hours will be eight-thirty to four-thirty but keep in mind that we may have to attend some presentations and business dinners." He closes the file and drops it on his desk.

"Thank you again, Owen. I look forward to working with you." I stand up and shake his hand.

Owen leads me out of the office by placing his hand in the small of my back. *Ugh, that's kind of creepy.* I shake it off. *Have I just landed my dream job? Wait until I tell Brooke!*

"I'm so happy for you!" Brooke pulls me into a hug. "We definitely have to celebrate. I work late Friday, but when I get out we're heading to Wildcats."

I can't contain the smile on my face. "It's a date." I bounce on my toes.

We both jump up and down and squeal.

Well, I better get my apartment back to normal. If I can live out of two suitcases for months, I can definitely organize this place. I set out all of my business clothes for the work week right behind my sexy new lingerie for the weekend. Saturday night will be unforgettable!

I clean up my room and do some chores around the apartment. Jeeze, I'm a horrible roommate. I left poor Brooke with all the work while I was touring with Van.

On tour, I didn't have to do anything other than wash my clothes. I didn't even have to make a bed. As I vacuum and clean the bathroom, I desperately miss those days. Yep, just another perk of living with Van in Kansas.

∞

It is almost five o'clock Friday; time to start getting ready for the night's celebration. I tie my black halter dress around my neck and pair it with high heeled boots. My brown curls hang down over my shoulders. I quickly glance in the mirror. Umm, my make-up is way too heavy; I tone it down a bit. No concerts tonight, just a college bar that we've been to many times over the past four years. Nothing elaborate, just a fun night with great friends at a familiar place. I step out of my room just as Brooke walks in from work.

"Wow, you look hot! I just need to freshen up and we'll be on our way." She tosses her purse on the kitchen table and high-tails it to her room.

"No hurry, we've got all night."

There are lots of reasons to celebrate tonight. Lightness fills my chest and the heat of the sun radiates through my body. In less than twenty-four hours I'll have Van in my arms. My heart beats faster. Wait until I get my hands on him.

Beep beep. I gasp and jerk my head back as the noise pulls me back into reality. Dean's here to pick us up.

Brooke hops out of her room, trying to put her shoe on as she walks.

I laugh. "If you keep that up, we'll be at the hospital instead of the bar."

"I always think I have more time than I really do," Brooke mutters as she grabs her purse and heads outside.

Yeah, I know exactly what she means.

Wildcat's is hopping tonight. I turn sideways and trudge through the crowd, brushing against the sea of bodies. Dean snags a table by the stage. Cool! An eighties band is playing.

"We need nourishment before we hit the dance floor." Brooke looks over the menu that we should have memorized for all the times we've been here.

"Let's go old school like we used to and split a bunch of appetizers," Dean suggests, looking over her shoulder.

"You've got a smart man." I wink.

Brooke gives Dean a quick kiss on the cheek. "I definitely do."

"Be right back girls." He heads to the bar as the waitress takes our order and returns with a small tray of shots. "Ready to celebrate?" He passes us each a drink and raises his shot glass. "First, an apple pie shot to commemorate Lexie's new job and achieving her *all American dream.*"

We burst out laughing. Is Dean really attempting to tie his choice of drinks to the reason for our celebration? He's actually doing a pretty good job. How clever. We compose ourselves, hold up our glasses, and down our shots.

"Next is a layered astro-pop shot, to commemorate Brooke and me moving in together and taking our relationship to the next level."

We both laugh again as we ponder Dean's analogy, then we down shot number two.

Good thing Dean's used to our appetites. We devour our food as soon as it hits the table while the lights brighten on the stage. The drum beat vibrates in my chest, followed by the guitar's catchy melody. Ah, some familiar tunes. Time to let our hair down and celebrate!

I glance around the room as I twirl my body around the dance floor. My muscles freeze. Please, let my eyes be playing tricks on me! I rub them and refocus. Nope, just my luck. Jesse and the blond he cheated on me with are at the table next to ours. Dean waves hello, but Brooke and I don't even give him a second look. Oh crap! He spots me, staring at my face as he gropes the blond, making out with her.

"He's the epitome of an asshole. Like I really give a shit what he does." I roll my eyes and shake my head.

Really? He's opening his eyes to see if I'm watching him. Jeeze, someone has issues; I know for a fact he's not fond of PDA but if he wants to put a show on for me, more power to him. I'm just counting down the seconds until noon.

"You ready to get out of here? It's almost two a.m. and you have a big day tomorrow." Brooke tugs at my arm, leading me toward the door.

"Yep, I'll need all the rest I can get." I stand tall with my head held high and walk toward the door, my heels click against the concrete floor.

Finally, time to hit the sheets and sleep. Morning will be here soon, thank God. I set my alarm for ten a.m. and lay out my red dress and hot new lingerie. Everything has to be perfect. Why can't I stop giggling? I lay and watch the clock as time passes slowly. Finally, I drift off.

The alarm sounds like an angel's choir. I leap out of bed and head for the shower. After a few final touches, I grab my keys and run out the door.

∞

Luck is on my side, I'm a half-hour early and Van's flight is on time. I twirl my fingers around my hair as I stare at the gate. Seconds seem like hours. Finally! The flight attendant grips the intercom and makes her announcement. Flight 947 has arrived! My heart races and my hands shake. Why am I so jittery? Van and I are far from strangers. The first few passengers walk out of the gate. My heart pounds out of my chest and my palms sweat. I wipe them against my dress, take a deep breath, and continue to stare.

Van runs his hand through his hair as he walks out of the gate. He stops for a minute glancing around the terminal, and then spots me. I'm frozen. A smile forms and spreads across my face as our eyes lock. He walks up to me, drops his bag at his feet, and grabs my face with both of his hands. I let out a low moan as he steps forward and slams his lips into mine. I pull him close, gripping the hem of his T-shirt with both my hands. My heart palpates as the familiar tingles surge through my body. I blush when a few people clap.

Van pulls away, picks up his bag and wraps his arm around me. "You're certainly a sight for sore eyes. I can barely control myself."

"Good thing we won't have to control ourselves for much longer." I place my head on his shoulder and slide my arm around his waist, trying to get as close to him as possible as we walk out of the airport.

"I know this isn't nearly as luxurious as a limo, but *your* chariot awaits." I point at my powder blue used Chevy and chuckle.

"The heartbeat of America." Van slides into the passenger side while I start the car. He touches my keychain, noticing the addition. "I hope you need this one a lot." He glides his hand across the keys to his house key.

"One of my favorite places to be." I brush my fingertips along Van's thigh. *God, it's great to touch his body.*

Apparently it's possible to make the short ride from the airport even shorter. I step on the gas and breathe deeply, trying to slow my heart rate. Van rests his head back against the headrest and exhales deeply. He turns his head toward me, his eyes burning through my flesh. I gaze into the emerald hue that can bring me to my knees, and then my eyes descend to the dark gray shirt clinging to every muscle in his torso. A bead of sweat forms on my forehead. *Is it hot in here?*

He runs his hands down against his jeans. *Oh, that lucky fabric!* I'm in severe withdrawal. The heat radiating off my body can rival a thousand suns. Is it wrong to pull over and have my way with him?

At last, we're here. The driveway resembles the Garden of Eden. I slam on the brakes and jerk the shifter into park. "We're here. You ready to come inside?"

"I'm more than ready." Van clutches his bag and high-tails it to my front door.

Damn it! I fumble with the keys. My hands shake uncontrollably. I take a deep breath and steady them, finally unlocking the door. I take Van's hand and guide him past the kitchen and living room and directly into my bedroom.

"Make yourself at home." I close the door behind us.

"Oh, I plan to." He drops his bag to the floor and places his hands on my waist, pulling himself against me.

My breathing is erratic. He presses harder, growing as we kiss. Can that thick denim fabric keep him from bursting through it? He slides his arms up to my neck, tugging at my zipper. He pulls down the thin metal tab and lets the dress fall to the floor, revealing my new undergarments.

"Sorry if I stare, but I want to burn this image into my mind." He takes a step back.

"You never have to apologize for staring at what's yours."

I pull my bra straps down so they're hanging over my arms then unhook my bra, letting it fall to the floor. His lips part and he continues to stare. I kick off my heels and walk toward him. Goosebumps erupt over every inch of my body. My heart pounds and my skin becomes ultra-sensitive. I run my fingers along the hem of his shirt and yank it over his head. God, his body is perfect. I gently glide my fingers down his chest and abs, following all the peaks and valleys, stopping at the waist of his jeans. He reaches up and caresses my breasts, rubbing and fondling them in exceptional ways. I tug at the button of his jeans, finally releasing him from the thick denim fabric and slide my hand over the front, rubbing and grabbing every inch of him. *How can someone be so impressive?*

I walk backwards, urging Van toward me, until the edge of the mattress meets my legs. He gently eases me onto the bed, removing my underwear and garter belt, and kicking off his jeans in one smooth motion. His talents are endless.

My body is hot. I moan as he presses against me, causing me to move my hips back and forth to allow him to enter me. I gasp and groan in ecstasy as he fills me, igniting sparks through my body. We move at a slow, steady pace, and gradually increase. Wow, my headboard is really banging against the wall. What a glorious sound!

I groan, yelling out Van's name as I climax. I exhale, catching my breath and roll on top of him. He deserves this same pleasure.

Our animal instincts take over, leading us to explore different positions and find new ways to pleasure each other. I find my release once more before he finds his. We're both dripping with sweat as we lay on the bed, catching our breath.

"You never cease to amaze me, and you're much wilder than I give you credit for." He runs his hand through his sweaty hair, slicking it back.

I bite my lip and wink. "I can be as wild as you want me to be."

"If all of our reunions are this great, maybe the next few weeks won't be so bad." He rolls me over on top of him, gently kissing my lips.

I raise my eyebrows "Next one might be better."

"I don't know if that's even possible." He grazes his fingers along my back.

We hold each other for a while, making small talk about the tour and the details of my new job. I sigh, two more weeks until I see Van again. It sucks that he has shows the next few weekends.

"Next time we see each other we'll be at the halfway point, only three more weeks until my tour ends." He rubs his nose along my neck, and then gently nibbles my ear.

A plethora of tingles engulf my body. "Hopefully I'm busy at work these next two weeks so my mind can be occupied with something other than missing you."

"It's not possible to get you off my mind." He runs his tongue along my lips.

Time for round two. Umm, it's probably better just to stay in bed.

We certainly worked up an appetite. Van throws on jeans and greets the pizza delivery man at the door.

"Next time, I'll make sure there's food in the house." I slide up on the bed.

Van places the pizza box between us and hands me a beer. "I'd rather order in; why spend all that time cooking when we could be here instead?" He twists off the cap and takes a slug.

"You've got a point there." I raise my eyebrows and pull a slice from the box.

He sets down his beer and rubs his hand on my thigh. "So, when do you plan on using your new key?"

There goes my appetite. My mouth becomes dry and my stomach flutters. Ugh, please don't let this turn into an in-depth discussion. "After the tour ends. It's easier for you to come here than it is for both of us to go to your house." I slug my beer.

"Yeah, that makes sense." He bites his pizza. "My tour ends on October 12th so I'll make sure you have a plane ticket to Kansas."

"Make sure there's plenty of food in your house because I'm not leaving those satin sheets." I reach over, kissing Van's neck, then ear, gently rubbing my tongue across his lobe.

"The fridge will be stocked." He places the pizza box onto the floor, leans over, and again gives me the pleasure only he can provide.

∞

I open my eyes and glance at the clock. Oh my God, its noon. Wow, I must have been exhausted from the night's festivities. Van's phone rings and buzzes, sliding across the night stand. He answers.

"It's Jenna for you." He stretches and rubs his eyes.

I sit up and hold it to my ear. "Hello?"

"Hey stranger, I want to talk to you really quick. I'm sure you're preoccupied."

"Actually, I am." I run my hand up and down Van's arm.

"I'm sure. Anyway, I want to plan a welcome home party for the guys when their tour ends. Are you coming to Kansas? Just say yes or no."

"Yes."

"Great. I'll fill you in on the details later."

"I'll talk to you soon Jenna." I hand the phone back to Van. *So much for spending my next trip to Kansas in Van's bed.*

He brushes his hand against my cheek. "I hate to say it, but we better get moving. My flight is at two."

I sigh and lower my head. "Ok. I guess you're right."

Why can't I erase this frown from my face? I can be depressed after Van leaves. No need to ruin these last few minutes. This will be the longest time we've ever been separated. *How am I going to do it?*

Van lifts my chin. "Don't look so sad. Next time we see each other, we'll be halfway through this." He gently slides his lips across mine. "Please start thinking about what you want to do. October will be here before you know it."

I nod.

Good ole, déjà vu. We head through the terminal and to the gate. I squeeze Van with all my might, kissing him and running my hands over his perfect body. Does security see me? If they do I may be arrested. I wave and watch him disappear through the gate as the final boarding call is announced.

Tears well up in my eyes, flowing down my cheeks on the short drive home; I can't be without Van! This is torture. How much more can I endure? What if I give up this dream job and he decides he doesn't want me? It seems like that wouldn't happen in a million years, but I don't have the best of luck with relationships. I wipe my eyes and take a deep breath as I park in the driveway. There's only one person that will understand. I dial the phone. Please be alone Jenna!

CHAPTER 22—UNCERTAINTY

"Jenna Crane, party planner extraordinaire."

I sniffle and swallow hard. "You got a minute?"

"What's wrong? Am I going to have to beat Van senseless when he gets back?"

I sigh and wipe the tears from my face. "I'm just having a hard time being apart from him."

"I know it sucks, but pretty soon you'll be together. Maybe we'll plan something fun for Halloween."

I clear my throat, trying to hide the fact that I'm starting to cry. "I'm nervous. I just landed this dream job which I'll have to quit if I move to Kansas. What if he decides he doesn't want to be with me anymore? Then I'm left with no job, no friends or family around, and nowhere to live."

"Wow, don't hold back the theatrics," she pauses, "I'm only kidding, I understand. I never did the college thing, but I did drop everything to be with Marcus. It happened to be the best decision of my life, but you need to do what's best for you. Don't worry about Van breaking up with you. He's like a lost puppy. It's actually pretty pathetic. I've never seen him like this before."

A small smile creeps over my face. "Is it wrong that I'm a little happy about that?"

Jenna chuckles. "You're a smart, independent woman. You can probably land a dream job any place you go. Did you talk about all of this with him?"

"I don't want to bring it up until I decide what to do. It's a big decision." I twirl my fingers around my hair.

"You've already got matching tattoos and a house key and I know you can get any other commitments you need from him. He really, truly loves you."

My smile widens. "Thanks Jenna, I appreciate the pep talk. It's what I needed to hear. I miss you. I'm sure the party you plan for the guys will be epic."

"I really miss you too. The party will be way over the top. I'll fill you in on all the details."

I hang up the phone and wipe a few stray tears from my eyes. *What am I thinking?* I didn't even start working yet and I'm already acting like I've landed the best job in the world. What if I hate the job? I need to wait and see how everything plays out before I stress myself. I guess I needed to hear it from someone else.

I take a deep breath and shake my head. Ok, time to focus. I need to clear my head and catch up on some chores. *Have I really neglected the laundry for this long?* I stare at my overflowing hamper.

∞

Finally, all finished! I push the dresser drawer closed and collapse onto my bed. The soft cotton sheets envelop my body. I press my head onto the pillow, inhaling deeply. Mmm. The aroma of Van is imbedded in the fibers. I breathe in deeper, trying to capture his essence. These next three weeks without him are going to kill me. What did I do to deserve this torture? My cell phone will be my lifeline, the only connection I'll have to the one I love. I exhale deeply and close my eyes. He's the last thing I think about before I go to bed and the first thing on my mind when I wake up. No doubt, Van Sinclair is my one and only soul mate.

The alarm sounds, jolting my body awake. I rub my eyes and launch myself out of bed and into the shower. First impressions can make or break you. The warm water trickles down, soothing my nerves as it consumes my body.

I wrap my hair in a towel and proceed to the closet. *What should I wear?* Uh huh, I pull out my black pencil skirt with a thin belt, a gray blouse, and a black blazer. Perfect! Some chunky silver jewelry and I'm all set. Professional, with an edgy flair.

Ding dong.

Who could that be? My heels click across the tile floor. I pull open the door and find a large bouquet of pink and white roses; the note attached reads:

Have a great first day. Love, Van

A few tears escape my eyes as I inhale the enchanting fragrance of the fresh cut roses. Ah, Van's a romantic at heart, even if he doesn't realize it. My fingers dance across the buttons as I send him a quick text.

Thanks for the flowers. So far my day is perfect!

I'm twenty minutes early, so I take a slow walk to Owen Jenkins's office, trying to soak in the golden rays of sun before I enter the building. My heart beats faster as I wait in the reception area. My palms are actually starting to sweat. I quickly run my hands down my skirt. Owen walks toward me carrying a newspaper.

"Good morning, Alexis. It's nice to know you're punctual. Please, come inside and I'll brief you on our plans for the day."

I follow Owen into his office and breathe in the aroma of leather and wood. My eyes travel across the impeccably organized space and scan the room for a place to lay my purse. I never want to be too far away from my cell phone. "Is there somewhere special I should leave my personal items?"

He picks up a file from his desktop. "You can leave anything you need on the chair. No one comes inside my office unless I'm with them so it will be safe."

I smile shyly and place my blazer and purse onto the hard leather chair.

"Ok, Alexis. We have a twelve thirty lunch meeting today with representatives from American Gemstones. Afterward, we will discuss our marketing plan and brainstorm some advertising ideas." He closes the folder and sits down at his desk.

"Great. I'm excited to get started. What shall I do until lunch?" I fidget with my fingers.

He delves through a stack of papers on his desk. "Get us some coffees and we can look over the files. I'll bring you up to speed on what was done so far."

I twirl my fingers around my hair. "How do you like your coffee?"

He lifts his eyes. "No sugar, a little cream."

I take a few steps backwards, turn and head to the reception area. The coffee sloshes right up to the rim of the cup. I steady my hands to the best of my ability and proceed forward. The secretary chews on her pen and watches me as I make my way back to the office. She's young, I would guess around twenty, beautiful and blond. *Huh, she must be new, I hadn't seen her the last time I visited Global Inc.* At least we have something in common.

"Hi. Sorry I didn't get a chance to introduce myself earlier. I'm Alexis Waters and today is my first day."

She drops the pen and smiles. "Hi, I think we spoke on the phone. I'm Simone. I've only been here a few months myself. Good luck on your first day."

"Thanks." I continue my journey to Owen's office desperately trying not to spill any coffee on my way. *Note to self, don't fill the cups to the top when you're walking in heels.*

"Alexis, I've outlined the main points of this account for you. American Gemstone has hired Global Inc. to create an advertising and marketing plan for their new line of yellow diamonds. Our job will be to filter the ideas of the marketing and advertising teams and come up with a business plan in the hopes of a more permanent contract." He takes his cup of coffee and sets it on his desk.

Once again, I'm way out of my league. *Well, he doesn't need to know that.* I tilt my head back and look him directly in the eye. "It sounds both interesting and challenging. I'm thrilled to be a part of it." I pat down my skirt with my free hand and sit in the sturdy leather chair.

He sips his coffee. "Brian from advertising and Marla from marketing will be here at ten to brief us on their ideas thus far. They will also be joining our lunch meeting with the American Gemstone reps. Right now, I'd like you to read over the outline so you're prepared. I'll be back." He hands me the paperwork, takes a few files, and leaves the office.

Wow, I'm really part of this team. How did that happen? The other new graduates are working in the mailroom. *Please let me keep doing whatever it is that got me here.*

I focus on the paperwork so I'll be well prepared for everything that we may discuss.

Footsteps click on the hardwood floor as Brian and Marla walk into the office.

I lift my head and smile. "Hello, I'm Alexis Waters."

"I'm Brian, and this is Marla. We'll take cream and sugar in our coffees." Brian flips through the papers in his file as if I'm invisible.

Owen walks into the office sipping his coffee. "Ah, I see you've met Alexis. She'll be joining our team."

Marla and Brian jerk their heads back in unison and look at each other, their eyes wide.

"My apologies, Alexis." Brian slightly shrugs his shoulders and turns away from me. "Owen, our slogan is: *American Gemstone's Yellow Diamonds: Forever Exceptional,*

Forever Chic. We plan to market with a commercial, magazine ads, internet ads, and billboard advertising."

"Great job! I have a short business meeting with our California office so I'll see the three of you at Antonio's at twelve-thirty." Owen glances at his watch, and rushes out of the office.

"Sounds like a great campaign. I'm excited to be working with the two of you. This is a dream job so far." I play with the corner of the file folder which is resting in my lap.

"Alexis, how long have you been working with Global Inc.?" Brian asked as he flips through the pages of the file.

"This is my first day."

Marla chokes on her coffee, spilling a little on the floor. "I'm sorry, it's just that I've worked for this company for eight years and this is the first account I've worked on at this level. Were you a prodigy in college?"

My face heats and my stomach hardens. "No, I guess I'm just lucky." I twirl my fingers around my hair.

Marla opens her mouth to say something more but quickly closes it.

Great! My coworkers can't comprehend how I landed this position either. I sigh. Oh well, I'm here so I'm going to do the best job I can.

Is it possible to learn this proposal before lunchtime? Noon is here way too fast. Thank God Marla offered to drive. The reps from American Gemstone wouldn't be too impressed with their advertising team stepping out of a beat up Chevy.

∞

The scent of garlic bread and pasta fills the air of the high end Italian restaurant. The reps from American

Gemstone are pleased with the advertising and marketing strategies and want a full presentation by Friday. How exciting!

We return to Global Inc. for a quick follow-up meeting.

"Great job everyone! We'll need a full presentation by Thursday so we have time to make revisions. I hope you're all ready to burn the midnight oil." Owen hands a file folder to each of us.

∞

I drop an overabundance of paperwork on the desk in my room. *Is it possible to read and organize these files before our deadline?* My mouth moves a mile a minute as I relive my exciting day for Brooke. I calm myself before calling Van to fill him in on my news. Damn, straight to voicemail. Hearing his voice makes my body tingle. God I miss him. Good thing I'm so busy with work. I gather all my paperwork and start reading through the documents. My phone chimes.

I'm so proud of my brilliant girlfriend.

Aw, he's the sweetest man in the world. This business opportunity is exciting, but it's nothing compared to the thought of getting my hands on Van. My heart races as I picture his perfect body. My fingers ache. Why can't he be here with me right now? There's no cure for Van Sinclair withdrawal.

I shake my head and regain focus. I need to read through the paperwork and familiarize myself with this whole process. It's a shame; I learned more about business in the last twenty-four hours than I did during my four years of college. Time sure flies when you're working seventy hours a week.

We nail our presentation. Now we have to elaborate on the financials and time frame for executing the plan.

Our next presentation is scheduled for Wednesday, so it's another long work week for me. At least the long hours keep my mind occupied. I sigh and lay back onto my bed. Van and I haven't talked much lately. *Ah, he'll be in my arms Friday.* It's like an eternity. I reach for my phone and dial his number. Did I calculate the time change right?

"Hello stranger."

"Hi." Ah, two simple words and my heart is about to beat out of my chest.

"So, how's the corporate world?"

"Great! We have another presentation. I think it'll be the last one for this account." I sink my head into the pillow.

"We can celebrate Friday. We're halfway through?"

"I know, thank God." Emptiness fills the pit of my stomach. I need to figure out my plans for the future soon.

"Gotta go, we're about to hit the stage. Love you."

"Love you too."

My face erupts in a cheek to cheek smile. What can I do to make this visit special? Hmm, I'm coming up empty. Maybe I used all of my creative energy on the diamond account. I rub my eyes and yawn. Who knows, an idea may come to me in my sleep.

"Hey, Alexis," Simone stops me before I make it into the office.

"Simone, please call me Lexie." I hold my files to my chest and turn toward her.

"A bunch of us are going to Martini's, the new cocktail bar, after work on Friday. It's kind of a tradition to celebrate after we finish an account. You in?"

I nod. "My boyfriend's coming in to see me so I'll have him meet me there."

"You'll have to fill me in about this boyfriend." She raises her eyebrows.

I chuckle. "Hey, should I invite Brian, Marla, and Owen?"

She shrugs. "You can but Owen never comes so don't take it personally."

My fingers race over the buttons of my cell phone on my way into the office. I give Van a quick text about Martini's before I step all the way inside. Brian and Marla are already reading through some paperwork.

"Alexis, good morning. I'm assigning each of us a piece of this presentation to ensure it's ready. You will handle the PR planning, Brian will take slogan marketing, and Marla will manage the plan of action. I'll take care of the financials."

My phone chimes before I have a chance to silence it.

"Do you need to get that?" Owen tilts his head to the side and purses his lips.

"Sorry. I'll shut it off." My face flushes and I look down.

"Brian and Marla, you two can get organized and then work together. Alexis and I will do the same."

Apparently, all those business worksheets and practice accounts I've worked on in college have come in handy. My presentation is professional and detailed, outlining the PR needed for this account, how to achieve it, and a time frame to our goal. I step out of the office to refill our coffees and quickly check my phone, scrolling for the text Van sent earlier.

I'll take a cab to the bar. We'll have a celebration of our own later ;)

My muscles quiver and my stomach flutters; I quickly text back.

**Can't wait to see you. Gotta get back to work. Love
you** ☺

Thank God I'm used to eating on the road. My dinner
consists of takeout in Owen's office. Jeeze, we've been
working for hours on end. I clench my stomach, trying to
suppress the loud growls. I grab my carton from the desk
and rip it open. Mmm. I take a deep breath and inhale the
sweet scent of chicken and broccoli.

Owen scoots his chair closer to mine. "We may be
dining with clients of different cultures. It's always a
compliment to embrace their ways." He hands me a set of
chop sticks.

Great, now I even have to work hard to eat. I tear open
the paper and separate the chop sticks. I place them
between my fingers and thumb, desperately trying to create
a uniform rhythm. No such luck. Three tries and I can't
even pick up a grain of rice. I huff.

Owen sweeps my hair behind my shoulder and moves
even closer. His soft breath blows a few stray strands
around my neck. He slides his hand over mine and adjusts
the wooden pieces. "Use your finger and thumb. Like this."

I lean away from him as far as I can. "Thanks, I think I
got it now."

"Alexis, you did exceptional work. I see a bright future
here for you at Global Inc." Owen rubs his hand down my
thigh as he speaks.

I grimace and shift in my chair as nausea fills my
stomach. I brush it off; maybe that's just how he is.

∞

I'm an hour early for work on Wednesday. No harm in
running through my portion of the presentation one more

time. It's flawless, definitely up to par. Rattling keys chime through the office. I turn to find Owen behind me.

"Alexis, you're early this morning." He cocks his head to the side and gazes at me from head to toe.

I swallow hard and try not to grimace. "I wanted to double check my part of the presentation. I'm all set." I twirl my fingers around my hair.

Footsteps tap through the hallway as Brian and Marla enter the reception area.

"Looks like we're all early. Wonderful, he who hesitates is lost." Owen smirks.

We gather our materials from the office and head up to the meeting room. It's way too quiet in this elevator; time to break the ice.

"Simone told me there's a party on Friday at Martini's to celebrate our successful account. She wanted to make sure you're all invited. I guess it's a tradition?"

"Yes, it is. Thank you." Owen lifts his eyes and flashes a quick smile.

He leads me out of the elevator with his hand in the small of my back. My scalp prickles causing a slight shiver to lift the hair on my neck. My stomach quivers and a sour taste invades my mouth. *Why is he so touchy-feely?*

The sun gleams through the wall to wall windows overlooking the cityscape. I stare at the fluffy clouds and light blue sky, taking in the breathtaking view. The fresh scent of the leather chairs fills the room. *Who would've thought I'd be here right out of college?* I organize and set up the materials for the meeting.

The reps from American Gemstone enter the room and take their seats at the table. I take a deep breath as the lights start to dim. It's show time. Owen pitches the presentation flawlessly, showing off his skills. He stands in front of the reps with his shoulders back and chest out, looking them directly in the eye. It's no wonder he's so successful. He could sell an Eskimo ice. Any onlooker would be mesmerized and impressed. He's in his element, a true business pioneer.

The lights brighten and the reps from American Gemstone shake everyone's hand, thanking us for our hard work. The campaign's a home run and I'm part of it! My face flushes and my eyes widen.

I skip through the door of my apartment, smiling from ear to ear, kick off my heels and pour myself a glass of wine. Here's to me! I sip it slowly, savoring the sweet flavor as a special present to myself.

∞

Finally, it's Friday! I fidget in my chair as I read the business plan for the millionth time. *Van's probably in the air on his way to me.* Lightness fills my chest and I take a deep breath. Goose bumps erupt throughout my whole body while I picture his perfectly flawless face and piercing emerald eyes. My heart races as I stare at the clock. Isn't the day over yet? It can't strike four-thirty fast enough.

"You coming to Martini's? I was hoping to meet your rocker boyfriend." Simone taps her ink pen against her desk.

"Yep, and Van's meeting me there so you're in luck."

Why is everyone so shocked that my boyfriend's a musician? I guess Simone pictured me with a man from the corporate world, as does my mom.

A neon martini glass flashes above a brick building. I push open the heavy wooden door and glance at several black leather stools surrounding a dark granite bar. The walls are illuminated with pale blue lights shaped like ice cubes, reflecting against the tan walls.

Hey, there's Brian and Marla. We push our way through the crowd of people, hoping to get a seat. No such luck; only one stool left which I offer to Simone. I don't mind standing, I sat all day and she's had a busy day at work.

"This place is great guys! Should we grab a couple of drinks and make a toast?" I glance over the martini list.

"The drinks are on me tonight, and I'm also making the toast." Owen Jenkins stands behind me, gesturing for the bartender to come over.

I hold my breath as he steps forward, less than an inch away from me.

"That's very kind of you, Mr. Jenkins. Congratulations on another success. It's wonderful that you're able to join us." Simone stares at Owen like a lost puppy.

"Yes, thank you." Owen finally catches the attention of a bartender. "I'll have a dirty martini, top shelf, two olives, and I'll be buying for all of these fine individuals tonight." He waves his finger around, motioning toward the Global Inc. employees.

Once everyone has a drink in their hand Owen raises his glass. "To another success. Thank you all for the hard work and dedication you put into this account. Here's too many more successes."

We all raise our glasses and sip our drinks. Owen brushes my leg as he orders another drink. It's like the third time in an hour. No way it's unintentional. I place my glass on the bar and swivel my stool. Lips slam against mine. I'm breathless as the smooth skin and familiar hand caressing my face sends sparks throughout my entire body. My heart's about to pound out of my chest. I reach up and tangle my hands in Van's hair. He pulls away slowly.

"God, I've missed you babe." He presses his lips against mine again.

I take a breath and focus on the flawless face in front of me. "It's been forever." I pull him into another kiss.

My rock god has returned! That was quite the entrance. I start to introduce Van to everyone when I glance over at Owen. He storms out of the bar, slamming the door hard behind him.

CHAPTER 23—IMPROPER

"That was my boss, Owen, who just left. Something must've pissed him off." I shrug.

"Yeah, I guess." Van narrows his eyes and pulls his lips into a hard line.

"Anyway, these are my friends from work," I finish the introductions while Van treats us to a second round of drinks. My self-control is drastically decreasing. I inhale deeply, taking in his sexy scent as we huddle together in the crowded bar. My heart races and my fingers ache; everything I want is standing three inches away from me. Small beads of sweat form on the back of my neck and heat floods my body.

Well, I've kept myself from ravishing him for an hour. I'm only human. "It was great hanging out with you guys, but we've got to split. See you all on Monday."

"Great to meet you all." Van follows me out the door, wrapping his arms around my waist as we walk outside. "Finally." He holds me against the side of the brick building, pressing himself against me.

The cool bricks sizzle against my hot skin. Our lips slam together, nothing but uninhabited animal passion flowing between us. My heart hammers against my chest. I grab the waist of his jeans and pull him forward, smashing him against me. Oh God, I need him. A low moan escapes from his throat. He slides his fingers beneath the hem of my shirt. Ah, skin to skin contact. Wait a minute! I don't want my co-workers to come out and see us. No need to be pegged as the office nympho.

I pull away, panting heavily. "Let's get back to my apartment. The sooner the better."

He rests his forehead against mine and catches his breath. "We'll see how fast this Chevy can go."

Van presses the gas pedal hard, running two stop signs and I'm pretty sure the speed limit isn't eighty. *Why is this ride taking so long?* Finally, he hits the brakes and jerks the car into park before coming over to my side like a true gentleman. That demeanor doesn't last long. He rips open the door and pulls me out of the car by my hips.

My breathing quickens and I'm pressed against the smooth metal side-panel. Soft lips travel over every inch of mine. My heart pounds and my nerve endings stir, like blazing sparks charring throughout my entire body. He glides his hands under my shirt, lifting it up to my bra. The cold metal sends goose bumps along my skin. I pull him as close as I can, smashing our bodies together. *He wants me just as badly as I want him.* How *can* the zipper of those jeans contain him?

Boom! Thunder roars through the night and cool drops of precipitation crash into my hot skin. Is it possible for steam to emit from my body? In a moment, we're thoroughly drenched! Thank God the rain doesn't hinder our unstoppable passion. Van lifts me up, his lips never leaving mine, and marches through the driveway and over to my apartment placing me back on my feet at the door.

My hands tremble as I fumble with the keys. Finally, I open the door. We kick off our shoes and start up right where we left off. Van scoops me up again and walks us to the bathroom. He sets me on my feet and steps back.

"I like that shirt even better when it's soaking wet." He licks his lips.

My white blouse, now see through, clings to my body. I slowly unbutton and remove it from my rain soaked skin.

"It looks even better on the floor." Van lets out a slight moan and reaches his arms around my waist, unzipping my skirt and letting it fall to the floor. "The view just keeps getting better."

I tug at the button of his jeans, finally releasing him from the constricting fabric. Our last few articles of clothing fly through the air as we rip them off each other and step into the shower. The warm water is no match for the fire burning inside me. I need Van's love now! My mouth becomes moist and adrenaline surges through my veins. I run my fingers down his chest, following the path of the trickling water down to his waist but he holds my hands and wraps my arms around him. I try to pull free, but he holds me tight. He slowly glides his tongue along my neck and breast, swirling it around my nipple. My heart is hammering and I can barely catch my breath. *Why must he drive me completely wild?*

"I can't wait any longer, I need you now." I pant and move from side to side, trying to free my hands.

"Haven't you heard that good things come to those who wait?" He holds my hands tighter.

Patience is a virtue I haven't been blessed with. I drop to my knees and wrap my mouth around him, moving my lips and tongue in an array of twists and turns.

"Oh God," Van groans and pushes me away from him. "You've waited long enough."

He lifts me up and pushes me against the wall of the shower, slamming himself against me. I moan as he enters me, my muscles quivering and twitching. I hook my leg around his waist, our bodies finding the perfect rhythm together. *How did I make it through these last three weeks?* The water hitting our flesh intensifies the electricity already flowing through me. I dig my fingers into Van's back, calling out his name as I let myself go, finding my release of pure pleasure. I pant as he continues to thrust himself hard inside me. Adrenaline rushes through my veins. I weave my fingers in his hair, gripping it firmly as desire builds within. The intensity returns with a vengeance, and I find my release again. He pushes himself deep inside of me and lets out a loud moan as he finds his.

We catch our breaths and dry off. *Is there anything in the world more amazing than Van?* My legs shake on the way to the bedroom. Van collapses on my bed. My eyes travel along the tan cotton sheets to the shirtless rock god in blue jeans, his head propped up with his elbow, and his hair slicked back, still damp from the shower. *What a breathtaking view!* I stand at the foot of the bed and stare at this beautiful man in front of me. He's all mine.

"Hey, earth to Lexie," Van says and throws a pillow at me.

I shake my head, pulling myself out of a trance as the pillow hits my arm. "Sorry, you look so damn sexy." I bite my lip.

He raises his eyebrows. "Really? Why don't you come over here and explain exactly how sexy I am, using as few words as possible?"

I run my tongue along my lips and throw the pillow back at him. "So far, I don't think we've used all that many words tonight."

Van flashes a wry smile. "Actions are better than words."

I crawl onto the bed and prop myself up, facing him. "Looks like we hit our halfway point. Are you sad the tour's almost over?"

"Are you kidding me? I can only be without you for so long." He brushes his fingertips along my arm.

A rolling flutter comes over my stomach. This conversation is destined to take a turn for the worse. "We'll be hitting those satin sheets the day your tour ends."

He moves his fingers in patterns across my hands, and then slowly lifts his eyes. "Any idea how long you'll be hitting those satin sheets with me?"

Oh no, here we go. "I guess that would be up to you." I flash a seductive smile.

"If it was up to me, we'd never leave those sheets." He places his hand on my chin and lifts it up, staring intently into my eyes. "Honestly, have you decided what you plan to do?"

Why do I always lose myself in those emerald eyes? My mouth is dry and I'm becoming faint. My heart pounds. I have to be with Van one way or another, but I love my job and I'm not quite ready to give it up. *How can I buy some more time?* "I find out the details of my new work assignment next week, Friday at the latest. Then we can make a plan, ok?"

Van exhales loudly. "Next Friday it is." His lips press into a hard line. "I need to plan my life too."

My chest tightens and I look down at the floor. Ugh, I'm probably holding back his future plans with the band. "Don't worry, we'll figure it out soon."

"I hope so." He pinches his lips together and rubs the back of his neck.

I sigh. *How am I going to save this night?* Time to use my imagination. "I promise." I kiss his cheek and slide off the side of the bed. "You hungry?"

"Sure." He shrugs, his lips still in a hard line.

"Be right back." I quickly make some sandwiches and bring them in; along with a bottle of wine, chocolate syrup, and whipped cream. "After we finish our sandwiches, I plan on getting creative with dessert."

"I prefer my dessert first," Van says, raising his eyebrows.

He sets down the sandwiches and grasps my waist, pulling me onto the bed and rolling over on top of me. My breathing becomes rapid as he pulls off my Devil's Garden T-shirt, which has become my new bedtime attire, leaving me naked and lying on the bed.

"I'm a chocolate lover." He takes the chocolate syrup and pops open the lid with his teeth.

He drizzles it over my breasts, down my belly, and onto my nether regions. Goose bumps arise as he runs his tongue slowly over my skin, licking off the chocolate from top to bottom, paying special attention to my more sensual areas. Adrenaline pumps through my blood causing me to release all of my intense energy one more time.

I catch my breath and rub my eyes, trying to get my bearings straight. *Whoa, that was intense!* Once I'm able to compose myself, I reach for the can of whipped cream.

"Everything needs to be topped off with some whipped cream." I squirt it all over Van's naked torso.

Hmm, yummy! I lick slowly and sensually, running my tongue across his chest and over his abs, until he grows enough to meet my lips. My tongue gently rolls against him, causing him to tense. He groans and his veins pulse. I continue my seduction until he calls out and I taste him over the sweet whipped cream.

We lay on the bed, sticky and completely satisfied. "I think we may need another shower." I hop off the bed and hurry to start the water.

We quickly rinse off one more time and make our way back to the bedroom.

"Sorry I didn't notice before, those sandwiches look great."

My mouth waters. "We'll need some nourishment if we plan to continue our weekend like this." I giggle.

If prison is this good I'll break every law! Who would've thought being confined for two days is pure paradise. Van and I hardly move from my bedroom as we enjoy each other, savoring every second we have. Is it even possible to get enough of one another to last us for the next three weeks? Definitely not, but it's worth a try.

Time defeats me once again. We're faced with Sunday afternoon, and I'm back at the airport bidding goodbye to Van. *Please, let this be the last time.*

∞

The alarm echoes through the room like a battle cry on Monday morning. I slam my hand around the night stand, desperately trying to reach the snooze button, but it continues to sound. I stretch and rub my eyes, finally focusing enough to shut off the alarm. I drag myself from the bed and gaze out the window upon a dreary, rainy day. *I just want to roll over and stay in bed; however, I have to work for a living.* No need to continue the fantasy, time to get ready for my day.

I wipe my feet and shake off my umbrella, fastening it in its pouch as I walk into the office. Simone is already hard at work. She hangs up the phone just as I make my way toward her desk.

"We had so much fun Friday night. Your boyfriend's great, and also easy on the eyes." Simone winks at me.

"He's the best." I blush as I relive a few moments from our weekend together. "I'm glad everyone was able to meet him. Well, with the exception of Owen."

"I can't believe he showed up. Word out on the street is that he's never shown up for an after work celebration."

I jerk my head back. "Really? He seemed like he was having a good time until he stormed out. What was that about?"

She shrugs. "Don't know, but FYI, his mood has continued into this morning so beware."

"Ugh, thanks for the heads up." I grimace and make my way into Owen's office.

Why does he look so miserable? He sits back in his chair and gazes at a few folders scattered across his desktop. He leafs through a file as I walk in.

"Good morning, Owen."

"Yes. Good morning, Alexis. It seems we're through with the American Gemstone account so from now on, you'll be working down in the mailroom with the other new hires."

My face gets hot and there's no air in my lungs. Have I been sucker punched? I gasp as my brain comprehends the words coming from Owen's mouth. "What do you mean? I don't understand. You told me you were going to teach me the ins and outs of advertising and marketing. I took this job to *avoid* working in a mail room."

Owen swivels his chair so he's looking right at me. His face is stern, his mouth in a hard line. "I believe I did teach you the ins and outs of advertising and marketing these last few weeks. Now that you know what lies ahead, you'll need to work your way up. New hires start in the mailroom, and that's where you should be. Please send my regards to your boyfriend. It's a shame we didn't get to meet." Owen reaches for his phone and goes back to work as if I'm not even in the room.

How can he do this to me? He didn't even tell me what I did wrong. My heart is racing so fast the blood is pounding in my ears. My throat is dry and my body begins to tremble. I grab my things and storm out of his office, yanking the door behind me.

Simone jumps as the metal door slams. "What happened?"

"That asshole just sent me to the mailroom. He said all new hires start there. I don't know what his problem is." My vision becomes cloudy as tears start to form. "I'll talk to you later, Simone."

She rushes over and gives me a quick hug. "Don't worry. Everything will work out."

Tears stream down my face as I proceed down the hallway to the stairs. No way am I going to be in a crowded elevator today. I wipe my eyes, take a deep breath, and walk slowly to the mailroom. *Please let me compose myself before I get there, no need for a bad impression if this is where I'm destined to be working.* I don't understand. We landed a huge account and I definitely did my share of the work. How can he just demote me?

Whoa! Wait a minute. Owen puts me on a team for a huge account on my first day, Marla and Brian are shocked that I'm already part of this type of team, Owen is constantly touching me and insisting I stay and work late with him in his office, he separates Marla and Brian onto a team so he can work alone with me, and he shows up at the bar for the first time ever and storms out when Van arrives. How could I have been so blind? Owen was trying to seduce me! Oh well, you can't always get what you want. The bastard's punishing me for resisting his advances. I guess seeing Van and I together at the bar pushed him over the edge. It all makes perfect sense now.

How do I keep getting myself into these positions with arrogant men? It's like déjà vu, except Jesse isn't even close to as powerful as Owen Jenkins. Good thing I've learned a few tricks from attracting men who are assholes. New goal;

make Owen as uncomfortable as I can before I leave. At least I don't have to stress anymore about my future. Now my decision is more than clear. I'll be on my way to Kansas with Van in three short weeks. Maybe I'll add the tune *Take This Job and Shove It* onto my iPod.

Now that I have a plan I need to find the means to execute it. Thanks for the lesson Owen.

I peek around the corner and gaze upon the desolate gray walls. The musty fragrance of mold and mildew greet me as I step inside. Ah, just as glamorous as I envisioned. Three other new hires sort packages onto carts while a woman passes out floor assignments for deliveries.

"Hi, you must be Alexis. I'm Tara, and I run the mailroom." She runs her hand through her sleek black hair streaked with red highlights.

I lift my head, stand with my shoulders back, and smile. "Please call me Lexie. I'm ready to learn the ropes."

Tara leafs through her paperwork. "It's pretty simple; just deliver the letters and packages to the specified floors and offices. We meet here at eight a.m., take a lunch at noon, and leave at four p.m."

"Sounds perfect." I walk over to the other new hires and get to work.

Wow, lunch time already. Time flies in the mailroom, at least there's one perk. I relay the tale of my short lived advertising career to Jane, Lisa, and Doug, my mailroom colleagues, over a salad and water. Yes! They agree to let me deliver all of Owen's mail to his office. Good! The son of a bitch can see exactly what he can never have.

Day two of my new career in the mailroom! I tug at my grey pencil skirt and unbutton the top three buttons of my white blouse, exposing a tight gray camisole. Hmm, it's much shorter than I remember. My curls hang down, gently brushing over my slightly exposed cleavage. No need to look professional anymore; Tara's not that strict in the mailroom.

Oh, two packages waiting to be delivered to Owen Jenkins. Well, I'll make sure they get to his office.

"Wow, you look hot. The mailroom must be hopping." Simone's eyes travel from my black heels to my crystal headband. "A few of us are going out again this Friday night. You in?"

"Give me a call and we'll make some plans." I flash a quick grin trying not to lose focus.

I scoot my cart past her and wheel it into Owen's office. My black stilettos click against the hardwood floor. He swivels his chair around as I enter. His jaw drops and his eyes just about pop out of his head as he looks me up and down.

"Hello, Alexis. You look splendid this morning." He runs his finger along his lips.

"Thanks." I turn away from him and bend over at the waist to retrieve his two packages. I slide them onto his desk and take hold of my cart, pushing it forward.

"I may have made a mistake by sending you to the mailroom."

"Oh, you definitely made a mistake." I wiggle my hips as I exit the office.

Day three in my new career in the mailroom. Ah, a short, fitted tank dress, with tights and boots is a splendid ensemble. Only two letters and a small package for Owen today; no need to fill the cart. I step into his office and drop the envelopes on his desk and the package on his chair.

"Alexis, nice to see you again."

"Uh huh. See you later." What a pig! Owen's eyes are on my ass as I walk out the door. Doesn't he realize I can see his reflection in the glass door? Someone's not as smart as they think.

No more excitement for today. Time for lunch. I step into the hallway. Crap! Owen is standing by the elevator. My eyes widen as he walks toward me.

"Alexis, would you care to join me for lunch?" He raises his eyebrow.

"I have plans." I walk past Owen and entwine my arm with the first male colleague I see, Doug.

Is it wrong to use Doug to make Owen jealous? Since Doug doesn't mind I guess it's ok. Ah, my plan is working perfectly. Men like Owen can't handle rejection. It's all about the game with them, and I've become an excellent player. Owen deserves it! I'm sure I'm not the first or last girl who has to put up with his crap.

Today I pull out the big guns; my red, strapless dress paired with high heeled boots and my diamond earrings from Van. Thin tendrils tickle my neck as I pull my hair back into a sexy ponytail. Definitely not appropriate attire for a business meeting, but hey, I look fine for the mailroom. Oh, four packages for Owen this morning. God, he's so pathetic he's probably sending them to himself.

I waltz into his office, standing as tall as I can and wheel my cart toward his desk. What a shame, all of his packages are on the bottom. I hike up my dress and retrieve them, one by one, placing them onto his desk. I grip the handle of my cart and slowly push it, swaying my hips to and fro. My eyes dart toward the glass. He's rubbing his chin and staring at my ass.

"Jeeze, you look ready to hit a club. Maybe we should go out after work tonight instead." Simone's eyes widen.

I pull my skirt down. *Please don't let Simone see my underwear.* "I'm going to a show with my roommate after work, but we're still on for Friday night."

"Have fun!" She flashes a quick grin and answers the phone.

So I told a little white lie. It's not like I can fill her in on what was really going on. Why is the mailroom busy today? Great, a whole bundle of packages and letters that need to be delivered before four. My feet are throbbing and aching, I'll be soaking them as soon as I get home. No one knows about my demotion as of yet. Maybe I'll tell them over the weekend. Tonight I'll relax in a bubble bath and soak my troubles away.

I dig in my purse as I walk through the parking garage. Where is the last place I saw my keys? Oh no, the desk in the mailroom. I sigh and head back inside to get them. I'd lose my head if it wasn't attached!

Perfect, there they are. I trot back toward my car, my heels clicking on the cement floor. Who's that? A figure stands in front of me, blocking my way. Oh crap, it's Owen.

"You've got my attention, Alexis."

My heart hammers. I inhale deeply and raise my eyebrows. "What are you're talking about?" I continue to walk to my car, my pace increasing.

Owen follows beside me. "Please don't insult my intelligence. You've been trying to get my attention all week. Now you have it."

I fold my arms and walk faster. "I only look for the attention of my boyfriend. You're obviously mistaken."

"Please, that's bullshit!" Owen's pace quickens to keep up with mine.

I fumble with my keys, trying to find the right one quickly. *Why is there no one else in this parking garage?* My jaw clenches and my body trembles as I walk up to my car. Please, just let me get out of here!

"What's the matter? Am I too reserved for you? I saw you with your boyfriend at the bar. I hadn't pegged you as a girl who likes it rough."

My heart beats faster and my whole body shakes. Damn it! I try to steady my hands and put the key into the lock. Maybe this wasn't the best plan for revenge. It's failing miserably. The lock clicks and I pull the door open. It's caught by Owen and he slams it shut. Sweat forms on my brow and my heart is about to beat out of my chest.

"I can give you what you like as well." Owen pushes me into the side of the car, pressing his body against me, hard.

How can I get out of here? I squirm and sway my body back and forth. He grabs both of my wrists and holds them above my head, against the car. *Oh God, please let me get away.* I gasp for air. He runs his nose along my neck, kissing it and slides his tongue along my skin. Ugh, a sour taste invades my mouth. I'm about to hurl.

"Help, Help!" I squeeze my eyes shut. Tears well up and fall down my cheeks as I continue to struggle. Owen is solid. Damn! He won't budge one inch. *Oh God, please make him stop. Get me out of here!* My body goes into survival mode. I thrust myself back and forth with all my might, screaming and flailing. My body smashes against the beat up Chevy, denting the side panel. Owen grips me tighter, pressing his fingertips into my biceps while screaming at me to keep quiet.

"Hey, get off of her!" A male voice yells from afar.

Lexie Waters does not go down without a fight! "Help!" Adrenaline surges through me. I push with all my might using every last ounce of energy. He shakes me harder, banging my head against the car. I thrust my head forward, but he slams it back against the hard metal. Extreme pain radiates in the back of my head. Suddenly, everything is dark.

CHAPTER 24—BLISS

Beep, beep, beep. I slowly open my eyes, blinking repeatedly to focus my vision. My head is killing me. What's that annoying sound? I turn and gaze at the flashing monitor against the pure white wall. The stench of bleach and alcohol burns my nose. *Wait.* I rub my eyes. *Am I hallucinating or is that Van?*

"You're awake." He scoots his chair closer to the bed and holds my hand, gently bringing my fingers to his lips.

I gasp. Oh my God, there's an IV in my arm. I shake my head and try to sit up. The room is spinning. *Dear God, please don't let me hurl.* I quickly lie down and sink into the pillow. Why won't this painful ache in my head subside? "What's going on?"

"Don't you remember?" He stares into my eyes while gently brushing my fingers with his thumb.

My God, those eyes can pierce an armored tank. Oh no! Like a freight train, the memory hits me hard and fast. My eyes water; I close them and clear my throat. "I got in a fight with Owen in the parking garage." A few tears escape.

Van leaps from the chair and runs both hands through his hair. They ball into fists as he drops his arms. "No, that fucking asshole attacked you. He's one lucky son of a bitch. If he wasn't in jail right now, he sure as hell wouldn't be walking this earth." Van's face flushes and his lips pull back. His white knuckles pulsate as he clenches his fists tighter.

"Why am I in the hospital?" How far did this go? Please, tell me Owen didn't have his way with me!

Van exhales deeply, sits back down, and holds my hand. Fire burns through his pure red face. "That asshole tried…" The chair screeches on the tile floor as he stands up and paces around the room, cracking his knuckles. He wipes his hands over his face, inhales deeply, and sits back down. "The parking attendant saw everything on the camera monitor. When you screamed for help that asshole, Owen, panicked and slammed your head off of the car. You have a concussion."

A river of tears well up in my eyes and stream down my face. I'm such an idiot! What the hell was I thinking? I drove Owen to this.

"Don't cry baby, it's not your fault." Van wipes the tears from my cheeks and brushes a few loose strands of hair away from my face.

The tears continue to fall. Heaviness fills my chest and my stomach knots. "This is my fault." More tears flow down my face. I clear my throat and take a deep breath. "Owen demoted me to the mailroom because he was pissed I didn't respond to his advances. For payback, I dressed sexy to show him what he can't have. I brought this on myself." A few sobs escape. *Please don't let Van be mad. I need him so much, especially now.* I lower my head and slowly lift my eyes up.

"Seriously?" He shakes his head and throws his hands in the air. Exhaling deeply, he rubs his fingers across his forehead and pinches the bridge of his nose. "That fucking asshole's hands should never be on you, not even if you're half-naked in a bikini." He covers his face with his hands and inhales deeply, slowly dropping his arms to his sides. "Everything's on video. He can't weasel out of this." He grinds his teeth together, baring them. "Too bad he didn't make bail. I'd love to get my hands on him." He slams his fist against his palm.

My muscles weaken as the tension releases from my body. He's not pissed at me. Thank God! "Wait, why are you here instead of on tour? Oh no, is everyone mad at me again?"

He narrows his eyes. "Brooke called me. I jumped right on a plane." He tilts his head to the side. "No one's mad, everyone's worried."

"Jeeze, you didn't have to drop everything. I'll be fine."

He moves closer and presses his forehead against mine. "Nothing's more important than you." He brushes his soft lips gently against mine.

Beep,beep,beep,beep.

I blush and cover my mouth with my hand, chuckling underneath. Is the heart monitor going to explode? I guess it's not equipped to withstand the power of Van Sinclair. Wow, even with the throbbing pain in my head my body still tingles from his touch. "So, when do you have to get back on the road?"

Van rolls his eyes. "Leave it to you to be worried about my next show. We postponed the tour dates by a week. I'm not leaving without you."

A huge smile erupts across my face. What hurts more, my head or my cheeks? "How long am I stuck here?"

"Excellent question. Let's find out." Van walks out of the room and over to the nurse's desk.

Unbelievable! Who would have thought Owen would react like a psycho? Someone has issues! I turn toward the window, stretch, and inhale deeply. The sweet fragrance of the fresh cut flowers on the windowsill catches my attention. What beautiful arrangements! I rub my eyes and squint, trying to read the cards attached. One is from Simone, one from Brooke, and the largest of them all is from Global Inc.'s corporate office.

"Hello Lexie, I'm Dr. Greene. How are you feeling?" She walks toward me with a chart in her hand. Her short blond hair brushes against her cheek as she moves.

I grimace, the pain still throbbing in my head. "I feel ok," I say as I stare into the brightness of her pen light.

"It looks as if your concussion is improving. I'm going to release you, but you need to get plenty of rest and stay in bed." Dr. Greene signs a few papers in my chart.

"No problem, it's my favorite place to be." I flash a suggestive smile at Van, even though the hospital gown I'm draped in is not the sexiest attire.

"No strenuous activity for at least a few days." Dr. Greene winks at me as she leaves the room.

My face flushes and I twirl my hair around my fingers. "Dr. Green's an intelligent woman."

"Finally, I can take you out of here." Van kisses my forehead, before gathering up my belongings and flowers.

Do I really have to be wheeled out in a wheelchair? I guess I can overlook the hospital's policy if it means I'm heading home.

Brooke and Dean are sitting at the kitchen table when we step inside my apartment.

Brooke hops up from her chair. "I was so worried. Thank God you're home." She charges me, pulling me into a tight hug.

"Hope you guys are hungry, Pizza Palace never disappoints." Dean stands up and put his arm around me, gently squeezing my shoulder.

"Starving! Hospital food sucks!" My mouth waters as I inhale deeply, taking in the aroma of tomatoes and fresh baked bread.

"Couch or bed?" Van asks, raising his eyebrows.

I graze my teeth over my bottom lip, catching it between them and wink.

Van rolls his eyes and shakes his head.

I sigh. "Bed. Our couch sucks." *Great, he's actually making me stick to the bed rest regime.*

Yay, pizza and monopoly; maybe this night is shaping up. The board game shakes and a few hotels fall over as I reach for another slice of pizza. Who would've thought that four people can fit on my bed? Dean wins, no shocker there. Is this the first time we've ever played without drinking? Apparently, alcohol consumption doesn't affect the outcome.

I yawn and lean back against the headboard. These pain meds are knocking me out. "Thanks for tonight. I love you all."

"Aw, we all love you too." Brooke pats my shoulder. "We'll show you more love tomorrow, right now you need to rest."

Dean and Brooke pack up the game and leave us alone.

"Global Inc. called me yesterday." Van tucks a few stray hairs behind my ear. "They want to have a meeting on Monday morning. I said we'd be there, but if you're not up to it we can cancel."

My face flushes and I cross my arms. "Oh, we're going! I'd like to tell them exactly what I think of that scumbag, Owen Jenkins."

"Don't get all fired up. You need to rest." He glides his fingers along my cheek.

My chest flutters, sending a shiver of pure pleasure to my core. My heart races, drumming in my ears. *I finally have Van in my bed again and I have to take it easy? When will the torture end?* I take a deep breath and try to suppress my burning need to ravish him. "I'll need my favorite T-shirt."

"You got it babe." A low growl develops in his throat as he hands me my Devil's Garden T-shirt. Deep red flushes across his face and his jaw clenches, causing his lips to tremble. His eyes protrude as he glares at my wrists.

What's the matter with him? I jerk my head back. My eyes follow his to the black and blue marks shaped like fingerprints around my wrists. "Stop it." I grab his cheeks and stare into his eyes. "Don't get mad over my war wounds. We'll just tell everyone I'm really kinky and made the handcuffs too tight."

Van exhales deeply. "You're a piece of work."

Am I in prison? Van watches over me like a hawk. Al-Qaeda isn't under this degree of heavy surveillance. I get it, he's just looking out for me but I'm not made of glass.

Finally, it's Monday. The sooner this meeting is over the better. What should I wear today? I peruse my closet. Ah ha, my gray business dress with black flats is good enough. It's not like I'm on the clock. Um, I can't do much to cover the bruises on my wrists or the one on my forehead, but letting the reps from Global Inc. see my injuries may not be so bad; maybe they'll understand the severity of what happened.

I grip Van's hand tightly as we march through the parking garage into the huge building. My heart races, faster with every step. I just want to put this all behind me, not relive it again.

Simone walks down the opposite side of the hallway leafing through a few papers. She lifts her head and stops in her tracks.

"I'm so glad you're ok." She rushes toward me and pulls me into a hug. She steps back and flinches. "That bastard." Her eyes travel along my forehead.

"I'm fine. Thank you for the flowers."

"Alexis Waters?" A woman at the front desk calls for me.

I wave to Simone and walk over to the woman glaring at me. "I'm Alexis Waters."

"Ms. Tucker will meet you in the third floor conference room. You can go right up." She turns her attention away from us after delivering the message.

My finger trembles as I press the button of the elevator. Van wraps his arms around me and kisses my forehead. The steel doors open, revealing light blue walls and a gray carpeted floor. My heart hammers against my chest.

He entwines his fingers with mine. "Walk with me."

I grip his hand tightly and nuzzle my cheek against his arm. I can do anything with him by my side.

Huh, I guess they all look the same. Déjà vu hits me as I glance around the room. The astonishing view from the wall to wall windows is obstructed by the handful of people seated in the leather chairs.

A woman at the head of the table stands. "Hello Alexis. I'm Victoria Tucker, CEO of Global Inc. Please, take a seat."

Oh my God. The CEO of Global Inc. is meeting with me. I begin to fidget "Thank you."

Victoria Tucker weaves a stray strand of blond hair back into her severe bun. *Wow, that black business suit screams power. Everyone around her hangs on her every word.* Well, there's one person in the room who could care less about her status. Van's not intimidated by anyone.

Victoria's eyes move up and down, assessing Van. He sits with his shoulders back and his chin up, dressed in a T-shirt and jeans, just like he would for any other occasion. Why should he try to impress the reps from Global Inc.? In this situation, shouldn't it be the other way around? Does it really matter what he wears? He has the tendency to dazzle people without any effort at all.

"You must be Van, we spoke on the phone." Victoria's eyes widen as she stares.

He nods and shakes her hand. "What did you want to see us about?"

Victoria pours us each a glass of water and sits in the chair directly across from us. "First of all, I want to make sure Alexis is alright. Second, I want to talk about the incident that occurred so we can see where we need to go from here."

I take a deep breath and slowly exhale. "I remember everything up to the point right before I blacked out." I twirl my hair around my fingers.

"The actual incident is all on tape, so there's no need to relive it. Is there anything that would have led you to believe that Mr. Jenkins was on the verge of this type of behavior?" She taps her pen against a yellow tablet.

Umm, other than the 'I'm-better-than-you-and–get-everything-I-want' attitude? "Not that I can pinpoint. I didn't realize Owen only made me part of a big account with the intent of seducing me. I probably seem naïve to everyone, but I really believed it was legitimate. When he demoted me for not returning his advances, I tried to torment him by showing him there are things in this would that he can't have. I guess I should have just worked in the mailroom and let it go." I sink down in my chair and look at the table.

She lowers her eyes to look into mine. "Alexis, none of this is your fault. Owen is responsible for his actions. I'm just trying to implement a plan to prevent this from occurring again in the future and your input is vital."

Maybe I *can* prevent this from happening to someone else. I exhale and raise my head. "I'm not sure if anyone can predict this type of behavior. I can only suggest a policy for new hires indicating a starting point with the company and a structured plan for advancement."

"That's an excellent idea and I will take it under advisement. Now, Global Inc. would like to keep this incident quiet, especially from the reps of American Gemstone." She sips her water. "Since you were unfairly demoted, we have a new job offer to propose to you."

I bite at my lips. "To be honest, Van is a musician who tours the country. I'm really not comfortable being alone anymore, so I've decided to travel with him from now on."

"I can understand your fears. Global Inc. is prepared to offer you a 'work from home' position which will allow you to travel. We will issue you a laptop with a broadband internet connection that will be accessible wherever a cell phone is usable. Your job will consist of creating strategies to implement new business plans. We're prepared to offer you a five year contract and start you out with $80,000 a year. Naturally, all of the benefits offered by Global Inc. will apply." She pushes a stack of papers across the table toward me.

Is she serious? I bite my cheek to ensure I'm not dreaming. Ouch! Yep, it's real. "I accept."

Victoria smiles. "Wonderful, Alexis. We'll be in touch. You're entitled to traumatic leave so you won't start this new position until November first."

"Thank you." I gather the paperwork, weave my fingers with Van's, and exit the room.

An irrepressible smile plasters across my face and I'm almost skipping down the hallway. Any ounce of stress or fear that once existed is banished to oblivion. *How did I become one of the lucky few who get to have it all?* "Winning the lottery can't feel this good. Does it get any better?"

"I can think of a few ways." He wraps his arms around my waist, pulling me close to him and nibbles on my ear. "I planned a surprise getaway for us; a beachfront bed and breakfast in Cape May."

The hairs on my neck stand on end as his tongue glides along my ear. Ah, a beach vacation, just what I need. I bounce up on my feet and kiss Van softly. "You're amazing. When do we leave?"

He presses his forehead against mine. "Tomorrow morning. Let's pack."

∞

The aroma of salty air blows through the vents of my Chevy as we pull into the parking lot of Rose's Bed and Breakfast. Ah, it's the offseason! The closest we can get to our own secluded beach. The Cape is so busy during the summer months. Well, there's still a few people strolling through the cobblestone streets, but it's like we're on our own private retreat. I close my eyes and listen to the sounds of the waves crashing onto the sand. For once, time is on my side, and I'm not wasting a second.

I grab Van's free hand as he pulls a bag out of the trunk and I rest my head against his shoulder. "Thanks for this trip." I step back and run my hands up his hard chiseled chest, wrapping my arms around him. "After everything that's happened, a long weekend with you away from the rest of the world is like paradise."

He drops the bag and gently tugs my hips toward him, pressing himself against me. "You deserve it." He lightly brushes his fingertips up my arms and to my cheeks, gently grabbing my face and kissing me softly. "I want this to be perfect."

I wet my lips. "Once we get in that room everything will be superb."

He glides his fingers back down my arm and holds my hand. "You're still supposed to be taking it easy." He raises his eyebrows.

I flash my sexiest smile and nuzzle my cheek against his arm. "I'll take it however I can get it." He kisses my forehead and then shakes his head.

Perfect, second floor and oceanfront! I gaze at the sea through an enormous picture window. The waves crash along the white sand. I step back and glance around the room. Have I traveled back in time? It's like I'm in a doll house, my eyes travel from the rose and cream lace curtains to the huge claw foot bathtub.

"You certainly have a gift for picking out exceptional hotel rooms." I strut toward him and pull him close, slowly grazing my fingernails down his back. I stop at the waist of his jeans and run my fingers along the rim of the thick fabric, making my way toward the front.

He backs up and gives me a quick peck on the lips. "How about a little shopping before dinner?"

Does he think I'm still on the bed rest regime and avoiding strenuous activity? Well, he's dead wrong. I plan on doing quite a few things in bed this weekend, none of them restful.

Hand in hand, we stroll through the gas-lit streets of Cape May, admiring the historic Victorian homes.

How amazing! Each is more beautiful than the next. "I love those huge porches. They remind me of your house in Kansas. I can't wait to start my mornings with coffee on your swing."

"You should consider it *our* place." He stops and looks over at me. "You know what's mine is yours, right?" He wrinkles his brow and stares, searching my face.

Huh, he's acting weird tonight. I shrug. "Yeah, I guess. I've never lived with a boyfriend before. I still have to get used to the terminology."

We browse through a few jewelry stores and antique shops. *Hey, is that Christmas music?* Up ahead is a holiday themed store.

"Come on, I have an idea." I drag Van by his hand into the store and peruse the selection of ornaments. This one's perfect. I hold it up. *Our first Christmas Together* with two reindeer enclosed in a heart. "For our first Christmas at *our* place."

Van holds it in his palm, a small smile creeps over his face. "We're gonna need a tree to hang that on. Are you a real or an artificial kind of girl?"

"I'm not fussy. Either one is good, as long as our lights can be seen from space." I giggle.

He shakes his head and slides his arm around me. "Should I invest in a windmill?"

"Wouldn't hurt." I slither my arm around his waist as we make our way out of the store.

I glance at my watch. Time is flying again; it's just about dinner time. "Where to next?"

"I planned an outdoor dinner." He bites at his lip.

He's full of surprises. "Wow, you're amazing." I pull him close as we walk back to our room.

Hmm, what outfit screams outdoor dining? Ah ha, my turquoise blue sundress, white sweater and white flip flops. The breeze from the ocean always wrecks my hair. Might as well try to look as good as possible, I pull it into a loose ponytail. The sunlight shining through the window reflects against my diamond earrings, casting a million rainbows against the wall. What a spectacular sight! I step out of the bathroom and stop dead in my tracks.

Van rises from the bed and runs his hand through his hair. Dear God, can he be any sexier? My heart's about to beat out my chest and electricity flows through me as if I've been struck by lightning. Whoa, where's the jeans and T-shirt? My eyes gravitate toward the dark gray pants that hang on his hips in just the right way. Damn! That green shirt accentuates every sculpted muscle in his torso. His eyes sparkle, reflecting off the emerald hue.

My jaw drops as I stare at my rock god. "I've only seen you out of your jeans at Sydney's wedding." I can't take my eyes off him.

He flashes a sexy half smile and raises his eyebrows. "You may have seen me out of my jeans a few other times too." He winks.

How am I going to compose myself during dinner? We cross the street to the beach and stroll along the edge of the gritty sand. The warm breeze caresses my face, causing a few loose strands of hair to tickle my skin. I gaze out into the ocean, watching the waves crash in a perfectly choreographed rhythm.

A bottle of champagne rests in a chiller atop a wooden platform covered with a blanket, surrounded by white candles in the sand. I squint and jerk my head back slightly. Did Van do all this for me?

I cover my mouth with my hands. My knees are weak, electricity jolts throughout my body. My lips part and I drop my hands to my side, staring into the emerald abyss. "This is the most romantic moment of my life."

Soft lips touch mine, breaking my trance.

He pulls away and rubs his hands down his pant leg. "Your favorite, picnic style."

I slide off my flip flops and sit on the soft blanket. Van fidgets, biting at his nails as he joins me. Two shiny silver domes cover our dishes. How fancy. What kind of meal awaits? Wait, those flowers scattered around the blanket are familiar. I pick one up and examine it. Asphodels, the flowers in our tattoos. I look over at Van who's biting his lip as he stares at me. *What does he have up his sleeve?* I lift my silver dome. Huh, there's no food on the plate, just a small silver gift bag with the most beautiful asphodel on top. I glance over at Van and narrow my eyes as I open the bag. I gasp! It's a small velvet box.

Van's already down on one knee. *Oh my God, is this really happening?* My heart bangs against my chest. Tears well up in my eyes as the warmth of the sun flows through my body. My cheeks flush and a smile that could light up the darkest night forms on my face.

Van takes the box from my trembling fingers and holds my hand. "My world changed the moment I met you. I never knew what was missing. Everything's better when you're here and nothing's right without you. I never feel as good as I do when you're by my side or as bad as I do when you're away from me. So far it's been a blissful tragedy. I love you, Lexie, and I'll love you forever. I promise you much more bliss and much less tragedy. Will you marry me?"

A tear rolls down my cheek as I stare into eyes that can bring me to my knees. Every moment we've shared flashes before my eyes. I'm not the same girl that I was before. Everything missing from my life is standing in front of me, asking for forever. I wipe the tears from my face. "Yes, of course I'll marry you."

Van exhales deeply, lunges forward, and slams his soft lips against mine in a frenzy of passion. My heart pounds. I reach around and wrap my arms around his neck, weaving my fingers through his hair. *Ah, most definitely the best kiss of my life!*

He pulls away and holds out the velvet box. "I almost forgot." He lifts the lid.

I'm breathless. My jaw drops and my eyes widen as they travel over the large, round, flawless stone. "It's the most beautiful ring I've ever seen."

"I can't take all the credit. Jenna helped me pick it out." Van laughs. "She was muttering something about wishing she waited longer to get engaged so she could have a ring like this one." He slips it on my finger.

Perfect fit! "Yeah, that sounds like Jenna."

He pops open the champagne bottle and fills our glasses. "May our tomorrows be as happy as today."

We clink our glasses and sip the bubbly.

I gaze out onto the ocean as I cuddle on the blanket with Van, occasionally looking down at the faultless diamond on my finger. The gentle breeze caresses my skin, as the sun descends and disappears into the water. I'm the luckiest girl alive!

"I made us a dinner reservation at a quaint restaurant on the beach." Van looks over at me, barely able to contain his smile. He stands up and holds out his hand. "Walk with me."

My heart palpates and my skin tingles as I take Van's hand and stroll through the sand, watching my diamond sparkle in the setting sun. "I will walk with you forever Van Sinclair."

I have the man I've longed for, a dream job, and wonderful friends and family. What more can I ask for? My life is suddenly and completely perfect. No tragedy, all bliss.

Coming Soon

Wrecked

Eighteen year old Layla Anderson has it all. She's queen bee of her high school, head cheerleader, and dates the captain of the football team, but all her popularity won't help expunge her tarnished record and help her win the scholarship to a prestigious culinary school she's been vying for. When she's partnered up with mysterious bad-boy Chase Cooper in traffic school she vows to steer clear of him and the trouble that seems to follow. Then tragedy strikes, pulling her from her perfect life and plunging her into a downward spiral. Can the most unlikely person turn into her hero? How can you pick up the pieces when your whole life's been wrecked?

About the Author:

Romance author by night, pharmacist by day, Amy Gale loves rock music and the feel of sand between her toes. She attended Wilkes University where she graduated with a Doctor of Pharmacy degree. In addition to writing, she enjoys baking, scary movies, rock concerts, and reading books at the beach. She lives in the lush forest of Northeastern Pennsylvania with her husband, six cats, and golden retriever.

Other titles published by
www.5princebooks.com

How to Have an Affair *Lindsay Harper*
The Soul of Jesus *Doug Simpson*
The Girl before Eve *Lisa J Hobman*
Courting Darkness *Melynda Price*
Owned By the Ocean *Christine Steendam*
Sullivan's Way *Wilhelmina Stolen*
The Library *Carmen Desousa*
Rebekah's Quilt *Sara Barnard*
Unforgiving Plains *Christine Steendam*
Love Songs *Bernadette Marie*
The End *Denise Moncrief*
On Thin Ice *Bernadette Marie*
Through the Glass *Lisa J. Hobman*
Indiscretion *Tonya Lampley*
The Elvis Presley I Knew *Robert C. Cantwell*
Finding Hope *Bernadette Marie*
Over the Edge *Susan Lohrer*
Encore *Bernadette Marie*
Split Decisions *Carmen DeSousa*
Matchmakers *Bernadette Marie*
Rocky Road *Susan Lohrer*
Stutter Creek *Ann Swann*
The Perfect Crime *P. Hindley, S. Goodsell*
Lost and Found *Bernadette Marie*
A Heart at Home *Sara Barnard*
Soul Connection *Doug Simpson*
Bridge Over the Atlantic *Lisa Hobman*
An Unexpected Admirer *Bernadette Marie*
The Italian Job *Phyllis Humphrey*
Jaded *M.J. Kane*
Shades of Darkness *Melynda Price*
Heart like an Ocean *Christine Steendam*
The Depot *Carmen DeSousa*
Crisis of Identity *Denise Moncrief*
A Heart Broken *Sara Barnard*

CPSIA information can be obtained at www.ICGtesting.com
Printed in the USA
LVOW13s2210160614

390337LV00001B/23/P